CH

... ns fun, contemporary romances. Internationally published, with books translated into more than a dozen languages, she is a two-time winner of the *RT Book Reviews* Reviewers' Choice Award and winner of the CataRomance Reviewers' Choice Award. Now living her dream, she resides with her very patient husband and Writer Kitty. When she's not plotting her next romance you can find her with a mug of tea and a book. Learn more at jenniferfaye.com

Despite a no-nonsense background as a West Point graduate, army officer and Fortune 100 sales executive, **Caro Carson** has always treasured the happily-ever-after of a good romance novel. As a RITA® Award–winning Mills & Boon author, Caro is delighted to be living her own happily-ever-after with her husband and two children in Florida, a location that has saved the coaster-loving theme-park fanatic a fortune on plane tickets.

Discover more at millsandboon.co.uk

FAIRYTALE CHRISTMAS WITH THE MILLIONAIRE

JENNIFER FAYE

CHAPTER ONE

CHRISTMAS WAS IN the air...

Cheerful holiday tunes played on the radio. The Manhattan storefronts were trimmed in shiny tinsel and twinkle lights. And right here on Holly Lane, the Stirling Apartments' foyer was decked out with lush garland and a pencil Christmas tree adorned with white lights and red satin balls.

This was hands down Alina Martin's favorite time of the year. She loved to sing the uplifting carols, all the while pretending she could carry a tune. She loved to decorate the tree. And she loved how the holiday season brought out the best in people. However, this year she was hoping for a Christmas miracle to keep her from losing her beloved home.

But at the moment, her immediate attention was focused on finding her apron. Mentally she recounted her actions the prior evening. The day hadn't been much out of the ordinary. She'd worked the morning shift at the restaurant tending to the party planning as well as helping out in the dining room before rushing home to do her second job as building manager. Even with a rent-controlled apartment, it wasn't cheap living in New York City. And yet there was nowhere else in the world she'd rather live.

"Mrrrr..."

She glanced down to find her ginger cat, who she'd affectionately named Prince. They'd first met at a local park.

She'd been out for a walk, trying to achieve her ten thousand steps a day, when she'd stopped at a local animal rescue adopt-a-thon. Long story short, Prince picked her out and the rest was history.

When Prince rubbed against her leg, she said, "Begging won't work. You already had breakfast."

"Meow."

Sometimes it was like he could truly understand what she said, "Sorry, sweetie, I can't hold you, either. I have to leave."

"Mrrrr..."

He strode away, probably headed back to bed. She wished she could join him.

Alina turned her focus back to her missing apron. She rushed over to the dryer, where she found it at the back of the machine. It was a bit wrinkled. She shook it out with a couple of quick snaps. Good enough.

She rolled up her apron and then stuffed it in her oversize purse. She threw on her red winter coat, a knit cap and her boots. Out the door she went. Noticing the elevator was at the top floor, she opted for the stairs instead. Hers wasn't a large building, not by New York City standards. But within its five floors, it housed the people she liked to refer to as her adopted family.

She exited the stairwell and rushed up the hallway. Meg, her best friend, stood in the lobby near the mailboxes. Her curly red hair was pulled back in a ponytail. However, instead of her usual sunny smile, she wore a distinct frown. Meg held up a letter. "Have you seen this?"

The worry in her friend's warm brown eyes drew Alina's concern. "What is it?"

"It's another letter about them throwing us out."

"What?" Alina rushed over to her mailbox. In her rush,

she fumbled with her keys. They fell to the tile floor with a loud jangle.

With a groan of frustration, she bent over to retrieve the keys. Once the little door was open, she withdrew her copy of the letter. Her gaze scanned down over it. The new owner was willing to pay them extra to move out by the new year. That wasn't going to happen.

With her back to the front door, Alina faced her friend. "Don't worry. There's nothing Toliver can do to rush things. He has to wait ninety days before he can begin eviction proceedings."

"But that's in February. Even that's not much time to find a new place to live."

One of their youngest and newest residents, Jimmy Greene, came rushing past them. He gave a quick nod in greeting but kept going. He must have another interview lined up at a software company. He'd inherited his grandmother's rent-controlled apartment and was now struggling to find a job in the competitive market of online video gaming.

The door creaked open and closed behind him, letting the cold winter air rush in around them. It also reminded Alina that she had to get a move on.

"We'll figure something out," Alina said, hoping her voice sounded encouraging. "Even if I have to go back to that awful man's office building and stage another protest in the foyer until he agrees to meet with me. From what I've read, he inherited his position and he doesn't know what he's doing. Well, that's obvious." She held up her copy of the letter as proof. "This isn't going to change Stirling residents' minds about moving. I've got to get to work. We'll talk later."

"I've got to get going, too. Remember, I have that week-long seminar in LA. And then I'm spending the next couple

of weeks in Wyoming with my parents. But I can cancel—
the family visit, not the seminar—if you need me."

"No. Go. Enjoy yourself. You haven't seen your family
in a year. I've got this."

Uncertainty showed in Meg's eyes. "You're sure?"

"Positive."

"Keep me updated."

"I will." Alina gave her a brief hug. "We'll talk soon."

Alina spun around and immediately bumped into a solid
force. She lifted her gaze, finding a tall man standing there.
It was his brown eyes that immediately caught her attention. They were dark and mysterious. And she found herself drawn in by them.

The more she stared, the more she noticed a glint of irritation. Well, it wasn't her fault he was standing in the
middle of the foyer.

"Sorry," she mumbled. And then she rushed right past
him.

She'd have to run if she was to catch her train. She set
off as quickly as she dared in the wet snow. As she kept
moving, her thoughts returned to the mystery man in the
lobby. Who was he? And what was he doing in her building? Well, it wasn't her building but it was starting to feel
that way because not only was she the building manager
but she had also been unofficially elected to lead the charge
to save the Stirling from being torn down and replaced by
a flashy high-rise.

Though she didn't relish the idea, perhaps it was time she
made another visit to Mr. Toliver's office. She'd been turned
away before for not having an appointment. The problem
was that every time she'd tried to set up an appointment, he
was either away on business or unavailable for the foresee-
able future. She was pretty certain they'd been delay tactics
and he'd been in his office the whole time.

And when she'd staged a peaceful protest with other Stirling residents, hoping Mr. Toliver would no longer be able to ignore them, the police had been called. Her blood boiled every time she thought of that man avoiding her—avoiding the truth about the damage he was doing to people's lives. The next time she wouldn't be chased away so easily.

His teeth ground together.

Graham Toliver couldn't believe those two young women had been bad-mouthing him—right in front of him no less. Surely they'd heard the outside door open when that young man held the door for him to enter.

Still, those women had kept talking, and not quietly, either. Hadn't they heard his approaching footsteps? It wasn't like he tiptoed around. Or hadn't they cared who overheard them?

His muscles tensed. It was bad enough not having the confidence of his board but to have perfect strangers judge his qualifications to run his family's business, well, that was quite another thing.

He was tempted to withdraw his very generous offer to get them to move out earlier. But he hesitated. He was a businessman above all else. He drew in a deep breath and then slowly blew it out.

He recalled the young woman with light blond hair and pink stripes streaked through it. When she'd bumped into him, their gazes had connected. For just a moment, it felt as though time had stood still. It was though he should know her, but he was positive they'd never met. He wouldn't have forgotten those blue eyes framed by long, dark lashes.

No matter how cute he might find her, he couldn't dismiss her words. Still, he shouldn't let that rude woman's words get to him. It was quite likely they'd never see each other again.

Instead of thinking of her mesmerizing eyes and how they'd made his heart jolt, he needed to focus on the reason for his visit. He was here to speak with the building manager. He withdrew a slip of paper from his pocket with a hastily scrawled name...

Did that say Al? He squinted. It didn't help sort the squiggly line into letters. Now he was left to guess at the name. Alan? It seemed like a safe bet. As for the last name, it was easier to read. Martin. Alan Martin? Perhaps.

When he glanced up, he found he was alone in the lobby. He wasn't used to people just strolling right by him like he was a nobody. At the office, people always wanted something from him. A signature here, an answer to a question there. It was always something. But at the Stirling Apartments, no one recognized him. Interesting.

For a moment, he wondered what it'd be like to not be the CEO of a billion-dollar business. A frown pulled at the corners of his mouth. That would never happen. Toliver Investments was his destiny. Without it, he'd be—well, he'd be nothing.

He made his way farther into the building. This Al or Alan guy shouldn't be too hard to find as he was the building manager. And just like that, Graham happened upon a door with a black plaque that read Building Manager.

Graham rapped his knuckles on the door. No response. He checked the time. It wasn't quite eight o'clock. Surely the guy would be at work by now. Didn't everyone arrive early? His employees did.

Just as he raised his hand to knock once more, a door farther down the hall opened. An older man stepped into the hallway. They nodded to each other, then Graham turned his attention back to the door and knocked louder this time. Again, no sounds came from inside.

When the older man ambled down the hallway, Graham

cleared his throat. "Excuse me. Do you know where I can find…" He glanced at the slip of paper once more. "An Al or Alan Martin?"

A smile lifted beneath the man's bushy white mustache. "Try the Christmas Café."

Why would he try there? But before he could formulate the question, the man had disappeared onto the nearby elevator. Graham glanced around for someone else to ask but the hallway was empty.

It would have helped if his investigator had left him a phone number for the building manager. After all, he had to find this Al guy. He was obviously getting the tenants worked up about not moving—as was evidenced by the two young women Graham had encountered in the lobby.

He once more glanced at his Rolex. Time was ticking by and he'd missed breakfast this morning. He supposed a quick stop at the Christmas Café wouldn't be so bad. He'd promised his board he'd make progress on getting the tenants to move out early—by the beginning of the year—because time was money and money spoke volumes at board meetings.

And so he set off for the restaurant. Once he tracked down this Alan guy, Graham was determined they'd come to some sort of resolution. He just had to find out the guy's price.

CHAPTER TWO

SHE'D MADE IT to work with literally a minute to spare.

Alina didn't like to be late for anything. Her father used to say it was a trait she'd inherited from her mother. Alina had to take his word for it because she'd been too young when her mother had passed for her to remember those sorts of details.

What she did remember of her mother was that she was kind and loving. She remembered her mother's smile; it was bright and glowing, warm and welcoming. But sometimes Alina wondered if that was a real memory or just something she'd picked up from staring at her mother's pictures—the ones she'd been able to salvage and hide from her wicked stepmother. Once Alina's father had remarried, her stepmother had rid their Manhattan apartment of everything that was a remembrance of Alina's mother—as though she could just wipe away the past.

But when it came to Alina, her stepmother couldn't just toss her out with the trash. Though Alina knew if she could, her stepmother would have done exactly that. Alina's father used to say Alina was the spitting image of her mother. Alina didn't see it. Not really. But everyone who had known her mother agreed. She was her mother's mini-me.

Alina pushed aside thoughts of the past because if she didn't start taking orders and serving up food, she wouldn't get tipped. And if she didn't get tipped, she wouldn't make her rent payment. And that would just be one more excuse for the new building owner to kick her to the curb as soon as possible.

Alina's mouth pulled into a distinct frown. How could someone be so cold and calculating, especially at this time of the year? Her gaze lifted, taking in the twinkle lights trimming the edge of the ceiling. This upscale restaurant went overboard with the decorations. It was part of its charm. The white walls were now adorned with Christmas prints. Large, red poinsettias were strategically placed about the dining room. A pencil tree stood near the hostess station with white lights and silver ornaments. And then there was Santa all done up in his red velvet and snowy white trim. Next to him were elves in their red overalls and pointed hats.

"Hurry up." Her manager, Sally, softened the order with a smile. "It's going to be a busy day."

"How can you tell?" Alina asked.

"When you've been working here as long as I have, you can feel it in your bones."

Alina arched a brow at Sally. She didn't believe her. There was more to the woman's reliable fortune-telling than feeling it in her bones. The woman definitely had a sixth sense about her.

Sally leaned in and said conspiratorially, "There are going to be flurries all day. No accumulation but enough to put people in the holiday spirit. They'll be out and about trying to put a dent in their Christmas shopping. Mark my words."

"I believe you." And with that Alina tied her apron, not having time to worry about the wrinkles.

The restaurant wasn't overly busy. The early breakfast crowd had moved on. But with this being the holiday season, shoppers would stop by the café off and on all day, in between finding just the right gift for that special someone in their life.

Not that Alina would know about that as her last boyfriend had broken up with her after just six months together. When the former building manager quit and moved to Florida where the winters were so much warmer, she'd taken on the building manager position to help pay off her credit card bills. But having two jobs took up a lot of time. These days she never had time in her busy schedule to go out on dates. She couldn't blame her ex for breaking up with her. When she wasn't working at the restaurant, she was on call to help the Stirling residents with all of their problems. Some she could help with, others she had to call in professionals.

Alina had just turned in an order when Sally walked up to her. "I have someone at one of my tables requesting you. At least I think it's you he wants."

Alina's brows drew together as she smiled at her friend. "You think?"

Sally shrugged. "Thought you'd want to check him out since he's awfully cute and he isn't wearing a ring."

"Let me guess. If you didn't have your own cute husband waiting for you at home, you would have kept him to yourself?"

Sally's smile widened. "How'd you guess?"

Alina shook her head. "I don't need you setting me up. I'm fine on my own. I promise."

"I'm not setting you up." Sally's expression was perfectly serious. "This guy was asking for Alan Martin. He said he was told he could find you here."

"Alan? Seriously?" A lot of people messed up her name but this was really bad. She sighed. "Okay. I'll see what he wants."

Sally pointed her in the direction of a table near the front of the restaurant. Alina wondered what this man wanted. She hoped it wasn't some sort of problem. She didn't need any more problems. She was up to her chin in them.

Her steps were quick. Her orders would be up in a few minutes. And she wasn't going to serve up food that had dried out under the warmer. She wouldn't want to eat food that had been sitting too long and she wouldn't do that to someone else.

With "I'll Be Home for Christmas" playing in the background, Alina approached the table by the big windows overlooking the busy sidewalk. The man had his head down as he read the menu. It gave her a moment to study him. His hair was dark and cut short. Every strand appeared to be in place. He wore a dark suit. It looked expensive.

"Excuse me," she said. "You asked for me."

When he lifted his head, his gaze met hers. Her heart jolted in recognition. She would know those brown eyes anywhere. They were the same ones she'd stared into that very morning in the lobby of her building.

His dark brows drew together as unspoken questions flashed in his eyes. Apparently, she wasn't the only one to remember their run-in. But why had he followed her here? Was he some sort of stalker? Worry sent her pulse racing.

"You. You're the woman from the building this morning." He set aside the menu.

"And you're the man who stood there eavesdropping."

"I did not. I was politely waiting to ask a question."

"If you say so. Still, you could have cleared your throat or said something." The man's gaze grew darker. Good. Let him be angry. She didn't like to be spied upon and she didn't have time to waste. "I have to get back to work."

"But where is Alan?"

"It's Alina. And I'm standing right here, but not for much

longer." Her brain said to turn around and walk away, but her feet refused to move.

"Wait." Confusion showed in his eyes. "That can't be right." He reached in his pocket and withdrew a slip of paper. "I'm looking for Al or Alan Martin. He's the building manager at the Stirling Apartments on Holly Lane."

"I'm the building manager."

The man stared at her for a moment as though trying to figure out if he believed her or not. "Can I ask you a question?"

She shrugged. "You can but it doesn't mean I'll answer."

A smile lit up his face, making him downright gorgeous. The breath hitched in her lungs. For a second, she forgot she'd been irritated with him. She took a moment to really notice him. He was wearing a charcoal gray suit with a brilliant blue dress shirt sans the tie. The top button was undone, revealing a silver chain around his neck. Interesting. Perhaps it wouldn't hurt to give him another chance.

Her gaze rose, taking in a squared jaw that was clean-shaven, until finally she met his dark gaze. She could sense he was quite observant, and right now, he was studying her. What was he seeing in her? And why was he interested in her?

Was he planning to ask her out? A bubble of laughter rose up in her throat. She swallowed hard. This man could easily grace the glossy pages of any magazine—then again, perhaps he already did. Either way, there was no way he'd be interested in plain old her—the memory of her stepmother's insults still lingered in the back of her mind.

"What is the deal with this place?" he asked.

She wasn't sure she understood. "Excuse me?"

"The restaurant, is it really called the Christmas Café?"

"Yes."

His eyes widened. "You mean all year-round?"

She nodded and smiled. "In here, it's Christmas year-round."

"Even in the summer, it's decorated for Christmas?"

"Well, Santa and his buddies do like to celebrate other holidays so they put up valentines, shamrocks, jack o'lanterns, and in the summer, Santa breaks out his board shorts and surfboard."

If it was possible, the man's eyes widened even further. "Seriously?" When she nodded again, he said, "That's a lot of Christmas."

"I take it you're not a fan of the holiday."

"No." There was no hesitation in his very firm answer.

What in the world had made him so grinchy? But she stopped herself from asking. She didn't have time to get to know this man, no matter how cute she might find him or how curious she was to know the man behind those dark, mysterious eyes.

"I really need to get back to work," she said. "Do you want to order?"

"In a moment, but first I need to speak with you about the apartment building."

"Listen, if you're looking for an apartment to rent, you've come to the wrong place."

"Why's that?" His brown eyes sparked with interest.

"Because some company is trying to force out all of the tenants."

"Trying to?"

She shrugged. "They've sent notices but the fight isn't over. In fact, it's just beginning."

"What does that mean?"

Her gaze narrowed in on him. "Why all of the questions? Are you a reporter or something?"

At first, the thought alarmed her. But as she rolled it around in her mind, she warmed up to the possibilities.

In fact, the idea of relaying her story to the press became downright appealing. Why hadn't she thought of it a long time ago?

"I'm not a reporter."

"You're not?" Disappointment assailed her. She made a mental note to contact a reporter. "Then what's with all of the questions about the apartment building?"

"I'm the new owner."

What? Surely she hadn't heard him correctly. Her gaze searched his. He seemed to be taking a sort of satisfaction in being able to catch her off guard. It wouldn't happen again.

Was it really that surprising?

Graham watched as Alina gaped at him. He hadn't intended to spring a surprise attack. In fact, he'd been expecting her to recognize him. Perhaps he'd done too good of a job ducking the press since taking over as CEO. The truth was that he'd never wanted to live a public life, not like his father, who made the news regularly.

His father had thought the more press coverage he received, the greater the confirmation of his success—his company's success. And Graham's mother, well, she would have gone along with most anything that would make his father happy. And his father had only been happy when his company was on top of the business world, when his son was on top of his class, when their family's name was on top of the headlines. Second place wasn't good enough.

"You can't be Graham Toliver," she said. "He's much older. I know. I've seen the pictures."

"That was my father, Graham Toliver II. I'm Graham Toliver III." As the light of dawning settled upon her, he hoped they could get down to business. "Could you sit down so we can talk?"

She shook her head. "I'm working."

"This shouldn't take long. I'd like to make you an offer."

She opened her mouth, presumably to refuse to speak with him. But then she pressed her lips together as though rolling the thought around in her mind before deciding. "I'm listening."

"Alina." A server rushed up to them, interrupting before Graham could respond. Her name tag said her name was Sally. "Are you available on Thursday? We just received a big reservation and we could use more help."

"I...I can't. I have work at the building to do."

"Please, Alina," Sally said. "You know how much these big groups tip. It'll really help you if that jerk kicks you out of your home."

Color rushed to Alina's cheeks. She didn't say anything for the moment. "Let me think about it. Can I let you know?"

"I'll mark you down. If it doesn't work out, you can let me know tomorrow."

This was the first time Graham had a chance to visualize the Stirling residents as flesh and blood and not merely as numbers on a spreadsheet. He thought she'd at least be appreciative of the extra money he was offering—money his company didn't have to hand out.

Alina acted as though he was kicking them to the curb with nothing but their belongings. He'd made them a fair offer to move. And then he'd upped that offer if they moved sooner. In fact, his board had balked at the size of the offer but that hadn't stopped him from making it happen.

Alina turned back to him. "I have to get back to work."

"I tracked you down so we could come to some sort of agreement."

She shook her head. "You wasted your time."

"I can wait, you know, until you have another break." He

had meetings all morning but they could be moved. This was more important.

"I won't have a break for hours. I just started my shift. And I can't just have you sitting here all day taking up space."

"Then have dinner with me." The words were out before he realized how they might sound.

Her eyes widened with surprise. "No."

Ouch! His ego took a direct hit. He wasn't used to being turned down by women. Not that he wanted to date Alina—or anyone else for that matter. He had enough issues to deal with at the office without having to figure out a relationship—something he was not good at, just ask his ex-girlfriend.

"Wait. I didn't mean that as in an actual *date* date." He noticed the color bloom in her cheeks and he couldn't help but think how beautiful she looked. As soon as the thought came to him, he dismissed it. He refused to get distracted. "What I meant was that we could have a business dinner."

She shook her head. "I don't think it's a good idea."

He wasn't going to let this go, even if it meant opening himself up to some pushback. "I thought you wanted to speak to the man who bought your building."

"I do," she said quickly.

"Good." He smiled satisfactorily. "I'll send a car to pick you up at six." He got to his feet.

"What? No."

"Are you saying you aren't interested in pitching your reasons for keeping the building as is?"

"I...uh...sure, I want to."

"Then this is your chance."

She hesitated. "Fine."

They exchanged phone numbers before he left.

The truth was that he didn't want to spend his time listening to all of her sentimental reasons why the building shouldn't be demolished for a new high-rise to be put in its place. He'd never conducted one of these meetings himself, but he'd witnessed his father conduct them.

His father had never been one for patience. He'd barely let the other party get a sentence or two out of their mouth before he'd shut them down. But Graham wasn't his father. And sometimes people just needed to feel as though they'd been heard. He would keep his word and hear Alina out. That didn't mean he would change his mind.

CHAPTER THREE

WHY IN THE world had she agreed?

For the remainder of the day, Alina could think of nothing else but her upcoming date…er, business meeting with Graham. So much so that she'd messed up two orders and received a gentle reprimand from her supervisor. Then upon her return home, she learned Grace Taylor's kitchen sink had a leak. When Alina went to work on it, she'd been distracted by thoughts of what to wear to dinner that evening. When instead of tightening the joint, she'd loosened it and ended up with water in her face. It'd startled her back to reality and she focused on the task at hand.

Once finished with the sink she rushed back to her apartment. Having no idea what to wear to a trendy downtown restaurant, Alina texted her friend Meg. Her friend promptly showed up at her door. "I can't believe you're having dinner with him."

"It's not dinner." When Meg arched a disbelieving brow, Alina said, "Well, it is dinner but it's not like you're thinking. It's all about business. That's it."

"Uh-huh." Meg's tone said she didn't believe her protests.

"It is." Alina ignored the way her heart raced and her heart pounded when she thought about sitting across the table from Graham and staring into his dark mesmerizing eyes as they talked. The enemy shouldn't be so handsome.

"Now what should I wear?" She held up a dark pair of jeans with a red cable-knit sweater. "What about this?"

Meg's brow rose high on her forehead. "Where did you say he was taking you for dinner?"

"Um… I'm not sure. The information is on my phone." She rushed over to her bedside table to grab her phone. "It doesn't give the name, just an address." She read it off.

Meg typed it into her phone. "That's not a restaurant. It's an office building. And not just any office building but the renowned Diamond Building."

Alina frowned. Of course he'd want to meet there. After all, he was only meeting with her to discuss the sale of the Stirling Apartments. That made her decision of what to wear easy because her attire didn't matter. There would be no dress code where she was going.

"Good. That's decided." Alina clutched the jeans and sweater.

Meg reached out and pulled the clothes out of Alina's grasp. "You can't wear that."

"Why not?" Alina frowned. "You just said it wasn't a restaurant, which means I get to feel comfortable."

"Not if you want to impress this guy."

"I don't want to impress him."

"Yes, you do." Meg's eyes implored her to be reasonable. "Why do you have to be so stubborn?"

"Why would I want to impress the man responsible for taking away my home and the home of my friends?" Yes, she thought of most everyone in that apartment building as her friends, except her stepmother and two stepsisters.

It wasn't that she'd always disliked them. In fact, in the beginning it was quite the opposite. She thought it would be nice to have a mother figure, not that anyone would ever replace her mother, but to have two sisters would be amazing. In the end, it had been an amazing disaster.

"Alina, listen to me. You need this guy on your side. He's the only one that can stop the demolition of the building."

As much as she wanted to argue with her friend, Meg was right. The end was in sight and her options were limited. If there was going to be a Christmas miracle, it would have to come from Mr. Scrooge, er… Mr. Toliver.

With the utmost reluctance, Alina asked, "What do you think I should wear?"

"Let me see." Meg rummaged through Alina's closet.

Hangers rattled together. There were a lot of no's and Alina had a feeling putting her friend in charge of her attire for the evening was a mistake.

All the while Prince laid on her bed, staring at her as though she were a traitor for getting dolled up for the enemy. Or maybe that was her own guilt. But if there was any chance of changing this guy's mind about where he built his high-rise, she would do what was necessary for the residents of the past, those of the present and the ones of the future.

Alina was ready to go promptly at seven.

It was already dark out but the inky black sky was clear—the big moon hovered overhead but there were too many lights in Manhattan for her to make out the stars.

A black sedan rolled to a stop in front of the Stirling. The driver got out and opened her door for her. She had no idea when Graham said he'd send a car that it would be chauffeur driven. She'd thought he'd meant he would send a taxi to pick her up. She climbed in. This black high-end sedan with tinted windows was quite a few steps up from a taxi. As her hand ran over the buttery-soft black leather seat, she realized it was way out of her league. With this sort of luxury, no wonder Mr. Toliver couldn't understand how an old building could mean so much to so many people.

She glanced down at her little black dress, the one she'd almost refused to wear. She was thankful Meg had been so insistent on her dressing up. Like it or not, if she wanted Mr. Toliver to take her seriously, jeans and a casual sweater weren't going to do the trick.

And maybe some inside information would help. "Excuse me."

"Yes, ma'am," the driver said.

"Do you drive regularly for Mr. Toliver?"

"Yes, ma'am. We should be there in five minutes."

"Thanks. But what I was wondering is, what is Mr. Toliver like?" She had no idea if the driver would speak to her about his employer, but it was worth a try because time was running out before everyone at the Stirling was out on the street.

"Mr. Toliver is the best boss I've ever had."

Now, that shocked her. Sure, she expected the man to say something nice about his boss. After all, he had his job to protect, but this man went above and beyond, saying that Graham was the best.

Maybe it was just that the man didn't know Mr. Toliver well enough. "How long have you worked for him?"

"I've worked for him and his family for eleven years."

Okay. So that wasn't the issue. Maybe it was that the man hadn't worked as a driver for anyone else and had no one to compare him to. "And before you became the Tolivers' driver what did you do?"

"I've been a driver since I graduated high school. My father owns a fleet of cars for hire. But once I started driving for the Tolivers, they requested me regularly. And then one day, the Tolivers hired me full-time. I've been with the family ever since. Mr. Graham is good people. Do right by him and he'll do right by you."

Alina was floored. She really wanted some dirt on the man. She wanted every reason to dislike him. After all, he was taking away her home. And then there was this man who was more than willing to sing the man's praises.

But that couldn't be the truth. She'd read some articles online about the Toliver company being ruthless in business. That was the man she needed him to be so they could go to war over the apartment building. So what if the driver had a different view of Toliver. It didn't mean it was the right view.

The car dropped her off in front of the Diamond Building and she stepped out onto the cleared sidewalk. She lifted her head, trying to see the top of the building. It rose higher and higher until the top floors got lost in the night sky. This man owned all of this? Wow.

Not that she was going to let herself be impressed. He owned all of this because he plowed over people's hopes, dreams and homes to be the biggest and the best.

The uniformed guard behind the impressive reception desk directed her to an elevator that took her to the top floor. She'd be lying to herself if she said she wasn't nervous. There wasn't one thing about this evening that didn't lead her to believe this man had untold power, from his fancy chauffeured car to his company's impressive building. But none of that was going to stop her from speaking her mind.

Graham Toliver might have a lot of power and even more money but he needed to be reminded that his actions had consequences. And though she'd much rather be at home watching a romantic comedy on television while eating Chinese takeout on the couch, she would stand here in her rarely worn little black dress and black heels. She would speak her mind. And she hoped he would really hear her.

She could do this. She thought of all the people in the building who were counting on her to save their homes. She had to do this.

The elevator dinged and then the door rolled back to reveal a big white lobby with a crystal chandelier. Whatever this place was, it was meant to impress people. She was impressed. But it wouldn't deter her from fighting for her home—for her family.

There was only one doorway, so she headed toward it. It was a long hallway that opened into a great room. The walls were black and the floor was white marble. It was quite stunning. And she was starting to suspect that she was in the wrong place.

The room was empty except for one long solitary table. But where was Mr. Toliver?

"You came."

The male voice had her turning to the left and there stood Graham Toliver. He was wearing the same charcoal suit and blue shirt that he'd been wearing earlier that day. How was it that he still looked as fresh as he had hours ago? If she'd have worn the same thing all day, it would look utterly disheveled.

And yet Mr. Toliver stood before her looking like he'd just stepped off the pages of a glossy fashion magazine. And for a moment, her mind stuttered. In that moment, she forgot he was the enemy. And for the briefest second, she imagined what it might be like to meet the man for a dinner date. Her heart picked up its pace. Oh, yes, he would make some lady very happy. But it wasn't to be her. Her feet came back down to earth.

"Of course I came," she said, blinking away her daydream. "We have things to discuss."

He approached her. His eyes were dark and unreadable. "Yes, we do. Please come this way."

She wanted to ask him where they were going, but she resisted the urge. She had no doubt it would be his office. His very big, very impressive office where he would try to bulldoze over her with what he needed and what he wanted.

"Come in," he said.

"What is this?" She glanced around.

"This is a conference room. All of the walls are removable so that the top floor can hold everyone in the office. It's where we host guest speakers and hold training seminars. But for tonight, I had them shrink the size of the room. I hope it's adequate."

"It's very nice." She was drawn to the wall of windows.

She gazed out over Manhattan, which at the moment twinkled with all of the city lights. "I don't know how you get any work done here. I'd be staring out the window all of the time."

He moved next to her. He was so close that she could reach out and touch him, not that she would, or anything, but her pulse raced just being so close to him. It was though an energy force pulsated off him.

"It's an amazing view." His voice was deep and rich, sending waves of awareness throughout her body.

She had to concentrate on anything but how her body responded to him. "Too bad you can't see the Christmas tree in Times Square."

"I'm afraid not. I take it you like that sort of thing."

"You mean getting into the Christmas spirit?" When he nodded, she asked, "Doesn't everyone enjoy the holidays?"

"No."

She turned to him and recalled their discussion at the restaurant. "That's right. You hate Christmas?"

"Hate might be a bit strong, but I could live without it."

He cleared his throat. "However, that's not what you're here to discuss."

She looked at him, taking in his serious expression. She felt bad for him and his complete lack of holiday spirit. She wanted to dislike this man. After all, he was tearing down her home, but there was a part of her that felt sorry for him. What had happened to him that he'd lost his joy of the season? Or was it possible he'd never been excited about Christmas?

An image of Graham as a little boy flashed in her mind. She just couldn't believe a man who came from a wealthy background would have been deprived on Christmas morning. There had to be a story there, but she resisted the urge to ask him about it.

CHAPTER FOUR

THE ROOM WAS devoid of Christmas decorations.

No tree. No twinkle lights. Nothing.

What was up with that? Maybe they didn't have a chance to get them out yet. It was still a few weeks before Christmas. Alina's gaze moved about the room with its immaculate presentation and perfectly arranged wall hangings. It felt cold and sterile.

It was then that she noticed the soft sound of music. She listened closely, expecting it to be a holiday tune. It wasn't. Interesting. Instead, big band music played. It was nice but not what she had been playing on her radio. From now until Christmas, she was listening to Christmas carols 24/7. There was just something about those festive tunes that put an extra pep in her step.

Graham moved to a small table. She followed, finding two black, thickly cushioned chairs placed on opposite ends of the small table. In the center was a white tapered candle. Its flame flickered. And there were two place settings of what looked to be real china. A private dinner for two?

Alina's heart pitter-pattered. Was this the way Mr. Toliver conducted all of his meetings? She doubted it. She didn't see him sitting across a candlelit table from a businessman to discuss a future deal. So why was he treating her different?

Immediately she wondered if he was interested in her. And just as quickly she dismissed the foolish notion. Why would he be interested in her? He didn't even know her. Worst of all, she was standing in his way of demolishing her apartment building. And she intended to keep on impeding his progress as much as possible.

So what was up with this dinner? Was he hoping some candlelight and good food would sway her? Did he think she'd be that easy? If so, he had another thought coming.

"Mr. Toliver—"

"Please call me Graham."

His friendly gesture wasn't going to soften her up. "All right. Graham, I thought you wanted to talk business."

"As a busy man, I multitask." His tone was matter-of-fact. "Since it is my dinnertime, I thought we would eat while we talk."

She didn't know how she felt about sitting down to a meal with the enemy. Still, at last she'd made it past his bulldog of an assistant, who had previously not let her move beyond the reception area. Perhaps some food might make him more congenial.

"Mr.—er, I mean Graham, our business shouldn't take all that long."

"Then we should begin the meal." He signaled to the server standing across the room.

"Please sit down." He pulled out a chair for her.

Part of her was still hesitant, but she knew it wouldn't help her cause. And without changing his mind about his proposed building site, she would be homeless in the new year.

She approached him. "Thank you." As he waited to help push in her chair, she said, "I've got it."

His eyes momentarily widened, but in a blink his reaction faded. "I didn't expect you to make this easy on me, but do we have to spend the evening in constant opposition? You don't even know me well enough to dislike me that much."

It was true. She didn't know anything about him, except what she'd gleaned on the internet. She hadn't even found a current photo of him, just something from when he was in college with long shaggy hair and a beard. Now his thick dark hair was clipped short around the sides with some longer curls on top. And his sun-kissed face was clean-shaven. The images of him then and now certainly didn't look anything alike.

This was the first time she realized how defensive she'd let herself become. She didn't like the thought that she'd changed so much and not for the good.

Maybe that had played a part in the reason she hadn't had a date in quite a while. Not that this was a date. Far from it.

She had been once bitten by her ex and now she was twice shy. People she could rely on—people she could trust—were hard to find. And she certainly didn't trust Mr. Designer Suit with his billion-dollar smile. He would say and do most anything to get her to move. And it wasn't going to happen—not without a fight.

Graham took a seat across the small table from her. Lifting her gaze, she took in his strong jawline, his straight nose and those very observant eyes. She wondered if he'd been studying her, as well.

When he smiled, her stomach dipped. She caught herself just before she smiled back at him. After all, she didn't trust him. Not at all.

Or was it herself that she worried about the most. All it took was for him to smile for her to forget that they were here to do business.

"So why do you have to build where the Stirling stands?" She wanted to get to the heart of the problem, hoping to find an alternative solution.

"You don't waste time getting to the point, do you?" He stared at her as though not quite sure what to make of her.

"These days I don't have time to waste."

"In that we have something in common."

She honestly didn't see where they had anything in common. She lived in a modest apartment while he sat here in one of the finest buildings in Manhattan—a building she'd heard he owned. And yet he longed for another building—a bigger one—a new one. No, they had no common ground.

"I doubt we have anything in common," she said.

Interest flared in his eyes. "Is that a challenge?"

A challenge? "No. It's a fact."

His gaze narrowed. "Do you know how much time and effort goes into running a business of this size?"

"No."

"I didn't think so or you wouldn't say something so careless."

She paused for just a moment, letting things settle. "I didn't mean to imply you didn't work hard."

"It certainly sounded like it."

She shook her head. This conversation had gotten off track. "Maybe we should get back to the reason I'm here."

His jaw visibly tightened as a tense silence filled the air. Then he nodded. "If you think that by us having this meeting means I'll change my mind about the fate of the Stirling, it isn't going to happen."

She didn't like that he could read her thoughts. She let his words hang in the air without a response. And then she once more asked, "Why do you have to tear down the Stirling?"

He leaned back in his chair and crossed his arms. "Not that I owe you an explanation, but my company already owns some of the surrounding properties."

"So you figured why not buy more and level the place?"

"It's a matter of using assets to their full value."

As she looked at him, she noticed there was something else in his eyes. Was that sorrow? Or perhaps regret? She couldn't be certain.

And what did he mean by their full value? She considered asking for clarification, but she already knew enough about him to realize he wouldn't be very forthcoming.

Just then the server returned with crystal stemware filled with shaved ice topped with a half dozen jumbo shrimp, a lemon wedge and cocktail sauce. It wasn't until it was in front of her that she realized she hadn't stopped to eat since that morning.

And then the rumble of her stomach filled the air. The heat of embarrassment swirled in her and rushed to her face, setting her cheeks on fire. She hesitated to eat, even if her mouth watered just looking at the food.

"Go ahead." Graham unfolded his white linen napkin. "Eat."

He didn't have to tell her twice. She was so hungry she could have woofed down the appetizer in no time, but she mustered her restraint, not wanting to give Graham a bad impression of her.

Between courses, Graham said, "Why are you fighting so hard to save an old building? That place quite honestly could use some updating."

Her mouth opened but her mind was unable to keep up with her rapidly firing fragments of outrage. She pressed her lips together as she formulated a cohesive response. "It's more than an old building. And what you might call flaws, I call charm."

"I know it's your home now, but that doesn't mean you can't make a home somewhere else."

Before she could respond, their salads and fresh baked bread were served. They quietly ate but all the while her mind was spinning so much so that she didn't even notice what she was eating.

She had to convince Graham that the Stirling was so much more than brick and mortar. But how? And why would he think that homes were so easily interchangeable? Was that the way all rich people thought?

Alina's fork hovered over her salad plate. "The Stirling is irreplaceable. It is full of family and friends."

"Nothing that can't be found somewhere else."

She inwardly groaned. He wasn't hearing her, not the way she needed him to hear her. If her words weren't enough, she needed to show him what the Stirling meant to her and its residents.

"Is that how you feel about your home?"

He took a sip of ice water. When he returned the stemmed glass to the table, he said, "I like where I live, but if there was a compelling reason to move, I'd do it without making a big deal out of it."

She looked at him in disbelief. "I think it's easier said than done."

"Are you doubting me?" His eyes challenged her.

She leveled her shoulders and lifted her chin ever so slightly. "I am."

His brown eyes grew dark as a muscle in his cheek twitched. "You presume to know me, but I don't care how much you've read about me, you still know nothing about me."

But that wasn't exactly true. She could see that he was a man who rose to a challenge. It was knowledge she intended to use to her advantage.

The main course consisted of a pasta dish served with marinara sauce and topped with fresh herbs. On the side was chicken parmesan with a thin but crispy coating and some steamed vegetables. It looked delicious and tasted even better.

As she savored each delectable bite, she considered how to open Graham's eyes to the fact that the Stirling was so much more than an old building—more than a hitch in his plans.

When she could eat no more, she pushed aside her plate. It was then that she glanced over at Graham. She noticed he didn't seem interested in his food as he moved it around his plate. He appeared lost in his thoughts.

"Thank you for the meal," she said. "It was very good."

"This was a mistake." Graham balled up his napkin and tossed it on the table.

"What do you mean? The meal?"

"All of it. I thought we could conclude our business over a friendly dinner but obviously that was a miscalculation." Graham stood. "I think we should conclude our business in my office."

She welcomed the excuse to get away from this cozy candlelit dinner. Because even though the room was quite large, Graham's larger than life presence made it feel so much smaller.

Alina nodded in agreement. She folded her napkin and then set it on the table. She noticed that he didn't wait for her as he took long strides toward the exit.

They went down one floor and it was a totally different atmosphere. Instead of being black and white, the foyer was done up in earth tones and royal blue carpet to muffle footsteps. A large reception area sat directly in front of the elevator. On the wall were gold letters that spelled out GH Toliver Investments.

He moved to the right and held open a glass door for her to pass by. And then he led her to the office at the end of the hallway. When he swung open one of the two oversize wooden doors, she wasn't sure what to expect, but it wasn't to find his desk stacked with files. When she looked to the side, there was a long table. It, too, was piled with files.

"I'm sorry for the disheveled appearance," he said. "Since I've taken over, there has been a lot to review and my father was old-fashioned, preferring paper files."

He walked ahead of her, picked up a hefty stack of manila folders and clipped papers and placed them on the table. He returned to his desk. "There. That's better."

She sat down in front of his desk, while he took a seat in a large black leather chair. She didn't like the way she felt at a disadvantage now because her chair seemed shorter than his and a large desk sat between them. She remained perched on the edge of the chair, trying to decide if she should stand.

She wanted this man to take her seriously. After all, this was a very important matter, not just to her but to everyone who lived at the Stirling. Those people were the ones that brought her chicken soup when she didn't feel well and celebrated her birthdays with her. They'd unofficially adopted her after her father passed on and she would do anything for them.

"Mr. Toliver—"

"I thought we were past standing on ceremony."

"There's a lot at stake here and I want you to take me seriously."

"And I won't do that if you call me Graham?"

She narrowed her gaze on him. Why was he making this so difficult? If he was trying to distract her, it wasn't going to work. She had an idea in mind, one that had come to her at dinner after learning a bit about her enemy. A sexy one but an enemy all the same.

She swallowed hard as she prepared to start again. "This

matter is very serious for the both of us. You have a building that you want to build. And I have homes I want to save."

Graham rested his elbows on the desk and leaned forward. "And how do you propose we resolve this matter?"

"It's obvious that both of us can't have our way."

"Agreed. You know I'm offering a generous bonus if all of the tenants agree to move out at the beginning of the year. And for that to happen, I need *you* to agree to it."

Her heart clenched. To agree to his plan would mean this would be the last Christmas in the place that had always been her home. "Why me?"

"Because my investigator says that people follow your lead. And from what I witnessed this morning, I would agree. I also know you led the protest here at the office—"

"The protest you avoided."

"I was caught up in important meetings all day, but that doesn't mean I wasn't informed of the disruption."

Disruption? Well, she supposed he could have called it something worse. But it also didn't escape her that she was situated in a very strategic position. She slid back on the chair until the cushion touched her lower back. All the while, she worked up the courage to lay down a challenge—a challenge Graham wouldn't be able to turn down.

"What is it?" His voice interrupted her thoughts.

She focused on him. The idea hovered at the forefront of her mind. Even if he was motivated to win a challenge, there was a distinct possibility he'd turn her down. But if she didn't take this chance—if she didn't challenge him—she didn't have a backup plan.

"Just say it," he said. His gaze searched hers as though trying to figure out what she was thinking.

He was wasting his time trying to guess her thoughts because she scarcely believed what she had come up with. "I'll make you a deal."

His eyes momentarily widened. "You want to renegotiate my very generous offer to have the Stirling tenants move out early?"

"Yes." She hoped her voice sounded more confident than she felt.

There was a noticeable pause. "I'm listening."

Inside she secretly cheered. She'd hooked his interest. "You'll pay for everyone's moving expenses."

"And why would I do that?"

"To get my help. I don't come cheaply."

He leaned forward, resting his elbows on the desk. "I'm figuring that out." He paused as though considering the pros and cons of the suggestion. "You drive a tough bargain. But you have a deal."

"Not so fast. You haven't even heard my final condition."

A muscle in his jaw flexed. He steepled his fingers together as his laser-sharp focus zeroed in on her. "You're pushing your luck."

She knew it, but she couldn't stop now. She leveled her shoulders and met his stare. "Do you want to hear my final condition or not?"

He visibly swallowed as the muscles of his neck moved. "And what would that be? A penthouse for you?"

"Um, no. But now that you mention it…" Suddenly a smile pulled at her face. She couldn't help it. If she didn't hurry with this, she was going to break out into an embarrassing fit of nervous giggles and any chance of making her idea a reality would be lost. And so she rushed to get out her unheard-of demand. "Forget the penthouse. I want you to work for me until Christmas."

A deep frown came over his face. "If you aren't going to take this seriously—"

"I'm very serious. I need to pick up extra shifts at the café and I don't have time to do everything."

"And you want me to do what?"

"I want you to be the building manager."

His eyes widened. "You mean with a toolbox, wrench and such?"

She struggled not to laugh at the look of horror on his face. "Exactly. If a tenant has a problem, you fix it, or if it's too big, you call in experts."

"It surely can't be that much work that you can't handle it in the evenings."

"That's the thing. With this being the busiest time of the year at the café, I'm working a lot of hours. I don't have the extra time like I normally do."

He shook his head as he sat back in his chair. "I don't think you understand. I'm the CEO of a large company. I don't have time to play janitor."

"It's building manager."

"Whatever." He waved off her correction. "The point is I don't have time."

If she didn't do something quick, she was totally going to lose him. "So what you're saying is that you can't do the job."

"That's not what I said." Frown lines creased his brow.

"I bet you don't even know how to work a wrench."

He sat up straighter. "I hate to disappoint you, but I do."

It was her turn to be surprised. She struggled to keep it from showing on her face. "Good. Then you don't have a reason not to agree." And then she reinforced the challenge by saying, "That is, unless you think it'd be too much for you."

He frowned as he crossed his arms. If he was going to outright refuse, he would have done it by now, right? So was he actually considering her totally off the wall idea? And if he did accept, would the people in her building agree with her actions? She hoped so.

Seconds passed in utter silence.

It was though a wall had gone up in his eyes, blocking her attempts to get a glimpse of his inner thoughts. So much for the eyes being the windows to one's soul.

He leaned forward. "I need a day or two to consider this."

Wow! Maybe it wasn't such an outrageous idea, after all.

She hesitated, not wanting him to know just how excited she was to have him take her proposition seriously. "Okay, then. I'll wait to hear from you. I should be going."

He walked her to the elevator. All the while, she wasn't sure what to make of him. Was he really going to consider her offer? Or was he just stringing her along?

When the elevator door slid open, she turned to him. "Thank you for dinner. And the view. I loved the view."

He surprised her with a smile. It lit up his eyes and made him look younger and sexier, if that was possible. His gaze lowered to her lips. "It is a spectacular view."

And suddenly she had the distinct impression they weren't talking about the same thing. Was he considering kissing her? Her heart pitter-pattered faster as she grew warm. They definitely weren't talking about the same thing at all.

If she didn't step on that elevator right this moment, she had the feeling things would spin completely out of control. And she'd done so well negotiating with him. She refused to falter now for what? A moment of desire? A quick flirtation?

"G-good night," she stammered as she forced her feet to move.

"I'll be seeing you soon." His deep voice sent a wave of anticipation humming through her body.

The elevator door swished shut. She pressed the button

for the ground floor. What had happened? One moment they were negotiating a business arrangement and the next moment it was like he was considering kissing her good night. Or had she imagined the whole thing?

CHAPTER FIVE

HIS DAY STARTED before the sun.

The truth was Graham had tossed and turned most of the night. His thoughts had been filled with memories of his dinner with the intriguing Miss Martin. The evening had not gone at all as he'd expected.

After giving up on sleep, he grabbed a hot shower. He leaned against the tile wall as steamy jets beat against his sore muscles. Trying to undo the tangled mess his father had left him at the office was taking its toll on him. And the last thing he needed was this very bizarre agreement with Alina.

When the water started to cool off, he got out of the shower, dressed and headed up to his office. The one thing about taking over his father's city apartment was that it was in the same building as his office.

He was determined to answer some of his emails before the workday officially began and new emails started to flood his in-box. It was tough for him to concentrate on the business at hand as Alina's alluring beauty kept stealing away his thoughts. What was it about her that captivated him so much? She wasn't the first beautiful woman to cross his path. Still, there was something wholly unique about her that drew his attention.

Maybe it was Alina's spunk. She was certainly feisty—

"Good morning." Mary Barnes, his dependable assistant, entered his office wearing a friendly smile. "It looks like you've gotten a jump start on the day."

"Morning." He gazed at the older woman over the top of his monitor. "I have a lot to do today and wanted to get an early start."

Mary shook her head as she laid a stack of paperwork in his in-box. "You work too hard."

"I have to right now. You, of all people, know that."

"Your father certainly left you in a bind, but do you have to do so much on your own?"

"I can't lose the faith of the board."

She nodded. "I understand. If there's something else I can do to help, just let me know."

The decision he owed Alina weighed on his mind. He liked a challenge in business and his personal life. It kept life interesting. It'd been a long time since he met a woman who didn't agree with everything he said.

"What would you say if I told you I was going to work away from the office for a few weeks?"

The woman's eyes momentarily widened. She glanced down at the signed contracts she'd withdrawn from his outgoing basket. "You're going on vacation?"

"Hardly." He paused, realizing if he were going to do this, he would need her help. "I have some delicate negotiations to take care of."

"But you have a meeting with legal next week that you can't miss. And the acquisitions team has been calling every day for an opening in your schedule."

She was right. He couldn't just stop working from now until Christmas. It was impossible. Still, to save the company money in the long-term and to earn the board's respect, he needed to get the residents of the Stirling to move. The sooner, the better. The other buildings in the vicinity had already been vacated. The Stirling was the last holdout.

His father had always talked of one day building a permanent home for Toliver Investments on that site. His father hadn't lived long enough to bring his dream to life but Graham would do it. Toliver Tower would be built upon the land where his father was born and raised. Graham had visited his grandmother in a building adjacent to the Stirling when he was young. He'd played with the neighbor kids just like his father had done.

"Is there any reason I can't hold the meetings with legal and acquisitions via video?"

Mary opened her mouth to say something, but without uttering a word, she closed it.

"In this day and age of technology," he continued, "I don't see why I can't work remotely. After all, you'll be here to scan whatever mail or documents I need to see."

"Are you sure you're willing to take a step back?"

"No." His voice was firm. "I still intend to be on top of everything. And I will be in the office, just not every day all day long."

Mary arched a brow as she cast him a doubtful look. "If you can do it, I think some time away from this place would do you good. You work too hard."

"But you'll help me see that nothing falls through the cracks?"

She again nodded. "I'll do my best. Shall I start canceling your in-person meetings and make arrangements to move them to video calls?"

"Not yet. But I'll let you know."

He didn't like the thought of stepping back from being in the office because Mary was right, running the business remotely just wasn't the same. And he was a man who liked to be in control of everything.

However, now that he had a plan to make this outlandish idea work, he had to make a decision. But what should it be? Stay in the office and accept the costly delay in the building plans? Or take Alina up on her offer?

One very slow day passed.

Alina spent the time organizing a meeting of the tenants, including her stepmother. It was the first time in Alina's life that her stepmother sided with her about anything. But when her stepmother learned the size of the bonus for moving out early, she was all for it. The catch was they *all* had to agree to move early in order to receive the bonus.

There were heated discussions, but in the end Mr. Merryweather, who was like a grandfather to her, and Mr. Jackson, a talented musician, were the firm holdouts. However, when Alina pleaded with them and told them she had a plan, they said they trusted her. In the end, the plan was a go on her end. However, she hadn't heard back from Graham.

Day two dragged on.

As Thursday evening settled in, blanketing the world in darkness, there still was no word from Graham. Thank goodness for the glow of twinkle lights. They buoyed Alina's spirits. Miracles didn't always happen overnight. Sometimes they took time. However, it didn't make the wait any easier.

Alina had worked the breakfast shift that day as well as coordinated an afternoon Christmas party. Now she was home, pacing the floor. She'd checked her phone off and on all day. It looked like he wasn't even going to have the decency to phone her and turn down her proposal. She groaned in frustration.

Knock-knock.

How was she going to tell the people she cared about that their last chance to save the building was gone? Defeat weighed heavy on her. Now she was out of options. And she had no idea how to tell any of them, not after she'd pleaded with them to give her plan a chance.

Knock-knock.

"Coming." Alina drew in a steadying breath before heading for the door. She glanced through the peephole but couldn't see the person's face, just part of a shoulder.

"Who's there?"

"Graham."

Graham? At this hour? What did it mean?

She unlocked the door and swung it open. "What are you doing here?"

His eyes momentarily widened. "Not exactly the greeting I was expecting."

"Sorry. I just didn't expect to see you. Here. Now. This evening." Oh, she was rambling and making a fool of herself.

"Can I come in?"

Heat swirled in her chest. If she'd have known he was coming to visit, she would have cleaned up. As it was, her dinner dishes were stacked in the sink and her party planning papers for the café were scattered over the couch and coffee table. But what choice did she have?

She backed up, pulling the door wide open. "Sure. Come on in."

When he stepped into her living room, it suddenly seemed to shrink. *Oh, my, this guy is tall.* Her mouth went dry.

She closed the door and then rushed over to the couch and started to collect her papers into a pile. She would sort them out later.

"I…I was working," she said, not wanting him to think she was always this messy.

"I'm sorry for just dropping by. I just out at a business dinner when I realized I left your phone number at the office."

"Oh." She gestured to the two armchairs across from the couch. "Please have a seat."

Still wearing his coat, he moved to the armchair and perched on the edge. He obviously didn't intend to stay long.

Just then her cat entered the room and sauntered straight up to Graham. Prince jumped up on the arm of the chair and stared at Graham, who stared back at him.

"Is he friendly?" he asked.

"Oh, yes. Prince loves everyone."

Graham reached out to pet him. Prince hissed and ran away.

"Prince," she called. The cat kept walking. "Prince, come here." His ears didn't even twitch as he disappeared down the hallway to the bedroom. He always did have selective hearing. If it was time to eat, he heard everything, otherwise he was likely to ignore her admonishments. Alina turned back to Graham. "I'm so sorry. He never acts like that. He really is a nice cat. I swear."

The look in Graham's eyes said he didn't believe her. He cleared his throat. "I've given your proposal serious consideration."

The crucial moment was at hand. The breath caught in her chest. Her mind said that he was going to turn her down, but her heart hoped he wasn't a cold, calculating businessman.

His steady gaze met hers. "And I've decided to take you up on it."

"You did? I mean, that's great." She hoped.

"The reason it took me so long to get back to you was that I had to push the agreement through legal."

Legal? He had his lawyers weigh in on their arrangement? Just then he withdrew some folded papers from his inner jacket pocket. Why was she surprised? Everything to him came down to looking out for what was best for his company.

Graham held out the papers. "They're just waiting for your signature."

She accepted the papers and stared at them. When she'd proposed the arrangement, she never thought he would take it this seriously.

He leaned back in the chair. "If you want your attorney to look over it, that's fine. But I can promise you it's straightforward."

As she looked at the agreement, she found it was only two pages long and on the second page was Graham's signature.

"Alina, it's okay—"

She held up her finger for him to pause. She started to read it, line by line. And she was surprised to find the language was indeed straightforward, so much so that she could easily understand it. There was nothing in it they hadn't discussed. And the agreement ran from tomorrow through Christmas Eve.

Alina reached for a pen on her coffee table. She signed her name and handed it over. "So you'll be here tomorrow morning?"

He nodded.

"But you realize you'll need to stay here." When his eyes widened in surprise, heat infused her cheeks. "Not here. Not in my apartment. I…I meant here at the Stirling."

He leaned forward, resting his forearms on his thighs. "Where exactly do you envision me staying?"

She couldn't let him back out now. Sure, they signed a formal agreement, but she was certain Graham's legal team could get him out of it. "All of the units are currently occupied. But there's the building manager's office. It has a bed in the back as well as a small bathroom."

He leaned back in the chair as though her words had knocked him off balance. "You're serious, aren't you?"

"Well, you live too far away with the congestion of city traffic. If a pipe bursts or there's a real emergency, you should be close by." And she needed him to spend some serious time here so he would get to know the residents and learn how special Stirling and its inhabitants were to her.

He hesitated. Was he trying to figure out how to back out of this unusual arrangement? Her body tensed as she waited for his next words.

"Fine. I'll be back in the morning." He got to his feet to leave.

The morning? That didn't give her long to make the manager's office presentable, but then again it was small, so there wasn't much to clean.

She glanced up in time to see Graham headed for the door. "Wait." She rushed after him. "Before you go, I should take you around to meet everyone."

"Everyone?"

"Sure. There's sweet Mrs. Hanasey in 504 with her little dog, Louie. And then there is Mr. Jones down in 306. He's always asking for help with his crossword puzzle. Come on. They're anxious to meet you."

"Now?"

"Sure. In the morning, everyone will be rushing around getting ready for work and getting their kids off to school. And we don't want anyone mistaking you for a burglar, do we?"

He hesitated. "I suppose not."

And so they set off to all five floors, knocking on door after door. Most people were hesitant but no one was hostile. Thankfully her stepmother and stepsisters had departed on vacation. Hopefully they wouldn't return before Christmas, but then again, they never checked in with her.

When they stopped outside the building manager's office, Graham turned to her. "Are you going to show me my new home?"

She resisted the urge to worry her bottom lip. If she were to show him that office in its current disheveled state, she was certain he'd bolt for the door. And she wouldn't blame him.

"I…I don't have the key on me." It was the honest truth.

"Well, it is getting late. It can wait until the morning."

"Sounds like a plan." She smiled at him. "You should go. After all, you having packing to do." And she had to make the office homey or at least as welcoming as possible. Was that even possible?

"You're right." Standing in front of her, his gaze met hers. It lingered a moment longer than necessary, making her heart race. "Good night."

Alina swallowed hard. "Night."

It was the only word she trusted herself to say. She worried her voice would betray the way his nearness caused her body to heat up with desire. Not that she was planning to act on those urges. After all, he was the enemy. She couldn't forget that fact.

CHAPTER SIX

AGAINST HIS BETTER JUDGMENT, he'd agreed to Alina's outlandish request.

And ever since, Graham had been working to streamline his business interactions using Mary as his point person in the office. In the end, he'd had to tell his key people the truth about negotiating an early vacancy of the Stirling—just not the whole truth about being the building janitor. His pride refused to divulge it.

Still, people were impressed he was willing to take this important project on himself and not assign it to an underling. He was certain if they knew the details of his agreement with Alina, they wouldn't be impressed at all.

With his earpiece in place, ready to pick up all of his office calls, Graham's chauffeur-driven sedan pulled to a stop outside the Stirling. It was Friday morning at precisely seven a.m. Exactly on time. This was a good way to start things.

On his way in the door, he got precisely three suspicious looks, one *hello* and one *so you really came back* comment. He stopped at the building manager's door. He tried the doorknob but it was locked. Time to visit Alina. There was an added bounce to his step as he headed for the elevator.

However, when he found the elevator was stopped on the top floor, he headed back down the hall and took the steps to the third floor. With his luggage in hand, he paused in front of Alina's door. He couldn't help wondering if he'd made the right decision to go along with her plan. Not giving himself time to answer the question, he knocked on the door.

A moment passed before Alina answered, surprise written all over her pretty face. He glanced down, making sure in his rush he hadn't put on mismatched shoes. Nope. They matched. And he had on pants, a shirt and a coat. He'd remembered everything, even though he'd been distracted all morning with thoughts of seeing her again. Although not in a romantic way, of course.

He raised his gaze. "You look surprised to see me. I did get the time right, didn't I?"

"You did. I...I guess I'm just surprised you're really going through with this."

His brows scrunched together. "Have you changed your mind? Because we have a signed agreement."

She shook her head. "We're good. Come in."

He entered her apartment, dropping his bag by the door. With the morning sun streaming in through her living room windows, the rays bounced off the Christmas decorations, from a snowman wearing a red scarf that was situated on an end table to a crystal bowl in the center of the coffee table filled with shiny red ornaments. The more he looked around, the more he realized the whole room was decked out for the holidays.

"I've done a little decorating," she said.

"A little?" The words popped out of his mouth before he could stop them. It looked like a lot of decorations to him. What else could she possibly add?

As though reading his thoughts, she said, "It's still missing the Christmas tree, but with trying to balance two jobs, I haven't had time to get one." She gestured for him to wait a moment. "Let me grab my shoes and I'll show you where you'll be staying."

While she finished getting ready, he continued to glance around the apartment. The furniture was old but it was well cared for. The modest living room and kitchen were a bit crowded but otherwise orderly. He wondered if they were always this way or had she gone to the extra effort because she knew he'd be showing up. No, of course she wouldn't. She didn't seem to care what he thought of her—and maybe that was what held his interest.

"I'm ready." Alina approached the door.

He joined her there. When he drew near her, he inhaled a light scent of berries and champagne. It was an interesting combination. Before he could breathe in that intoxicating scent again, she exited the apartment. Disappointment assailed him.

He followed her to the elevator. She was quieter than she'd been in the past, but then again, she'd gotten what she'd wanted—him agreeing to play along with her plan— but if she expected this arrangement to change his mind about tearing down the Stirling, it wasn't going to happen. The tower and all it implied was just too important.

She pressed the down button and immediately the door slid open. He stepped inside, noticing just how small the elevator was compared to the bank of elevators at the Diamond Building where the Toliver offices were located.

Though rumor said that the Tolivers owned the Diamond Building, they didn't. And with the building fully occupied, there was no space for the company to expand. As it was, they had employees doubling and tripling in offices. It was getting bad. They needed the new building up and operational as soon as possible.

As the silence dragged on, Graham grew uncomfortable. He said the first thing that came to mind. "I wonder if there's enough work around here to necessitate me living here."

A knowing smile lit up her face. "You'll see."

Before he could respond, the elevator stopped, the door squeaked open and Alina was on the move again. She paused outside the building manager's office and inserted the door key. And then she swung open the door.

"Home sweet home." She stepped aside, letting him enter first.

He wasn't sure what he was expecting, but it certainly wasn't this. There were no windows in this room. Just one solitary light fixture overhead, which didn't illuminate the room all that well.

The gray walls were bare. There was an old metal desk with a few dings on the side. Though it had been cleaned off, probably by Alina, it was still not welcoming. It was about half the size of his sleek new desk at his office. There would definitely have to be some adjustments made if he were to work here, and he most definitely needed to work while he was here.

"I know it's not much," Alina said, "but I've moved most of the clutter to this big walk-in closet."

He turned around to find a door behind him. He followed Alina inside. A single light bulb hung overhead, illuminating two stepladders, a hot water tank, a couple of shelving units with some home improvement items and an assortment of other items.

"You weren't kidding about me being the building janitor—"

"Building manager," she corrected. "Most everything you'll need should be here. If not, let me know and we can work something out."

"I think I can manage."

"There's one more room to show you." Alina moved to the back of the unit and opened the door. "This is your bedroom."

As he stepped into the room, he noticed the minimal furnishings. Beneath a window was a twin bed and next to it was a nightstand with a lamp. Wait. A twin bed?

He hadn't slept in a bed that small since he was a kid. And to make matters worse, there was a pink comforter with large white polka dots. The pillow propped up against the headboard had a pink pillowcase with a unicorn. He inwardly groaned. He felt like he'd just stepped into a girl's dormitory.

"I know it's not fancy like what you're accustomed to, but I can assure you the entire place is clean. When some of the residents found out what I was doing, they offered to help."

He drew in a deep breath, smelling a fresh lemony scent. That should have made him feel better, but he still was having a very hard time adjusting to the accommodations. This wasn't going to do. Not at all. Not for a few weeks. Not even for a few days.

Yet he kept his thoughts to himself. He didn't want to insult Alina after the trouble she'd gone to. But hopefully she wouldn't mind him making this unit his own. After all, he did own the building. And he wasn't accustomed to asking anyone's permission to do as he pleased. He didn't plan to start now.

He stepped toward the small bed, barely big enough for his six-foot-three frame. He settled his bag on the end of the bed, causing the comforter to become disheveled. When he went to straighten it, he noticed it was double-sided. The bottom side was gray. Thank goodness. He'd flip it over, problem solved.

Ring-ring-ring.

Graham turned to Alina.

"It's the phone on the desk," she said. "I can get it for you."

He was tempted to take her up on her offer, but he said

he would do this and he refused to break his word. "I'm on it."

He didn't even want to imagine what problem awaited him. He picked up the phone with a friendly hello. The conversation was short and straight to the point. There was no small talk, just the problem laid out. Was this how his next few weeks were going to be?

"Yes, Mr. Merryweather. I'll be right there." Graham hung up the apartment phone.

"What did he want?" Alina asked.

"It appears there's a leak in his bathroom."

A smile came over Alina's face and though Graham already thought she was beautiful, when she smiled, it took his breath away. There was something about this woman that was very special.

"What are you smiling about?" He wondered if he had some breakfast stuck in his teeth.

"Nothing."

"It's something."

"It's just that I never imagined a big CEO like you would be willing to fill in as the building maintenance guy." She glanced at her fitness tracker. "I don't have much time before I have to leave for work, but I can go with you."

"Don't worry. I've got this."

He hoped. He wasn't going to mention that he'd been guided to YouTube videos by his assistant. When he'd checked it out, he'd found they had how-to videos on most every subject. He just hoped the tutorials were enough.

"Okay. If you don't need anything else, I should be going." She started for the door before turning back. "Oh, I forgot. You'll need this."

When she handed over the key, their fingers touched. Her skin was warm and soft. His gaze met hers. There was a spark of emotion in her blue eyes—cornflower blue like the flowers in the sunny field, a place where you could lose track of time—and he could easily get lost in her beautiful eyes. She withdrew her hand and the connection was broken.

As she walked away, he stood in the doorway staring at her retreating form as though hypnotized by the gentle sway of her hips. It wasn't until she stepped out of sight that he snapped out of his trance. He gave himself a mental jerk. He couldn't let himself get distracted—no matter how sweet the distraction.

CHAPTER SEVEN

WHAT HAD HE been thinking?

He shouldn't be here. Being a building manager was way outside of his skill set. How Alina managed it all plus her work at the café was truly impressive. Thankfully his very first job was really quite easy and no YouTube video was necessary. All it took was a few turns of the wrench.

Graham carried the red toolbox into the living room. "All fixed."

"Thanks," Mr. Merryweather said from his spot on his brown recliner, a sports station playing on the television while he held a book in his hands. "I used to be able to do those things but I can't get down on my knees the way I used to."

"No problem."

Mr. Merryweather gazed at him over his reading glasses. "You taking over the maintenance job from Alina?"

"Only temporarily. She's busy working holiday parties at the restaurant."

Mr. Merryweather nodded. "Glad to hear she'll be back."

"Why's that?"

"She always has time to talk." *Wasn't that what he was doing now?* Mr. Merryweather continued. "And she usually brings a treat?"

"A treat?"

Mr. Merryweather nodded again. "She makes the best cookies."

The man really thought he was going to take time out of his busy day to bake? Not a chance. "Sorry. I don't bake."

Mr. Merryweather's face grew serious as his bushy white brows drew together. "Because you're too busy kicking people out of their homes."

Ouch. This man certainly wasn't worried about pulling his punches. Was that why Alina had smiled when he'd told her who was on the phone?

Regardless, he still needed to get through to the man. "Mr. Merryweather, wouldn't it be nice to get a new place? Maybe one where the plumbing is updated?"

Hmph! "The plumbing here is just fine. And the name is Merryweather."

"That's what I said, Mr. Merryweather."

The man sighed. "There's no mister. It's just Merryweather."

"Okay, Merryweather. I'm no expert but even I can see that the building needs some work."

Right then Graham's earpiece buzzed, signaling an incoming call. But whoever it was would have to wait. This conversation was important.

Merryweather frowned at him. "Just because things get old doesn't mean they should be disregarded."

Graham opened his mouth and then promptly closed it. He wondered what it'd take to get the man on board with the sale. Because Graham was beginning to realize he was going to have to win over the tenants one at a time.

"You could pick out wherever you want to move." Graham's gaze moved to the television. "Maybe somewhere close to sporting events so you could see them in person instead of having to watch them on television."

"I like my television. I can see the game better than if I were there in person."

It seemed as though Mr. Merryweather—er, Merryweather—was determined to argue with him, no matter what Graham said. The best thing for him to do now was to pick up his red toolbox—er, Alina's red toolbox—and head out the door.

"I should be going," Graham said.

"You won't be back, right?"

What? That was a strange comment. "Not unless you call."

"No. I mean, next time Alina will come to do the work, right?"

"I'm going to be filling in for Alina until Christmas."

"Oh." Talk about a deflated sound.

Graham shifted his weight from foot to foot. He couldn't help but wonder if this was what his employees thought with him stepping in to fill his father's place at the helm of the company. He didn't do things like his father had done for many years. And he knew it bothered a lot of employees.

However, his father's resistance to change had put the company in a bind. There was no room to grow. And building a new home for Toliver's was the only way to secure its future.

"What if I were to bring a treat the next time I visit?"

Interest lit up the older man's face. "What sort of treat?"

Graham didn't realize details would be necessary. "What would you suggest?"

"Well, I don't know. You're the one that mentioned it."

Technically, Merryweather had been the first to mention a treat. This was all Alina's fault. Whoever heard of a handyman bringing baked goods to the tenants? Wasn't it enough to fix whatever may be broken? Leave it to Alina to raise the bar. No wonder no one wanted to move.

"How about sugar cookies?" Graham suggested. "After all, it's the holiday season."

"No. Alina bakes the best sugar cookies."

Graham sighed because the big toolbox was growing heavy and he didn't want to put it down as that might signal he was staying for a while and that wasn't the case.

"I know, gingersnaps." Merryweather smiled. "My mother used to make them. They were just right with a punch of flavor and they snapped when you bit into them."

Were those Christmas cookies? Graham wasn't up on his Christmas fare, but then again, did it really matter so long as Merryweather was happy? He just wondered if the Polka Dotted Bakery made them. "Gingersnaps, it is. Goodbye, Mr. Merryweather."

"Tell Alina I said hi."

"I'll do that."

Graham let himself out of the apartment and headed toward the elevator. Then, realizing that every time he stepped in it he could run into a tenant that inevitably needed something done around their apartment, he opted to take the stairs.

But when he opened the fire door and stepped into the hallway of the first floor, there was an older woman standing outside the building manager's door. He inwardly groaned.

It was probably another tenant that needed help with something or other. And he really didn't have time. He had five reports that needed reviewed and two memos to sign off on. How Alina maintained another job in addition to managing the building was totally beyond him. This position seemed to be full-time and then some—and he'd been here less than two hours!

"Can I help you?" he asked.

The older woman turned to him. Her bright red lips pursed together as her eyes narrowed behind black framed glasses. "Do I know you?"

He didn't recall her from his brief tour the prior evening. But it had gotten too late to meet everyone. "No, you don't."

"Then what are you doing in this building?" And then her gaze lowered to the toolbox in his hand. "You borrowed Alina's toolbox?"

"Worse than that, I'm filling in for the building manager."

"Oh." Her eyes widened. "For a moment, I'd forgotten about Alina's arrangements."

"Do you need something fixed?"

"Come with me." She crooked her finger.

His business would have to wait a bit longer. Perhaps he should have asked Alina more questions before agreeing to her terms. From his point of view, she definitely got the better end of the deal.

He was the sexiest building manager ever.

As soon as the totally inappropriate thought of Graham came to Alina, she dismissed it.

The next morning, Alina couldn't think of Graham as just another man. He was anything but the usual guy that passed through her life and it was more than his devastatingly handsome looks. He held the keys to her future. He decided if she stayed or left—of whether she clung to the makeshift family that had surrounded her through the loss of both of her parents. And it was for that reason she had to keep her wits about her.

Showered and dressed for work, she moved to her bedroom door to find Prince waiting for her. He lifted his head and blinked.

"Mrrrr..."

He got up from his spot at the end of the bed and rubbed over her ankles. Alina bent over and picked him up. Prince stretched his neck, pressing his nose to hers. Alina's heart swelled with love.

She ran her hand down over Prince's back as his deep purr emanated. Holding him with one arm, she opened the door. She carried the still purring Prince to the kitchen, where she lowered him to the floor.

"Mrrrr..."

"Okay, I'm getting your breakfast." She reached in the cabinet and grabbed a can of cat food and one of Prince's bowls.

Once Prince was taken care of, she turned and filled the coffeemaker with water and added a pod. With a press of a button, her morning caffeine was under way. And boy did she need a nice big mug of coffee this morning.

Prince sat next to her as he woofed down his breakfast like he hadn't been fed in days. When the bowl was licked clean, he looked up at her. His eyes begged her for seconds.

"Sorry, buddy, that's all you get. The vet said I had to quit spoiling you." When she bent down to soften her words by scratching behind his ears, he dashed past her. He definitely didn't like his new diet.

Knock-knock.

Alina opened the door to find Graham standing there. "Good morning."

"I need more time."

"Time? Time for what?" She had no idea what he was talking about.

He smiled at her and then pointed at the earpiece. "I don't care what you have to do to make it work. I'm not signing off until I have a chance to review the details. And yes, I know it's Saturday. I have to go." He glanced at her, looking a bit sheepish. "Sorry about that. It was the office."

"Come in. Why are you working on the weekend?"

"Business waits for no man."

She shook her head in disbelief. He needed a break more than she thought. She gave Graham a quick once-over, finding him dressed in jeans and a red sweater. At least it was a change from his designer suits and ties. Although she couldn't decide which look she preferred. He looked good no matter what he wore—

She stopped herself. What was it about being around him that muddled her thinking? She just got done telling herself that she wasn't going to be susceptible to his good looks. This was important. He had to take her seriously.

"Is something wrong?" He glanced down at his outfit, then lifted his head, his brows knitted together in confusion.

"Uh. No, I...I was just thinking that I had to make time to get a Christmas tree before all of the good ones are picked over." She busied herself by pouring him a cup of coffee. "I'm sure you already have your tree."

He accepted the cup. "I told you I'm not a fan of Christmas."

"Oh, that's right." Alina couldn't imagine not doing anything at all. She loved Christmas. The joy of the season was so infectious. "Not even when you were a kid?"

Graham shrugged. "My father said it was nothing more than a marketing scheme."

"That's so sad because it's so much more. Maybe you'll see it differently this year."

"I don't think so. I have my business to run and it takes up all of my time."

"You know what they say about all work and no play."

He took a sip of coffee. "Are you implying I'm boring?"

She held up both hands in innocence. "I don't even know you yet." Alina filled her to-go coffee mug. "I have to go to work now. Was there anything you needed?"

"I was wondering if you'll be around for dinner." He

rushed to add, "It'll be a business dinner as I'm sure I'll have questions about the building."

"Sorry, I'll be late. I'm going to work as many hours as they'll give me throughout the holidays."

"Because of me?"

She busied herself, checking for her keys and purse, in order to avoid his pointed gaze. And then she decided that they couldn't just dance around this subject. She lifted her head and met his gaze straight on. "Yes. Rent in this city is going to cost a fortune. And even with everything I'm saving, I don't know if I can afford to live someplace else. And I have it better than other people in the building who are retired with no means of raising additional income."

He frowned. "I'm giving out bonuses."

"But how far will they go? Let me tell you, not very far at all."

Graham rubbed the back of his neck. "I don't know what to say."

"I don't expect you to say anything. I just need you to understand—really understand—the ramifications of your actions." She shrugged on her red coat. "Is your new building really this important?"

"Yes." Graham's voice was firm.

It was not the answer she wanted to hear. She grabbed her stocking cap, decorated with a design of white snowflakes, from her coat pocket. She couldn't get upset. She had to remain calm. After all, her plan to change his mind had barely begun.

She forced a smile to her lips. "I've got to get going. I'll see you later." Just then Prince returned to her side. She bent down to pet him. "I'll see you later, too. Be good."

Prince turned around to walk away. He paused in front of Graham and looked up at him. Alina would love to know what Prince was thinking. When Graham noticed, he moved to pet Prince, who once again scurried away. What was up with that? Was it possible Prince was jealous? Laughter bubbled up in her throat.

"It's not funny," Graham said. "He just won't give an inch."

"Hey, he didn't growl at you this time. That's something."

He held up the still full cup. "Mind if I bring this back later?"

"Not at all."

Graham headed for the door, but she was standing between him and the door. As he passed by her, their bodies briefly brushed against each other. Her heart slammed into her chest as awareness set every one of her nerve endings a-tingling. So much for telling herself that she could treat Graham like everyone else.

"I'll see you later," she said as she put the lid on her to-go mug.

"I'll be here."

And then the door closed. She could at last take a full breath. This was going to be a very long few weeks. Very long indeed.

CHAPTER EIGHT

HER FEET ACHED.

Her knees ached.

Her arms ached.

Okay, so there wasn't a part of Alina's body that didn't ache. She'd worked a ten-hour shift. Ten hours of being on her feet, carrying heavy trays of food to table after table, was exhausting. She couldn't wait to get back to her party planning. At least then she'd be seated.

After this very busy week, all she wanted to do on this Friday evening was kick off her rubber-soled shoes and climb in a bubble bath with a couple of candles and a captivating thriller. She wanted to get lost in the pages as the heroine outsmarted the killer.

But when she entered the foyer of her apartment building, she breathed in the most delightful aroma of... What was that? And where was it coming from?

She inhaled again. The scent of oregano and garlic called to her. Her stomach rumbled in response. She'd been too busy at work to stop and eat. But on the plus side, she'd received the biggest tip that night. And it was going straight toward her future rent/deposit.

Graham stepped into the hallway. Upon seeing her, his eyes widened. "You just saved me a trip."

She approached him. "How did I do that?"

"I was headed to your apartment to leave a note on your door."

"About what?"

"Dinner." He went on to tell her that he had had dinner delivered from one of Manhattan's poshest restaurants.

"Wow. I've heard how hard it is to get a table. No one ever said they have delivery service."

"They don't."

"But you—"

"Know the owner."

"Lucky you."

Alina took a step back. "I'll let you eat before it gets cold."

"But I got enough to share. Unless you already ate?"

"There wasn't time. We were too busy."

"Well, come in." He gestured her inside his apartment.

She didn't know what she was expecting to find, but it was though the unit had had a complete makeover. In the past week, he'd certainly made himself at home. There was a new desk with two large computer monitors side by side and a black leather desk chair.

"I hope you don't mind that I made a few changes."

She shook her head, still taking in the changes. "Not at all."

Against the other wall were a couple of comfy-looking chairs and a small fridge with a microwave atop it.

"This—" he gestured to the wall behind him "—is for anyone who wants some coffee or doughnuts in the morning."

"So you're having an open-door policy, literally."

"Something like that."

She stared at the small table by the doorway with a new coffeemaker and a big white baker's box with the Polka Dotted Bakery logo. There was only one doughnut left and a bunch of crumbs. Wow. He really had made himself at home. And it looked as though he was trying to win over the Stirling residents, one doughnut and coffee at a time.

"Have a seat." He gestured to the chairs.

"I can help get the food."

"You are my guest. I've got this." He turned and set to work.

The man was certainly stubborn. She looked on as he pulled out plates and utensils from one bag and food containers from a second bag. She grew uncomfortable with him waiting on her when she was perfectly capable of doing it herself.

"This isn't necessary," she said. "I can do it."

"Yes, it is necessary. You look exhausted."

"I'm fine." *Liar.* "I can help you."

He arched a disbelieving brow and stared at her until she sat down. She stifled a sigh as she got off her feet. Her pride refused to let Graham see that he was right about her needing to sit down.

He made short work of serving up the food. When he handed her a plate, her mouth watered.

Graham sat down. "There. Was that so hard?"

"What?"

"Letting me do something for you?"

She placed the plate on her lap. "I don't know what you're talking about."

"You are always going out of your way to help people, but you refuse to accept help in return."

Heat flared in her cheeks. "I don't need people going out of their way for me. I'm fine on my own."

"How about just letting someone do something nice for you because they want to?"

Had she spent so much of her life waiting on others that she'd learned to ignore her own needs? She dismissed the thought. Graham was putting wayward thoughts in her very tired brain.

For a few minutes they ate in silence. Alina smothered a moan of delight over the food. "This is delicious."

"So glad you like it. See. It doesn't hurt to let someone do things for you."

"Really?" She couldn't believe what she was hearing. "You make it sound like my being self-sufficient is a fault."

His gaze lowered to his plate. "I'm just saying sometimes you have to consider yourself."

She didn't like the turn in this conversation. It reminded her too much of how her stepmother used to needle her with snide little insults here and there. The food was overcooked, the laundry was too wrinkled—it went on and on.

Her gaze narrowed on him, and she became intent on turning this conversation away from what he viewed as her shortcomings. "All this advice from a man who wrote the book on being stubborn."

"Stubborn?"

She nodded. "You insist on doing things your way."

"This from the woman who refuses to accept that this apartment building is going to be demolished. Instead of making plans for the future, you're clinging to the past."

Her gaze narrowed on him. "The past is important. And it's not just me that thinks so. Haven't you learned anything by working around the building this week?"

"I've learned that Mrs. Campbell in 203 has a cute little dog that is very curious. I've learned that Mr. Merryweather prefers to be called Merryweather minus the mister. He also has a sweet tooth and he misses your visits. Apparently I'm not nearly as good of company as you. And I know there's some really nosy woman on the first floor that refuses to change her own light bulb. She asked a lot of questions about you."

Alina had a sneaking suspicion she knew who it was. "Did the woman have bleached blond hair?" When he nodded, she asked, "Did she have on a lot of makeup, especially eye makeup?"

"How did you know?"

"Because it was my stepmother. Although I thought she was supposed to be on vacation. I must have gotten my weeks mixed up."

"Your stepmother?" When she nodded, he asked, "Do you two get along?"

Alina rolled her eyes. "Not at all."

"Wow. That bad?" When she bobbed her head, he turned his attention back to his plate of food. "Is she the only family you have?"

"Yes. My father married her after my mother died. He was the building manager—"

"That's how you learned to do everything."

She nodded. "I always followed him around. He showed me how to replace pipes, paint apartments and everything else." When she noticed Graham smiling, she asked, "What's so amusing?"

"I'm just imaging you as a little girl with a wrench in one hand, a hammer in the other and a smidge of grease on your cute little nose."

He thought her nose was cute? She wondered what he thought about the rest of her, but she didn't dare vocalize her thoughts.

She swallowed hard. "That was me. A total tomboy. After some comments from one of the busybodies in the building, my father got it in his head that I needed a female role model—someone to teach me how to be a young lady. And so he married my stepmother."

"I bet you weren't happy about it."

"In the beginning, she seemed nice enough, but once they were married, everything changed."

Why was she telling him all of this? She never talked about her family with anyone. At least, she tried not to, but when they lived in the same building, it made it extremely difficult.

A yawn escaped her. And now with her stomach appeased, her eyelids grew heavy.

"You should go," he said.

"I think you're right. Thank you for dinner. It was delicious."

"You're welcome."

On her way to her apartment, she replayed her dinner with Graham. Had they moved from adversaries to friends?

Because only a friend would order her dinner and from an A-list restaurant no less. And only a friend would wait on her. Then there was their conversation; it was the kind that was far too personal to have with her enemy.

She would have to maintain her distance going forward. Because falling for Graham would be the biggest mistake of her life. All she had to do was look at what he'd done to his temporary home. New furniture. New electronics. And a new coffee machine with daily doughnut delivery.

It was a life far from hers. Hers was so much simpler. So much so that he wouldn't even have bothered with her if it wasn't for their agreement.

CHAPTER NINE

AT LAST A day off.

A morning to sleep without an alarming rousing her. Much to Prince's chagrin.

While lounging in bed, Alina decided how she wanted to spend her Saturday. A big smile pulled at the corners of her mouth. Prince marched up the bed and meowed loud and long.

"Okay. Okay." Alina ran her hand over his head and down his back. "I get it. You're hungry."

She rushed through her morning shower and dressed. She and Prince shared breakfast. He had seafood supreme while she opted for two frozen waffles and juice. As she ate, she thought of her plans for the day and then she got an even better idea—one that would hopefully fill Graham with some holiday spirit.

With her dirty dishes in the sink, she grabbed her purse and coat. She rushed out the door. She was a lady on a mission.

She stopped outside Graham's door. She didn't have to knock because the door was already open with a sign that said Free Coffee and Doughnuts.

Graham glanced up from his computer, a smile lighting up his face. "Good morning." His gaze momentarily dipped to her outfit before returning to her eyes. "You aren't dressed for work."

"I have the day off. And we have plans."

He tilted his head to the side and looked at her. "Do I even want to ask what you have in mind?"

A smile tugged at her mouth. "Don't you trust me?"

"I don't know. I'm having visions of replacing plumbing or something even worse."

That made her laugh. "What if I told you there were no repairs involved in today's activities?"

"Then I'd ask if you made sure all of the building's residents were on board with your plan."

She couldn't stop smiling and it was all his fault. There was just something about him that made her happy when she was around him. "Stop being so difficult. If someone needs you, they can leave a message. Now grab your coat."

"Not until you tell me where we're going."

His pointed stare let her know that he was serious. She sighed. "Fine, if you must know we're going to get a Christmas tree. It's past time to put it up. And I just can't wait any longer."

"Why me?"

"Because you need some holiday spirit. Don't you want to put up a Christmas tree?"

He shrugged. "I don't know."

"Come on." She headed into the hallway, hoping he would follow. This man needed some Christmas in his heart. And she couldn't think of a better way to start his transformation than by picking out an evergreen.

She slipped on her winter coat. She wanted to glance back and see if Graham was following her lead, but she resisted the urge. She'd done all she could. If he didn't want to have some Christmas fun, she wasn't going to make him. But she would feel bad for him. Who didn't enjoy the holiday festivities?

She'd just pulled on her knit cap when Graham said,

"Are you going to just stand there all day? We have to get a Christmas tree."

The smile returned to her face and so did the hope that there would be a Christmas miracle this year—that Graham would find his holiday spirit and her home would be saved.

Christmas tree shopping.

He didn't have time for this.

Graham thought of the budgets he had to review, trying to cover the endeavors his father had obligated the company to participate in while trying to secure the necessary funds to cover the mounting expenses to build Toliver Tower.

He had a plan to bring on a new partner who would take over some of the investments, freeing up Toliver funds. But finding the right partner was difficult. And now that he'd found someone who would be a good fit with Toliver, they were hesitant to commit in the current economic climate.

But he also realized the importance of making Alina happy. She was the key to having the Stirling residents moved out by the beginning of the year. It would give his contractors an extra two months to clear the land so they could be ready to break ground in the spring.

And most of all, she was finally doing something for herself. He hadn't known her for long but it was long enough to know that she truly did put others' needs before her own. Today would be different. He'd see to it.

As they headed out into the cold, crisp morning, Graham couldn't help thinking of his father. He would say buying a Christmas tree was an utter waste of time and money. His priority needed to be on the company and fixing the financial mess he'd inherited.

But Graham's mother would be all sorts of happy to see him doing something that wasn't work related. He thought of calling her. His hand moved to his pocket to grab his phone. *She would be happy to hear from me, wouldn't she?* He hesitated. The last conversation they'd had was harsh and some words were said that just couldn't be taken back.

"What has you so quiet?" Alina said. "Did I pull you away from something important?"

She had but he wasn't going to admit it. "Nothing that can't wait until later."

His response brought a smile to her face and it was then that he knew he'd chosen the right answer. Because when she smiled, it lit up his whole world. He didn't even know something like that was possible. He'd certainly never felt something so intense before. And he had absolutely no idea what to do about it. And so he ignored it—pretended like it had never happened. Like any of that was possible.

"We're almost there," she said.

"Almost where?"

"At the tree lot where I've been getting my Christmas tree since I was a kid."

"That's a really long time. Wouldn't it be easier just to buy an artificial tree?"

She scrunched up her nose. "I know it works for some people. And that's great for them. But I love having a live tree. There's just something about the pine scent and the look of it that really sets off the holiday."

He actually never heard of anyone so enthusiastic about a Christmas tree before. He couldn't help but wonder if she got this excited about everything in her life.

She glanced over at him. "I know you don't celebrate Christmas now but what was it like when you were a kid?"

"My father thought the holiday was a waste of time, but my mother insisted we at least have a small artificial tree. It wasn't much. It sat on a table in our living room. My father sighed every time he looked at it." Graham remembered those days and how he didn't understand how his friends would have these big fancy trees with all of the lights but they only had an itty-bitty tree. "The day after Christmas it went back into storage and life went back to normal."

"Is that what you wanted?"

He didn't want to answer. He didn't like to think about the past. "It doesn't matter. We're here to get you a tree."

She stopped just outside of the tree lot and turned to him. "But it does matter because unless you've decided to give in on our deal, we'll be sharing the holiday season."

Give in? Him? Never. He was in it to win it. Everything was riding on him lowering Toliver's financial obligations and creating space for their growing workforce—something his father put off for far too long.

"Fine," Graham said, "if you must know, back then I wanted a real tree—a tall tree—like my friends had. But it doesn't matter anymore."

"It matters," she said with an understanding tone as though she could see right through him.

He wanted to argue the point but decided it was better not to. He followed her into the tree lot. With it still being early in the season, the lot was filled with trees—to the point where it was difficult to walk down many of the paths.

There were short chubby trees, tall slender ones, short needles, long needles, some greener, some bluer. He honestly never stopped and paid enough attention to realize just how many different types of Christmas trees were available.

He followed Alina around the lot. She paused to give some a closer inspection before moving on. He wondered what she was inspecting but he didn't ask. He didn't want her to get the impression he cared all that much.

Christmas was just another day. Or at least it should be. Instead it was a day where no work got done. A day where his plans to prove himself to his mother, to his board, to the world, were put on hold. If anything, Christmas should be for the children, but let the adults get on with business.

Alina carried the top of the tree.

Graham held the trunk.

With a light snow falling, they walked home. Not that the tree was heavy. Graham offered a couple of times to carry it all by himself, but she wouldn't hear of it. After a bit of back and forth, they agreed to share the task.

However, now that they were back in her apartment and had the tree set up, Alina realized she might have been a bit overly ambitious when it came to the size. The top of the tree touched the ceiling. It hadn't looked that big in the tree lot. There were lots of other trees that were so much bigger.

And it was wide—very wide. The corner she'd cleared, next to the window, wasn't big enough. The couch had to be moved. Again. And an end table had to be put into her bedroom in order for people to be able to move about the room.

Still, it was a pretty tree. She stopped and stared up at it. It was going to take her stepstool to reach the top. Then again, she might have to borrow the stepladder from the building manager's office, erm, from Graham.

"Do you want me to cut the top off so it fits better?" Graham's deep voice drew her from her thoughts.

She turned to him. "Definitely not. You really don't know anything about Christmas trees, do you?"

"What's that supposed to mean?"

"That you never cut the top of a tree. If you want to shorten it, you do it from the bottom."

He shrugged. "Same difference."

"No, it isn't. If you cut off the top, it'll look funny. And you won't be able to add the angel."

"Do you want me to cut the bottom?"

She stepped back, taking in the sheer magnitude of the

tree. There was no room in her tiny apartment to cut it. They'd just have to make do. "It's good just the way it is."

Graham moved up next to her. "It is?"

"It is. Now we have to decorate it."

He shook his head. "I'm out. I'm no good at that kind of stuff. Besides, I have work to do."

She pressed a hand to her hip. "Don't you ever take a day off?"

"Listen to who's talking—"

"What's that supposed to mean?"

"That you work all of the time. If not at the café, you're working here."

She huffed. She wanted to argue with him, but it was true. She worked as much as she could to save money for her uncertain future. But she didn't want to ruin the day arguing with him over the future of the building because day by day he was beginning to make friends with the residents of the Stirling. But would it be enough to change his mind?

"Okay," she said. "Go do your work. I'm going to turn on some Christmas music?"

He shook his head and headed for the door.

She turned her back to him and started opening the box of decorations closest to her. She lucked out, finding it was the box with the light strands. She plugged them into the wall to make sure they still worked before she started stringing them at the bottom of the tree. It wasn't an easy task when the tree was so large. She couldn't even come close to wrapping her arms around it.

She had made a couple of rounds when she stretched as far as she could to place the bundled light strand on the tree branch before repositioning herself to pass it around the back when her fingers brushed Graham's. Her head jerked up, surprised to find he hadn't left, and their gazes met. A current of attraction pulsed up her arm and set her heart pounding.

CHAPTER TEN

THE BREATH STILLED in her lungs.

For a moment, it was though time came to a sudden halt.

Alina stared deeply into Graham's eyes. She could see the future—a future with him in it. She could imagine this was just the first of many Christmases where they'd decorate the tree together. In her daydream, she envisioned him pulling her close and kissing her, not just any kiss, but one filled with passion and…and love—

She jerked her hand back. That was not going to happen. She wasn't going to put her heart on the line. She wouldn't get hurt again, because she knew whoever she loved would eventually disappear from her life. And that was agony she couldn't live through again. She refused to put her tattered heart on the line. The price was just too steep.

And once Graham got what he came for—the residents' agreement to move out early—he'd be gone. Her apartment would be empty. And her stepmother would be right—she wasn't worthy of love.

"I've got this." Alina put a respectable distance between them.

His confused gaze searched hers. "I'd like to help. Will you let me?"

She wanted to argue the point but didn't. Instead she nodded her reluctant agreement.

This time she made sure their fingers and any other body parts didn't touch. However, as the silence stretched out, the more awkward it became. She glanced through the full branches at Graham. What had happened for him not to enjoy the holidays? She was curious about that and so much more about him.

"Tell me more about the holidays when you were young." The words came tumbling out and then she froze, wondering if she'd overstepped.

He shrugged. "I already told you."

There was something he was holding back. And by the way the muscle twitched in his jaw, it was something serious. But she couldn't drag it out of him. She had to wait until he was ready to talk about it.

They finished wrapping the tree in lights and then sat down on the couch. Graham turned to her. "What were your Christmases like?"

She smiled as the memories came flooding back to her. "They were happy. My mother loved the holiday. She used to say she wished it was Christmas year-round."

"That's a lot of Christmas."

Alina nodded. "She used to decorate the entire apartment," she said, gesturing at the space around them.

"This apartment?"

She nodded. "You didn't know I grew up here?"

"I had no idea." He leaned forward and retrieved one of the red glass ornaments and affixed a hook to it. "Did you ever want to move away?"

"I thought about running away after my father remarried. I wanted to be anywhere but here."

"You and your stepmother never got along?"

"We did, in the beginning. But looking back now, I think it was a show to impress my father so he'd think it was all right to remarry. But once she had that ring on her finger, things changed. There were rules for me and extravagances for my stepsisters. She claimed I was spoiled and unruly.

But I wasn't. She lied." Alina pressed her lips together, realizing she shouldn't have said all of that.

"She was jealous of you?"

"I don't know. I can deal with a lot of things, just not lying. Why do people have to lie?"

"She wasn't the only one that lied to you, was she?"

Alina shook her head. She'd said too much. This was a subject she never discussed. It was easier just to keep it to herself.

"When my father had a heart attack and passed away, I'd just turned eighteen. I inherited the apartment. My stepmother was furious and took me to court, but it was ruled that the apartment and the rent control lease were rightfully and legally mine. I was hoping it would be the last I saw of that woman and her daughters, but she used the life insurance money to move into a larger apartment in the building."

Graham reached out and gave her hand a squeeze. "I'm sorry you went through all of that. I'm sure you were a great kid."

"Why are you so sure?"

"Because I see how you are with people you care about. You go out of your way for them, from baking cookies to fighting on their behalf to save their homes. It takes a very special person to do those things. Not to mention sharing your Christmas traditions with someone you consider the enemy."

Heat rose in her cheeks. "I never said you were the enemy."

"But you thought it. And I understand because if I was in your place, I'd feel the same way. But with all you've been through, did you ever consider moving?"

"I can't afford an apartment in the city without the rent control and I like my neighbors. They're like family. Considering I have none of my own, I need them. And I know they need me, too—especially some of the older residents who don't have family or their families have busy schedules and don't visit very often."

"You try to fill in the gaps. And that's why you don't complain when their faucets leak more than is normal."

"Something like that."

She never talked about this stuff with anyone. It was too personal, too painful. But she knew for Graham to understand the significance of the Stirling, she would have to bare her soul, no matter how much it hurt to pull back the scabs on her past.

They'd trimmed the tree.

And by the time they'd finished, it felt as though a bond had grown between them. They were no longer strangers. They were friends.

Graham found comfort in the thought of Alina being his friend. But in the next breath, he had to wonder if friendship was the right terminology. Because he'd never longed to kiss any of his friends.

There was something about being close to Alina. They didn't even have to be touching for him to feel her draw. It was like she was the sun and he'd been pulled into her orbit, soaking up the rays of her smile.

But he knew that none of this was going to last. It was all an illusion created by their temporary closeness and the magic of the holidays. Once Christmas passed, he'd be back in his sterile and cold apartment. And Alina would never want to see him after he tore down the Stirling. So it was best not to let himself get drawn in.

Graham paused to look up at the tree. In his hand he held a white, glittery glass ornament. And for the life of him, he couldn't find a spot to hang it. The tree was covered with lights, ribbon and ornaments.

He wanted to say it was overdone, maybe even gaudy, but he couldn't say any of those things. There was a method to Alina's madness and, in the end, the tree looked amazing. It sparkled and shined like fine jewelry.

And at the same time, it was filled with memories. Graham knew this because Alina had told him the history of each of the unique ornaments as she hung them on the tree. In the end, the tree was like the story of her life. No wonder she liked it so much.

He didn't have anything like that, but in the next breath, he realized that wasn't true. He had the company his father had left to him. It was filled with memories, from the first time he could remember sitting in the CEO's chair when he wasn't even big enough for his feet to touch the ground to interning when he'd been in college.

And then there was the time he'd gotten to shadow his father throughout the day. It had been bring-your-child-to-work day and he'd badgered his father until he'd agreed to take him to the office. It was that day Graham had sworn to himself that one day he would run the company just like his father had done. He just never thought that day would arrive so soon.

He also remembered his mother's reaction to the reading of the will—the part that gave Graham controlling interest in the company. His mother had begged him to sell it. He'd refused.

She'd told him that in order to successfully run the company he would have to make sacrifices. Back then he'd thought he'd had all of the answers. He told her he was man enough to make all of the sacrifices necessary. He hadn't wanted to hear a word his mother said if it was contrary to him living up to his duty as the Toliver heir.

"What do you think?" Alina's voice interrupted his thoughts.

He blinked and turned to her. "What?"

"The tree. Do you like it?"

He paused to take in the tree once more. "I think it's amazing. It's you."

"It's me?" Her fine brows scrunched together. "You think I look like a tree? A skinny top and a fat bottom—"

"No! I don't mean you as in you literally, but it's made up of little pieces from your life."

Her brows smoothed and then a smile lifted her pouty lips. "Yes, it is. I never thought of it that way. Is that the way your little Christmas tree was?"

He shook his head. "We always had the same designer ornaments that came as a set."

"What was Christmas morning like? Or were you so rich growing up that you didn't care about Santa bringing you presents?"

"I wasn't as spoiled as you might imagine. My father believed I needed to earn what I got. I don't even remember how young I was when he started saying that. For all I know, he could have said it as soon as I was out of diapers because I can't remember anything else."

"Your father sounds like a tough man."

Graham shrugged. "He had his moments of softness, like when I had pneumonia. I never saw him so worried. But once I was better, things went back to normal."

"Well, Christmas at the Stirling is all about family."

"But you're not related to these people."

"Not biologically, but they're my family by choice. So we celebrate the holiday by having a potluck dinner and doing a Secret Santa exchange."

"That sounds nice."

"It is. It's not about the extravagance of the presents.

It's about the company. And you're welcome to join us this year. That is, unless you're spending the holiday with your mother?"

"Uh, no." He shook his head. "My mother and I haven't spent the holidays together since before my father died. We…we had words." He picked up a small silver ball ornament and rolled it around in his hand. "She accused me of turning into my father."

"I take it that's not a good thing."

"Not the way she meant it. She said I was going to let the business take over my life. I told her I could balance things, but she didn't believe me."

"Is she right? Or do you have more dates than you can count?"

He arched a brow. "Why? Are you planning to ask me out?"

Her asking him out?

The idea didn't sound as preposterous as it should.

Immediately heat flamed in Alina's cheeks. "Of course not. I just wondered if your mother was right. Do you have a life outside the office?"

Graham placed the ornament back in the box. "I don't have time." He got to his feet. "Why can't anyone understand that it takes a lot of time to run a company the size of Toliver? Once I get a firm hand on everything, things will change. I'll have more time."

She knew he wanted to believe that, but she had her doubts. "My father used to say you had to pick what was important in life and then make a concerted effort to make time for what makes you happy."

He frowned at her. "So you're siding with my mother."

"I'm not. I'm just trying to understand."

"Never mind. It doesn't matter. Once this agreement is

over, you'll never have to see me again." And with that he started to walk away.

"Graham, wait. That isn't what I meant."

With his back to her, he waved her off and kept walking right out the front door.

Ugh! That had gone totally wrong. She hadn't meant to upset him. She shouldn't have said anything, but she thought they'd reached a point where they could talk to each other openly, like friends. As his friend, she worried that his mother might be right.

Not that she wanted him to date her or anything. Far from it. They were too different from each other. She loved Christmas. He couldn't care less about it. He loved working at all hours. She only worked the long hours out of necessity. She craved a big, loving family. He seemed happier being alone. They definitely didn't belong together.

But that didn't mean she didn't feel bad about the way the conversation went. It was getting late, maybe they were both tired. She'd apologize to him in the morning.

Oh, who was she kidding? There was no way she'd be able to sleep with things left like this. And so she stood and headed for the door.

She pulled open the door to find Graham standing there. His head hung low as he shifted his weight from one foot to the other.

"I'm sorry," they both said in unison. And then they both smiled.

"I shouldn't have said anything," she said. "I know you're doing your best."

"And I shouldn't have let it bother me. It's true. I work a lot. But it won't be forever."

She wanted to ask if that meant he was planning to marry and settle down with a family of his own. Suddenly the image of his arm around a tall, slender woman with perfect hair filled Alina's imagination. The thought stirred unease in the pit of her stomach. Refusing to acknowledge what it might mean, she shoved aside the thought.

"Well," she said, "I'll just go clean up and call it a night."

"I'll help you."

"You don't have to—"

"I want to." His tone was firm.

"Thanks. That would be great."

She breathed easier as together they walked back to the living room. She was starting to see that this challenge of getting him to see the apartment building as something more than an obstacle to his goals was going to be more difficult than she'd originally envisioned.

How did she draw him into the charm of the building without making things personal? Because they needed to keep their distance. No matter how handsome or thoughtful she found him, they came from different worlds.

Even with that warning in mind when she glanced over at him, she felt a flutter in her chest. This was going to be so much harder than she'd ever imagined.

CHAPTER ELEVEN

HE'D NEVER BEEN so busy.

And yet Graham found himself happier than he'd ever been.

Monday morning he'd slipped away from the Stirling for a very important meeting. He was hoping to persuade a couple that owned a sizable company to go in on a project with his company, considerably lowering Toliver's financial obligation. However, when the topic of the holidays came up, he soon learned they loved Christmas celebrations.

And when they'd mentioned spending Christmas in New York, there had been a miscommunication. They thought he was inviting them to a party. What was he supposed to say to that?

He'd known that this was his chance to solidify their relationship so of course he had to invite them to his big Christmas gala. The only problem was he didn't have one planned. His company never held or sponsored holiday events. And now Graham had exactly eighteen days to plan a huge Christmas party.

He thought of handing it off to his assistant, Mary, but he just couldn't bring himself to do that to her—even though he knew she wouldn't have complained. She was a newly-wed and she already had her hands full picking up some of his work while he was working from home.

He would deal with the party himself—something he'd never done in his life. He figured he'd start with the location but that was proving impossible. Venues large enough to hold such an event had been reserved a year or two in advance.

It was late in the afternoon when Alina stopped by his place. "The restaurant was busy all day and I had not one but two Christmas parties. I just came home to change my clothes before heading back." She gestured to a large red stain on her white blouse. "It was a rough day."

He stared up from where he was sitting on the floor leaning back against the wall with papers scattered around him. "You're going back so soon?"

She shrugged off her coat, then draped it over her arm. "It's fine. It'll slow down after the holidays. How was your day?"

He closed his laptop, giving her his full attention. "I'd rather hear about your day."

She studied him for a moment. "What's the matter?"

"Why would you think something's wrong?"

"Because you get those little lines between your brows when you're worried about something."

"Wait. Are you saying we've spent that much time together that you can read me?"

"Yes. Now, tell me what's wrong. Is it Merryweather? Is he giving you a hard time?"

"No. I picked him up some cookies on the way home from the office and he loved them. It has nothing to do with the building."

"That's a relief." She resisted the urge to point out the fact that he'd referred to the Stirling as his home.

He rubbed the back of his neck. "I have a problem at the office."

"Anything you want to discuss?" She sat across from him on one of his new chairs. It would be nice to focus on someone else's problems for a change.

Graham hesitated. "I have potential clients coming into the office the week of Christmas and I really need to impress them."

"You're the best at what you do and your offices are beautiful, so I'm not seeing the problem."

"It's not enough. I know a couple of other companies are courting them. So I need this visit to stand out in their mind."

"I take it we're not discussing your business presentation."

He shook his head. "That's already under control. But I sort of invited them to a Christmas party that doesn't exist."

Her mouth gaped. "How in the world did you do that?"

"I'm not exactly sure but now they're making plans to return for this impressive Christmas gala."

"Graham, do you know how close it is to Christmas? People make these plans months or a year in advance."

His frown deepened. "Now what am I supposed to do?"

"You have a nice apartment. You could throw an informal party there."

He shook his head. "They're flying in from Phoenix. They're expecting something spectacular. Not a little dinner party."

"Hmm… I see." She racked her brain for an easy solution. "I can't even offer the Christmas Café. It's booked solid."

Graham lifted both arms and raked his fingers through his hair. "What am I going to do? This account is very important."

"One of the things I ask clients before planning a party is about their likes and dislikes. Have you researched these people to find out their interests?"

He nodded. "I didn't learn much."

"There was nothing about what organizations they support?"

"Well, I did find this." He opened his laptop and started typing. It took him a moment. "Here it is."

She accepted the laptop from him and started to read. A few minutes later, she said, "This is great."

"How do you get that?"

"It says that Mrs. Cortinas is a proud sponsor of the arts."

"And…" His dark brows knitted together in confusion. "You want me to make a donation to one of her causes?"

Alina shook her head. "Let me think on it and I'll get back to you."

"On what? The party? But you said it was too late."

"I didn't say it was too late. I said most places will already be reserved. So we'll have to think of someplace less traditional. And it'll have to accommodate artwork because if the wife is impressed, she'll make sure the husband gives your presentation more attention."

"I hear you," he said. "But it's not going to work."

"But why? Are you afraid they'll learn you're a grinch?"

"I am not."

She crossed her arms and arched a brow. "Remember, I've been to your office. I know it's devoid of decorations."

"My father didn't believe in wasting the time and money on decorations when everyone was supposed to be there to work, not to have a party."

"I hope you don't mind me saying that your father was way too serious."

"How could I mind when I agree with you?"

"You do?" When he sent her a crooked smile and nodded, her heart fluttered. Refusing to let him see how he affected her, she turned her attention back to the laptop.

"I found another article that says the Cortinas decorate

their home for the holidays." She followed the link he gave her. "Here. See."

He leaned over to look at the monitor. In the process, he grabbed the other chair and pulled it up next to hers. She pretended like his closeness didn't bother her as she clicked through the online photos. But her heart was pitter-pattering as her pulse raced. She had to think about something other than the way his shoulder was brushing against hers.

"Do you see all of the artwork on the walls?"

"I do. But how does knowing she likes artwork help us?"

"Those pieces aren't classic pieces of art. I'm not an expert, but I'm thinking those were all created by up-and-coming artists."

"And that helps us how?"

"I don't know yet. Let me think about it."

He sat back. "Alina, this isn't your problem. I don't expect you to fix it."

Alina glanced at the time on the monitor. "I have to go."

"Already? But you just got here. You haven't even had time to eat or rest."

"I'll be fine. It's a big event. Do you know the Hulligan Group?"

He nodded. "They're a big financial firm."

"And they rented out the entire café for a holiday party. I was told it was going to run late."

He reached out to her. His fingertips caressed her cheek, making her heart pound. "You look tired. You're on the go from first thing in the morning until you collapse in bed at night. There are lunch parties and evening parties on top of your regular shift. This is, what, your eighth party this week? Just quit. I'll pay you to plan my holiday party."

"No." She pulled away from his touch, angry that he'd disregard her job so quickly.

"My job might not be as important as yours but I like it and there are people counting on me. Now I have to go."

She jumped to her feet when Graham said, "Alina, wait. I'm sorry. That's not what I meant."

Her back was to him. Her mind said to just keep walking, but another voice said to let him explain himself. She turned to him and found him standing there with a frown on his face.

"I don't have a lot of experience talking with women. Not like this." He raised his gaze to meet hers. Uncertainty showed in his eyes. "The last woman I was involved with, well, I thought things were going good. We'd been together more than a year when she dumped me."

"I'm sorry. That must have come as a shock."

He nodded. "It did. When I asked her why, she said I was too focused on my work and she felt invisible. I don't want to make that mistake again. Not that we're dating or anything."

Was he trying to say he'd spoken out of actual concern for her? She didn't want to jump to conclusions. She'd done that with her stepmother and stepsisters and look how that had turned out.

Graham's gaze met hers. "I just meant I was concerned about you. If there's anything you need me to do, just say the word."

Her heart fluttered in her chest. He cared about her. "Thanks for the offer. If I think of something, I'll let you know. For now, I need to go change."

She rushed out the door and headed for the steps. All the while her heart was pounding. Graham really cared about her.

A voice in her head said to be cautious. After all, he was the enemy, poised to take away her home. She wanted to say that was business, this is different—it's personal—but could you separate the man from the business?

While the CEO was away, the party planner could scheme.

Okay, so maybe *scheme* was too strong of a word. But this Christmas party was nearly impossible to plan. Even though Graham thought finding a location to hold the event would be the hardest part of this last-minute party, it was in fact the easiest since he owned the venue.

The Toliver conference space on the top floor of the Diamond Building was perfect for his purposes. Though Graham thought it was too cold with the black-and-white decor, she knew the right decorations could change the starkest room into a cozy Christmas setting.

The more she thought about taking on the task of planning Graham's party, the more she saw an opportunity. Not just for Graham but for herself, too. If living here in the apartment building and interacting with its residents hadn't changed Graham's mind about the pending demolition, she was going to have to work harder. And she thought she had an idea. The only question that remained was whether or not Graham would go for it.

She knew she was going out on a limb here because planning an elaborate party in just a few weeks, well, it was a crazy notion. And yet, she found herself willing to take on the challenge because she was running out of options.

First, she'd have to come up with the theme for the party. And then it came to her: the Snow Ball. Other party details would prove to be more challenging…that is, unless you lived in an apartment building full of talented people. She just hoped everyone had the time and interest in helping her. After all, it would be asking a lot of them to help Graham, of all people.

Still, what would it hurt to ask them? And that's why

she'd called the residents she was closest to and asked them to meet in her apartment.

"Thank you all for coming," Alina said. "I really need your help."

Mr. Jackson glanced around. "Where's the handyman?"

Alina smiled at the CEO of Toliver Investments being called a handyman. "Graham had a meeting at the office. I told him I would handle things here while he took care of his other work."

Merryweather crossed his arms over his chest. "Is he at the office plotting to kick other people out of their homes this holiday season?"

"He's not like that." As soon as the words were out of her mouth, Alina felt as though she was having an out of body experience. Since when had she started defending Graham?

Pearl Sanders, the sweetest eighty-year-old woman, sent her a knowing smile. "I understand, dear. He is quite handsome. If only I was a few years younger, you'd have a challenge on your hands."

Challenge? There would be no challenge. Graham wasn't hers. And she didn't want him to be. Did she?

"What I want to know is why we would help someone who's kicking us out of our homes," Grace Taylor asked.

"I don't have anywhere to go," one person said.

"Neither do I."

As other residents chimed in with their discontent at helping the enemy, Alina felt caught in the middle. It was a very strange and uneasy place to find herself.

Because she was beginning to really know Graham as a man, not the high-powered CEO. He wasn't the big mean monster that people wanted to think about him. He was fun. He was caring. And he was hot. Very, very hot.

"I understand your hesitation," Alina said. "But what if

in exchange Graham had his people track down affordable housing for all of us?"

"He agreed to do this?" Merryweather asked.

"Well, uh, no." Alina worried she was about to lose any chance of them agreeing to help. "But he told me how important this party is to him. I think he'll be agreeable to our term. Trust me. I'll work it out."

Mr. Jackson frowned. "I still don't like it. No matter what they find, it won't be home. Our home."

"I know." Alina's heart ached at the thought of them all being separated. "But I haven't given up hope that he'll find an alternative building site." She'd seen Graham take to the people in the building. Tearing down this building was no longer going to be a case of faceless numbers on a report.

For a moment, everyone chatted among themselves. Alina hoped they'd see it as an opportunity to win Graham over.

"What do you say?" Alina asked. "Are we going to do this?"

Though they lacked enthusiasm, they all agreed.

"Thank you." Alina smiled at the people she thought of as family. "Let's get to work."

Everyone stated their special talents. The people who claimed not to have any talents befitting a grand party were relegated to the decorating committee. Their first task was tracking down a live Christmas tree that was relatively slender but tall, something close to twenty feet. And second on their to-do list was buying an enormous amount of twinkle lights in blue for the ceiling and white to drape about the various support posts in the ballroom and the Christmas tree.

"I know the Stirling has some snowmen in storage," Alina said. "I'll pull them out and see if they're usable."

"I'm assuming you'll want music for the event," Mr.

Jackson said. He played the sax professionally until he retired. Now he and his retired bandmates played local venues. When she smiled and nodded, he said, "I suppose I could see if the band is available."

She'd wanted to ask him, but she hadn't wanted to pressure him. "Thank you. Your band is amazing. I'll mark you down. Let me know if there are any problems."

Mr. Jackson nodded before adjusting his bifocals. He started to type a message on his phone.

Merryweather offered to check with the theater where he used to work and see if they could borrow some props. Someone else had connections with an art gallery and was going to see if they could track down a bunch of winter-themed pieces to decorate the walls. Piece by piece and person by person this event was coming together.

She hoped when it was all pulled together that it would live up to Graham's expectations. She knew this event had to be high end and she planned to do everything to make it so.

CHAPTER TWELVE

A DAY OFF.

Today would be Alina's day to catch up with everything that hadn't been done around the apartment building—that is, whatever Graham hadn't been able to complete. She was expecting a really long list. She knew Merryweather always had problems—lots of problems—though most of them were quite minor.

Merryweather's family didn't live in the state and so he didn't get many visitors. And now that he was retired, he stayed in his apartment most of the time. He was lonely and she couldn't blame him.

As she rushed through her Wednesday morning routine, her thoughts returned to Graham. She'd heard from some of the residents that Graham didn't appear to have a clue about the difference between a nut and a washer, but he'd persevered. More times than not, he'd called in outside help. That wasn't surprising. She had to do that, too, when a task was beyond her ability. But what surprised her was that he stayed and observed the hired help, even asking questions. The man was certainly full of surprises. She smiled.

When she moved to the kitchen to feed Prince, her gaze strayed over to the calendar. Time was running out before everyone had to move. Her good mood dimmed, but she wasn't giving up on a Christmas miracle.

With her coffee made, she headed for the door, planning to stop in at Graham's office. She would check to see what messages the tenants had pinned to the punchboard on the outside of the door to the building manager's office. It wouldn't hurt to give Graham a helping hand.

But no sooner had she opened her apartment door when Graham appeared before her. "Hi. I was just heading out to see you."

"Look no further." He held up a pastry bag. "And I brought goodies from the Polka Dotted Bakery. Thought you might enjoy the treat after your exhausting week."

How did he know she had a soft spot for pastries? Lucky guess. Still, it did have her retreating back into the apartment. "I can't stay long. I have to see what needs done around the building."

"Nothing."

"What?"

"Nothing needs done. I'm on top of everything."

Surely she hadn't heard him right. "Everything?"

He smiled at her. "I can tell by your one-word responses that you expected me to fail miserably at this building maintenance stuff."

Even she couldn't stay on top of everything in the building. "What about Merryweather? He always has a leak or a clog or a squeak."

"All of his faucets and drains have been tightened. His bathroom is just fine. And his door hinges have all been · lubricated."

Her mouth gaped. She caught herself and pressed her lips together. "That must have taken you forever."

He shrugged. "I think that was the point."

"So you noticed he's lonely."

Graham nodded. "I started taking him cookies and staying to chat. Once I started stopping by every day or so, the repair requests slowed down."

"You know, I've been thinking of getting him a rescue dog. I figured they could help each other out. The pup would get a good home. And Merryweather wouldn't be alone and he'd have a reason to leave his apartment."

"That's a good idea. I bet he'd love it. You should do it."

Alina sighed. "I can't."

"Why not?"

And then she explained her reasoning about the move and the possible restrictions on pets. "I just couldn't do it to him. I couldn't imagine him getting attached to a dog and then having to give it up."

"And it's my fault."

She didn't say a word. Now that she was getting to know Graham, he was no longer the big bad monster she'd originally imagined. She didn't want to like him, but it was difficult not to when she found out what he'd done for Merryweather. I mean, how can you dislike a man that indulges a lonely retiree and goes out of his way to get him cookies?

In an effort to change the subject, she said, "I've been giving your problem some thought."

His brows scrunched together. "What problem?"

"Impressing your prospective partners with a big splashy party."

"Oh." His brown eyes lit up. "What did you think of?"

"How about a Snow Ball?" She smiled at her pun. "Get it? Snowball as in something to make Frosty out of. And a Snow Ball as in a winter dance."

"Cute." He smiled but it didn't reach his eyes. He didn't like it. "I'm sure they'll be invited to scads of parties."

Though her excitement had been punctured, she wasn't giving up. He hadn't heard the whole idea yet. "Perhaps, but this would be a chance to show them that you support local artists."

His eyes widened and she could tell she had his full interest. "What exactly do you have in mind?"

"I don't have any specifics but it can't be that hard to get a bunch of local artists to come together for a party. It would be free publicity for them. Who would pass that up?"

"I don't know. There isn't much time until the party. They might already have other plans."

She wanted the party to also represent some of Graham's interests. "What do you enjoy about winter? Maybe something you liked to do as a kid."

He shrugged. "When I was a kid, I'd go sledding."

"What about going to the tree lighting at Rockefeller Center?"

He shook his head. "My mother hated the noise and rush of the city."

"Oh." Alina couldn't imagine anyone not loving the energy of New York City. There was no other place she wanted to live. Ever.

"About this party," Graham said, "I just don't see being able to make it work. There's too much to do and not enough time."

"What would you say if I were to tell you I already started planning it?"

His brows rose. "You did?" When she nodded her head, he asked, "But how? This is *the* party season. Everything is going to be reserved."

He was right. If she were to pull this party off, it would have to be by nontraditional methods. But then again, when had that ever stopped her? When Mrs. Campbell's oven had died, their prior landlord refused to replace it per the lease agreement, and Mrs. Campbell didn't have the money to replace it, so Alina had taken it upon herself to locate a gently used oven. She'd bartered her services to plan the seller's birthday party for their five-year-old daughter in exchange for the oven. In the end, everyone had been happy. It wasn't the only time Alina had negotiated to make things work. This would be no different.

Desperation to save her home—and to save the homes of her beloved neighbors—drove her onward. "Let me worry about the details. What would it be worth to you to pull this off?"

His gaze met hers. She saw the doubt in his eyes but she wasn't backing down. "It'd be worth a great deal."

"Then I propose I plan your party while you seriously consider another site for your high-rise."

"There is no other site."

"You aren't even trying!"

"Don't you think we did that before we started buying up property here? I can show you all of the paperwork, if you don't believe me."

It was worth a try. And with a heavy heart she said, "I believe you."

"I'm sorry." His deep voice sounded sincere.

She wasn't giving up. She had a backup plan. "Fine. If I do this, if I plan you a grand holiday ball, I need you to find affordable housing for all of the residents of the Stirling." Her gaze met his. "Can you do that?"

"I…I don't know."

She pointedly stared at him. She wasn't going to back down. This party was going to be the biggest and most challenging of her career.

When he looked at her, she crossed her arms, pressed her lips into a firm line and narrowed her gaze. He had to know that she meant business. She wouldn't budge from this demand.

After a moment of tense silence, Graham said, "Okay. I'll get some people at the office started on it, first thing in the morning. But I can't promise you'll like what they come up with."

"All I'm asking for are some legitimate options for people who didn't ask to have their home demolished."

"I understand. I'm just surprised you didn't ask for something for yourself."

She shook her head. "I don't need anything special."

There was a look in his eyes—was it respect? She wasn't sure. But she hadn't done anything more than someone else in her position would have done.

"Alina, you're the most giving person I know, but sometimes you have to slow down and do what's best for you."

She waved off his concern. "I'm fine. Prince and I will land on our feet. We always do."

This time there was concern in Graham's eyes. "You can't ignore your own needs forever."

If he was talking about her lack of a boyfriend, she was too busy. She'd date again. Someday.

Her stepmother's voice echoed in her mind. *"You're too chubby, Al."* She always called her Al because she knew it bothered Alina. *"Men will never notice you. What kind of woman wears overalls and carries around a toolbox? Honestly, Al, you're embarrassing."*

Right now, she didn't want to examine what was missing from her life. "We better get started on the party," she said, hoping her voice didn't betray the way he unnerved her. "We have a lot of details to go over."

And so they got to work. The more they dove into the details of the party, the more she was able to push away the disturbing memories of the past. It seemed Graham was a good distraction, in more ways than one.

CHAPTER THIRTEEN

THEY'D BEEN BURNING the candle at both ends.

Since assuming the CEO role, Graham was used to really long hours. It was nothing, though, compared to balancing his business and the needs of the Stirling residents. Even he was getting a bit burned out.

And then there was Alina's nonstop schedule. To make matters worse, Christmas was her favorite time of the year and she was missing most of it. He blamed a lot of it on himself. In his rush to please a potential business partner, he hadn't considered how much effort the party would take.

He promised himself that, going forward, he would make things easier for her—as much as he could. He'd start with a bit of fun and, after that, he'd make sure she had a warm meal waiting for her each evening when she got home from work—whatever hour that might be.

And he was going to put his plan into action today.

Alina might not believe it, but he did know how to have a good time. After all, he'd grown up in the country. He'd learned how to pass the time, even if it had been a lifetime ago. Somewhere along the way, he'd forgotten those good times. Somewhere along the way, it'd become all about proving himself to his father, which led to a distance between him and his mother.

His mind reached for those foggy memories that he'd pushed away many years ago. The faces of those childhood friends came back to him. In the winter, they were always outside when it snowed. Winter had been one of his favorite seasons. So when had it all changed? When did the fluttering snowflakes change from something exhilarating to something aggravating because it would tie up traffic even more than normal?

"Alina?" he called down the hallway. "Alina, hurry up."

It was Thursday and she'd finished working early. She was now changing out of her work clothes, but it seemed like it was taking her forever. And now that he remembered how much fun winter could be, he was anxious to share some of that fun with Alina.

"Alina—"

"Okay. Okay." She stepped into the hallway in jeans and a green sweater with a Christmas tree on the front with gold jingle bell ornaments. "What's with the rush?"

"We have things to do. Come on." Graham shrugged on his winter coat.

Alina moved toward him with a confused look on her face. "What has gotten into you? I thought you had a report to get to your board."

"It can wait. This can't."

She arched a brow as her gaze studied him. "You are acting mighty strange."

"Not strange. Mysterious. Yes, mysterious sounds a lot better."

In no time, they were bundled up and headed out the door into lightly falling snow. Graham adjusted his black knit cap. He couldn't remember the last time he'd set aside an important project to go play in the snow.

He glanced over at Alina, all bundled up in a red coat with a matching knit cap with the design of white snowflakes. There was just something about being around her that reminded him of the person he used to be many, many moons ago.

"Where are we going?" Alina asked.

"You'll soon see." He took her gloved hand in his as he led them through the maze of people crowding the sidewalk.

A quick subway ride and a short walk later they arrived at Central Park. The area was a bustle of activity. Young and old alike were out and about, enjoying the holidays.

As they made their way to the edge of the ice rink, Alina looked at him. "We're going ice skating?"

He smiled and nodded. "You wanted to know what I used to do at Christmastime."

Her gaze moved to the ice with people of all ages gliding along the ice and then her attention returned to him. "You can skate?"

"Don't look so shocked. I used to do a lot of things before I became a busy executive. When I was young, my mother would take me to a local ice rink. And when I got older, I would go skate with a friend on their pond." When he saw Alina staring at him with surprise in her eyes, he said, "You surely didn't think I was born in a three-piece suit, did you?"

"No. It's just that you're all about business 24/7. It's surprising seeing you in a different light."

With her hand still in his, he said, "Let's go rent skates." When he turned to start walking, she didn't follow. He turned back to her. "What's wrong?"

"I can't skate." When a smile lifted his lips, she said, "It's not funny."

"I'm not laughing. It's my turn to be surprised. Who'd have thought there's something you don't know how to do."

"What's that supposed to mean?"

"That you, my darling, are a jack-of-all-trades." It wasn't until he finished speaking that he realized he'd called her "my darling." Where in the world had that come from?

"When you lose a parent, you learn to help out. When you lose the other parent, you learn really fast how to provide for yourself—even if it means slinging a tool-box."

He gave her hand squeeze. "I'm sorry you lost both of your parents."

"I am, too." Her voice was so soft it was more like a whisper that floated away in the breeze.

As they stood in line to get skates, Graham said, "Don't worry. I'll teach you to skate."

"You might regret making the offer. I can just see me falling face-first and taking you down with me."

"It won't happen."

She arched a fine brow. "How can you be so sure?"

"Because I'll be there to make sure it doesn't."

Once they had their skates laced up, Graham helped Alina out onto the ice. This time she was the one reaching for his hand. She wrapped her fingers around his and squeezed like a steel vice. His fingertips started to lose sensation.

"Relax," he said.

"I can't."

"Listen to the music. It's a Christmas song. And we all know how you love the holiday classics. Maybe you could sing it."

She frowned. "What does a song have to do with me skating?"

"Because if you don't relax a little, my hand is going to lose all blood flow."

Her mouth formed an O as she eased up her hold. "Sorry."

He stretched his fingers. "All I'm saying is that you can't skate when your muscles are tense. I promise this isn't that hard."

Her eyes narrowed. "You keep saying this is easy, but I still haven't seen you skate."

"Is that a challenge?"

She eagerly nodded. "It is."

"Are you fine staying there against the wall?"

She nodded again.

"I'll be right back." He took off around the rink. Luckily it wasn't too crowded.

It'd been a while since he'd been on skates, but for him it was just like riding a bike. He took a couple of warm-up passes. Then he moved to the center of the rink where there were fewer people. He attempted a jump. He didn't have much height and his landing was a little off, but he was still impressed he was able to do that good considering how long it'd been since he'd been on skates. Next, he tried a spin and did marginally better. Hopefully it'd be good enough to convince Alina to trust him.

He skated up to her, noticing her death grip on the wall. He smiled at her, hoping to ease her anxiety. "So what did you think?"

"I think you must have been a professional skater in another life."

His smile broadened. "Not even close. But do you now trust me to guide you around the rink?"

Her eyes held doubt, but she placed her hand in his. "Let's try it."

He moved behind her, placing his hands around her waist. "I've got you." When she let go of the wall, he said, "Keep your skates shoulder-width apart." She adjusted. "Good. Now bend your knees just a bit." When she did, he said, "Not so much. There you go. And now push off with your right leg."

When she pushed off, he let her go—let her glide on the ice by herself. But when she slowed to a stop, he was right there to lend aid. They worked together on her skating as they made their way around the ice.

He let go of her hand, picked up speed and then turned so he was skating backward. Alina smiled at him. She looked adorable with her cheeks pink from the cold.

"Are you having a good time?" he asked.

"I love this. I never knew what I was missing."

"Good. We'll have to come back."

It wasn't until he'd spoken the words that he realized he'd implied they had a future. And he knew that wasn't the case. When he bulldozed her home, any thought of them doing anything together would also be demolished. The thought saddened him because he couldn't remember the last time he'd had this much fun and it was all thanks to Alina.

"I'd like that," she said, making him feel even worse.

He shoved aside the troubling thoughts of the future. Instead he focused on the here and now. He slowed to a stop, but Alina wasn't so good with stopping. She ran into him. He absorbed the impact, keeping them standing. Her soft curves leaned into him and instantly there was a chemical reaction.

When he looked down at her, he couldn't remember what he was about to say. His gaze lowered. Her rosy lips beckoned to him.

His heart lodged in his throat. He was about to live in the moment and deal with the consequences later. He lowered his head and claimed her mouth. He wasn't sure what sort of reaction his hasty action would receive, but Alina didn't push him away. Her lips moved beneath his. And in that moment, he realized he'd never had a kiss like this one, where it warmed him from the inside out.

He knew all of the reasons this shouldn't be happening, but the pounding of his heart drowned out those reservations. There was just something so special about Alina, from her determination to her thoughtfulness. How could any man resist her charms?

As her smooth lips moved over his, he wished their circumstances were different. He wanted to follow this kiss up with another and another. Because as sure as he was standing there, he would never get enough of Alina. That was a complete and utter impossibility.

The laughter of kids nearby had him pulling back. Even though it felt as though time had stopped, their kiss had been brief—much too brief.

His gaze met hers but he couldn't read her thoughts. This had been a moment of weakness. He knew to consider it anything else would be a big mistake. In the end, he would hurt Alina when inevitably her home was replaced with Toliver Tower.

"I think we should call it quits for today," he said.

She averted her gaze. "I agree. It's been a long day."

The ramifications of his spontaneous action were already sinking in. They skated over to the other side of the rink, where they'd left their belongings in a locker. This time he didn't hold her hand.

There had been a distinct shift in their relationship. He hadn't just tiptoed over the line of common sense, he'd barged right over it with both feet. There was no taking it back. No changing history.

And as much as he'd like to see where this relationship would lead them, he couldn't do that. To follow that kiss up with more would lead Alina to believe this was the beginning of something and that wasn't the case. As it was, their time together was quickly drawing to a close.

His phone buzzed.

The following day, Graham was in no mood to speak to

anyone. All he could think about was how Alina had gone out of her way to avoid him since that kiss. And he missed her—missed their friendship.

His fingers pounded harder than necessary on his laptop keyboard. He'd been on a roll and actually making a dent in his email. Maybe if he ignored the call, they'd give up and not call back. He knew he wouldn't be that lucky. Still, he continued typing.

Graham had forwarded the calls and texts from the Stirling to his phone. By doing this, he freed himself from having to sit in the manager's office at the apartment building. It had come in handy the day before when there had been important meetings at the office about the new building.

He checked his phone, finding whoever had rung had left him a voice mail. He listened to it and found it was from the tenant in apartment 104—Alina's stepmother. If he didn't take care of it now, he knew she'd come knocking on his door. It was best to just get it over with.

He finished an email to his assistant, closed his laptop and then grabbed his toolbox—er, Alina's toolbox—and headed out the door. The one thing he'd learned since taking on this arrangement was that he wasn't so bad at multitasking. He used to like to work on one project until it was completed, but he was finding periodic breaks gave his subconscious a chance to work out problems. When he returned to his project, he had a fresh perspective.

He stepped into the deserted hallway. It was the middle of the afternoon and most people were still at work. He made his way to 104. The door was still plain, whereas most of the doors in the building had holiday wreaths or bows affixed to them. Maybe Alina's stepmother hadn't gotten around to it yet.

He raised his hand and rapped his knuckles on the door. "Maintenance."

The door immediately swung open. A tall woman with short platinum blond hair frowned at him as though she'd been standing there waiting on his arrival. It must be something serious. He inwardly groaned because he had notes about an important contract to finish typing.

"It's about time," she snapped.

Wait. What? He'd just gotten the message a few minutes ago. "I got here as fast as I could. What's the problem?"

The woman glanced past him, into the hallway. "Where's Al… Alina?"

If she thought she was going to rattle him, she had another thought coming. "She's not available. But if you'll just show me the problem—"

"It's Alina's job!" The woman's eyes darkened with anger. "I told you this the last time you came. It's what she gets paid for. I'm not going to have one of her boyfriends—"

"I'm not her boyfriend."

The woman's eyes widened. Either the news that he wasn't Alina's boyfriend was a surprise or the woman wasn't used to anyone interrupting her when she was yelling. Either way, he didn't like the woman at all.

Suddenly her demeanor changed. A smile plumped up her drawn cheeks. "My daughters aren't here at the moment, but I know they'd love to meet you."

He didn't know where this conversation was headed, but he had an uncomfortable feeling.

"Come inside." She stepped back. "I just put on some coffee."

So much for there being an emergency. It was time to make a quick exit.

He held up a finger for the woman to wait and then he pressed on his earpiece, pretending he had an important phone call.

"Yes, Mary." He paused for a moment. "Yes, I have those

numbers on my laptop. I'll get them for you. Hang on." He turned back to the woman. "Sorry, its important business."

The woman's mouth gaped as her brows gathered and her eyes revealed her utter disapproval at being dismissed.

He immediately turned and strode away. His dislike for Alina's stepmother was intense. Behind him a door slammed shut.

The funny thing was that most of the people in the building were super friendly. Others weren't as talkative, preferring to keep to themselves. But that woman was the meanest person in the building. He felt sorry for Alina—not only because she had to deal with that woman on a regular basis, but also because it was the closest Alina had to family.

CHAPTER FOURTEEN

FOUR DAYS HAD PASSED...and neither of them had said a word about the kiss.

Alina was proud of the way she'd avoided Graham. It hadn't been easy, not with him living in the same building as her. When she'd made the deal for him to live here and work here, it'd seemed like such a good idea. Now, she utterly and totally regretted it.

Because the memory of his kiss was never far from Alina's mind. She thought about it in the shower, when she was supposed to be working and when she went to bed at night. How could she let herself be drawn to the enemy?

She felt as though she'd betrayed her friends and neighbors, who were counting on her to save their homes. And she'd betrayed herself by letting her guard down with him. In the end, he'd end up disappointing her like others had done.

Even so, it didn't stop her from keeping her word about organizing the Christmas party. She spent every free moment that week working on Graham's upcoming party. The Snow Ball was taking shape.

With the aid of some of the Stirling's residents as well as a handful of Graham's employees, they'd worked tirelessly to bring Alina's brainchild to life.

The conference room was a mix of fake snow, snowballs, lighted snowmen and a tall elegant tree with homemade ornaments from a local second grade class. One of the Stirling residents was a teacher and had offered to have her class help. Considering the ball was meant to feature up-and-coming artists, Alina couldn't think of anything better.

And now she wanted to do a little something for the people who had been such big helpers with this project. She'd stopped at the store and picked up some chocolates because who didn't love chocolate? She also wanted to add some Christmas cookies to each plate. She thought of buying them, but it didn't feel right. She would bake them.

Just then she heard a knock on the door. It wasn't uncommon for some of her neighbors to stop by in the evening. As the kitchen was right next to the front door, she called out to them to come in.

When she glanced up, the breath hitched in her throat. She blinked but Graham was still standing there staring back at her. How was it possible he looked even better since the last time she'd seen him in person?

"Graham, what are you doing here?" Realizing how that might sound, she tried again. "I'm sorry. What I meant to say was, is there something I can help you with?"

"I wanted to let you know that Beverly Williams has an electrical short in her kitchen. I've turned off the breaker and called in an electrician. I just wanted you to know in case you saw a stranger in the building."

Disappointment assailed her. For just a moment, she'd hoped he was there to see her. "Thanks for letting me know."

"Should I inform anyone else?"

She shook her head as she moved about the kitchen, clearing the countertop. "We may be a smaller apartment building, but people are used to service people showing up."

He nodded. "I just wanted to check."

When he didn't move to leave, Alina felt compelled to fill the awkward silence. "Is everything going okay?" She grabbed a dishcloth to wash off the countertop. "I mean, is everything okay between you and the tenants?"

"It's fine." He arched a brow. "That is unless someone complained. Have there been complaints?"

"No. None at all."

For the first time since he'd entered the apartment, she paused and really looked at him. Graham wore a pair of low-slung blue jeans. His hair was a bit mussed up, making him look so cute. As he yawned and stretched, his gray T-shirt lifted, exposing a glimpse of his washboard abs. She inwardly groaned at being so close and yet so far away. It was all she could do not to drop the baking sheet in her hands.

Before he noticed her staring, she turned her attention back to placing the baking sheet on the counter. Finding her mouth had gone dry, she swallowed hard. "I…I'm, uh, going to bake some Christmas cookies."

"For Merryweather?"

"Some for him, but most are for the people helping with the Snow Ball."

"That's a nice idea. I hope you'll have extra so I can try one."

"There should be so long as I don't burn them."

He sat down at the breakfast bar. "What can I do to help?"

She shook her head as she got out a cutting board. "Nothing. I've got it."

"Really? There's nothing I can do?"

He seemed quite intent on staying, but why? Was it possible he wanted to move past that kiss? She chanced another glance at Graham. He appeared to have forgotten all about it. But could she?

It wasn't like she was an infatuated teenager. She could control her emotions and do what needed done. After all, they couldn't keep avoiding each other. Perhaps she should follow his lead.

"How are you with sprinkles?"

"Decorating is my thing." He got up and washed his hands. "Where are they?"

"In the cabinet next to the fridge." In the meantime, she retrieved some of the cookie dough from the fridge.

When she glanced over to make sure he'd found the sprinkles, he was stretching to reach the top shelf. His shirt had ridden up once more. She swallowed hard as she averted her gaze. This casual relationship was going to be so much harder than she thought.

"Wow. You have a lot of them. In almost every color."

Alina smiled. "I like them. They're bright and fun."

"The only thing I don't understand is that you said you weren't good in the kitchen." The plastic bottles rattled as he removed them from the cabinet. "Yet you bake."

"Maybe there are a few things I can do in the kitchen," she admitted. "I just prefer not to."

"Ah...so the truth comes out now," he teased. He moved to sit down on a bar stool and then placed the collection of sprinkles on the counter. He glanced up and his gaze landed on the plastic roll in her hand. "What's that?"

She cut open the plastic wrap and peeled it back. "It's cookie dough."

His brow arched. "No, it's not. It's store-bought."

"It's still cookie dough." She took a sharp knife and sliced off a sugar cookie.

"I don't know about this. This might be considered cheating." His brown eyes sparkled with merriment. "Does Merryweather know about this?"

"Oh, listen to you." A smile pulled at the corners of her mouth as her guard started to fall. "You, mister, have no room to talk."

He crossed his arms as a smile played on his lips. "What? I don't hand out fake cookies."

"They aren't fake!" *Oh, this man!* The more he got her worked up, the more he smiled. And the more he smiled, the more she fell for him. "Your cookies aren't any better than mine. I've seen the Polka Dotted Bakery boxes in the garbage."

"You did?"

She nodded.

The smile vanished from his face. "Oh, well, you keep my secret and I'll keep yours."

"It's a deal." Alina placed the last cookie on the sheet and pushed it toward him. "You start decorating this one."

He looked at the plain round circles and frowned.

"What's wrong?"

"I'm not sure how to decorate them."

"They don't have to be fancy. Just add a few sprinkles. They'll look fine but taste even better." She started to fill the second tray with cookie dough.

She could get used to this—used to spending the evening together. It was like they were a couple. As soon as the thought came to her, she halted it.

They weren't a couple. They were far from it. Weren't they? Her heart beat faster. Because then she thought of how they'd decorated the Christmas tree together. And how they'd gone ice skating together. And the kiss, oh, the kiss. Heat flamed in her cheeks. What did she call this thing between them? Because there was something. Of that she was certain.

The cookies were decorated and baked.

The kitchen was cleaned up.

Graham didn't want the evening to end. Sure, he had reports to go over, emails that needed responses and directives to send out, but for the first time ever, he had no drive to spend his evening in front of his laptop.

His gaze moved to Alina as she settled on the couch next to the Christmas tree. That's where he wanted to be, next to her, continuing to make her smile. Thoughts of work slid to the back of his mind.

He poured two glasses of cold milk and placed a few freshly baked cookies on a plate. With the excuse of sharing a snack, he moved to the living room. He sat down on the couch, leaving a modest space between them, resisting the urge to slide up next to her.

He chanced a glance at her. His gaze drifted downward to her pink lips—her very tempting mouth. Talk about your sweet treats. But he held back because Alina wasn't just anyone. He knew she'd been hurt by people in her past and he didn't want to be added to that list.

He cleared his throat. "Time to sample the baked goods."

"But those were to hand out to the residents."

"I don't think they'll mind if we eat a few." He held out a glass to her. "And I grabbed some milk."

She smiled. "Something tells me you used to have this as a bedtime snack when you were a kid."

He hadn't thought about those times in quite a while. These days he tried to keep his focus on the future. "I did. My mother would give me cookies and milk when I couldn't sleep."

"Did that happen often? The not-sleeping part."

He sat his glass on the coffee table alongside the cookies. He leaned back on the couch, letting his thoughts roll back in time. He'd purposely blocked those memories from his thoughts.

But Alina had opened not only her home but also parts of her past to him; how could he not do the same for her? It wasn't like she knew what she was asking. How could she know when from the outside the Toliver family looked like they should have everything? But they hadn't. Far from it.

And the thing was that Graham hadn't even known how deep some of the lies had gone until long after he'd stepped in to run the family business. And now he was in so deep that he just had to keep up appearances while he realigned the business.

"When I was young my parents for the most part lived separate lives. My father was all about living in the fast lane in the city. He wanted to be around for business dinners and arrive early at the office before the other employees."

Graham had never told any of this to anyone else, including the woman he'd almost married. Maybe that should have been a warning flag to him that their relationship wasn't as strong as it needed to be to pledge forever. But they weren't discussing that right now. "My mother preferred the calm serenity of the suburbs. She said it was better for raising a child."

"Was it?" Alina asked. "I mean, did you like living outside of the city?"

"I never really thought about it, but I didn't dislike it."

"I couldn't imagine living anywhere else. It's like this city gets in your blood and you're lost without it."

"Now that I've lived here for a number of years, I understand what you mean."

"So you don't miss the quiet of the burbs?"

"Sometimes the silence just gives way to deeper thoughts."

"And what thoughts did you have?"

"That appearances can be a front for hiding secrets." He stopped there. What was he doing digging up all of this family drama? He could feel Alina's curious gaze on him. It was his fault for starting this conversation. He might as well finish it. "My parents were all about appearances. My mother prided herself on being the perfect wife and mother. My father prided himself on being a shrewd businessman. And none of that in and of itself is bad, not until you let it rule your entire life."

In that moment, he felt Alina's touch. She wrapped her soft fingers around his hand and squeezed. "I think everyone wants to show the world the image of a perfect family."

He turned to her. "But what happens when, behind the scenes, it's anything but perfect?" He turned his focus back to the blank wall in front of him. "My mother was alone with me all week. My father would come home Friday evenings. I don't know why he bothered because all he wanted was to be left alone to concentrate on the reports he'd brought home with him. And my mother was lonely and wanted his company."

"And what about you?" Alina's voice was soft. "You must have missed him terribly. I know that I loved spending time with my father, even if it included fixing a clogged pipe. Not one of my favorite tasks."

Graham shrugged. "I had my friends."

"But they couldn't replace your father."

He recalled the past—the real past—not the snippets he often referred to when asked about his youth. "I never lived up to my father's expectations."

"I'm sure you did. Maybe he just didn't know how to communicate his feelings."

Graham shook his head. "I tried to impress him with my grades in school, but all he could see was the one mark that wasn't the best. And then I participated in sports, most any sport, hoping it would be a bridge for us, but my efforts were never enough. My father said you needed to be the best or not even bother trying."

Graham glanced at her, seeing the sympathy in her blue

eyes. It made him feel uncomfortable. He didn't want people's sympathy. That's why he never opened up.

"Don't," he said.

"Don't what?"

"Feel sorry for me. I'm fine. I'm better than fine. I run one of the biggest companies in the world." Though it didn't fill the hollow spot in his chest. He told himself that if he reorganized the company, overcame his father's business errors and built Toliver Tower, it was all he needed to feel fulfilled.

"But you're not fine," Alina said in a gentle voice.

He jerked away from her hold and slid over on the couch. When he turned to her, he saw the pity in her eyes and it ignited his anger. "How can you say that? You're the one who is still living in her childhood home and refusing to move out—refusing to see what the world has to offer."

No sooner were the words out of his mouth than he regretted them. What was he doing lashing out at her? He sounded just like his father when his mother told him that he worked too many hours.

Alina gasped. Pain and disappointment shimmered in her eyes.

"I'm so sorry." He moved closer to her. "I didn't mean that. I...I wasn't thinking."

When he reached out to her, she immediately recoiled. Whatever connection they'd been building, he felt as though he'd destroyed it in one outburst.

He jumped to his feet and moved to the window that looked out over quiet Holly Lane. He raked his fingers through his hair. All the while, his jaw was clenched tight. How could he hurt Alina of all people? She was the sweetest and kindest, just ask anyone in the Stirling.

"My mother was right." His voice was soft. "I am turning into my father. No wonder she doesn't bother with me."

Guilt weighed down on him. He wanted to make this up to Alina, but he had no idea how to do it. His mother had given him an ultimatum—selling the company and having a life that included her or running the company alone. His mother would never know how much that decision had cost him. And now he doubted Alina wanted him, either.

A hand touched his bicep. "It's okay."

He turned to find Alina standing there in the glow of the Christmas tree. He wanted to wipe away the sadness from her face. "You don't know how much I want to rewind time and take back my words."

"But you're right. I am stuck here. Without any true family left, I just can't imagine letting go of the Stirling and the people in it. They make me happy. They make me feel needed."

"And I have a company but no one to share it with."

Alina reached out and cupped his face in her delicate hand. "You don't have to be alone, if you don't want to be."

Wait. Had he heard her correctly? Was she saying what he thought she was saying? Every fiber of his body longed for her—to be close to her—to breathe her essence in. But first he had to know if that's what she really wanted because he just couldn't make any more mistakes where she was concerned.

His gaze searched hers. "Alina, what are you saying?"

It was then that she lifted up on her tiptoes and pressed her lips to his. Whoever said actions spoke louder than words must have been referring to this very moment. Because as her lips moved over his, he had no doubt what she'd been saying. Her lips were definitely doing all of the talking. And he was more than happy to be on the other end of that wordless communication.

He reached out and drew her to him. Her soft curves fit perfectly to his hard planes. But now he took the lead, heating up their kiss. Her hands reached up past his shoulders, wrapping around his neck as her fingers combed through his hair.

He no longer felt alone. With Alina right here next to him, he felt as though together they could take on the world. And for the first time in his life, he knew what it was to have someone truly believe in him.

Alina didn't judge him as not good enough like his father had done. And she didn't hold things against him that he hadn't even done yet like his mother. Alina didn't pressure him to be anyone but who he was.

In this moment, he wasn't the head of a billion-dollar corporation. He wasn't the heir to a mess of accounts that had been mismanaged. And he wasn't the mean landlord that was kicking everyone out of their homes.

With Alina in his arms, he was just a man—a man that felt worthy just by being himself. He felt the weight of the world fall away. And he stopped worrying about the future or looking over his shoulder at mistakes of the past. In this moment, he just wanted to savor the here and now for this one special evening in the twinkle of the Christmas lights.

They pushed aside the coffee table and then he grabbed the blanket from the back of the couch. As he spread it out over the floor, Alina tossed down the throw pillows.

And then with the lights off except those of the Christmas tree, Alina was once again back in his arms. He claimed her lips—her full, soft lips.

Santa had come early this year. Graham wasn't sure he was worthy of such a sweet gift. He was pretty certain he wasn't. But he was totally caught up in the moment—caught up in Alina's addictive kiss.

And so he would unwrap this most special gift. He would savor this evening and the twinkle of desire in Alina's blue eyes.

CHAPTER FIFTEEN

OH, WHAT A NIGHT!

Alina woke up smiling, remembering how attentive and loving Graham had been during the night. Like a cat after a sunny nap, she stretched. She enjoyed the way her body still tingled all over.

But when she looked around, she didn't see Graham anywhere. She paused and listened for sounds of the shower. There was none. He was gone?

It was then that she checked the time. It was after eight. *After eight!* She never slept this late. But she did have a good excuse. The best excuse.

She wrapped a blanket around her from the makeshift bed on the living room floor and jumped to her feet. She'd requested the day off from working at the Christmas Café. Everyone was meeting at the Diamond Building at nine a.m. to make the final touches on the conference room.

She still couldn't believe she'd forgotten to set her alarm, but then again she'd been utterly distracted the night before. A smile pulled at her lips. But it soon disappeared when she realized Graham had left without saying a word to her.

What did his silent departure mean? Did he regret their night together? Her heart tumbled clear down to her frosted pink shimmery painted toes.

Unshed tears pricked the backs of her eyes. She blinked them away. Whatever his reason for disappearing, she'd

have to deal with it later. Right now, she had people waiting for her. And Alina wouldn't let them down.

She rushed to the kitchen and found the coffeemaker was
filled with water and ready to go with a fresh pod already
loaded. She hadn't left it like that. It had to have been Graham being thoughtful. A smile lifted her lips. All she had
to do was close the top and press the power button. And
then she saw the note from Graham.

> Sorry I had to go. You were so tired I didn't want to
> wake you. I had an important meeting at the office
> with the Cortinas.
>   I'll see you later, G.

She smiled. Maybe it wasn't a love note, but he hadn't
pulled a disappearing act. For that she was grateful.

Then realizing the lateness of the hour, she ran down
the hallway and hopped straight into the shower. It was the
fastest shower she'd ever taken.

After she dressed and threw her damp hair up in a messy
bun, she realized Prince wasn't yelling at her for his breakfast. In fact, he wasn't anywhere in sight. That was strange.

"Prince? Prince?" She rushed into her bedroom, looking for him.

There was no Prince in her bed or under it. She was on
her way to the kitchen when she spotted Prince in the living
room stretched out on the couch. Not far away was Prince's
licked-clean blue bowl with white fish ringed around it. She
never fed him on the couch.

She smiled and ruffled Prince's fur. "Seems like you
and Graham have made up. Huh, boy?"

Prince squeaked as he stretched. Then he settled on his
other side.

It looked like she wasn't needed here. It was a strange

feeling, sharing her cat. She'd never done it before. But she liked that the two males in her life were getting along.

She leaned over and kissed the top of Prince's head. "Love you. I'll be home later."

But not for long. Tonight was the Snow Ball and she had every intention of dancing with Graham. In fact, her heart was set on it.

The pep was back in her step as she gathered her thank-you gifts and then headed for the door. She'd been worried about nothing. Things between her and Graham were the best they'd ever been.

This room was amazing.

It no longer resembled a conference room.

Graham stood in the doorway, admiring the fake snow settled around a snow people family. There was even a small snow hut made out of white foam balls. He smiled. Why had he ever worried about letting Alina run with this plan? She did amazing work. She needed to start up her own party-planning service and do it full-time.

He strolled around the room, taking in all of the artwork on the walls, from snowy mountains to quaint snowy store-fronts as well as some abstract pieces. It was very impressive. He needed to thank Alina. In this case, words wouldn't be enough. It needed to be more than helping the residents of the Stirling find appropriate housing. It needed to be something special just for her.

He thought of the prior night and a smile pulled at the corners of this mouth. No matter how long he lived, he'd never forget this time with Alina. The night had been more than he dared to imagine it would be—she had been more special than he deserved.

But with their agreement about to come to an end, he knew their paths in life would lead them in opposite directions. The thought immediately deflated his mood. Even though the company was headed in the right direction, he had other things that needed his immediate attention. He finally acknowledged running a company this size would always be demanding of his time, and there was no way he wanted to end up in an unhappy marriage like his parents had endured.

And no matter what had happened between them, Alina was going to look at him differently after the Stirling was gone. The thought caused an uneasiness in his chest.

But before all of that happened, they had tonight. And he wanted to show her how much their time together meant to him. He rushed to the bank of elevators. He had a meeting with the Cortinas and then he was slipping out to find Alina a memento to remember tonight—to remember him.

Things like this just didn't happen to her.

And yet Alina stood in front of her bathroom mirror in a white evening gown that she'd picked up at a secondhand shop. She didn't have the money for a fancy, new dress. It had needed a few adjustments, the torn lace mended and a stain removed. But she'd done it.

If someone didn't know about those issues, they wouldn't notice them, right? She turned in front of the mirror and assured herself the dress would do just fine. After all, it wasn't like she would stand out in a crowd.

As her anxiety rose, so did her insecurities. Words from the past came roaring back in her mind. *"Al, you have to accept that you just aren't pretty." "Al, no one will notice you."*

She pushed away the negative thoughts. It wasn't like she was going with the intent of impressing anyone—well, maybe just one person. What would Graham think of her appearance?

She glanced at the time. There was no time for a debate. If she didn't hurry, she was going to be late. And she didn't want to miss a moment of Graham's big night. She hoped it all worked out for him. She knew how much he was counting on it.

Her makeup consisted of the usual powder and mascara. But she couldn't decide about her hair. Should she wear it up? Or down? As she lifted her hair and turned to the side, her insides shivered with nerves. Maybe down would work—

Buzz-buzz.

That was probably someone with last-minute questions about the evening's events. As she continued to ponder her hair dilemma, she pressed the phone to her ear.

Before she could utter a word, she heard, "Alina, you have to come quick."

The sound of her stepmother's voice had Alina releasing her hair. "Dorian, is that you?"

"Of course it is. Now hurry." And with that the line went dead.

Alina frowned as she stared at the phone. What could be such an emergency? And it didn't escape her notice that this happened the night of the ball. Could her stepmother be low enough to want to ruin it for her? Surely nobody could be that mean.

She glanced back in the mirror at her reflection. There was no time to debate. She opted to put her long hair up in a neat and formal French twist. Once it was secure with an army of bobby pins, she gave it a light mist of hair spray.

And then Alina, knowing Graham was occupied on this big night, went to investigate what was bothering her stepmother. Hopefully, it wouldn't take long. Graham was sending cars to pick up the Stirling residents and she didn't want to miss her ride.

Knock-knock.

The door immediately flung open. Her stepmother stood there in a sparkly navy-blue dress, but it was the frown on her face that drew Alina's attention. Her stepmother made a point of taking in Alina's dress.

"Al, what are you wearing?"

Alina struggled not to roll her eyes. "You know perfectly well that everyone in the building was invited to the ball tonight."

"But not you."

"Of course I was included. I helped plan it."

Her stepmother's face creased with deep frown lines. "But you have a building to manage."

"And it will be fine for one evening. Now if that's all you wanted, I have to go finish getting ready." Alina went to turn away.

"Not so fast," Dorian said. "You have a mess to clean up."

Dread churned in Alina's empty stomach. She would not let her stepmother ruin this evening for her. She'd been looking forward to it since they'd come up with the idea. And Graham had made her promise him a dance.

"What mess?" Alina's insides knotted up.

"Mother." Juniper, Alina's oldest stepsister, rushed into the room. She wore a hot-pink dress that was short on the hemline and long in the plunging neckline. "You have to do something. I can't get ready in the bathroom."

"Your stepsister was just about to fix the problem. Go finish getting ready in your room." Then Dorian turned back to Alina. "You, come with me."

Alina didn't want to go anywhere with the woman. She knew when Dorian felt crossed or believed Alina was getting away with something, there was a price to be paid. What did she have in store for Alina this time?

As Alina entered the living room, she noticed her youngest stepsister, Gretel, sitting on the couch in a fluorescent green dress. Her red curls were pull up with a big green bow. She glanced at Alina and scowled.

"It's in here." Dorian pointed into the bathroom.

Alina moved to the doorway and found the toilet was overflowing. She looked at her stepmother. "You couldn't have turned off the water?"

"That's not my job. It's yours." She looked at her expectantly.

Alina inwardly seethed. This woman was going to let the bathroom flood and not care about the damage it would do to her apartment. Luckily the water pressure was low as a result of the old plumbing.

Alina gathered up her long dress, keeping it from getting wet. And then she moved slowly over the floor to the shutoff valve. It took a little bit of juggling to keep her gown safe and turn the tight valve. But at last the water was off. The crisis had been averted. And her dress had been saved. She could still make it to the ball.

She turned for the doorway. If her stepmother thought she was going to stay and clear up this mess, she had another thought coming. When Alina looked at the doorway to tell her stepmother just that, she found the woman had disappeared. It was quite fine by Alina. The less she saw of the woman, the happier she was.

Alina had just stepped into the hallway and turned for the living room when she bumped into someone. The next thing she knew hot liquid hit her chest. The liquid seeped down to her abdomen. Alina glanced down. A coffee stain spread from her chest down over her stomach and flowed onto her skirt.

"My dress!" Tears stung the backs of her eyes.

Alina blinked repeatedly. No way would she let these

people see how upset she was over her dress. Her pretty dress. The dress that she'd searched for days to find. The dress she'd dipped into her savings to buy. The dress she'd worked so hard to make presentable. The dress she was going to wear to the ball where she'd hoped to dance with Graham.

Juniper sneered at her. "Look what you did. You spilled my drink."

"You're a jerk!" The emotionally charged words clogged in her throat. Alina pushed past her. If she didn't get out of that apartment immediately, she would lose control of her emotions. And then her stepmother and stepsisters would get what they wanted, to see Alina upset. She simply wouldn't give them the satisfaction. They'd already cost her enough emotional harm.

In the background, she heard Dorian calling out to her, insisting that Alina finish her work. But Alina kept her shoulders straight and her head held high as she walked through the doorway and turned toward the stairs. With all of the anger bubbling in her veins, she had plenty of energy to burn off.

CHAPTER SIXTEEN

IT WAS RUINED.

Alina didn't need a mirror to know the extent of the damage to her dress. She also didn't need an admission from her stepmother or stepsister to know that they'd done all of this intentionally. They just couldn't stand for her to have a little bit of happiness. They had to ruin it.

This evening had meant so much to her. Someone like her didn't get invited to big, splashy parties. She was the person in the background seeing to all of the details and helping to clean up when it was over. But at last she wasn't going to be ugly, chubby Alina carrying around her toolbox. But in a blink, the opportunity slipped through her fingers.

She'd just reached her floor and yanked open the door when she ran into Merryweather. At first, he smiled at her but then his gaze moved to her dress. His eyes widened.

"Alina, what happened?"

"My stepmother and stepsisters."

"But the ball. It's time to go. I came up to escort you. The cars are waiting."

The prickling of tears started again. She glanced away from his concerned gaze and continued walking toward her apartment. "I'm not going."

"What? But you have to. You planned this whole night. Without you, none of us would get to go."

She knew Merryweather was sweet, but right now she just wanted to be alone in her misery. "You'll have to go without me. I…" Her voice crackled with emotion. She glanced down at her stained white cloth heels. A tear splashed onto her cheek. She swiped it away. "Please, just go without me."

Merryweather quietly followed her back to her apartment. All the while he muttered, "This isn't right. This just isn't right."

At her door, Alina paused and turned to him. "It's okay. I'll be fine. You should go. Enjoy yourself."

A determined look came over him. "Not without you."

"But I can't go like this."

"You aren't the only one with contacts. Go grab your stuff while I make a couple of phone calls."

She'd never seen this determined side of Merryweather. She had no idea what had come over him. There was no way he was going to fix this. She glanced down at the brown stain on her dress. It was completely ruined.

But she wasn't sure she should argue with him. This was the most animated she'd ever seen the man. Maybe it would be good to indulge him just a little. She would ride with him to the Diamond Building so he didn't have to go alone. But she wasn't getting out of the car—not like this. And then she'd come and wallow in a heaping of self-pity.

She went into her apartment and grabbed her coat and purse. She turned off the lights, locked the door and then joined Merryweather in the hallway.

When they stepped outside the building, it was snowing. And the cars that Graham had sent were gone. Alina felt bad because she didn't want Merryweather to miss the ball. He'd worked hard to help pull the event together. It was like his being involved in the planning had brought back his zest for life.

"I'm sorry I caused you to miss your ride to the ball,"

Alina said, wondering if she could get a taxi to take him to the ball in time.

"You didn't cause anything, my dear. Our ride will be along shortly."

Had he called for a taxi while she was in her apartment? He must have. "Merryweather, I know you want to fix things but I'll be fine staying home." She was deeply disappointed, but that was her problem, not his. "But if you could go and make sure there aren't any problems with the party, I'd be eternally grateful."

"I'll make sure the party runs smoothly. But you're going, right? It's your night to shine."

"I don't think so. Not dressed like this." She wouldn't do anything to embarrass Graham.

Just then a Rolls-Royce pulled to the curb. The unblemished white paint and polished chrome gleamed. But what was it doing here?

"Our ride has arrived." Merryweather gestured to the car.

"What?" Alina was utterly confused. How could Merryweather, with his secondhand furniture and worn clothes, afford to hire a prestigious car like this? "You hired us a car?"

"In a matter of speaking. Now we have to hurry."

"But I can't go to the ball like this." She gazed down at the stain that was beginning to dry.

"I have a plan. Trust me." He winked at her.

And for a moment, she'd swear his eyes twinkled. What did she have to lose at this point? When he realized the stain was never going to come out of this delicate fabric, she would find her way home.

The driver, in full uniform including a black hat, opened the back door for her. She got in and slid across the seat. Merryweather climbed in next to her. And off they went.

She noticed how Merryweather never gave any directions or an address.

The next thing she knew, they were pulling up to the back door of a theater—the same theater where Merryweather had worked.

"What are we doing here?" Alina asked.

"You'll soon see, my dear. Come. We don't have time to waste."

And so she followed him through the back door. Lights were dimmed and voices could be heard. There was a performance going on. As Alina listened to the voices, she recognized the lines to *Scrooge: The Musical*.

Merryweather stopped outside a dressing room. A woman approached them. She wore a friendly smile. "I'll definitely have something to fit her. I've also asked Heather to do her hair and Veronica volunteered to do her makeup."

"Perfect," Merryweather said. "But remember, we have to hurry."

"Then we best get to work."

Alina was ushered into the room. And then things moved in a flurry of activity. She tried to tell them that she couldn't pay them much but they dismissed her. They said they wouldn't accept a dime from her.

Dresses were held up to her. Brows scrunched up. There were hems and haws. And then one by one each dress was dismissed. It thoroughly confused Alina because each and every dress was absolutely stunning. But for whatever reason, these women didn't think they were fitting.

"I know," the older woman said. "I have the perfect dress. But first, we have to get her ready."

Alina's hair was brushed out and redone. Her face was cleaned off and repainted. The women talked among themselves and told her not to worry, they knew what they were doing.

With her hair done in barrel rolls held in place with sparkly pins and her face made up in neutral shades that shimmered in the light, she almost didn't recognize herself. They helped her out of her stained gown. All it was good for now was the garbage bin.

And then the older woman walked back into the room with a gown in a white protective cover. Alina would be lying if she said she wasn't anxious to see the chosen gown.

Once the dress was hung on a high hook and the zipper was undone, the protective covering was pulled back to reveal the most magnificent light blue gown. Alina's mouth gaped. Her gaze took in the spaghetti straps that led to a plunging V-neckline, and a fitted bodice, the tiny crystals sewn to the gown twinkling in the light.

The upper back was bare. The lower back was fitted and would hug her body. And the lower portion had a short train of light blue tulle with sparkles. Alina was speechless. They surely didn't mean for her to wear that. It was much too fancy for her.

The remaining piece was a sheer shawl that looked as if it was spun of the finest silk. Though it lacked crystals, it still shimmered. Altogether, it was quite a showstopper.

"It's so beautiful."

"Almost as beautiful as you," the older woman said. "Now hurry. We don't have much time."

"But I…I can't wear something this fancy." All she could think was if she spilled something on it she'd be horrified, not to mention working for the next year—no, make it two years—to pay for it.

"Don't be silly. This gown was made for you. Now hurry."

For a moment, Alina wondered if she'd meant the gown was literally made for her. But that was totally impossible. They didn't even know she'd be showing up until just moments ago. The woman must mean the dress would be flattering on her.

She stepped into the new gown. The women all said it brought out the blue of her eyes. Alina never believed they would have a dress that would fit her, but this dress accentuated her bust, drew in her waist, and the hemline... well, it touched the floor because she was in her bare feet. Surely no one would notice if she were to wear her stained heels, would they?

But before she could retrieve them from next to the makeup chair, Veronica brought over a pair of azure blue heels with rhinestones. They were gorgeous. And they looked so delicate.

"I couldn't possibly wear those," Alina said, still unable to take her gaze off them. "They probably won't fit."

"But you must. They match the gown." Heather knelt down to help her put them on.

Seriously, the chances they'd fit were zip, zilch, zero. But what would it hurt to try them on? They were so pretty. The most beautiful shoes Alina had ever seen. And they definitely cost more than her month's pay and then some.

And yet as Heather slipped the shoes on Alina's feet, they fit perfectly. How could that be? Tears of happiness blurred Alina's vision. How was all of this possible?

"Oh, no. You can't cry now," the older woman said. "You'll ruin everything. And Merryweather is waiting just on the other side of that door to whisk you off to the ball."

"But how can I ever thank you all?" Alina was so touched by the acts of generosity toward her—a perfect stranger.

The older woman smiled. "It's our Christmas present to you."

"Now go. Hurry." Veronica waved her off.

"Yes, go. And have a marvelous time," Heather said.

Alina hugged each of them before heading for the door. When she swung it open, Merryweather was waiting in the hallway. Her mouth gaped as she took in his transformation. It was as though he was ten years younger and he was now done up in a fine black suit and tie. He looked quite dapper.

"Merryweather, you look downright handsome."

He blushed. "Well, I couldn't escort the prettiest belle to the ball in my old suit." He held out his arm to her. "Shall we go?"

She placed her hand in the crook of his arm. "How will I ever repay you?"

"There's nothing to repay. It is I who owes you. You've always been there for me when I was lonely and when I was being contrary. You could have given up on me, but you didn't. Instead you brought me fresh-baked cookies."

"I...I didn't know it meant that much."

"It meant the world. Now there's one thing you should know about all of this. You have to be back at the theater by midnight. That is when the guard locks up for the night and the dress must be here by then."

Her heart swelled with love. She stopped walking and turned to him. Happy tears blurred her vision. She blinked them away. And then she leaned forward and pressed a feathery kiss to his freshly shaven cheek. When she pulled back, she said, "Thank you."

Where was she?

That's all that kept going through Graham's mind as the Snow Ball commenced. This was Alina's brainchild. Without her, none of this would have been possible.

He'd put off greeting his guests and officially kicking off the party for as long as possible. He checked the time. It was five minutes past seven and the room was crowded. He couldn't delay any longer.

Graham made his way to the stage. He stepped up to the microphone and waited as silence swept over the room. All the while he searched for Alina's beautiful face, but she was nowhere to be found.

He cleared his throat. "Thank you all for coming. First, I want to wish you all a merry Christmas. And I want to thank the residents of the Stirling because if it wasn't for them, we wouldn't be here at this wonderful party. I pride myself on setting business goals and surpassing them, but when it came to planning a holiday party, well, I must say that I dropped the ball. And the residents of the Stirling quite literally came to my rescue. Thank you each and every one of you."

And then his gaze spotted Alina standing at the back of the room. The breath caught in his throat. He forgot that he was giving a speech. All he could think was *Wow!* His gaze took in her striking beauty from her golden curls to the figure-hugging sky-blue dress that shimmered like it was covered in jewels.

Suddenly he didn't care that she was late or that he'd been worried about what might have happened to her. Right then all he wanted to do was to drink in her beauty. She was magnificent. As his gaze rose, he noticed the small smile pulling at her lips. When his gaze once again met hers, there was amusement in her eyes.

He wanted to go to her, but he suddenly recalled that he was still standing on the stage and people were looking at him expectantly to finish his speech.

He swallowed hard. "Please give a hand to Alina Martin and the wonderful people of the Stirling."

Graham stepped back from the microphone to lead a rousing round of applause. Cheers rose as the joyous sound of appreciation reverberated throughout the room.

He stepped back to the mic and signaled for everyone

to quiet down. "There's some amazing food in the back. Please help yourself because if you don't, I might eat it all. No, I *will* eat it all. It's so good." Laughter filled the room. "And make sure you dance. You know, it'll help make room for more of that delicious food." There was more laughter. "Again, I hope you all have a very merry Christmas."

He turned to the band and Mr. Jackson beamed as he nodded, and then with his saxophone in hand, he turned back to his band and signaled for them to start playing "White Christmas."

As the piano started to play, Graham exited the stage. He made a beeline for the back of the room—for the spot where he last saw Alina—but when he got there, she was gone. But that couldn't be right. He turned in a circle, his gaze searching the crowd.

And then he spotted her. She was surrounded by a group of his associates—his male associates. Intense discomfort came over him as he watched her smile and chat with the men. It took him a second to identify the feeling. It was jealousy—something he'd never experienced where a woman was concerned. But it was most definitely the green-eyed monster.

"You aren't just going to stand here and let one of them get the first dance, are you?"

Graham glanced over to find Merryweather standing next to him, dressed in a black suit and white dress shirt. He didn't look anything like the man that had Graham fixing nonexistent leaks and had used a cane to get around. Tonight, there was no cane and the man looked fit as a fiddle. How was that possible?

Graham turned his attention back to Alina as she laughed at something one of the men had leaned in close to say. Graham's body tensed.

His instinct was to march over there and sweep Alina

away from all of them, but did he have the right to do that? Because when it came down to it, he still had a job to do. And Alina wasn't going to be happy with what his engineers and inspectors had uncovered about the Stirling.

Merryweather said, "Graham, don't let tomorrow ruin tonight. Sometimes dreams really do happen."

"I...I don't know." All the while Graham couldn't take his gaze off Alina.

"She didn't get all fancied up for those men. You're the one she talked about on the way over here. You're the one she wanted to impress."

"She's certainly done that."

"Then why are you standing here talking to me instead of her?"

Merryweather had a good point. Why bother with the possibilities of tomorrow when there was tonight to live?

With that thought in mind, Graham headed for Alina. He bypassed people wanting to speak with him, putting them off until later. And then, at last, he was standing in front of her. His group of associates parted.

"Graham, the party is wonderful." Alina smiled at him, causing a warm fuzzy feeling in his chest. He was certain there was a name for that feeling, too, but he didn't want to delve too deeply into his feelings. Right now, he just wanted to live in the moment.

"You are absolutely breathtaking." He couldn't take his gaze off her. "But you're missing one thing."

"I am?"

He smiled as he withdrew a small velvet box from his pocket. "Here."

When her gaze zeroed in on the box, her eyes widened. "Graham, what have you done?"

"It's just a little something that made me think of you."

He held it closer to her. "Go ahead and take it. I promise it won't bite."

He just hoped she'd like it. The salesclerk in the jewelry store assured him that any woman would love it. He hoped she was right.

Alina accepted the box and opened it. She gasped as she stared at the necklace. "It's beautiful." Then she closed the box and tried to hand it back to him. "I can't accept this. It's too extravagant."

He moved his hands behind his back. "But you have to take it. There's a no-return policy."

"I'm sure the jeweler will make an exception."

He shook his head. "I mean, I have a no-return policy. I really want you to have it."

Her eyes shimmered. She blinked repeatedly. Then she once again opened the box. "It's so beautiful." She ran her finger over the diamond-encrusted snowball suspended on a white-gold box chain. "I'll never forget this night."

"Let me help you put it on."

She carefully took it out of the box and handed it to him. And then she turned her back to him. She swept her long golden curls off to the side. It took him a few tries but at last he had it fastened.

When she turned around, he said, "Beautiful."

"It certainly is."

"No." His gaze met hers. "I meant you."

Her cheeks pinkened. "Thank you."

"May I have this dance?" he asked, wanting a chance to talk to her without a rapt audience.

"I'd like that."

There was an audible groan from the men as they turned and moved off. A smile lifted Graham's lips. He got the girl—the most beautiful girl in the room. Lucky for him, it was a slower song and he was able to hold her in his arms as they made their way around the dance floor.

"Thank you," he said.

She arched a fine brow. "For dancing with you?"

His smile broadened. "Well, that, too. But I meant for tonight. This entire event was your vision. You really pulled it off. Everyone is impressed."

She glanced around, taking in the smiling people. "They do seem to be enjoying themselves. But I can't take any credit. It took a village to create this evening."

"And I owe you all a debt of gratitude."

"Does that mean you'll reconsider tearing down the apartment building?" Hope shone in her eyes.

"I've given it a lot of thought, but now isn't the time to discuss it."

The sparkle in her eyes disappeared in a blink. "You're right. I'm sorry."

"There's no reason to be sorry. I know how much the building and its residents mean to you."

They continued moving around the dance floor. He loved holding her close.

His gaze met hers and it was as though the world moved slightly off its axis. He couldn't quite explain what had happened in that moment, but he knew nothing in his life would ever be the same. He also realized that imagining anything more than this moment was a fool's errand. But it didn't keep him from hoping there would be some sort of Christmas miracle.

CHAPTER SEVENTEEN

SHE FELT LIKE a princess.

And Graham was her prince.

His hand felt natural pressed to the small of her back. Her hand fit within his other hand. It was though they were dancing among the clouds. She never even felt her feet touch the floor.

If this was a dream, she never wanted it to end. His warm smile made her heart trip over itself. How did she get so lucky to be here with him?

And to think she'd almost missed out on it all if it hadn't been for Merryweather. She still had questions for her dear friend. She wanted to know how he made all of this possible. But those questions would have to wait until later.

When she glanced over his shoulder, she noticed they were the only ones now dancing. What in the world? But the music continued to play and they continued to move to the beat.

Their audience had formed a circle. And then she caught sight of her stepmother. If looks could kill, Alina would be nothing more than a little sooty spot on the floor. On each side of Dorian were Alina's stepsisters, who looked as though they'd each sucked on a lemon. She never understood how people could live their lives being so nasty.

But tonight, nothing could ruin her good mood. Nothing at all. She was on cloud nine and she had no interest in coming back to earth. Tomorrow would come soon enough.

She leaned closer to Graham. "We have an audience."

He glanced up. "So we do."

"Maybe we should stop. I don't feel right taking up the whole dance floor."

"I agree about stopping, but how about we give them something to look at first..." Graham stopped dancing but he kept his arms around her.

What is he doing? Her heart pounded.

He bent his head and captured her lips with his own. Her breath hitched in her throat.

Oh, I know exactly what he's doing.

Suddenly it didn't matter who was watching, she was quite content right here in his strong, capable arms. His kiss was light and tender, but oh so stirring.

And she knew she shouldn't let herself fall for him. But it was too late. She'd fallen hard. It was as though they were fated to meet and she couldn't imagine her life without him in it.

When the music stopped, Graham stepped back. He lowered his arms and she immediately missed the warmth of his touch. She didn't want to let him go so soon.

But it was as if the spell had been lifted and she glanced around at all of the curious onlookers. Some people had their phones held up as though they'd been filming them. Others whispered back and forth. What in the world had gotten into them to put on such a public display of affection? Heat swirled in her chest and rushed up her neck, setting her cheeks ablaze.

Once they'd moved to the side of the room, Alina fanned herself. Her face felt sunburned, as though she'd been lying on a sun-drenched beach for hours.

"Come on." Graham reached for her hand. "Let's get a little air."

Alina had no idea where they were going, but some cool

air and privacy sounded perfect. They walked to the far side of the ballroom and that's when Alina remembered about the overlook.

Graham pushed open the door and they stepped out. A glance around assured her that, at last, they were alone. For the party, Graham had set up portable heaters out here, making it comfortable.

They moved to the edge. With the evening sky for a backdrop, the Manhattan skyline twinkled with lights. It was like a stunning piece of art, only better.

"This is so beautiful," she said.

"Yes, you are." Graham's voice was deep and throaty, making her pulse race.

She turned to him, finding him smiling at her. "Shouldn't you be inside with your guests?"

"But I like it so much better out here with you."

He was saying all of the right things to make her heart go pitter-patter. "I hope the evening is meeting all of your expectations."

"It most definitely is." Desire burned in his eyes.

She swallowed hard as she tried to keep her train of thought. "I was talking about the party. You know, so you can sway your business associates to join you in that new venture."

He continued to stare at her, making her heart beat erratically. "But I'd rather talk about you and me."

She smiled and shook her head. "You're impossible."

"Am I? I guess you'll have to do something about it." He reached for her, drawing her near.

Her gaze moved to the glass door that led straight to the party. Anyone could see them standing out here. "Graham, don't you think we put on enough of a show for one night?"

The smile fell from his face. "I suppose you're right." He

released her. "You wouldn't want to skip the party, would you?"

"Graham, you can't leave early after all of the hard work everyone put into this event."

"You're right, again." He sighed and turned back to gaze out over the city.

"Your business associates are having a good time, aren't they?" She'd yet to meet the people, but she hoped they approved of all the hard work to put together the party.

"They were at the office most of the day. I gave them a preview of the Snow Ball. They loved it. And we closed the deal. It was more than I ever could have hoped for—in fact, it's the biggest deal in the history of Toliver."

"Graham, that's wonderful!" This time she was the one who moved in close. When she went to place a kiss on his cheek, he turned his head. Her kiss landed smack-dab on his mouth.

It was with the greatest regret and effort that she quickly withdrew. She arched a brow at him. "You cheat."

"I like to think of it as not wasting a precious moment."

"Uh-huh."

"Anyway, after the papers were signed, they said they had to leave early. There's a snowstorm moving in and they didn't want to get stuck here for the holidays. So you have nothing to worry about. Everything worked out. And I thank you for all of your hard work."

"It's a shame they missed the ball," Alina said. "It really is special." It wasn't the dance she was thinking of as she stared deep into his eyes. This whole evening was like something straight out of a fairytale.

Graham reached out swiping a flyaway strand of hair from her face and tucking it behind her ear. She instinctively leaned into his touch.

He lowered his head, pressing his lips to hers. This time

his kiss was full of raw desire. She met his touch with a roaring need of her own.

She never wanted this night to end, but sadly she only had until midnight. So she best make the most of the time she had left—

Someone cleared their throat. "Excuse me, Mr. Toliver."

Graham pulled back slightly, resting his forehead against hers. "I'm sorry for the interruption. It's my assistant. It'll only take a moment."

"It's okay." Disappointment assailed her. "Do what you need to do."

Graham straightened. He drew in a deep breath and blew it out, as though subduing his irritation at the ill-timed interruption. He moved toward the doorway where a woman was waiting for him. "Yes. What is it?"

"The members of the board have arrived."

Alina watched Graham's facial expression change from one of utter irritation to one of curiosity. She could only surmise the board's appearance was a surprise for him— hopefully a good one.

He turned back to her. Regret was in his eyes. "I'm sorry. This is important. Would you mind if we picked this up later?"

"Not at all. I have some people I need to speak to." She thought of all the Stirling residents that helped make this evening possible.

"Make sure you save me a dance. Make that a few dances."

Heat warmed her cheeks. "You've got it."

He hesitated as though he were thinking of kissing her goodbye, but then he thought better of it. He turned to leave with his assistant. And with him went any answers to her unspoken question about what was happening between them. Because there was something happening, right?

And did that mean he'd changed his mind about tearing down the Stirling? Hope took flight in her heart. Before tonight, she would have said it was too much to hope for. However, this evening had shown her that magic could happen, even in the most dire circumstances.

There had to be a way for Graham to have his impressive tower and her to keep her home and family. She was more certain now than ever before.

The evening was flying by.

And it couldn't have gone any better.

Graham had impressed the board, not only with the new partners that would alleviate some of their financial obligations but also with this party that every board member thought should be an annual event. He fully agreed, which in and of itself was startling. Alina had brought some Christmas joy to his heart.

But his board was continuing to press him about the new tower—the one that he'd said he could start ahead of schedule. And that would mean breaking Alina's heart.

His gaze strayed to where she was speaking with her friend from the Christmas Café. They were smiling and laughing as they held flutes of champagne. He'd never seen her look so happy.

And that's why he refused to say anything about the dismal findings about the Stirling. He didn't want to tell her that the whole building needed to be replaced, whether by his high-rise or by another apartment building. In its current condition, it just wasn't safe.

But for tonight, he would keep that news from her. If she were to find out, her brilliant smile that lit up the entire room would disappear. It would be like the life had been snuffed out of the party.

Who was he kidding? It wasn't the party he was worried about, it was himself. He knew once Alina heard the news—that her home was going to be destroyed—that she would never forgive him. Could he blame her? Not really. He'd probably take the news a lot worse than her if the situation was reversed.

The hour was growing late when Alina's stepmother approached him with questions about the bonus for moving out early. This was not a conversation he wanted to have here in a crowd where anyone could overhear what was being said. And it was not a subject he wanted to get into tonight.

"This is not the place to talk about business," he said.

The woman's gaze narrowed as her shrill voice rose. "If you're trying to worm your way out of this deal, you can forget it. I have my attorney on speed dial—"

"Stop." He tried to rein in his anger. This woman was nothing but rude and mean, especially to her own stepdaughter. The fact she and her daughters were even at the ball was a mistake—a big mistake—but there was nothing he could do about it now.

Anger flared in the woman's eyes. "If Alina convinced you to renege on our agreement, you are mistaken. So what if her dress got ruined. It was an accident. I see that she got another one."

"You ruined her dress?" He was astonished that someone could be so mean and petty.

"What are you getting so high and mighty for? I told you she got another one."

"You need to stay away from her—"

"She's the building manager, even if you're playing the part for now. We both know that isn't going to last. And when you get tired of my whiny stepdaughter, one of my daughters would be a much better match for you."

He swallowed the bile that rose in his throat. The thought

of having anything to do with this woman or her daughters was nauseating. He needed them to go away—far away from Alina, where they could no longer hurt her.

He had an idea. It was an idea he'd toyed with before but always hesitated about acting on. He didn't believe anyone should be rewarded for bad behavior, especially not this woman and her two daughters, who both had their arms crossed as they stood behind their mother wearing the same evil scowls.

But there was another way to look at what he was about to do—a view from Alina's side of things. Getting rid of this woman with her angry tone and nasty comments would make Alina's world so much better. Alina wouldn't ever again have to wonder if she'd have to deal with her stepmother that day or her sniping stepsisters. And for that reason and that reason only, he was willing to make a concession.

"If you're willing to be moved out by the end of the weekend, I'll double your bonus."

Immediately the woman's face lit up but just as quickly her narrowed gaze returned. "What's the trick?"

"There's no trick. I just want you gone."

The woman's dark gaze narrowed. "Are you offering this to everyone?"

"No. This is a one-time offer."

"But the building is still being torn down, right?"

"Yes."

Gasp!

Graham's jaw clenched as he turned, hoping it wasn't Alina standing there. His hopes were dashed. Alina's face was ashen. But instead of the anger he'd expected to see on her face, there was disappointment in her eyes. And he knew that disappointment was directed right at him. He'd let her down.

If only her stepmother hadn't gotten him so angry, he'd have kept his cool. He'd have followed his plan to speak with Alina first about the dire circumstances with the building.

But now, his plan was out the window. He had to think fast. But all he could think about was how devastated Alina looked and it was all his fault. Would she ever forgive him?

CHAPTER EIGHTEEN

THE BUILDING IS being torn down. It's really going to happen.

Alina's heart sank right down to her fancy high heels. Even the thought of the designer shoes couldn't lift her spirits. Everything she thought she'd accomplished by convincing Graham that the building was so much more than a nondescript apartment building had been a lie.

He'd just been putting in his time to fulfill their agreement—an agreement that was at its end. And he didn't even have the decency to tell her the bad news first. What in the world?

She wanted to ask him, really she did. But at that moment, her mind was in complete disconnect with her mouth. She opened her mouth but no words came out. She promptly pressed her lips together.

Sally, her manager from the café, moved to her side. "You said to remind you when it was almost midnight. It's a quarter till."

Alina was still staring at Graham as though in a trance and not the good kind—this was the kind where you are stunned because someone you cared about did something utterly astonishing and oh so hurtful.

"Alina?" Sally asked. "Did you hear me?"

She nodded.

And then with what was left of her pride, Alina straightened her shoulders, turned and headed for the door as fast as her legs could carry her. Tears pricked the backs of her eyes but she blinked them away.

In the background, she heard Graham call out her name. She didn't stop. She couldn't stop. She was a moment away from losing control. And she would not let him see her cry. No way.

As she exited the ballroom, she heard someone call out to Graham. Good. Maybe he would get distracted. Because she had nothing to say to him. The fairytale had come to a disastrous ending.

The elevator ride was slow and agonizing. When at last she made it to the ground floor, she rushed for the exit. She burst through the outer doors and into the night air. She didn't notice the fluttering snowflakes or the plummeting temperature. She started down the first set of steps toward the road, hoping a taxi would come to her aid. But she didn't see any in sight. How could that be? This was Manhattan, after all. There would be one shortly. There had to be.

"Alina, wait!" Graham's voice carried through the evening air.

He hadn't waited to tell her the news about the building first, so she didn't feel any compulsion to wait for him now. Her vision blurred with unshed tears. She kept moving. And then the Rolls-Royce pulled up to the curb. How was this possible? It's as though he'd been waiting for her.

She'd just reached the car when a sudden gust of wind swept over her. It chilled her to the bone and the strong air current swept off her shawl. She turned to see it flutter in the air and float away.

There was no way to catch it while avoiding Graham. She hopped in the car. "Please go."

The car immediately pulled out. She leaned her head back against the leather seat. What had she been thinking all of this time? Like there was something serious going on between her and Graham? For him it was all business. She was the only one letting her heart get in the way.

How had such a perfect night gone so terribly wrong?

The next morning, a vision of Alina at the beginning of the ball filled Graham's mind. It was quickly replaced with the devastated look on her face when she'd heard him say he was tearing down her home. He groaned in frustration.

He hadn't slept all night. After Alina had driven off, he'd caught a taxi and gone immediately to her apartment. When she wasn't there, he figured she'd gone to a friend's place and he'd have to try and speak to her tomorrow instead.

He hadn't wanted to, but he'd gone back to the party to make sure it was shut down properly. He knew it was just an excuse not to go to his apartment alone. Because he knew when he did, he'd never get any sleep.

Graham glanced down at the shimmery wrap that Alina had lost when she'd left the ball. He'd thought for sure the gust of wind would have swept it halfway across the city, but instead the wind stopped when the wrap reached him and, as if planned, it'd landed in his hands.

He wrapped it around his hands and unwrapped it as he tried to decide the best form of damage control. He was good at it when it came to the business, but when it came to his personal life, well, that was another story.

He'd never been successful at personal relationships because he'd never been invested. But things were different with Alina. She was different. And he was different when he was with her—for the better, he liked to think.

He lifted the wrap and inhaled. A jasmine scent clung to the delicate material. He inhaled deeper and smiled. He knew as long as he lived that he'd never smell jasmine again without thinking of her.

But he wasn't a man to give up without a fight. Sure, she'd been shocked last night when she'd heard the news, but after some sleep, maybe she'd see things in a new light.

And so he took a quick shower and dressed. With damp hair, he rushed out the door. He didn't care that it'd snowed overnight and there were a few inches on the ground. Or that below those few inches was ice.

He pulled out from his underground parking spot and set off for Alina's apartment. Not all of the roads were plowed, especially the side roads, so it was slow-going. If he hadn't been in such a rush, he'd have realized that public transportation would have been far faster. But he wasn't exactly thinking clearly.

When he finally made it to the Stirling, he rushed up the stairs to Alina's floor. He hoped she was there. With rapid strides, he approached her door. He knocked. When the door didn't immediately open, he knocked again.

"Alina, please open up. We need to talk."

"Graham, go away. There's nothing to say."

He wasn't a quitter. "Not until you hear me out. I'm going to keep standing here and keep yelling through your door until you give me five minutes." When she still didn't open the door, he said, "And I brought back the wrap you lost last night."

The lock clicked and then the door opened. Alina stood there in her red-and-white flannel pajamas. Her hair was mussed, but it was the shadows beneath her eyes that drew his attention. It appeared she hadn't slept any better than him.

"May I come in?" he asked.

She opened the door fully and stepped to the side. He moved past her and into the living room. He noticed that for the first time since they'd decorated the tree that it was darkened. And that was his fault.

Alina took a seat on the couch, crossed her legs and threw a throw blanket over her legs. "Say what you have to say and then go."

Her tone was flat, which was the exact opposite of what he'd been expecting. It wasn't a good sign. If she was angry and yelling at him, he could have defended himself and hopefully gotten through to her. But it was like all of the fight that she'd had in her the whole time he'd known her had gone out of her.

He took a seat in the armchair opposite the couch. He held out the wrap. "Before I forget, here you go." When she didn't make any effort to reach for it, he placed it on the coffee table. "I'm sorry about last night."

Her gaze met his, but it was like a wall had gone up between them because he was no longer able to read her thoughts. "What are you sorry about? That I overheard part of your conversation? Or sorry that I found out you'd already made up your mind to tear down the building?"

His eyes pleaded with her. "I'm sorry about all of it. But you know that our agreement lasts until Christmas Eve, right?"

She shook her head. "It ended last night. I'm not going to let you make a fool of me, especially not with her."

"If you mean your stepmother, I…I was just trying to get her to move right away—to make things easier for you."

Alina's bloodshot gaze met his. "Nothing can make this easy."

"Listen, if you'd hear me out, you'd understand that the building is beyond saving. It failed too many inspections and needs too many repairs."

"What I hear is you making excuses to push through your plan to build your tower here." Alina got to her feet.

"I don't think we have anything else to discuss. You need to go. I have your things packed. They're downstairs."

He got to his feet, too. "Alina, don't do this to us."

"Why?"

His mouth opened but wordlessly it closed again. Silence filled the air as his eyes begged her to forgive him. "Is this really what you want?"

She nodded. "I can't be with someone that isn't honest with me."

"But I didn't lie to you."

"It feels that way. You said you'd wait until Christmas Eve and yet it's days before it. And then to overhear you tell my stepmother, of all people, that your mind is made up about my home, about the home of people that considered you their friend, people that went out of their way to make sure you had the best Christmas party." Her voice cracked with emotion. "Go."

Her words were like rocks being thrown at his heart. He hadn't stopped in that moment with her stepmother to realize the mistake he was making. He'd merely acted rashly to solve a problem—the way he did things in the office— figure out a solution and then act accordingly. Only this wasn't exactly an office problem, it was something much more important.

"I'll make it up to you," he said, "if you'll let me."

"Does that mean I get to keep my home—the homes of my friends?"

He couldn't make that promise because he was already obligated to his board and so many other people. And he had a feeling even if he said she could have the building that things wouldn't go back to the way they used to be between them.

"I'm sorry," he said. He'd never been sorrier in his life. He moved out the door with a heavy heart. All the while, he felt as though there were still things left unsaid. But when he paused and turned back, the door swung shut with a resounding thud. She obviously didn't feel the same way.

On the elevator ride downstairs, he told himself it was all for the best. He knew that marriage and business didn't mix. He'd witnessed enough arguments between his parents.

They might have remained married but he wasn't sure it was for the best. Neither of them seemed happy. And he didn't want to make Alina as miserable as his mother had been. Alina would be better off without him.

CHAPTER NINETEEN

IT WAS OVER.

It was all over.

And Alina had never been more miserable in her life. She was about to lose her home and she had no idea where to move. And with this being Christmas week, there were no real estate agents to help her.

Graham said his company had already contacted some people and would be forwarding information about available units by the new year. But she didn't want to wait that long. If she had to move, she just wanted to get it over with—the sooner, the better.

She was never one to just sit around and wait for things to happen, she liked to take the lead, but for the moment, she had to work. Even though some people were able to take off for the holiday, she was previously scheduled to work up to and including Christmas Eve.

It was the day before Christmas Eve that Alina stopped by Merryweather's apartment. She'd realized that she'd forgotten to give him the shawl that went with the beautiful gown she'd worn to the Snow Ball.

"I'm really sorry for not returning this sooner," she said as she handed it over. "I...I don't have a good excuse. I forgot." The truth was she'd been so upset with Graham and the fact she'd let herself fall for him that she hadn't thought of much else.

"It's all right, my dear." Merryweather studied her. "You haven't been sleeping well, have you?"

Was it that obvious? She'd have to start using more makeup to hide the shadows beneath her eyes. She didn't want anyone else questioning the reason behind her restless nights.

"I'm okay." *Liar. Liar.*

"I've noticed that Graham hasn't been around since the party."

She swallowed hard. This was why she'd been avoiding people, but she'd have to explain to them sooner or later. "Our arrangement is over." The breath hitched in her throat as she prepared to tell her friend the worst of it. "And… and Graham has decided to go ahead with the demolition of this building."

For a moment Merryweather didn't say a word. His face didn't give away his thoughts, but she knew he had to be as devastated as she felt. After all, this was his home, too. She wasn't quite sure how long he'd lived here, but he'd been here her entire life and then some.

"I'm sorry." She felt like she'd let down everyone in the building—the people she cared about, the people she thought of as family.

"Are you sure about this? He seemed like he really liked it around here."

"I'm sure. I overheard him talking to my stepmother at the ball."

Merryweather's bushy white brows rose. "I'm surprised he'd bother with her."

"I am, too."

"And that's when you heard he was going ahead with his plans to put the new tower here?" Merryweather didn't seem to want to believe what she was telling him and she couldn't blame him. It was a lot to take in.

"Yes." Her gaze lowered to her laced fingers. "I just thought…" She shook her head. "Never mind."

"You thought what? That he'd changed his mind? You thought you'd opened his eyes to just how special this place was with such friendly and caring people?"

She lifted her gaze to meet his. "That's it exactly. And then to find out that he confided his plans to my stepmother, of all people."

"You thought he should have talked to you first?"

She nodded. "Don't you think so? I mean, we did have an agreement."

"But did he promise you that he would speak to you first?"

"No. I just assumed that since it was our deal, I'd be the first to know."

"And did he say why he told her first? Was it possible he'd uttered the words in the heat of the moment?"

She thought back over the tumultuous confrontation at her apartment. She'd been so hurt—so devastated—that she hadn't given him much time to explain himself.

Her stepmother knew exactly how to press people's buttons. Was that the reason Graham had said something to her? Had he found out that her stepmother and stepsisters connived to make her miss the ball? Would he have cared enough to come to her defense?

The possibilities raced through her mind. Had she not given Graham enough credit? Had she just jumped to the conclusion that he would let her down like the other people in her life had done? Had she judged Graham too quickly?

She gave herself a mental shake, trying to clear her head. "I don't know what to think."

"You won't know until you ask. But I did happen by Dorian's place this morning on my way to Joe's apartment to drop off a book he'd asked to read and imagine my surprise when I saw her door open and the apartment empty of furniture. No nothing."

"They've moved out already? Even with the bonus for an early move out, we don't have to be out of here until after the beginning of the year."

"I don't know but something sure got them moving fast." There was a twinkle in his eyes as though he knew something he just wasn't saying. "You might want to give Graham another chance. There might be more going on here than either of us knows." His gaze moved to the plate of sugar cookies she'd placed on the end table. "Would those happen to be for me?"

She glanced over at the plate. She'd totally forgotten that she'd brought them for him. "Yes, they are. But they won't be as good as the ones Graham brought you."

"Don't be so sure. Things baked with love always taste the best."

Tears stung her eyes. She blinked repeatedly. "You always know just what to say."

"Now stop wasting time here. Go find Graham and this time listen with your heart."

She pondered his words as she walked to the door. She honestly didn't know what she was going to do where Graham was concerned. She hesitated to go see him, as much as her heart urged her to do so. She still didn't know if she could love a man who destroyed her home and took away her family.

She hadn't said anything to Merryweather because she hadn't wanted to upset him, but she was convinced that this would be their last Christmas together.

Nothing had gone according to plan.

Not one single thing. And Graham had no one to blame but himself.

Before Alina had entered his life, he was driven by one thing—success. He'd told himself the most important thing was proving himself to the board, but deep inside he knew he had to prove to himself that he was capable of stepping into his father's shoes.

He'd been in awe of the man growing up. After all, his father was regularly in the paper for making one successful deal after the next. And he'd been named Man of the Year by one of the most renowned financial publications. His father was certainly well-recognized and well-respected in the business world. To live up to his memory was a daunting task.

And then to learn that his father's successful career was in part a charade. In later years, the company had been in trouble, had been playing a shell game, trying to hide its deficiencies.

There was nothing harder than stepping into a new job and finding nothing was as it seemed. And just when he'd been about to turn it all around, Alina stepped into his life. She was all spunk and determination. And she was the roadblock to his success. But at the time, he hadn't realized she was exactly what he needed to open his eyes to the fact that there was more to life than business and success. A happy life isn't about the big things that happen now and again, but rather it's about the little things you do on a daily basis that bring a smile to someone's face.

She'd also showed him how much family meant. Alina clung to her apartment because it was the last tangible link she had to her parents. And she was willing to do whatever it took to hang on to it.

And yet here he was standing on his pride, unwilling to admit that his mother might have made some good points about making room in his life for both business and family. She'd been so sure he'd end up like his father and he'd gone right ahead and proved her right.

But it wasn't too late to change. If he wanted to be the man Alina deserved, he needed to do more than talk the talk, he needed to walk the walk.

He grabbed his phone. Before he could talk himself out of it, he dialed an old but familiar number.

The phone rang once. Twice.

"Graham, is that you?"

"Yes, Mom. It's me."

It wasn't until then that he realized how much he missed hearing his mother voice. And he was surprised to find that she didn't sound mad at him. She didn't bring up their last argument or throw his words back in his face. She was just genuinely happy to speak to him.

He couldn't believe he'd put this conversation off for so long. "Mom, I'm sorry it's been so long since we talked."

"I'm sorry, too. I should have tried harder to understand how important the business is to you."

"Are you saying that you now understand?"

There was a pause. "I didn't want to, not at first. Your father always told me when he retired he'd make more time for us—that we'd travel the world. And then we lost him—and his promises died with him. I was so angry that I blamed the business. And because I loved you, I didn't want to lose you to the business, either. But I pushed so hard that it's exactly what I did."

"I should have been more understanding. I'm sorry. I was so caught up in proving to myself that I was good enough to fill Dad's shoes that I didn't realize what you were going through."

"And now?"

"Now, I have the biggest dilemma of my life."

And so he told her about Toliver Tower—tying the past

to the future. It was meant to be Graham's mark upon the company, pulling him out from behind his father's shadow. And then he mentioned how it was destroying his relationship with the woman he loved.

Yes, he loved Alina. The problem was he'd figured that important bit out a little too late.

"If you love this woman as much as you say you do, you'll find a way to work things out," his mother said.

It wasn't the solution he'd been hoping for. In fact, it wasn't a solution at all. It left him in the same position he'd been in at the start of this conversation.

"I've been trying to find a compromise to make everyone happy, but I don't think there is one." He'd barely slept for days, trying to find a way to fix things with Alina. "No matter what I decide, people are going to be disappointed and angry."

"Then it sounds to me like you might as well follow your heart."

Or follow Alina's heart. If she were to know all of the details of the Stirling's physical condition and the projected plans for the new building, would she make the same decision?

He wasn't sure, but a plan was starting to form. "Thank you, Mother. You've been a huge help."

"Can we get together over the holidays?" she asked with a hopeful tone in her voice.

"I'd like that." He thought of Alina and hoped she'd be a part of it, too.

"Graham?"

"Yes."

"Thank you for calling. It means the world."

"I'm just sorry it took this long."

And he meant it. He'd let his pride get in the way of their relationship. It wouldn't happen again.

Now, he had a very serious decision to make. Because through it all, he'd learned that he was a better man with Alina in his life. She made him see the bright side of life even on the darkest day and she made him laugh, even at himself. He needed her. He just hoped she needed him, too.

So his big decision really wasn't such a big decision, after all. It didn't matter how many times he considered the proposal, he'd choose Alina every time.

And it wasn't just Alina that he'd grown fond of. It was also the people of the Stirling—well, most of them. Thankfully he'd given Alina's stepmother and stepsisters a strong enough incentive to move out. Hopefully they'd moved far away.

So how did he make Alina and the Stirling residents happy? By keeping their building standing. But even if he wanted to do that, there were problems. The whole building needed to be replumbed, rewired, new windows...the list went on. It would cost more to fix than to rebuild.

But the more he thought about it, the more he felt certain his plan would work. He rushed to grab his coat on his way to the door. He didn't care how late it was. He started dialing his employees. He had a plan and he needed their help. This couldn't wait.

CHAPTER TWENTY

SHE'D MISSED HIM.

Alina didn't know that it was possible to miss someone so much, but she felt the loss from her life clear down to the depths of her bones.

Amid her misery, Christmas Eve arrived in a flurry of activity. Everyone was making plans to move out. Moving boxes had been piled in the hallways, waiting to be filled so that Graham's people could move them to either storage or their new apartment.

Alina hadn't packed one solitary item. Just the thought of it turned her stomach. Instead she'd taken every single shift available at the café. She'd had to stay busy. It'd been the only way to get through the pain of losing Graham. And that was why she'd agreed to take over someone else's shift on Christmas Eve.

The café was about to close early when the front door opened. Alina turned to tell whoever it was that they were closed, and her gaze met Graham's. Her words hovered at the back of her mouth and then dissipated. What was he doing here?

Alina stared deeply into Graham's eyes, drinking in his very essence. But was it possible to move past everything that had happened? Could she truly love a man who took away her home—the place where her most precious memories lived?

Her heart pounded out its hope. It wanted Graham back

at all costs. But her mind said to move cautiously because he'd hurt her once and she didn't know how she'd live through another heartbreak.

She continued to stare at him as he approached her. She dug deep and found her courage. She swallowed hard. She hoped when she spoke that her voice didn't give away her nervousness.

"Why are you here?" she asked as they stood in the middle of the Christmas Café. She hadn't seen him since he'd returned her shawl.

"I had to come. There's something important you need to see."

Her eyes widened. "Has something happened? Is it the building?"

"Calm down, Alina." Graham went to reach out to her—to comfort her—but then he hesitated and lowered his arm back to his side. "It's nothing like that."

Relief rushed through her body. "Then whatever it is, you don't need me." She just wanted him to go away. Seeing him—being so close to him and yet they'd never been so far apart—was killing her on the inside.

"But you don't understand, you're the key to everything. Please come with me."

"I...I can't." She glanced around to find her coworkers staring at them. "I have to close up."

Sally stepped forward. "It's okay. We can manage. Why don't you go find out what he wants?"

Alina turned to her friend and glared. She was supposed to be helping Alina out of this extremely awkward position with her ex—wait, was Graham her ex? They'd never really talked through the specifics of their relationship.

"Please, Alina. I think you're going to like this." Graham's eyes pleaded with her.

"I don't know."

Just then her coworkers started with a low chant of "Go. Go. Go." It grew in volume. Alina's mouth gaped. These people were pushing her to do something her mind said was a mistake even as her heart longed to find out what he wanted. What was so urgent?

Sally handed over her coat and purse. Alina's mouth opened to protest but Sally gave her a gentle push toward the door.

"Have fun," Sally said. "And merry Christmas."

Alina begrudgingly walked to the door. When she paused and glanced back, everyone was still staring at them. The chanting had stopped and instead they all wore pleased grins. They were traitors. Each and every one of them.

She shrugged on her coat and then walked through the door Graham held open for her. Once they were on the sidewalk, she noticed a black sedan with the driver opening the door for them.

"Where…" Her voice wavered. She swallowed hard, willing her nerves to calm. "Where are we going?"

"Back to the past."

"The past?" She was confused. He was talking in riddles.

"And the future."

He was absolutely no help. What was he trying to tell her? And why was he being so cryptic about it all?

"Please, Alina. I promise it'll be worth it."

She got in the car. They slowly made their way through the congested streets. She felt as though she should make conversation to break the awkward silence. But then, just as quickly, she realized that none of this was her idea. If he didn't like the quiet he could do something about it. But for the moment, he seemed inclined to ride along in silence.

Frustrated, she turned away from him to stare out the

window. With each passing block, the scenery became more familiar. If they made a right up here, she was certain where they were going.

And then they turned right. They were headed home—back to the Stirling. Did this mean he'd changed his mind about tearing it down? As excitement lifted her heart, reality brought her back down to earth. If he'd changed his mind, he would have told her by now.

So if this meeting wasn't about the apartment building, was it about them getting back together? The thought tempted and teased her.

But to give in to her desires—to even consider getting back together—she needed more than he'd been willing to give her before. She needed a commitment that she—that their relationship—would come before business. She had to know he loved her. Anything less wasn't enough. Anything less wouldn't be fair to either of them.

And Graham had already told her he couldn't make the commitment a marriage needed to survive. So this was all just a painful waste of time.

She turned to Graham. "I don't think this is a good idea."

He stared deep into her eyes. "Do you trust me?"

This was such an important question. Without trust they didn't have any chance of a future. She didn't have to debate the answer to this question because it was something she knew instinctively.

She nodded.

He smiled and reached out to take her hand in his. And that's how they were sitting when the car pulled to a stop in front of the Stirling.

"Come on." Graham opened the door before the driver could do it. He stepped out and then turned back to offer her his hand.

She stepped outside the car as a light snow started to fall.

"Graham, I don't understand. What can you say to me here that you couldn't say back at the restaurant?"

"It's not what I can say, it's what I can show you." His eyes pleaded with her not to fight him. "Just give me five minutes. If you don't like what you see, I'll go away and you'll never have to see me again."

Five minutes. In some instances, that was no time at all. But with her heart hanging on his every word, it was agonizingly long. And yet, she was dying to know what had him going out of his way. After all, if this was about the sale, he had everything he wanted. Every resident had agreed to move early.

"Okay." Her heart raced. She didn't know what he had planned but she hoped it was something good.

CHAPTER TWENTY-ONE

WHAT WAS HE up to?

As they quietly made their way to her apartment, Alina's stomach shivered with nerves. Graham was acting so strange and she had no idea what to make of it.

Once she stepped inside, she was surprised to find the Christmas tree lit up. Prince was stretched out beneath the tree, quietly observing them. Alina knew she hadn't turned the lights on. The tree had been dark since the night of the ball. She stepped toward the tree to turn them off and saw two large Christmas presents sitting on the coffee table with a smaller package sitting in the middle.

She turned to Graham. "Did you do this?"

He nodded. His serious expression didn't give anything away. It wasn't like they'd parted friends, so why would he buy her Christmas presents?

Once their coats were off and they were seated in the living room, she turned to him. "You shouldn't be buying me gifts."

He stared at her with regret in his eyes. "I'm sorry it took me so long to figure things out."

What was he saying? Was he saying he wanted them to get back together? She tried to subdue her excitement when she reminded herself that it was going to take more than a present to fix things. Still, she wondered what he'd picked out for her.

He handed her the smallest of the packages. She stared

down at the red-foil-wrapped box with a satin bow. It was very light, as though there was nothing in it. What was it?

The paper was so pretty that she wanted to unwrap it carefully to save it but her fingers were clumsy with nerves and her need to see what was inside had her ripping it off to find a plain white rectangular box. Her questioning gaze lifted to meet Graham's.

"Go ahead. I promise it won't bite."

It was all the encouragement she needed. She lifted the lid and then pulled back the red tissue paper, finding a large gold key ornament. She lifted it by its thin red satin ribbon.

She held it in front of her. It was pretty enough. She turned her attention back to Graham. "I don't understand."

"You will."

He moved to the other side of the coffee table. He knelt down. "That key goes with one of these." He reached out to the first package and lifted the box.

What was beneath the fancy wrapping was a model of a building. She could only surmise that it was a replica of Toliver Tower. She wanted to hate it, she really did. But it was a pretty building. It had modern lines but historical characteristics. It wasn't the cold, nondescript building that she'd imagined. Someone had taken their time in designing it.

Then without a word, Graham lifted the lid on the other package to reveal a model of the Stirling—the place she'd called home all of her life. She marveled at the exactness of the miniature, right down to the bushes next to the front door.

Her gaze lifted. "They are amazing."

He nodded and then came to sit beside her. "The man who makes them is a real artist. But I didn't bring them here for you to merely admire. Back when you made me that deal, I was so sure I knew what I wanted in life. I knew I didn't want to repeat my parents' mistakes. And truth be told, I didn't repeat theirs. I made all of my own mistakes. I thought for so long that I could have only one thing or the other, but I never thought I could have both."

Her heart started to beat faster. She told herself not to get too excited because she didn't want to get her heart broken. But she knew it was too late for that. She was totally invested in this—in them. But she needed him to spell it out to her in detail.

"Graham, I don't know what you're trying to tell me. Have both what?"

"The business, it's all I've thought of since I was a kid. I needed to prove myself to my father, but most of all, I needed to prove to myself that I was good enough to be CEO. And I did, but I found out that being a success in the business world wasn't as fulfilling as I'd thought it would be. I need someone to share it with."

"But you did it. You pushed through the sale of the Stirling in record time, and your building—" she glanced at the coffee table where the replicas sat "—will be completed ahead of schedule. It's everything you wanted. Your name will be on the building and your board has to be duly impressed."

"But they aren't who I want to impress. That's what I'm trying to tell you in my fumbled way. It means nothing without you. I love you, Alina."

Had she really heard him correctly? "You...you do?"

He nodded. "I fell for you that first day in the café."

"You did?"

He smiled at her as he took her hand in his, his thumb gently stroking her skin. "Why else would I take you up on that arrangement to take over the handyman duties when I didn't have a clue what I was doing?"

"You didn't seem terribly lost."

"That's because I had YouTube videos to guide me and real handymen on speed dial when I got myself in a jam."

"But you never complained."

"And take a chance of you firing me? No way. I was having too much fun getting to know you. The better I got to know you and the residents of the Stirling, the more everything started to change."

"You mean you finally figured out what's so special about this place?"

He nodded. "I did. Now I have a question for you. In which of these two—" he gestured to the buildings "—would you like to spend your future?"

She looked at him. Then she turned to the building models. And then she gazed back to him. "I thought you'd already made up your mind. The Stirling needs too many repairs."

"And if you want to remain here, I'll see that the repairs are done. It may not be pretty for a while and I can assure you it will be noisy, but I will make it happen."

Her gaze searched his. She had to be imagining all of this. He couldn't be serious. "But all of your plans…"

"Plans are made to be changed."

With each word he spoke, she was falling further in love with him. "But this is your chance to make your mark on the company."

"And you've taught me there's more to life than business. Something my mother tried to tell me years ago, but I was too stubborn to hear."

Hope bloomed in her chest. "Does this mean you spoke to your mother?"

"I did. We had a long conversation and we're getting together for the holidays. She's eager to meet you."

"I'm so happy for both of you."

He stood and then held out his hand to help her to her

feet. When they were both standing close, he stared into her eyes. "Alina, you've shown me what's important in life. And it's not business or making a name for myself, it's so much more than all of that. It's having people in your life that want to spend time with you—people that are there for you through the good and bad. And most of all, it's people like you that give me time to figure out that I'm wrong."

"What were you wrong about?"

"Love. I thought that having a successful career meant having to choose it over love. But you showed me that it's not an either/or proposition."

She smiled. "I did all of that?"

"You did. I love you, Alina. And I can't imagine my life without you in it."

"I love you, too."

He pulled her close and claimed her lips with his own. Her heart soared. This was the best Christmas ever. Her feet felt as though they were floating.

He pulled back, ending the kiss much too soon. "I have one more present for you."

He moved to his jacket and withdrew a wrapped box from the pocket. The breath caught in Alina's lungs. Could it be?

She told herself that she was getting too carried away. But she couldn't stop herself from hoping they would be together forever. Even then, it wouldn't be long enough.

He turned back to her and held out the gift with the tiniest gold bow. "This is for you."

It wasn't until she accepted the box that she noticed the tremor in her hands. Her mind raced for all of the things that could fit in the little box. Each time she thought of a diamond ring, she pushed aside the thought. It had to be something else. Maybe a bracelet to match her snowball necklace.

With her hands not quite cooperating, she obliterated the wrapping paper. Inside she found a little aqua box. As she read the name of the famous jeweler printed on the lid, she gasped.

She lifted the lid and found yet another box. But this box was made of black velvet. Tears of joy rushed to her eyes. She blinked them away. For a moment, she just stood there staring at the little box that fit in her palm.

Graham reached for the box. "Perhaps I should take it."

Her gaze met his. She had so many questions but her mouth totally refused to work. Of all the times for her to be speechless.

Graham opened the box. The overhead light caught the brilliant diamond and made it sparkle. Her heart was beating like crazy. Was this really happening?

And just to prove it, Graham got down on one knee. "Alina, I didn't know it for so long but you are what I've been searching for. You are the morning sunshine that lights my days. You are the comfort I seek after a long day. And you are the best friend that I've ever had. I love you with all of my heart. Will you marry me?"

Tears of joy splashed onto her cheeks as she nodded her head because she was afraid her voice would fail her once more, but she tried to speak, anyway. "Yes. Yes, I will."

He drew her back into his arms and this time when he kissed her, it was so full of love. She'd never been happier in her life.

And she knew that no matter where she went in the world that her home would always be with Graham. It wasn't a building. It was the memories. And they would make plenty. And it wasn't the hallways or the rooms. It was the love in her heart that had room enough for everyone she cared about...most especially her real-life Prince Charming.

EPILOGUE

Two years later... Toliver Tower

HOME AT LAST.

Alina Toliver placed the last table setting on the long row of tables that stretched from her living room into the dining room. Graham had had his people deliver the tables and chairs from his office the day before and now it was all set for this evening's Christmas Eve dinner.

Prince took a bit to adjust to his new surroundings, but now he thought he was in charge. He rubbed over Alina's ankles as she straightened each place setting. She smiled at how everything was at last falling into place. She hoped everything would go perfectly this evening. After all, this was their first Christmas in their new home.

In the past couple of years, the Stirling residents had been split apart as there was no one place available in the city to accommodate so many dislocated residents. She had dearly missed her friends, but Graham had kept her distracted planning their wedding. She glanced down at her sparkling diamond engagement ring. One month ago to the day, she'd received the matching diamond wedding band. It wasn't the ring's beauty that meant so much to her, it was the promise it carried—Graham would love her forever. And she him.

"Still admiring them, I see." Graham's voice interrupted her thoughts.

She lowered her hand to her side. "I was just thinking that today's our one-month anniversary."

"That long already?" He stepped up close to her, placing his hands on her waist. "It's only the first of many anniversaries."

"Do you know how nice that sounds?"

He leaned down, placing his lips on hers. She immediately leaned into his embrace. It didn't matter how many times he kissed her, it still felt like the first. Her heart pitter-pattered as desire pumped through her veins.

"Hey, you two newlyweds, aren't we supposed to be getting ready for a party?"

Alina immediately jumped but Graham refused to let her go. He wrapped his arm around her waist, pulling her to his side. Prince scampered over to hide behind them.

"Hello, Mother," Graham said. "We didn't hear you arrive."

"Obviously." His mother smiled. "You two look good together. Any news about grandchildren?"

"Mother." Graham frowned at her. "Stop pushing."

"Who's pushing? With the way you two look at each other, it's a safe bet."

Alina smiled. She enjoyed seeing Graham reconnecting with his mother. It was long overdue. She moved out of her husband's hold and went to greet her mother-in-law. Sharon Toliver was tall and slender, her dark hair the same shade as her son's. When Sharon smiled, it lit up her brown eyes. Alina realized that Graham may have inherited his father's business acumen but he'd also inherited his mother's warmth.

Alina reached out and hugged Sharon. "Welcome."

As Alina took Sharon's coat, his mother looked around. "This place is beautiful. Not like that stone-and-granite mausoleum that Graham stayed in at the office building.

This place has warmth. It looks like a home, not a show-piece. Alina, you have done a marvelous job."

"Thank you. But we—" she motioned to Graham, who was now standing beside her "—did it together."

"You are good for my son."

"And he's good for me," Alina quickly added, meaning it wholeheartedly.

Sharon's gaze moved to the collection of tables. "My, you're expecting a lot of guests. People from the office?"

"Just family," Alina said.

Ding-dong.

Prince dashed back to the bedroom. Alina smiled and shook her head. He might be bossy with her and Graham, but when it came to strangers, he made like a ghost and disappeared.

"And there are our guests now." Alina moved to the door, anxious to see her family all together again.

And this would be just the first of many such occasions because Graham had invited all willing Stirling residents to move into the top two floors of the newly finished Toliver Tower. They were a family once more.

Alina swung the double doors wide open and there stood her family in their Christmas sweaters, Santa hats and smiles. In the front stood Merryweather, carrying a bottle of wine with a red bow on it as he held the leash to his sweet rescue dog, Bentley. Her heart swelled with love for both of them.

"You all came," she said.

"Of course we did," Merryweather said. "Where else would we be on Christmas Eve but with family?"

Alina turned back to her mother-in-law. "Sharon, do you remember my family from the wedding?"

"Yes, I do." Sharon smiled as she moved to Alina's side to greet everyone.

After everyone arrived, Alina stepped back, taking in the happy scene. For a moment, she watched as the people interacted. It was then she admitted that she'd been wrong. Having a new building hadn't changed anything. They were still the people she loved. And she was blessed enough to be loved back.

Just then Graham moved up beside her and slipped his arm around her waist. "Something on your mind?"

"How did I get to be so lucky? Our family isn't bound by bloodlines. It's made up of the people of our hearts."

He turned to her. He pointed up. She lifted her head, finding that they were standing under the mistletoe. A smile pulled at her lips. She lifted up on her tiptoes. "I love you."

"I love you, too."

And then she leaned into his arms and they kissed. It didn't last long but it was filled with love and a promise of more to come. But first they had a potluck dinner to enjoy followed by their Secret Santa gift exchange. Everything was as it should be that Christmas. Everyone was home.

* * * * *

FOR THIS CHRISTMAS ONLY

CARO CARSON

This book about perfect strangers is dedicated to all the people who did their best during the pandemic to protect their families, their friends, their neighbours and, perhaps most generously of all, perfect strangers. Thank you.

Chapter One

*Never meet your heroes. Wait until they are
your equals.*

—How to Taylor Your Business Plan
by E.L. Taylor

It was her twenty-ninth birthday, and she was sinking in quicksand.

Literally.

Mallory Ames flailed about, trying to keep her balance as wet sand sucked her into its depths. Had this been a movie, a handsome and heroic Harrison Ford might have come out of the darkness and tossed her one end of his bullwhip to pull her to safety. But no—this was Mallory's real life, which meant she was flailing about like an idiot in a town park while a children's choir chirped Christmas carols and a massive Yule log burned brightly in the black night. At least she was flailing on the fringe of the crowd and not detracting from the little choir's moment of glory.

Because this was not a movie, she stopped sinking. After one more wild windmill of her arms, she stood upright, breathing heavily from the sudden exertion. She tried to lift her right foot free of the wet sand. Her rain boot didn't budge.

"Damn it, damn it, damn it," she hissed under her breath as she kicked her right foot back and forth, back and forth, a quarter inch in each direction, trying to get loose. She couldn't vent her frustration any louder than that, not with all the tiny tots running around the park with their eyes all aglow.

It was a big family night here in Masterson, Texas, home of the Masterson University Musketeers. The Yule log was always lit by the mayor on the first Saturday of December. This park had a huge, square sandpit. For most of the year, it was used for volleyball courts, but in the cool December weather, the nets were taken down so a massive tree trunk could be laid across the sand. A bonfire was built under one end for the celebration. Each night, the bonfire would be lit again, a couple of feet farther down the log, until the last of it was burned on January sixth, the traditional date of Twelfth Night and Epiphany. The university's spring semester would begin, and the regular rhythm of life in a college town would resume.

For safety, the fire department had soaked the sand with a gazillion gallons of water for tonight's kickoff.

With great, purposeful strides, Mallory had walked right into the deep, wet sand on the dark side of the pit. She was stuck now in mid-stride, each of her boots mired in the muck.

Back and forth, back and forth, she kicked. Her foot slid around inside her rubber rain boot, but the boot itself was still firmly stuck, shin deep. "Damn— *darn* it. Darn it, darn it, darn it."

"Hey, beautiful. Got a problem?"

Because this was not a movie, the person who stopped on the edge of the sandpit was not a sexy, rugged man. He was an overgrown boy, undoubtedly one of the university students, because he wore an athletic team's burgundy hoodie with the crossed sabers of the Masterson Musketeers printed in white on the sleeve.

He threw his arms open wide as if he were revealing an S on his chest, but it was only the university's initials, MU. "I'm your solution, baby."

He was the problem. She'd been hoping to lose him and his two buddies when she'd started walking with such confidence toward the Yule log and the temporary stage.

She'd come to the park for the anonymity offered by the night. On one side of the Yule log, Christmas lights sparkled, the temporary stage glowed, and rows of booths sold holiday crafts and treats. But on this side of the Yule log, there was no artificial lighting and people were sparse. Mallory wanted peace and privacy to watch the yellow flames while she thought through her plans for the new year ahead of her—only ahead of her. She wouldn't look back.

These blockheads had spotted her as she'd leaned against a pecan tree, alone, and they'd started with the "hey, beautiful" type of catcalls. Nothing to do but ignore them, she'd thought at first.

When their comments had gotten more persistent and they'd begun to zero in on her, she'd decided the best course of action would be to lose them by blending into the light and action on the far side of the Yule log for a little while. But, as she'd started skirting the wet volleyball sandpit, she'd taken her eyes off her goal to look back over her shoulder.

Never look back. Whatever you left behind is of no benefit to you now.

It was one of her favorite maxims from her favorite book by her favorite hero, the multi-millionaire entrepreneur E.L. Taylor. Two Decembers ago, she'd received *How to Taylor Your Business Plan* as a birthday gift from her godparents. Her godmother had looked at Mallory's online wish list and gotten her something she genuinely wanted.

Her brother had given her a gift more typical of the rest of her family, a pillbox with Bluetooth technology that reminded one, through cell phones and smart watches, to take their medicines. Mallory didn't need any medications; her brother had explained that it was a gift for her, because it would make her role as their grandfather's live-in caregiver so much easier.

Their grandfather. *Her* role.

Pill dispensing wasn't her passion. Business was.

Profit and loss statements, fixed and variable assets, supply chain operations—all of it fascinated her. She had finished her junior year at Masterson University's College of Business when her father had been seriously injured, his leg crushed in an accident. She'd been asked to take the next semester off to go back to Ohio to live with him, to dress his wounds, to cook his meals, to clean his clothes and his house, since he'd lived alone after her mother had moved out.

He'd been expected to recover within six months. That December, Mallory had spent her twenty-first birthday driving through an early Ohio snowstorm, chauffeuring her father to the clinic, counting the days until the spring semester began in January and she could go back to Masterson University and the mild Central Texas winter. The doctor, however, had crushed those plans. He'd confirmed what she'd suspected, what she'd been hoping wasn't true: her father's leg hadn't healed enough yet for him to regain his mobility—and for her to return to college.

After his appointment, her father had directed her to drive his car through Sonic for milkshakes to celebrate her birthday. He might have thought she'd wolfed down that milkshake in happiness, but she'd been binge eating ice cream for her heartbreak.

Six months had turned into two years. Her father had regained his health just as her great-aunt had fallen ill and required in-home care. Mallory's entire family had looked to her. Her final year of college, her dream to climb a corporate ladder to a position of respect and financial security—all of that could wait, her family reasoned. She was still so young, and Aunt Effie had *cancer*. What were a few college classes in the face of her battle?

By the time Aunt Effie had gone from surviving back to living, another relative had needed care. Mallory had become the *de facto* choice at that point. After all, as it was pointed out to her, she wasn't doing anything else, and she had so much experience now...

She'd received her crisp, new hardcover copy of *How to Taylor Your Business Plan* two years ago on her twenty-seventh birthday. Once she'd started reading it, she couldn't stop until she'd finished the whole book in the middle of the night. When she'd turned out the bedside lamp, she'd lain in yet another spare bedroom in yet another relative's home, and she'd admitted the truth to herself: she was an unpaid laborer assigned to ill or aging relatives, not their cherished daughter or niece or cousin. Somehow, one delayed semester at a time, one relative in dire straits after another, six months had turned into six and a half years.

When despair had threatened, she'd turned the light back on and picked up her book. The chapter that began with *Never look back* had saved her sanity. E.L. Taylor had been so confident that she, his reader, would succeed in the business world if she followed his advice, regardless of her past. In firmly worded prose, he told her to keep looking forward to her goals, so Mallory had created a plan, mapping out the steps she needed to get where she wanted to go. This September, she'd finally returned to Masterson to finish her bachelor's degree.

This was, finally, December of her senior year. She should have been turning twenty-one. Her family obligations had stopped her life in its tracks as surely as this quicksand had stopped her boots, so instead, she was turning twenty-nine and spending her birthday kicking her way out of a mess of her own making.

Never look back.

Yeah, well, she'd looked back tonight, physically taking her eyes off her goal. That hadn't been what E.L. Taylor meant, but it applied: she'd caved when she'd been faced with a tiny moment of insecurity, and she'd blundered right into this sucking-sand situation. Served her right. She should know by now not to ignore any *Taylor-made* advice.

"I'll be your knight in shining armor." The ringleader of the trio struck a pose, punching one fist in the air. It was Superman's pose, nothing like a knight's, and only when Superman was about to fly away. If this guy wanted to fly away from the scene, that was fine with her.

The other two told him to stop being such a dick.

Charming heroes, all three of you.

"There are children everywhere," Mallory said in her most motherly tone. She was dressed like a student—bright blue ski cap pulled over long hair, jeans tucked into colorful rain boots—but she felt old enough to be their parent.

The second boy, surly in corduroy, sneered at her parental tone. "Like I give a flying f—"

"*Dick* isn't a bad word," said the third. "Relax. You're a pretty girl. Smile."

She kicked her boot a little faster, back and forth, back and forth, *darn, darn, darn.*

The one who'd posed with his fist in the air still fancied himself a hero. He stood on the grassy edge of the sandpit and reached for her. "Give me your hand. We'll get you loose and go party."

"No, thanks. I'm almost loose. Go enjoy your party. Don't worry about me."

He grabbed the sleeve of her pink peacoat and started hauling. She clutched at his forearm as he pulled her off balance.

"Stop! Stop. I was almost—" Her right boot chose that moment to finally pop free from the sand.

Did the hero catch her?

Of course not. Real life was never like the movies. He kept pulling, so onto her butt Mallory fell. Her rear end landed on the cold, grassy edge of the sand court, but her left foot was still stuck in the quicksand, so her left ankle was stretched to its absolute, painful limit.

"Damn it!"

"Watch your language," the corduroy-wearing dude sneered. "There are children everywhere."

"Let go of my arm."

The ringleader finally realized that he'd done more harm than good. "Oh. Sorry. Yeah. Here."

He let go of her, then reached over the wet sand and snagged the top of her left boot. He pulled it free. Since Mallory had been pulling hard herself, the sudden release sent her own knee banging into her chin.

Her teeth clacked together and she fell back, but she didn't curse this time.

"Sorry," the ringleader said again.

Mallory lay on her back in the grass while three dudes who didn't know their own strength leaned over her, looking almost comically confused at how she'd gotten there. The one who'd told her to smile now offered his hand. When he pulled her to her feet, he pulled her knitted mitten all the way off her hand.

"Whoops," he said, laughing.

When she grabbed for her mitten, he held it over his head. "I'll give it to you when you agree to come party with us. It's for your own good. You need to have some fun."

"I'll buy you a drink," the ringleader said.

Mallory held her hand out, palm up, for her mitten. "You can't. You're not even twenty-one."

They all seemed faintly surprised at her statement. Offended, too. "We've got plenty of booze at our house."

The ringleader narrowed his eyes and studied her face a little more closely in the faint light from the too-distant bonfire. "How old are you?"

"Old enough to buy my own drinks." Or she could, if she had the spending cash. She made another quick grab for her mitten, but she wasn't fast enough. *Damn, damn, damn.* The mitten was a blue cable-knit, like her hat. She wanted it back, but she wasn't going to beg while they watched her jump for her own mitten.

"Come with us. We'll show you a good time."

The stage, the crowd—light and anonymity—were at her back. So was the ringleader. The other two were in front of her, nothing but darkness beyond them. It galled Mallory to have to be polite to them, but she fell back on one of the little white lies women used in these situations. "No, thanks. I'm meeting my boyfriend here."

All three scoffed at that. Apparently, they knew the game better than she'd thought.

She pulled her ski cap down firmly over her ears. "Really, he'll be here any moment."

"Bring him, then. Where is he?"

The ringleader walked around her to join Corduroy Boy and Mitten Stealer, so the three stood shoulder to shoulder with their MU letters on their puffed-up chests. They'd called her bluff, and they knew it. However, with the three of them in front of her, she could now back up freely. She glanced back over her shoulder.

Never look back.

Yeah, well, she was playing a role here. She pretended to spot her boyfriend in the crowd behind her. "I think I see him. Gotta go."

"Aw, don't be that way."

She turned her back on them and walked fast, heading toward the light and the crowd. One guy called out, "Your mitten will be at the Kappa Lambda house. Come and get it, beautiful."

She didn't look back until she'd skirted the sand courts and reached the stage. The children were filing off. The university's string quartet members were climbing up, cellos and violins in hand. She'd lost the trio of athletes, but now she was surrounded by other people's families, other people's holiday happiness, so much noise and chaos when she'd craved some time alone.

A line had formed in front of the Yule log. People stopped at a card table, scribbled their hopes for the coming year on little pieces of paper, then waited for their turn to throw the paper on the burning log. Their wishes for the new year were carried by the smoke up to the stars.

The fire department had erected a waist-high fence to keep anyone from getting too close. Little pieces of evergreen were tied to the paper notes, so the paper could be tossed more easily into fire. Some people were throwing hard, trying to hit the actual Yule log, but most of the papers were falling short, landing in the bonfire.

A little boy threw his note, but it barely cleared the fence. One of the firemen quickly used a fire iron as a golf club to chip-shot the little folded paper into the bonfire. "Close enough for a Christmas wish," the fireman assured the little boy.

Mallory would aim for the Yule log, just to be certain.

A donation jar sat on the table amid the clutter of paper slips and stunted golf course pencils. Its handwritten sign indicated which charity the money would go toward. *Donations requested but not required.* Not required meant free.

Free was right in Mallory's price range—temporarily. She made a mental note of the charity. She would donate to them when she started making money. She merely had to stick with her plan. *Never look back*, never this, never that. There were a lot of *never*s in a Taylor-style business plan, but if she could just follow them all, financial security would be hers.

It was working. She was here; that was proof. Her very first step had been to reconnect with the Masterson University admissions office by signing up for their email newsletter. Because of that step, she'd seen an announcement that their esteemed alumnus, entrepreneur E.L. Taylor, was going to be the Executive-in-Residence the next academic year. He would spend the spring semester as a guest professor for the university's College of Business. *Her* college.

That had seemed like fate. It had ignited a fire under her, at any rate. She'd accelerated her timeline to free herself from the endless family obligations and win readmission to MU. Parts of that had been painful, but she'd started her senior year this September. She had just one more semester to go. When it began in January, E.L. Taylor himself was going to arrive on campus, and she was going to be here to meet him. Before her graduation in May, she would take the next-to-last step: she was going to ask him to look at her Taylor-inspired business plan.

And then, Mallory Ames was going to execute her final step. She was going to ask E.L. Taylor to invest in her first business venture.

He would, because he'd be impressed with her business plan. He just had to be, for she'd followed his book precisely. She would present it with the confidence he'd assured her she deserved…unless her nerves killed her first.

Not nerves. *Anticipation.* The anticipation was killing her. What if he said no? What if he laughed at her plan?

What if her hero didn't even like her?

Mallory picked up a pencil stub and a blank slip of paper, one with a tiny pine cone attached by a ribbon. She refused to blush as the woman to her left and the man to her right each dropped dollar bills into the jar and gave her pointed looks for not doing the same.

Mallory knew her coat made her look more affluent than she was. She'd found it in her grandmother's closet. Peacoats never went out of style, and although the color was a Paris Hilton pink from a previous decade, the hand-me-down was high quality. Let the locals judge her for being cheap tonight. Someday, her donation to that charity would dwarf theirs.

She'd barely finished scribbling a single sentence when she heard Corduroy Boy's unwelcome voice.

"Well, well. Look who's here."

She stuffed the paper and its mini pine cone into her pocket. She wasn't going to wait in line, getting harassed the entire time by three meatheads who didn't know the difference between flirting and pursuing someone relentlessly. She headed toward the opposite side of the park, where hundreds of square hay bales were stacked three high, far enough away from the Christmas festival that no spark from the Yule log would be carried on the wind to ignite them.

As the crowds came nightly to enjoy the Christmas lights, the hay would be spread to keep the field from turning to mud. During Mallory's first three years as a Masterson Musketeer, she'd watched the stacks of bales get shorter and shorter as the holiday break had gotten closer and closer. She'd associated the smell of fresh hay with Christmas and college, anticipation and excitement, every year that she'd been away.

What would she answer if Mr. Taylor asked her about that huge time gap between her junior and senior years? *I never look back*, she'd say with confidence, and then she'd move on to her business plan. It would be the right answer. It was the only possible answer she could give him.

E.L. Taylor would never invest in Mallory's ideas if he knew the truth. She was practically thirty and definitely broke. What kind of person let herself be told what to do, where to live, with whom to live for so many years? A weak person. So weak that three young men had instinctively singled her out as their easy target tonight.

They'd stolen her mitten, and her hand was cold— and all of a sudden, she was fighting back tears. She shouldn't feel like crying over something as trivial as a stolen mitten, but it was the only pair she owned.

Since those guys could afford luxury extras like fraternity fees, they probably had parents supporting them. They were athletes, so they probably had sports scholarships covering the cost of their dormitory and dining hall. But Mallory? Familial caregiving paid nothing. She was poor enough to qualify for a work-study job that helped pay her tuition and gave her a dorm room at a reduced rate, but it hadn't covered her textbooks or the mandatory meal plan for those who lived in dorms. This one year of room and board had eaten up her meager savings—her *minimal assets*, in business lingo—and her hand-me-down car as well. Those rich boys couldn't imagine how valuable that mitten was to her.

Did life have to always be so unfair?

Never expect life to be fair. You must continue to play when the game isn't fair, or you'll never win.

E.L. Taylor was right, but Mallory was losing the game tonight, sinking into despair as surely as she'd sunk into the quicksand—and all over a mitten.

With her cold hand, she wiped hot tears from the corner of her eye before they had a chance to fall. In the future, when she wore a sharp suit and high heels and sat behind an executive desk that would be polished to a shine, that mitten would be insignificant. Therefore, it was insignificant now.

Dry-eyed, she left the crowd behind her, determined to find a quiet spot to watch the Yule log's flames in peace. That had been her plan, and she was sticking to it. *Never abandon a solid plan.*

She squinted at the hay bales. There was someone out there. A man? He was standing so still, she wasn't certain she was really seeing a person in the shadows.

She didn't take her eyes off him as she got close enough to see that he was real—and definitely a man, arms crossed over his chest, shoulders filling out his leather jacket. Alone in the night, he made a compelling figure. Had this been a movie, she would've assumed he was the brooding hero, reluctant to get involved but capable of saving the day if he must, Bruce Wayne on a dark sidewalk, a soldier off duty in a civilian dive bar.

The golden light of the Yule log's flames touched his profile. His features were strong, his expression fierce. He hadn't shaved for a day or two. His hair was thick and a little too long, only a shade less dark than the night. He might make a better villain than a hero, a young Rickman in a bank vault, Tommy Lee Jones on a battleship, the kind of anti-heroes that had made her father's favorite action movies pleasurable to watch with him.

But this wasn't the movies. This was real life, so Mallory didn't know if this man was a good guy or bad guy. Only one thing was certain: this was no college boy.

From behind her, three specific college boys sounded too close. "Don't be like that. Wait up."

Leave me alone.

The angry man ahead of her looked like he felt the same way toward the whole world. He glared at the fire, looking a little feral. Unapproachable.

The trio behind her started to sound more irritated than amused. "We know you can hear us."

Never look back. Everything that mattered was ahead of her.

"What's the problem? Boyfriend didn't show up, huh?"

"Boyfriend," the mitten-stealer said in a voice

meant to carry. "As if someone would want a bitch like her."

So much for *Smile, beautiful.*

Mallory kept pretending she didn't hear them, but her bare hand was clenched into a fist of frustration. It was always the same, wasn't it? If a woman didn't act flattered by a random man's attention, then he assumed she had a problem, not him. Mallory had turned twenty-nine today, twenty-*frigging*-nine. Was there an age where she wouldn't have to deal with this kind of crap? She lengthened her strides as best she could in loose rain boots on poorly lit, uneven ground.

Behind her, they laughed. "Is she trying to run away? From what? A party?"

Mallory kept her eyes on the man ahead of her. There was arrogance in his stance. If Mallory's anger made her look as forbidding as he looked, no college boy would mess with her.

They wouldn't mess with him, that was for certain, which would make him an excellent pretend boyfriend for the next ten minutes or so. She just had to stand next to him and make a little small talk, get him to smile politely in response.

Actually, he didn't look like he knew how to smile. A nod, then. A few polite words from her, a nod from him—that would be enough to convince those three jerks she wasn't alone. They'd turn away, she'd tell the angry man to have a good night, and that would be that. She could return to the pecan tree and ruminate on her future in peace. It was an excellent plan.

Her future boyfriend was winning his staring contest with the Yule log. Mallory wasn't even two steps away from him now, so close she could see the flames dancing in his eyes, so close she could see—

Her boots dragged to a stop as if she'd stepped into quicksand again. The fine lines in his face, the grim set of his mouth, those eyes—

Nothing anyone said or did would faze this man. He wasn't arrogant. He was...hardened.

She chickened out.

But as she took her first step past him, the book's maxim roared inside her head: *Never abandon a solid plan.*

She spun to face the flames, standing shoulder to shoulder with the man she'd chosen.

Chapter Two

Never show your doubts to the world.
—How to Taylor Your Business Plan
by E.L. Taylor

The man was so damned intimidating, this close.

That was precisely why Mallory had walked up to him, though. She took a few silent, calming breaths through her nose, the way every free online yoga class had taught her to do.

He didn't acknowledge her existence.

After a few seconds, once Mallory was certain that she wouldn't sound even the tiniest bit alarmed, she made a polite observation. "The Yule log is a real giant this year. That must have been some tree. I heard it was uprooted by a tornado this summer."

He didn't respond with so much as a flicker of an eyelash.

She leaned forward just far enough to peek past him. The three guys were still making their way toward her, hollering and fake-punching each other, practically buzzing with all the heady power of being young, financially secure, and free to raise hell on a Saturday night.

Mallory tried a little harder, smiling her friendliest smile at the man—or rather, at his profile. "Chilly tonight, isn't it?"

The man might as well have been a statue.

She was left smiling in his direction like an idiot, feeling as stupid as if she'd stuck her hand out to shake and he'd just left her hanging.

She leaned back this time, just enough to look past his shoulders toward the frat boys. They'd slowed down, but now the ringleader was ducking and weaving around his friends, imitating the way Mallory was peeking around someone to see them.

Mallory wasn't playing peek-a-boo, damn it. She put her bare hand on the stranger's sleeve, her cold palm on colder leather that had nothing but hardness underneath. Of course, a statue's arm would be hard. "I've got sand in my boot. Can I just use you for balance for a second?"

Without waiting for a reply that wouldn't come, she stood on one foot, clinging to his sleeve as she started to push one boot off. Then she thought better of it. She'd keep her boots on in case she needed to take off again. Instead, she brushed the sand off the outside of her boot, an operation that got sand stuck in the knitted wool of her remaining mitten, but at this point, it hardly mattered since—

"Who are we trying to make jealous?"

She hopped in surprise. *The statue speaks!*

"Is he sufficiently jealous yet?"

She quit slapping her boot and stood on two feet once more. "Who?"

"The man you're looking for while you force yourself to talk to me."

How he'd seen her look anywhere was anybody's guess, since he still hadn't taken his eyes off the fire. The corner of his mouth had twisted into a sort of mocking smile to match the disdain in his voice, but Mallory didn't let go of his arm. Not yet—not while she could see Corduroy Boy out of the corner of her eye, smacking her mitten against his palm, making her feel like she was twenty, not twenty-nine.

Never expect life to be fair.

"I'm not trying to make anyone jealous," she said.

He scoffed at that, a shocking amount of derision packed into a short snort. He thought this was a joke, just like the boys who were currently treating her mitten as their toy.

They would treat her like a toy, she was sure, if she were stupid enough to go to their party to get her mitten back. They were the kind of young men who'd be utterly, genuinely surprised when a girl yelled no and pushed them away. They wouldn't have had any idea she hadn't been willing to accept the attention of popular athletes—why would a girl object to that?—and they'd act shocked that she hadn't appreciated being pushed off the dance floor into a corner, so the one she'd been dancing with could grind his hips against hers, just a little fully dressed public foreplay, so his bros would know he was a stud who'd be getting laid later that night. In the movies, every girl understood Sandy pushing away Danny at the drive-in.

But real life wasn't the movies. When her no made him look bad, they'd all get mean. They'd call her a tease as she walked out of their keg party. They'd make fun of her every time they saw her on campus for the rest of the semester.

Mallory had been through it all. She'd been labeled a bitch at a party on her twentieth birthday, then jeered at on Tuesdays and Thursdays the next semester, when she had to cross paths with one of the guys in her microeconomics class. She'd gone to the student services center to see if there was some school equivalent of a restraining order, but the boys hadn't been violent at the party. They hadn't tried to stop her from leaving when she'd so boldly said no and walked off the dance floor, and they weren't making threats when they saw her in class. They were just loud and rude.

It hadn't mattered in the end. Her father had fallen off a ladder and shattered his leg and pelvis, and Mallory had needed to leave campus, anyway.

She'd let her hands freeze solid rather than put herself in that kind of situation again. She was worth more than a million mittens. She'd known it then, and she knew it now.

She let go of the leather jacket. Her uncooperative fake boyfriend uncrossed his arms and straightened his sleeve with a tug on his cuff, as if she could wrinkle a bomber jacket made with leather so high quality, James Bond could have worn it. The man might have been like her grandparents, investing in one quality piece of clothing every decade or so, but his hands were leather-clad, too, in driving gloves that looked painted on. His dark jeans fit exactly right over boots that looked as perfectly made as his jacket. Even his hair was stylish despite being shaggy, evidence that it had been cut very, very well in the past, and no doubt would be again.

Money.

This wasn't a movie, but in real life, there were people made of money. He was one of them.

Mallory stuffed her hand into her coat pocket, wrinkling her paper wish, and wriggled out of the sandy mitten. It was better to look like she hadn't bothered with gloves at all tonight than to look like a beggar who had only one.

She wasn't a beggar. She was this rich man's equal. She just hadn't built her own company yet. Every trait she needed to do so was already within her, as her book had so wisely pointed out. When Mallory Ames was the CEO of her own company, she'd be the same person she was right this minute.

So, she returned the intimidating man's scoff with one of her own. "That's an incredibly high opinion you have of yourself. You're certain that being seen just standing next to you is enough for a woman to make any man jealous."

Finished with his cuff, he crossed his arms over his chest once more.

Mallory crossed her arms over her chest, too, but not to imitate him. She just wanted to tuck her hands under her arms for warmth. "It's more likely a man would feel sorry for the woman standing next to you, with the way you're giving her the silent treatment."

"I'm not giving you anything."

"I noticed."

"You walked up to me for a reason," he said, still watching the fire. He had yet to spare a glance for the peon beside him. "It wasn't because you had a sudden desire to talk about the weather. Then you leaned on me instead of a hay bale to get the sand out of your boots, yet you didn't take them off. You barely bothered to brush off one. It's obvious that you wanted someone to see you touching me. Once he did, you stopped. We're done. Take your sandy boots elsewhere."

Her mouth fell open at his rudeness.

After a moment of silence, he spoke again, sounding weary. "Did you think you were the first woman to try this with me?"

Beyond him, the ringleader broke away from the other two and started walking toward her, shaking his head at her like she was a disobedient puppy. Her ruse hadn't worked. The stranger beside her was too obviously not interested in her as a human being.

Damn it, damn it, damn it. It looked like she was

going to spend her twenty-ninth birthday just like she'd spent her twentieth, yelling no and pushing away a college boy who'd then go tell his entire team what a bitch she was.

She didn't bother trying to hide her frustration. "I'm trying to fend someone off. Fend them off, not toy with them. Not make them jealous."

Out of the corner of her eye, she saw the ringleader hesitate. Arguing made her look like she knew this stranger well, didn't it?

The irony wasn't lost on her, but it only fed her irritation. She shouldn't have to play these games. "You know, if I could help out another woman just by letting her stand next to me for a few minutes, I would. I *have*, more times than most men seem to believe is possible. All you had to do was say, 'Nice weather. Not too chilly.' That was all that was being asked of you." She raked her gaze over his oh-so-casual, oh-so-expensive clothing, from his shoulders to his boots. "Would it have hurt you to spare so little?"

At last, a reaction: he clenched his jaw. "You want someone to think you have a male protector?"

She blinked. "That's kind of a medieval way to put it, but yes."

He finally looked down at her. His eyes were silver, startling—a mirror that reflected the flames. In one smooth motion, he uncrossed his arms, placed his hands on her waist and picked her up high enough that her head and shoulders were above his. She squeaked in surprise and grabbed his shoulders for stability, but he dropped her onto the stack of hay bales, leaving her sitting five feet off the ground with hay poking her rear right through her jeans.

Oh, she didn't have to fake an argument now. "What are you *doing*?"

"You wanted safety. Done." His gaze dropped to her feet as they dangled above the ground like a child's. "And your boots won't get any sandier."

"You idiot. Now I'm sitting up here where anyone I'm trying to avoid can see me."

"He'd already seen you, had he not?"

She threw her hands up. "What now? I'm supposed to wait here until he comes to pull me down? You've made me more helpless. All you had to do was act like I'm your girlfriend, not a bale of hay. Really, was that so difficult for you? *Really?*"

The fire framed him from behind. It gave him a dark-angel kind of appeal, a sinfully handsome Lucifer with striking eyes. She glanced toward the last spot she'd seen the trio—they'd stopped and were huddled over one glowing cell phone screen—and back at him.

He turned around. She thought he was going to walk away, but instead, he leaned back against the hay bales. *Her* stack of hay bales—so she wriggled back and pulled her right knee out of his way. He rested against the hay bale, its edge just below his shoulder blades, which meant she now was sitting with a man's shoulders between her knees.

Mallory gaped at the back of his head.

"But—" she started.

She stopped. But what, really? With his shoulders

between her knees, it certainly looked as if they knew each other well.

Fine, then. She rested her forearms on top of his head, like he was that executive desk she'd have someday.

"What," her desk asked, sounding furious, "are you doing?"

"I'm acting like you're my boyfriend."

"You've never had a boyfriend, have you?"

She stuck out her tongue at the top of his head. "You've never been one, have you? You seem to think sticking me on a pile of hay bales and turning your back on me is a normal thing to do on a date, but let me tell you, it's not."

He spoke through gritted teeth. "There wasn't time to buy you flowers."

She snorted, unwillingly amused, even as she kept an eye on the trio. They were all looking at her once more, clearly shocked that she hadn't lied, although she had. They turned to go, but first, the ringleader hit his hero pose, holding her mitten up high in one fist, then flipping her the bird with his other hand.

She stayed cool, even blasé, as she lazily raised one hand and flipped him the bird right back.

She was hoping he'd be so incensed, he'd throw her mitten down. *Step on it, leave it the dirt, I don't care. I can wash it. Please, leave my mitten behind. Please, please, please...*

They left with her mitten. She'd lost the game. It was utterly unfair.

*You must continue to play when the game isn't fair,
or you'll never win.*

She had to come up with a plan for replacing that
mitten.

From across the sandy courts and the open field,
she heard the string quartet playing "Good King
Wenceslas." Mallory knew the lyrics by heart, of
course. *When a poor man came in sight, gathering
winter fuel.* She knew how the poor man felt, hoping
he could find what he needed for free. If she could
find a pair of mittens on the ground...

That was it. Tomorrow, she'd check the lost-and-
found box in her dorm building. A set of gloves or
mittens could have been there long enough that they
were now free for the taking. If not, she'd check the
lost-and-found box in the College of Business's main
building, where she worked. If not there, then she'd
check every building on campus until she found an
abandoned pair. The stolen one had matched her ski
hat, but she'd have to take what she could get now.
Beggars couldn't be choosers.

A beggar.

Her plan was to beg for mittens. The truth of it
weighed her down. She'd never impress E.L. Taylor
or any other investor. She was worse than a beggar;
she was weak. She'd spent the better part of her birthday evening letting three guys dictate where she'd
go. Make that four guys—she hadn't decided to sit
on these hay bales.

The violin notes carried on the night air. One tear

broke free from Mallory's lower lashes, making a warm run down her chilled cheek.

That fourth man grumbled up at her. "How much longer is this date going to last? It's like having a damned bird nesting on my head."

She chuckled despite herself, but the sound hiccupped and ended with something like a sob.

"Are you—are you *crying* on me?"

She shook her head no, which made a few more tears roll down her cheeks, but he couldn't see that. He could only hear her voice, and since her voice would give her away, she stayed silent.

Never look back. She'd pushed so hard to be here. She'd suffered through lectures from her brother and his wife. Gotten guilt trips from every other relative. Driven from Ohio to Texas in a hand-me-down car, then sold it to buy the annual meal plan at the college dining facility.

She'd burned all her bridges.

And for what? The coming Executive-in-Residence had sent his preferred schedule to the business college this week. The only courses Mr. Taylor would be teaching were exclusively for MBA students, not for those finishing their bachelor's degrees. Not for her, the woman who'd hugged his book to her chest in the middle of the night and vowed that she would be a success someday.

Her plan hadn't accounted for the possibility that she'd be denied access to Mr. Taylor as a professor. But her plan hadn't totally failed her, either. She'd seen Mr. Taylor's schedule because she worked in the administrative offices of the College of Business. She had that job because she *hadn't* been weak.

The financial aid she was receiving required her to work on campus. She'd been assigned a job bussing tables in the student dining facility. Collecting dirty dishes didn't fit any of her plans, so she'd gone over her financial aid contract with a businesswoman's sharp eye. The work-study program was ostensibly designed to give students experience related to their field of study, and she'd found a single sentence in the document that stated students could suggest their own jobs. So, dressed like the young and successful CEO she would be someday, Mallory had walked into the College of Business's administrative offices to ask where she could best help them.

They'd created a position for her, an assistant to the administrative assistants. A secretary for the secretaries, essentially. She wanted to believe they'd hired her because she exuded that Taylor-coached confidence, but she suspected the permanent admins had merely been happy to get a student as old as she was. Maturity had, for once, been an advantage.

Maturity and confidence were getting harder and harder to hold on to. A minute ago, she'd just flipped off the mitten-stealing trio.

Because I had a plan. I wanted them to be so angry, they'd throw my mitten down.

So many plans. So much stress. But if she hadn't had a plan, then she wouldn't have pushed herself to scramble for her office job. If she hadn't done that, she'd have zero opportunity to speak with E.L. Taylor this coming semester. She couldn't take his class, but she could leverage her job to gain access to Mr. Taylor. She'd look for opportunities to deliver his messages or print out his lesson plans. She'd stay alert, she'd hustle, and she'd *make* those opportunities happen.

Just thinking about it made her feel exhausted.

Two years of hoping and planning had really been two years of running into obstacle after obstacle. The cost of the textbooks and the dining plan, for example, had been a staggering five thousand dollars. Since practically everything in the town of Masterson was within walking distance from the campus, selling her old car had been the right solution. Now, she never had to fear where her next meal would come from, three meals a day, seven days a week, not until after she received her diploma. She hadn't run into that obstacle. She'd *surmounted* it. That was what E.L. Taylor would want her to tell herself.

But…

But, just for tonight, as she stared at the flames of a Yule log, she wanted to stop trying so hard. She wanted to stop pretending she was unfazed by every obstacle. She had doubts. Doubts about her plan. Doubts about her future. Doubts about herself.

The man she was resting on looked like he'd weathered so much, nothing could faze him. Were all these disappointments and worries, her self-doubts and stolen mittens, weathering her, too? Making her hard? Did she want to become that tough?

The alternative was to let her life be steered this

way and that at the whim of others. That hadn't been a happy life, either, and she'd chosen to leave it.

Never look back.

The stranger didn't ask her anything else. He just stood there like a rock, so she kept leaning on him, not like a child sitting on her father's shoulders, not like she was getting a piggyback ride, just…leaning on him as she sniffed back her tears and did her calm yoga breathing.

He took off his gloves and held them up. "Here."

Surprised, she took them, wiped her cheeks, and gave them back, dangling them in front of his face.

"Put them *on*." He sounded like he couldn't believe he had to spell it out. "Your hands are freezing."

She sat up straight, embarrassed that her freezing fingertips had been brushing his forehead. The gloves were like a second skin on him, so they weren't too terribly loose on her. Her fingers slid into the luxurious warmth gladly.

Now that her arms were off his head, he ran his hand through his hair, as if that would restore order to the untamed layers. He turned just enough to look at her out of the corner of his eye. "How much longer are we going to be here?"

She rubbed her gloved hands together. "You should have asked me that a minute earlier. I'm not really incentivized to send you and your warm gloves away now." She leaned to the side a bit, so he could see her expression and know that she was only teasing.

He remained serious. She felt a moment of concern for him. Poor man, so grim. Hardened.

Relax. Smile. You need to have some fun.

On the other hand, maybe he was content just as he was. If he didn't want to smile, he didn't have to smile.

She sighed as she sat up straight again. "I'm just kidding. You were a very effective imaginary boyfriend. They've gone."

He faced forward once more.

She frowned at the back of his head. Maybe he thought she needed more time to compose herself. It was embarrassing to realize she probably hadn't fooled him about the crying any more than she'd fooled him about getting sand out of her boots. Only a few tears had actually fallen silently, rather attractively, like an actress's single tear in a black-and-white movie. At least Mallory hoped so. At any rate, she'd sniffed most of her tears back, not sobbed them all out. If he assumed she needed more time to pull herself together, he assumed wrong.

"They actually left a little while ago." She didn't want to admit that being tossed onto a haystack had done the trick. "I didn't mean to keep you this long."

"I know."

She waited, but that was all he had to say.

She rolled her eyes behind his back. "So…should I leapfrog over your head now, or would you care to move aside, so I can jump down? Take your time deciding. My fingers aren't warmed up yet."

He stepped to the side, but before she could wriggle to the edge of the stack to drop to the ground, he kicked the heel of his boot back into the hay to make a step and hoisted himself onto the stack next to hers, a six-foot-something man landing right beside her. Had this been a movie, she would have been Debbie Reynolds, aghast that Gene Kelly had just dropped out of nowhere into her convertible.

This man had such a physical presence. He was big, and he was *built*. He had a body that vaulted to the top of a tall stack effortlessly, a body that had picked her up like she weighed no more than a bag of sugar. A muscled, masculine body.

Bodies. It had been so long since she'd thought about bodies as anything but frail. Injury, cancer, extreme old age—she'd worried about those bodies for so long. It had been the career she'd fallen into, easing their aches and pains, finding ways to get them to eat when they weren't hungry and drink when they didn't thirst, to walk when walking hurt.

At the university, she was surrounded by bodies that were so jarringly at the other end of the scale. Barely out of adolescence, they filled college classrooms with more energy than they could contain, boisterous bodies that could withstand the abuse of all-night study sessions and day-long keg parties.

The man beside her was neither of those extremes. He had strength and control, a man who had a body that he could rely on to perform. Need to lift a woman over his head? Done, without thinking twice about it. His demeanor wasn't arrogance, perhaps, but confidence that he could handle whatever physical task he needed to.

She let her eyes roam over his shoulders, his

thighs, his hands. The confidence that made him look untouchable to men would make women wish he wanted, *needed*, to touch them. Mallory had no doubt he knew how to handle that kind of physicality, too. Some people just had sex appeal, and they never really lost it, Paul Newman with silver hair and laugh lines.

Her fake boyfriend had it in spades, but no silver hair, not yet. Not for a while. He looked to be in his early thirties, a body near the same age as her own. He was just right for her.

For me?

What could she possibly do with a man whose body was...oh.

He turned to her, and it was a fresh little shock to look him full in the face. His days-old beard looked rough and dark, his hair fell forward after he'd pushed it back, but he was undeniably handsome. Had this been a movie—

He smiled at her, a polite, practiced, obligatory stretching of the lips, and she felt a little déjà vu.

Strange. If she'd seen him before, she wouldn't have forgotten him. No woman would. Yet there was something vaguely familiar about his stiff smile, except nothing about this man fit the word *vague*.

"You must want to get back to the festival," he said, a surprisingly courteous hint for her to be gone. "Your family or friends must wonder where you've gone. Your real boyfriend, perhaps."

Now he wanted to make polite small talk? She was used to him being all broody and curt. Her sudden sexual awareness of him—of her own body—made her broody and curt, too. "If I had a real boyfriend here, I wouldn't have needed to borrow you, would I?"

His smile became just a tiny bit more real at her comeback.

She looked away, hoping this flushed feeling inside wasn't a visible blush on her face. She was a grown woman sitting next to a grown man, not a flustered teenager who didn't know how to respond to a cute boy in class.

"I came by myself tonight," she said, determined to sound her age. "There's nothing at the fair for me."

It all costs money.

She'd planned for that. This evening, she'd been one of the very few students in the cavernous dining hall for dinner on a Saturday night, as usual on the weekends. She'd celebrated the start of the holiday season with one of those foil packets of instant cocoa, reconstituted with the hot water from an institutional coffee brewing machine.

She hadn't come to the park for food or cocoa, because she could get those on campus. She'd come for the rest. The Yule log was free. The music was free. Reflecting on one's future under a pecan tree was free. Maybe the powdered instant hot cocoa wasn't as tasty as the hot chocolate she remembered buying here years ago, but it had been prepaid. Beggars couldn't be choosers.

She squinted at the distant booths as if she wanted to read their colorful signs much more than she wanted to look at an appealingly rugged man. "There was some amazing hot chocolate over there, if memory serves. I don't see it from here."

"You come every year?"

"No, it's been a while. I went to college here." She left it at that. It was embarrassing to have gone to college but have no degree. Even worse to be living in a dorm on her twenty-ninth birthday. "How about you? Do you come here every year?"

"No."

If she rolled her eyes at yet another curt answer, he'd see her do it, this time. She rolled them, anyway. "So, what brings you here this year? Did you go to college here?"

"Of course."

That could be the reason behind that déjà vu. They might have had a class together—or she could have just admired him from afar. He must have been eye-catching at nineteen, too.

"When did you graduate?" she asked. "Maybe we were here at the same time."

"Don't you think you would have remembered me?"

Her mouth fell open again. Hot body or not, the man had an ego the size of Texas. "Do you think you're so amazing that I would remember if our paths had crossed between classes?"

He scowled at her.

She held up her hands and laughed a little. "I'm sorry, but you really do have an astonishingly high opinion of yourself."

It could have been a trick of the flickering fire-light, but he looked almost confused.

"It's okay," she said. "I envy you, actually. It's better than being full of self-doubts. Trust me."

"I find it hard to believe you harbor a single self-doubt," he said, with a very clear, very arrogant scoff.

She'd imagined that look. He'd probably never been confused about anything in his life.

He elaborated. "You say anything you want to say, fearlessly. You're confident that you have the right to tell me what's wrong with my own opinion of myself. Don't pretend now that you've been quaking with fright in your sandy boots for even a minute."

This time, her laugh was directed at herself. "Wow. I must be doing a good job of behaving the way I wish I already was, all fearless and what-not." She clapped her boots together to send some dried sand showering down, but it was a halfhearted effort, and she gave it up after a few tries. "Honestly, I'm second-guessing myself all the time. If I fooled you, I must have that whole 'fake it 'til you make it' thing down pat. That's something, I suppose. Some kind of achievement."

Sitting side by side, they fell into silence as they stared at the bonfire. From the stage beyond it, the string quartet began "O Come, O Come, Emmanuel." It was a slow and haunting carol, a song of yearning for someone to come and change a hard, unhappy world. Such longing for things to get better, someday...

Someday.

Never show your doubts to the world. If you must indulge your doubts, do so alone. You will be con-

*fident when your plan succeeds. Eliminate the pos-
sibility of having witnesses to any earlier version of
yourself.*

"Fake it 'til you make it," she repeated quietly.
"What happens if you never make it? You'll have
spent your life being a fake. Maybe being the real
you, flaws and all, would have been better than pretending to be something you never became. You'll
have missed the chance to find out."

Every inch of the body beside her went still.

"Sorry," she said. "I don't expect you to stay and
talk philosophy with me. I just came to see the Yule
log and debate my future with myself. I didn't expect
to have a human to talk to."

Not that the human was talking back much, but
still…

*Eliminate the possibility of having witnesses to
any earlier version of yourself.*

She shouldn't have admitted her doubts out loud.
But did a stranger she'd never see again count as a
witness to her weak moments?

Her book would say he counted. E.L. Taylor hadn't
even made exceptions for family members. When
Mallory's brother had snooped out her plans, she'd
needed to pretend she was confident that she'd be re-
admitted to MU—and that she'd win the financial aid
her brother informed her he would not be providing,
although she hadn't asked. If she'd admitted she was
worried, her brother would have been even harder to
deal with. As usual, her book had been right. *Never
show weakness.*

Mallory sighed. "The real me isn't usually so maudlin. It *is* my birthday, though."

"That makes you sad?"

"My twenty-ninth birthday."

"Ancient."

"You sound like every smug, grouchy octogenarian in my family. 'You're young. You have plenty of time.' Easy for them to say. Every single one of them, from my great-aunt to my brother, was married with a job and a house at my age."

Her fake boyfriend lapsed back into silence. It irked her after his sarcastic *Ancient*.

"You must think you have plenty of time, too," she said. "You don't look very domesticated yet. No offense."

"I have the house."

Mallory shrugged. Of course, he did. *Money* meant ownership of real estate, almost always. When she had money someday, she'd invest in property, too—a house, a townhome, a condo. Anything. She couldn't wait.

"And the job?" she asked.

"If you want to call it that."

Don't ask, Mallory, don't ask, don't ask…

"And the marriage?"

He slid her a very knowing look.

Okay, maybe she had been fishing for information. "Since I'm wearing your gloves, I see you have no wedding band."

He didn't bother to confirm the obvious. Mallory was happy she hadn't imposed on someone else's husband to stand in as her fake boyfriend; that was the reason she felt a little relieved that he was a bachelor. Not that she would ever begrudge another woman the space to stand next to her own husband someday, if that woman needed shelter. In fact, her future husband would have to be the kind of guy who'd help out any person who needed help.

Not that she was looking for a husband. First things first. She didn't have her bachelor's degree yet…at almost thirty.

Never look back.

It was hard not to on her birthday. The mournful Christmas carol was killing her. She'd lost so much time, waiting for her degree, waiting for her real career to happen, waiting to have her own home and—well, if not her own husband, at least a madly passionate relationship. Waiting, for years, for everything, while she'd traveled down the caregiver detour that she'd never seen coming.

She fell back to lie on the hay bale and stare up at the night sky. The smoke from the Yule log made a little plume of gray in the distance, but the stars above were bright in the clear night, white sparks of infinity that obeyed the laws of physics, not wishes.

She didn't need a Christmas wish. There was no mystery to the way her life was unfolding. Her path was the result of her own decisions. Why wasn't she where she'd expected to be at twenty-nine? The fault lay not in her stars, but in herself.

"I let too many birthdays slip by," she explained to the night sky. Maybe to herself. Not to the stranger's back. "I won't let that happen again. Every year will be a milestone year from now on. I'll make every single one count."

The string quartet's next song was more lively, all Santa Claus and toys and childhood, a better melody for tonight's crowd.

Mallory sat up again. She swung her rain boots in time to the children's song.

The man next to her did not. He didn't seem to have anything childlike left in him.

"Are you waiting for someone?" she asked.

He was silent.

"I'm just trying to make conversation so that I can wear your gloves a little longer."

More silence.

She didn't have to worry about him being a witness to her weakness. He'd never say a word to anyone.

She took her time as she took in his strong profile, the grim set to his lips. *Stoic* was a good word for him. Stoic, the way her grandfather looked when his body hurt and he didn't want to admit it was holding him back from some task he still expected himself to do, like hunkering down to put air in his car's tires. *I can do that for you, Grandpa. Let me help you stand. That asphalt has to be hard on your knees.*

Mallory tried again. "Why are you out here, staring at a fire by yourself?"

"Not because I'm sad." *Unlike you*, she practically heard him say.

"Hey, don't judge. Odds are, it's not your birthday."

He didn't smile at her flippant comment, not exactly, but his mouth sort of relaxed.

She picked at a piece of straw. "I'm not sad that I'm twenty-nine. It's just that, each birthday, I have an appointment with myself to stop and evaluate if I'm where I want to be."

Never allow your actual timeline to lag behind your projected timeline. She could hardly admit she was letting a business manual direct her entire life, could she?

"This time two years ago, things were not good in my life. I listened to a—a—"

A book.

"To a friend, and I made changes. Hard ones."

My book gave me the resolve I needed to object to my family's plans and make my own.

"So, this birthday, I'm actually right where I had always wanted to be. Finally."

"Congratulations." His tone was somber. The sarcasm was missing, for once.

"Yeah. Thanks." She laced her fingers together, warm now in his gloves, and let her hands rest in her lap, palms up, cupping…nothing. "I just thought I'd be happier once I'd gotten what I wanted."

She could feel the intensity of his gaze.

She kept looking at the gloves. "Do you know what I mean?"

The music stopped. She looked up from her hands to his unsmiling eyes.

Yes, you do. Poor man, so grim.

The quartet pushed chairs aside to place their instruments into black cases. In the absence of music, the crowd got louder. Families were talking, friends were meeting up. So much noise. So much connection.

The only connection Mallory had made tonight was with a stranger who barely spoke. She decided to fake some confidence—it really had become a habit in the past two years—and make him a little less of a stranger. She held out her hand to shake his. "My name is Mallory, by the way. What's yours?"

He didn't take her hand. Just as she'd suspected when he hadn't returned her first friendly smile, he was the type who'd leave somebody hanging if they approached him while he wasn't in the mood to be bothered.

Well, she was bothering. She kept her hand out, ready to shake, and raised one eyebrow at him in challenge.

"Eli," he said, and waited.

For what, she didn't know.

"Well, Eli, it's nice to meet you." She grabbed his hand with both of hers and pumped it up and down a few times. He let her, watching their hands as if she were performing some exotic ritual from another civilization.

But as she let go, he abruptly adjusted his grip so he was shaking her right hand properly. His handshake was firm, decisive. All of his physical confidence translated, unsurprisingly, into an impeccable businessman's handshake.

Or not.

He didn't let go.

Chapter Three

Never let anything take you by surprise.
                        —*How to Taylor Your Business Plan*
                                        by E.L. Taylor

The woman had no idea who he was.

E.L. Taylor let go of the hand that was wearing his glove.

She dusted her hands off on her jeans. "Well, now that I've been a Debbie Downer, I should get going."

Not Debbie. *Mallory.*

Mallory was the first person in at least two years who hadn't recognized him. She hadn't even started with the *Don't I know you from somewhere?* line of questioning he got from strangers who needed an extra moment to place him.

Yes, they knew him from somewhere.

From birth, Erasmus Leonardo Taylor had been well-known. Announcements had appeared in all the right places. From the first private kindergarten class, everyone at each of his prep schools had known whose son he was, students and faculty alike. He was called Eli by his immediate family, because Erasmus Leonardo was an asinine name for a child. He was called Taylor by everyone else, but he wasn't plain Taylor. He was *Taylor, Harold and June's oldest son—yes, the Dallas Taylors, the ones with the summer estate outside Galveston; you know the ones.* For the first eighteen years of his existence, everyone in his world had known who he was.

Then, he'd come to Masterson. The town was small, but the university was large. Thousands of students were not from Dallas, thousands had never spent their summers in their family's oceanfront vacation home in Galveston, thousands had never played the traditional round of golf with their father's business partners on their sixteenth birthday. Most had never played a round of golf at all.

He'd loved it.

He'd kept *Eli* a secret and ditched the ludicrous *Erasmus* entirely, using E.L. Taylor on every term paper, signing *E.L. Taylor* on his first legal contract, which had been his dormitory agreement. One of his many-greats grandfathers had founded one of the fraternities in the mid-1800s, guaranteeing his progeny membership in perpetuity, but Taylor had ignored that legacy and chosen a fraternity that none of his ancestors had ever belonged to, then been elected president of it. He'd aced his classes while leading the men's record-setting crew team, rowing in the first seat, the man with the most power, the man who led the team.

The end result was that everyone at Masterson University had known him by the time he graduated. Everyone in the world of collegiate crew had, too, and he'd attracted the attention of Olympic recruiters for rowing. To fly across the surfaces of rivers and lakes around the world, using his own body to power the fastest, cutting-edge racing shells… That would have been something.

However, Harold and June's son was not expected to spend two years training for any sport at an international level. He'd been named after two legendary geniuses. From birth, Erasmus Leonardo had been expected to have a brilliant mind and to nurture it, so that he would, one day, bend numbers and legalities to his will and become master of his own fortune. A gentleman's competence at sports was expected, but to devote oneself entirely to a physical pursuit was not.

So, he'd done what he'd been raised to do. He'd graduated from Masterson and gone to Harvard for his MBA. Harvard had an outstanding rowing team, as well as an infamous policy that barred all graduate students from competing in varsity sports. With that temptation out of the way, he'd mastered his master's degree, allowing himself one physically challenging outlet by returning to the fencing he'd first learned at his prep school, competing only at a club level, not intercollegiate. Not international.

He'd graduated and promptly invested in a winning array of stocks and real estate. He'd performed as spectacularly well as expected, accruing his first few millions, but he'd been in his mid-twenties, a little reckless. Tracking the stocks of long-established companies wasn't as thrilling as taking bigger risks in unknown start-ups. Instead of holding a stock that increased by a mere tenth of a single percentage point, he could invest in companies that grew by one thousand percent or more.

Most start-ups failed, however, becoming money pits until they finally dissolved, but Taylor had a good eye for new products and an even better judgment when it came to predicting which fledgling entrepreneurs would grow into successful CEOs of new companies. His millions had turned into tens of millions. Everyone in the world of venture capital knew him.

Fortunately, the world in general did not. He'd always been able to ditch the suit, don a leather jacket and ride a motorcycle across Texas like any other man. Stop and get gas without being photographed. Stop for a plate of barbecue without giving an autograph. He'd been able to stop being E.L. Taylor whenever he wished to.

Then, he'd written a book.

It had given him name recognition outside the world of high-stake investments and black-tie charity galas, so a few television producers had come to call. He should never have agreed to be a guest millionaire on a few episodes of *Shark Tank*. It had made his face as recognizable as his name, so a famous female recording artist had come to call—and come to his bed. He should never have agreed to escort her to the Grammys. The added exposure had sold more books. Their breakup had sold even more.

Taylor could not go anywhere or do anything without being watched, pointed at, photographed, whispered about. Anyone who had attended Masterson University during any part of the four years he'd been there invariably recalled that they'd been close friends.

This fall, Taylor had found himself on a private airstrip with one of those alleged school buddies. The man had proudly pointed out his private plane, a two-seater with a single propeller. It was laughably small compared to Taylor's personal jet, the equivalent of a go-cart next to a Ferrari. On that unimportant evening in September, Taylor had been inconvenienced by a change in plans and was impatient for his jet's return. The man he barely recalled from college had been happy, even eager, to take him from Houston to Dallas. *I'll fly; you buy*, he'd offered. He'd wanted Taylor to pay for the fuel, less than $150.

E.L. Taylor had spent that much on his lunch that day. The whole idea of returning to Dallas in a hobbyist's prop plane had been absurd, but it must have appealed to Taylor on some level. For whatever reason, Taylor had tossed the pilot a couple of hundred-dollar bills, and they'd taken off.

The plane had crashed.

There'd been a harrowing emergency landing into a lake rather than a residential street, an attempt to spare the people on the ground from being killed. Taylor had gotten out alive. The pilot, who'd only been flying to Dallas because Taylor was famous, was still in the hospital three months later.

E.L. Taylor wished he'd never written that book.

"Maybe I'll see you around town, Eli." Mallory started pulling at the fingers of one of his gloves to take it off. "If not, have a nice holiday."

Incredible. She didn't want to hang on to him. She was leaving, as if he were just any stranger at the park, and she didn't care if he remained a stranger.

He never went by Eli publicly, but he'd given her the name just to see if she'd raise that eyebrow and chastise him for being untruthful. *Oh, come on, we both know that's not your name.* That was what he'd expected her to say.

She hadn't. Had his appearance changed so much since the crash? He'd pulled all the necessary strings to ensure the world didn't know he'd been in a crash, so no one would have a reason to look for any changes. His physical and mental health couldn't be questioned, or the stock value of the companies he oversaw could fall. He was unrecognizable to himself on the inside, but he hadn't thought the world noticed any difference at all.

Mallory pulled off one glove and started on the next. Whether he liked it or not, she'd hop down and be gone in seconds.

He didn't like it. "Where are you going?"

That comment did earn him one of her raised eyebrows, and he realized he'd asked it as if she needed to account for leaving his boardroom in the middle of a meeting without being dismissed.

He made an effort to modify his tone. "To get that hot chocolate, I assume."

She stopped tugging at the glove. "I doubt the same church is still selling that particular hot chocolate."

She spoke softly, sadly—absurdly so, given the circumstances. By her own admission, she had whatever it was she'd worked hard to have. She did not have nightmares of oil burning on the water's surface as she struggled to get free of the wreckage of a plane. She had no idea how much worse life could be. Sure, she'd said she wasn't as happy as she thought she'd be, now that she'd gotten what she'd wanted, but *not as happy as I thought I'd be* was different than *sad*.

"What is so sad about hot chocolate?" he asked. Or tried to ask. Perhaps he'd said it more like he was demanding that she explain it to him.

"I haven't been back to Masterson for a long time." She paused as if she needed to steel herself against something. "I never graduated. I came back this fall to complete my senior year."

His first impression had been correct: she was a college student.

"Do you think that's dumb, to come back after so long? To be a twenty-nine-year-old woman living in a dorm? They put me in the dorm that houses foreign students, since they tend to be older, and there are a few graduate students going for their MBAs and PhDs, but I think I'm still the oldest. I'm definitely the only one taking bachelor-level classes. No one has any classes with me. They don't even study in the same library."

He didn't know what to say. He was only three years older than she was. He couldn't imagine the humiliation of moving back into a dorm.

He shouldn't say that.

You didn't face death in a plane crash.

He shouldn't say that, either.

She jerked her head away, like his silence was criticism, a little blow. He felt badly about that, but she recovered quickly enough, sitting up and tugging her cap lower on her forehead. "It doesn't matter. Everything is going great. I just mentioned it because it's been eight years since my last Yule log lighting. I'm not going to waste my time on a futile hunt for the hot chocolate of my youth. I planned to do something else tonight."

"Masterson's a pretty small town beyond the university," he began, trying to be reassuring. "I doubt any new churches have been built in the last eight years. I'm certain none have been knocked down. There's a good chance your hot chocolate is still there."

What am I doing? I don't cheer people up.

He shrugged—at her, at his thoughts, at his uncharacteristic attempt to make conversation when the subject wasn't business. "You should at least walk over and take a look, if it tasted so good that you remember it after eight years."

"Yes. Um…yes. You did me a favor tonight, so I do owe you a cup."

This was a novelty. A woman was going to buy him a cheap cup of hot chocolate at a small-town festival.

She ducked her chin, a little bashful. "But I'm afraid I don't have any money with me at the moment."

Ah, so she did know who he was.

Every light dimmed, inside him and out. He didn't bother to hide the derision from his voice. "No, of course you don't have any."

He knew women, and he knew this routine. She wanted him to buy her something. *Just look, Taylor, isn't that the most adorable set of earrings? I wish I had my credit card with me…but I don't.* He'd have to be a tight-fisted Scrooge not to pick up the tab. He'd never miss ten thousand, and women knew it. Men did, too—who else but E.L. Taylor should buy the round of overpriced, under-the-table Cuban cigars on the golf course? Women, men—everyone knew it, including Mallory.

"You don't have to sound so sarcastic." She pulled the empty glove through her bare hand slowly, no doubt gauging the value of the supple leather. "I just meant—"

"I know what you meant."

Did you think you were the first woman to try this with me?

He should never have told her his name was Eli. That was private, a family nickname, one only his sister and brother still used. If word spread that E.L. Taylor went by *Eli*, then business associates who wished they knew him better than they did would try to call him *Eli*. It would become a constant reminder that he'd been a sucker at a stupid Christmas fair.

He pushed off the edge of the hay bale stack and dropped to the ground, then turned to Mallory. He'd stuck her up there. He'd get her down, and then she could remove herself from his vicinity—and no, he wouldn't pose for a selfie with her before she went.

He reached for her denim-clad hips and pulled her to the edge of the hay bale.

"Hey—I can get down on my own."

She pushed him with her hands on his shoulders, but he'd already lifted her off the edge, so instead of landing on the ground, she ended up sliding down his front, her chest in his face for a moment, followed by a puff of her body heat escaping from her coat at her throat, then her smooth cheek brushing his unshaven one. A few strands of her long hair caught on his lower lip as she landed with her boots between his and her ski cap soft against his neck.

Sex.

Two seconds of accidental contact, and his body suddenly woke up from months of hibernation. Hips, waist, heat, hair—hair that would trail across his chest when she purred her way down his stomach.

Sex.

He stayed as he was, his hands on her waist, her hands on his shoulders. She tilted her face up to him, their gazes locked, and her indignation changed to something else. Her lips parted on a little intake of breath, her eyes went wide as she focused on him, on his mouth.

Sex—she was thinking it, too.

The sensation swamped him, as foreign as if he'd just now discovered how primal desire could feel. He'd had no interest at all since the crash, none whatsoever, but if there was anything good about being recognized as multi-millionaire E.L. Taylor, it was that any woman he wanted would happily come to his bed—and this woman, he wanted.

"Goodbye, Eli."

That was a laughable thing for a woman to say.

"Goodbye? This is the end of our date?" He kept one hand on her waist and braced his other on the hay bales by her head. His arm blocked the light of the bonfire from reaching her face, but the sight of her wide eyes and parted lips was already burned into his mind. He leaned in, bringing his mouth closer to those parted lips. "Then it must be time for the good-night kiss."

"This was a fake date. You didn't even buy me flowers, remember?"

He stopped cold. "I need to buy you something. Of course."

He should have pushed himself away from the hay bales, turned his back on her and walked away.

Instead, he drew her closer. "Kiss me nicely then. Prove to me I should spend my real money on my fake girlfriend."

Her sudden little breath wasn't arousal. It was—

she was—*laughing* at him as she leaned back on the hay bales, putting space between them. "You really think you're God's gift to women, don't you?" She started jerking off the remaining glove, pinky finger, ring finger, middle finger.

He scowled. The woman was not lingering over the middle finger. Surely not.

She moved on to her index finger as she made her point. "You don't know anything about women. We don't like to be dropped on hay bales, and we don't like to be told to perform before you decide whether or not we're worthy of your time or your money. You have no idea how to date a woman at all. No wonder you're so grouchy."

"I'm not dating you. You're the one who demanded that I be your boyfriend."

"I know, and you did me a favor. I understand why you were hinting that I should buy you a cup of hot chocolate in return. I owe you. I get that."

Hinting? He didn't hint about anything. Ever.

"Trust me, I would love to be able to buy you a hot chocolate. I'd love to be able to buy anybody a hot chocolate, but I don't have any cash in my pocket. I was going to offer to do something different for you, instead."

Skip the kissing, straight to bed? He could work with that.

"But you're being so rude, forget it." She pulled off the second glove and slapped the pair against his chest. "Take your gloves and move, so I can go do what I'd planned to do before all of this."

He didn't attempt to take his gloves. "What, exactly, was that?"

"I'm going to find myself a nice, out-of-the-way pecan tree where I can brood about my own life in private." She stuffed his gloves in the open collar of his jacket. "And not watch you brood about yours."

She stepped right around him and walked away.

Taylor stared at the hay bale where her face had been. She truly did not know who he was. She hadn't wanted him to buy her anything. She was just an attractive woman in a ski cap who'd wanted to stand next to him for a few minutes. Nothing more. And now, she was gone.

He turned around. He didn't want to brood alone by these damned haystacks. He wanted to brood in the company of—

"Mallory."

He barked out her name in the only tone he knew, the one that demanded a person drop everything for him. It worked on his staff. It worked on everyone's staff, every place he went. It even worked on his little sister.

Mallory kept walking. She waved her hand by her ear in annoyance, flicking away his command like it was a pesky, harmless bug.

How dare she?

He had power. It had nothing to do with the bedroom. He had power where it mattered, in boardrooms. He could bankrupt a company by voicing a doubt. He could kill someone's career with a word. If E.L. Taylor told anyone to stay, they stayed without question. Did she not know with whom she was tangling?

She did not.

She thought he was Eli, and the part of him that was Eli desperately wanted to be with the woman who had no idea who E.L. Taylor was.

"Mallory, wait." But his words still sounded like an order, and she kept walking.

He yanked the gloves free from where she'd stuffed them in his jacket and started after her.

Chapter Four

Never let an opportunity pass you by.
              —How to Taylor Your Business Plan
                                    by E.L. Taylor

Taylor caught up with Mallory easily.

He was taller, so his strides were longer. He also wasn't hampered by clunky rubber boots. She plodded along in a fairly silly way, looking from behind like all the nineteen-year-old girls on campus who favored cheap, colorful rain boots. He'd assumed she was one of those girls when she'd first grabbed his arm and started babbling about sand in her boots.

She'd gotten serious quickly. He'd heard the unmistakable experience in her voice when she'd talked about fending off a man. In his peripheral vision, her long hair and ski cap had reminded him of his little sister. If his sister had needed to stand next to a stranger in a similar situation...

With that mindset, Taylor—*Eli* Taylor, the big brother—had put Mallory behind him, where no one could reach her without going through him first. But, as he'd lifted her to the top of the hay bales, he'd looked at her face full-on in the firelight. He'd realized immediately she was no college student.

She was a woman. He was a man. Since the dawn of time, that was how trouble began.

Trouble—for example, there was no reason for him to feel this stupidly compelled to fix her first impression that he was a jerk.

He caught up to her and matched her stride, trying to think of the right thing to say, trying to figure out what he even wanted to say. This compulsion to make things right wasn't trouble; it was a nuisance. Annoying. Uncomfortable.

She stopped abruptly. "What?"

He stopped, unprepared. "What?"

Her hands made a few random, angry gesticulations. "This. You. Following me, all broody and silent. What do you want from me?"

"I want..." He didn't know what he wanted. She fascinated him, that was all. Her face was so expressive, even prettier in the brighter light, now that they were closer to the bonfire. He could see more details. She had very feminine, feathery eyelashes. He liked the little dip in the center of her upper lip.

She threw her hands up and started walking.

So, he walked. "My first impression was that you wanted to make somebody jealous. My conclusion was that you wanted to spend the night with me."

"Sheesh. Your ego. Amazing."

It wasn't ego when it was true. Most women his age did want to spend the night with him. Younger women, too. Older women. That didn't mean he slept around casually. He was too damned busy at work. He was too damned picky at leisure. But he'd always known an interested woman when he saw one—until tonight.

"It was my mistake. I've been…" He was not going to say he'd been a celibate recluse the entire fall, which had apparently made him lose his accuracy when it came to picking up on the signals that a woman wanted him. "I've been misreading everything since the moment you first walked up to me, and I apologize for it. You don't owe me a cup of hot chocolate. I owe you one."

She clomped along beside him in silence.

He couldn't blame her.

He did possess the social graces expected of Harold and June's son; he just so rarely needed to be charming to anyone, anymore. This was one of those rare occasions. Mallory would be gone in a moment if he didn't change tactics.

"If you don't want to have a cup with me, you could tell me which church sells the good one you remember. I've been making an ass of myself all night, and I need to drown my sorrow for screwing up a fake relationship with a genuinely interesting woman."

"St. Margaret's," she muttered unwillingly—but she stole a look at him.

That tiniest of victories made his heart pick up speed unnecessarily. "If you don't want to drink hot chocolate with me, I'd still like to pay for your cup."

"How? You'd give me cash? Don't do that. It's weird to pay a woman who wouldn't kiss you. Almost as weird as demanding she kiss you before you paid for anything."

"I meant we could do what every college student does. You fly, I'll buy."

As soon as the words were out of his mouth, the memories flashed. Oil burning on the water's surface. Wreckage. Fear.

She laughed. "I haven't heard that all semester. Everyone in my dorm must be broke. Lots of us willing to fly, but nobody to do the buying. So, you'll give me the money, but you expect me to bring you back a cup for each of us?"

No one will face death, here on the ground. A chill slid down his spine, anyway.

"Plus, I'd bring you the change, naturally."

He shoved down his past and focused on the here and now—on Mallory's expressive face. He had her full attention now, no more sneak peeks. "Correct. Then we can find a couple of pecan trees, and we'll go back to brooding alone."

"Alone, while we drink hot chocolate together? Am I getting this right?" She looked amused, even while doing that imperious lift of her eyebrow.

"Yes. We'll drink the same thing at the same time,

side by side, but under separate trees, so we won't be obligated to exchange ridiculous niceties, like 'gee, this hot chocolate is delicious.'"

"What's ridiculous about that?" she asked.

"It's a given. Hot chocolate is never bad. There's no need to state the obvious."

She stopped at the edge of the sandpit. "True. I'm tempted."

His heart had no reason to beat so strongly.

"But I'd be getting the harder part of the bargain," she said. "I'd have to wade through a crowd of families with rowdy, cranky children, looking for a booth that may or may not be manned by the same chocolate-loving nuns I remember, and then I'd have to carry two cups all the way back here without getting bumped and spilling anything."

He didn't want to go into the crowd. He was afraid he'd be recognized, and that would be the end of Eli's anonymous night and the resumption of the rest of E.L. Taylor's unsatisfying life.

Mallory didn't want to go into the crowd, either. She was afraid she'd get bumped and spill her drink.

Not the same thing.

She had no idea how lucky she was to be able to strike up a conversation with a perfect stranger who didn't assume they already knew everything about her. No idea how lucky she was that every single person she met didn't expect her to make their financial dreams come true, from ten thousand dollars in jewelry to a million dollars in venture capital—or even

$150 in plane fuel. How lucky that she hadn't learned to avoid strangers like the plague, the way he did.

Lucky…except the only reason she'd struck up that conversation with a stranger tonight was that she'd needed Eli—or any stranger—to discourage another man's unwanted attention. That was why she was going to say no to hot chocolate. She was afraid she'd run into the person she'd tried to fend off before, and this time, the fake boyfriend who'd helped her would be out of sight, waiting under a pecan tree.

She gave him that no. "The hot chocolate probably only costs a dollar. Sorry, Eli, but that's not worth the amount of time and effort I'd have to put into it. Besides, the hot chocolate would cool off too much by the time I got all the way out to the pecan trees. It's pretty cold tonight."

Finally, he was prepared. That was not the real reason she was declining, and he knew it. Her need outweighed his, hands down.

"In that case, we'll have to go get the hot chocolate together. We don't have to talk. I'll drown my sorrows in silence."

"If we're going to do that, then we might as well find a seat over there in the pavilion. We can brood alone, together, there, instead of wasting time looking for the perfect pair of pecan trees while our cocoa gets cold."

"Sharing a bench is problematic. I have it on good authority that everyone would feel sorry for a woman by my side, if I gave her the silent treatment. It might look like our date is going badly, if we don't speak."

It would also keep them in an area where there were more people, more chances of him being recognized. But her lips were twitching; he'd made it hard for her not to smile at him, which made it hard for him not to smile back.

"Okay, then," she said. "We'll talk just enough to make our fake relationship look realistic. Deal?"

"Agreed. And you're right, it is getting colder. Put these back on." He handed her the gloves. The satisfaction he felt as she slipped her hands into their protective leather was unreasonable.

Woman. Man. Trouble.

This wasn't trouble. This was a cup of cocoa with an attractive stranger, a half hour out of his life, at most, until the novelty of being Eli, of being with a woman who called him *Eli*, wore off. She'd muse a little more about her birthday; he'd listen. It couldn't possibly lead to trouble.

They skirted the wet sand easily as they began their quest to find the chocolate-loving nuns of St. Margaret's.

This was the quietest date Mallory had ever been on, real or fake.

Eli hadn't been kidding when he said they'd talk as little as necessary, without exchanging any banalities like *gee, this hot chocolate is delicious*. They sat a polite distance apart on a park bench under the pavilion in silence.

"Gee, this hot chocolate is delicious," she said.

Eli continued scrutinizing everyone who ventured near their bench.

"Those nuns are absolute connoisseurs of chocolate," she said. "Cocoa sommeliers."

Someone drifted their way. Eli raised his cup for a drink as if he were using it to hide his face.

"Am I your fake girlfriend?"

He lowered the cup and frowned at her. His stunning eyes weren't silver, but blue, now that they were in better lighting. Paul Newman blue.

"You appointed yourself to that role," he said.

Paul Newman blue, minus the laugh lines.

"No, I appointed you to be my fake boyfriend. Are you now using me as a fake girlfriend?"

He had to be using her as a decoy or defense of some kind. That made so much more sense than buying her hot chocolate as an apology for being rude. She was the one who'd imposed on him, after all, barging in on his privacy by the hay bales.

She didn't mind being imposed on in return, particularly because she had no objection to sitting beside the sexiest man she'd ever seen in person—which made him the sexiest man she'd ever seen, period. Sex appeal could be so strong that it jumped right off the silver screen—or off the television screens in various bedridden relatives' homes. But when it was coming from a man with a powerful body—a living, breathing man who had strong hands that had warmed up these gloves—the appeal was magnified a thousand times. This evening was a little birthday present to herself, a chance to play make-believe for a while, with herself cast in the starring role as the object of adoration for six feet of glowering gorgeousness. He needed to do more adoring to make anything look plausible, though.

"Don't get me wrong. If you think I'm enough to make a woman jealous, then I'm flattered. But you might want to look at least mildly interested in me instead of constantly looking for her."

"There's no *her.*"

"Who are you looking for, then? Am I helping you fend off a whole group of women who might start begging for your attention, otherwise?"

"Something like that."

"No kidding? Tell me more. Is some sorority determined to descend upon you and make you their mascot—I mean, their official sweetheart?"

"God, I hope not." He looked somewhat appalled at the idea of being attacked by a flock of nineteen-year-olds. That was a point in his favor.

The fact that she was the one doing all the talking was not. She held her disposable cup of hot chocolate in one hand and used her other to start counting off his words. "'There's no *her*. Something like that. God, I hope not.' That's ten. An even ten words. I don't know who you're on the lookout for, but she's not going to believe this setup if you only start talking to me after you spot her. Or the group of hers. Or whatever."

Without taking his eyes off the crowd, he slid closer and put his arm across the back of the bench, just behind her shoulders.

"Happy?" he grumbled.

"Eleven."

He smiled around the edge of his cup before closing his lips to take a sip.

Do that again.

She was fascinated. When he didn't have that grim set to his mouth, his lips looked softer, especially in contrast to the heavy black stubble around them. She'd never kissed a man with a beard. It had to be rough. A high school marathon make-out session would surely leave a serious red rash on the girl's face. Good thing most boys in high school couldn't grow a beard.

But this man had left boyhood behind long ago. A big, solid body like his would be so thrilling to snuggle into. If this were a real date, her hand would fall naturally to settle on his thigh. She'd feel more through denim than leather; his thigh would be as hard as his arm. She'd turn her face up to his, and he'd kiss her, chocolate kisses, hot kisses. Eli, her fake boyfriend with kissable lips—

"You're staring."

"Twelve and thirteen." She kept her chin up, faking confidence despite her embarrassment at being busted for staring. "That's some peripheral vision you have. You never look at me, yet you keep track of where I'm looking and what my hands are doing." She realized her hand was resting mostly on her thigh, but her pinky finger had drifted to his jeans, a touch of authenticity to her fantasy. She moved it quickly.

"When my hands are brushing sand off my boots, I

mean. You kept track of how many boots you thought I had to brush off to make a man jealous." She could feel her cheeks heating, which he probably could also see with his super side vision. "Which isn't what I was doing, because there's no *him*."

"One," he said.

It took her a second. One boot, he meant.

"Fourteen," she answered.

He smiled again at her word count, a lift of just one corner of his mouth, which made her wonder what it would feel like to be kissed by him.

You could have found out by the haystacks.

With a sigh, Mallory straightened up and refocused on the holiday scene. A high school choir had taken the stage. Their director was conducting them with intense motions, ensuring each *fa* and *la* cut off on the beat. An overabundance of little children, most still wearing the construction-paper reindeer antlers they'd worn onstage, crowded around the fence in front of the Yule log to throw their wishes on the fire.

Wish after wish was hitting the sand. An indisputably handsome fireman was using a fire iron to whack them into the fire as he made each child laugh. If that guy wasn't already married, then a dozen single women who dreamed about white picket fences were probably drooling over each swing. He looked like he'd make such a good dad someday—a handsome one, too. All in all, it was a wholesome little vignette, *It's a Wonderful Life* if George Bailey had been a hot hunk.

Was it bad form to notice a hot fireman while on a fake date with a fake boyfriend?

Her fake boyfriend was certainly scowling at the fireman as if he were a rival. Eli had nothing to worry about. The white picket fence wasn't Mallory's dream. She'd spent almost all of her twenties living behind everyone else's white picket fences.

He's not jealous of a fireman, Mallory Ames. This isn't a real date.

Eli simply scowled at everything, even sweet little children and their hero.

"Isn't it cute how the kids' faces light up when the fireman talks to them? Did you ever want to be a fireman when you grew up?"

"No."

She waited a moment.

"Fifteen," she said.

Nothing, not even a flicker of reaction as Eli stared hard at the bonfire scene.

She nudged his knee with hers. "Hello? Anybody home?"

He frowned a little—or rather, his usual frown deepened a little—but he closed his eyes, turned his head away, and resumed scanning the crowd.

She tried again. "It looks like he's as much of a hero to them as Santa Claus. That's good, since you can't aspire to be Santa Claus. You can aspire to be a firefighter. If your hero is real, you can make a plan to become just like him."

Just like she had. It was only a matter of weeks now before she'd arrive at work to find the office down the hall, which had been empty all fall, occupied by none other than her very own hero.

She knew what he looked like, of course. In the black-and-white photo on the back of the book jacket, he was handsome in that clean-cut, prosperous way, with short hair and a cashmere sweater over a button-down. The photo had been taken outdoors. He looked a little bit impatient. She imagined he'd paused for that photo on his way to a polo match, or perhaps just before he'd boarded his yacht. It was hard to picture a multi-millionaire like him in the administrative offices of the business college, even in one of the private offices—but he'd be there. Soon.

It was unnerving.

"Have you ever met one?" she asked Eli.

"I try to meet as few firefighters as possible."

Mallory had meant heroes, not firefighters specifically, but Eli's aversion to them struck her as odd. She'd assumed everyone admired firefighters, if for no other reason than they raised money for good causes by posing for calendars with kittens. Eli would probably just stick a kitten on top of a hay bale and consider the job done.

"I guess nobody wants to meet a fireman who is working. That would mean your house is on fire."

She paused.

"And you actually own a house, so is that why you avoid them?"

Still nothing.

She sat back with a huff, which would have knocked his arm off the edge of the bench's back behind her, had he not been as unyielding as a statue. "You know, if I were your *real* girlfriend, I wouldn't put up with this cryptic crap. I'd be talking to you all the time. You'd have to talk to me."

"How very fortunate that you're only my fake girlfriend, and therefore we are brooding in silence together, talking only as much as necessary."

"Was that a complete sentence? You're positively witty when you use a complete sentence." She batted her eyelashes. "I have faith in you, Eli. You can get the hang of this if you keep practicing tonight. Maybe you'll go on a real date someday, and you'll just knock her socks off with your complete sentences."

His smile increased from a sexy half to two-thirds. Good God, the man was devastating when he smiled. So far, *she* was the only reason he'd smiled at all tonight, which made that sex appeal factor go off the charts. A dark and dangerous man whose smiles were exclusively for her? *Happy birthday.*

Maybe if he'd smiled at her like that when they'd been by the hay bales, she would have handled that almost-kiss differently. When she'd slid down his body, he'd looked at her like he wanted to make her his, right there in the night, consequences be damned. He'd given her permission to kiss him with a level of breathtaking arrogance, the kind an alpha-male bad boy would have in a woman's fantasy.

In a fantasy, Mallory could take what she wanted from a man like that. In reality, there'd been an undeniable thrill in being seen as sexually desirable, but the chance to indulge in a moment of pure lust had been too much for her. In a split second, she'd chickened out, stepped back and laughed. After all, who would kiss a man in the flickering firelight, just because he was drop-dead gorgeous and intensely focused on her?

Not Mallory Ames, apparently.

Never let an opportunity pass you by. Of course, E.L. Taylor hadn't been giving her advice about carnal indulgences, but she'd missed the opportunity to be kissed the way she'd fantasized about, by the kind of man she'd fantasized about.

She'd gotten a free cup of hot chocolate, instead.

E.L. Taylor would not be impressed.

Mallory watched the fireman pose for a photo with a little boy in reindeer antlers. That boy was no worse off for having met a hero. Then again, he was a child, and no one expected him to be his hero's equal.

Never meet your heroes was her hero's crystal-clear edict, and his advice hadn't been wrong yet. On the other hand, he'd also said to never let an opportunity pass her by. She had to seize the chance to learn from him in real life. She couldn't obey both *never*s.

"Tell me something, Eli," she said. "Have you ever met one of your heroes?"

Chapter Five

Never divulge more details than necessary.
                    —How to Taylor Your Business Plan
                                          by E.L. Taylor

"Never."

Eli said the word with finality.

It sounded like the perfect way to say out loud what E.L. Taylor wrote. The inflection was exactly right: he knew best, end of debate, move on to the next chapter. If Eli narrated the audio version of Mallory's business book, she'd probably fall asleep in the dorm with it playing in her headphones every night.

She wanted to hear him say it again. "Did you say *never*?"

Eli gave her that look out of the corner of his eye,

the one that meant he didn't answer unnecessary questions. She'd asked, he'd answered, and he knew she'd heard him. Move on.

It was so deliciously bossy, it made her a little weak in the knees, not that she'd want him to sense that. *Never show weakness.*

"'Never' isn't a complete sentence." She pulled off her ski cap and shook back her loose hair. "Everyone has a hero at some point in their life. You must have had one as a child."

"Never." He said it differently this time, quietly, nothing like E.L. Taylor at all. This poor stranger. He really was too grim.

She angled herself on the bench to face him more fully. "Didn't you have a favorite teacher when you were little?"

"They were all excellent."

That could have meant he'd had dozens of hero teachers. Instead, it sounded like he'd had none.

"What about a coach?"

"No."

"Hey, Eli?" She leaned in close and waited until he looked up from his hot chocolate. "We're having a conversation here. Don't make me start counting again."

After a moment's staring contest, Eli smiled maybe a tenth of a smile, just a crinkling at the corner of his eyes, a look as devastating as...well, every other expression he had. She was getting used to this feeling, though, being constantly but pleasantly flushed beside him, all of her senses jazzed up by this physical awareness of him.

"I don't need a lot of words," he said. "In this situation, I can describe you in only one. *Fearless.*"

Her heart contracted. Those half smiles were sexy, but this, *this*, was her undoing. A confident man, admiring her confidence…which was, unfortunately, fake.

"If I were fearless, I wouldn't be so nervous to…" *Kiss you.* "To meet my hero."

"Don't meet her," he said, the voice of authority once more. "The timing isn't right to meet her if you're uncertain. It may never be right."

"It's not a *her*. How would you know whether or not I should meet mine, if you've never met yours? You can't know whether it would be good or bad."

"Touché."

He said it curtly, quickly, *toosh*. He said it like he was impressed with her counterpoint, which made her feel so light she might as well be full of champagne bubbles instead of hot chocolate.

But she pointed at him. "I wasn't trying to score a point. I'm proving to you that you are wrong. What about family? What about your dad? My brother idolizes our dad."

Displeasure touched his face. "We're talking more than necessary to keep up appearances."

"No, we're not. This is what a real girlfriend would do, you know."

"No, it isn't."

"Seriously, it is. You're not supposed to toss your

date onto haystacks without warning. You *are* supposed to talk to her over drinks, even nonalcoholic drinks. You truly have never had a girlfriend, have you?"

He gave her the *unnecessary question* look again—with a good dose of that alpha arrogance.

Right. There was no way this man was an untouched virgin.

"Fine," she said. "Then what kind of weird girlfriends have you had? What do you even do on a date, if you don't talk?"

He gave her a look: *Really?* Then he sat back and let his gaze roam over her hair. Without the ski cap, her hair had to be messy, even a little wild. He took his time, studying her hair from the crown of her head to where she'd tucked it behind her ear, tilting his head as if he were deciding whether or not he was satisfied yet with how wild it looked.

Yet. If not, he'd undoubtedly take her for another tumble to get her looking thoroughly debauched. He'd probably start by whispering a sexy something into her bared ear.

Mallory felt naked without her hat. If this was how he looked at a woman's hair on a public park bench, how would he look at a woman in his bedroom, when she was all his and completely exposed to his gaze?

Eli's gaze glanced over her heated cheeks, before he raised an eyebrow. *Any more questions?*

"In the park?" she asked, incredulous.

Silence.

"On a bench?"

He gave her the hint of a purse of his lips, the faintest imitation of Zoolander, spoofing a supermodel.

Mallory burst into laughter. "How many of your dates end by being jailed for public indecency?"

He couldn't sustain the smolder. She caught the twinkle in his eye just before he looked down at his cup, but his shoulders gave him away.

"Eli, is that an actual chuckle? Are you laughing? You are." She poked him in the chest. "You are trying so hard not to smile."

He caught her finger mid-jab and pressed her gloved hand to his chest. She tried to pull her hand back, but he held tight.

She reversed course and pressed her hand into his chest. "Is that a heart I feel beating? You do have a heart, Tin Man. You've just gotten rusty when it comes to smiling. You need an oilcan, that's all."

"You do have a brain, Scarecrow. You just need the diploma, that's all."

Oof. Mallory had walked herself right into that one. In the movie, the Scarecrow hadn't really needed a diploma, but it had been part of his happily-ever-after.

She didn't let her confident façade slip. "They just hand them to you in Oz, apparently, as long as you can prove you murdered a wicked witch."

"You'll earn yours."

He spoke like her success was a foregone conclusion. He really would be a great narrator for her book. She supposed a business planning guide would be an odd choice for a bedtime story, but if he were reading it, she'd go to sleep feeling hopeful that she had what it took to change her world for the better, drifting into a night of happy dreams as she snuggled against his chest, listening to that deep voice...

He let go of her hand and slouched a little, stretching his legs out in front of him, crossing his ankles in those classic boots. "If this date requires more talking, then go ahead. Tell me about your childhood hero, instead of demanding to know about my nonexistent one."

"My childhood hero? Singular? I had many."

He nodded toward the last remaining children and the firefighter. "Tell me about one you met."

"The first one I remember was when I was six. I met Cinderella at Disney World, and I'm telling you, I thought I'd explode from the excitement. She asked me what my name was, and then she acted delighted to hear it, like it was the most special name in the world."

Eli smiled fully.

Finally.

With Christmas lights and music all around her, and with a handsome leading man beside her, the evening was taking on a magical glow. It felt like a real date, even though she knew it was not. She hadn't forgotten for a moment, but he'd placed her hand on his chest as if he didn't mind at all if she touched him, and now he was relaxed and smiling because he was enjoying their conversation.

This was such a luscious little evening of make-believe. He would smile at her like this when she tossed that bedtime book aside and spread her hand on his chest—on his bare chest.

"You remind me of my little sister," he said.

Ugh. No. Stop.

"I think she was in kindergarten when she met Cinderella. She went crazy, too." He shook his head at Mallory like she was in kindergarten herself. "What is it with you girls and a sparkly blue gown?"

"A gown?"

"That's what girls love about Cinderella. A big, sparkling, blue gown." The authority in his voice edged closer to derision. "It's probably behind the wedding gown mania later in your lives."

His smile was for himself. He was so satisfied with his dissection of a children's hero—worse, a *girl's* hero. It reminded Mallory too much of her brother's visits during his college breaks, as her one semester off had dragged into two. He'd take control of the TV as if only he knew how to operate it. Then he would dismiss her movie suggestions as silly girl-stuff. Her father would agree, although he'd enjoyed all the movies Mallory had watched with him to keep him company while he was a housebound invalid.

She didn't want Eli to be like that. "We weren't excited about a blue gown. It was about the hero who was wearing the blue gown. She was—"

"Hero*ine*."

She narrowed her eyes at him. "*Hero* can be gender neutral, and that was the most trivial big-brother thing to interrupt me with. I'm not your little sister.

I'm your fake girlfriend." *You're my birthday fantasy. Don't ruin it.*

"All true." He polished off his cup of hot chocolate.

Mallory might have chosen to spend her birthday with a hot guy, but she wasn't going to be patronized as if she were a child, not even by the hot guy. "The reason girls love Cinderella isn't because she wore a pretty dress. Girls aren't that shallow. Cinderella's moment of victory isn't her arrival at the ball in a glass carriage. It's at the end of the story, when she doesn't have a magical disguise. That's when she wins. It's about being seen, being valued even when you're dressed in rags, not only when you're in a sparkly blue gown."

"*That's* what you're thinking in kindergarten?"

"Well, no. I don't mean that kindergartners analyze a hero's journey, but that's when those ideas are being formed. Subconsciously, girls are excited to meet Cinderella in her sparkly blue gown, because they recognize that it's a symbol that Cinderella is a winner."

"You said she wore rags when she won. They sell more dolls in sparkly blue gowns because that's what little girls like, and it doesn't matter whether or not the doll accomplished anything in the blue gown."

"It's not about dolls." Her frustration was real, but she faked being cool. "How about this? Soldiers earn medals when they are filthy dirty on a battlefield, but we dress them up in sharp uniforms and pin the medals on them later, while they're looking their best. Cinderella won when she wore rags, but we like to see her looking her best, now that her battle is won."

Eli leaned in closer, a smile still flirting with the corners of his mouth as if he found the whole awful conversation entertaining. "A handsome prince noticed her while she wore a blue gown, then a second time while she wore rags. Is that a battle victory? It's not much."

"You're right." Mallory didn't have to fake her sarcasm. "Thank you for proving that having a handsome man notice you isn't all it's cracked up to be."

"Touché, once more."

His approval wasn't thrilling now.

"You think I'm handsome, at least," Eli said. "I also fulfilled the requirement to notice you while you were not wearing a sparkly gown."

"I'm not wearing rags." She said it as if it hadn't taken forever to get the mothball smell out of her grandmother's peacoat. It was humiliating to be only a mitten away from scrounging through a lost-and-found box. Mallory could feel a knot of old and new sadness clogging her throat. This whole evening had been terribly emotional, all quicksand and broken plans. "The only reason you noticed me was because I decided you would. I gave you no choice."

"I'm glad you didn't." He raised his cup in a toast. "I would have missed out on some excellent hot chocolate."

With that meaningless bit of polite charm, he ended the subject. He'd torn apart her childhood hero for sport. End of discussion. Move on.

I'm not done. Mallory crumpled her empty cup and threw it at the nearest trash can. It hit the side of the metal barrel and fell to the plank flooring. "Cinderella doesn't care that the prince is rich. The important thing is that he loves her. She'll have an ally from now on. A champion."

Eli looked bemused. "An affluent champion. One who can buy her sparkly blue gowns and put her up in a castle."

"Should she aspire to keep her rags and remain in her family's attic? Do you know anyone whose life goal is to be poor?"

"Yes." He held up his empty cup. "The nuns that made this hot chocolate. Who knew women living in poverty would make something this rich?"

"You're being insufferable." She crossed her arms, rounding her shoulders so that she wouldn't be leaning against his arm on the back of the bench any longer. "You wouldn't know a hero if one sat right next to you. Cinderella, for your information, was a hard worker even when life wasn't fair to her, even when her own family wasn't fair to her. Her prince and her castle and even that sparkly gown were what she deserved. She worked hard, and she got what she deserved after all her hard work."

"Hard work? It was servitude. She was treated like a servant by her own family, performing every chore they didn't want to do themselves."

"I..."

Servitude to her own family...

Eli uncrossed his ankles and pushed himself out of his slouch, a leisurely lion toying with a mouse. "Worse than a servant. She wasn't paid for all that hard work you admire. She got some food and a bed in a room where her family didn't want to sleep."

"I…"

Spare bedrooms and food…her own family…

"She was being used," he said, "and she was allowing herself to be used."

"Allowing it? Where was she supposed to go? A homeless shelter?"

Cinderella hadn't had any options. Mallory understood that. For years, she hadn't been financially free to return to school. Her father had needed to pay for his medical bills instead. Her own savings had slowly dwindled down to nothing. It hadn't seemed right to add something like a bottle of nail polish to Aunt Effie's grocery cart, or even necessities like maxi pads or toothbrushes. Mallory would do Aunt Effie's shopping for her, then purchase her own things separately.

Mallory had been frugal, but her savings couldn't last forever, and she couldn't get a paying job to fill her account back up. Her family wouldn't allow it. They'd needed her with them full-time. Who else would help an invalid get to the bathroom and back, day and night?

Mallory had believed it would be impossible to go back to college without her family's financial help, because they'd said so. Missed semester after missed semester, medical bills and home repairs, new televisions and used cars had taken priority over her.

Worst of all, she'd been lied to by her own father. He'd told her he wasn't getting disability payments from the government any longer, until the month that a paper check had arrived in the mail rather than being electronically deposited. Her father had claimed that he hadn't realized he was still getting monthly payments. If the checks kept coming, he'd be able to send her back to school next year, he'd said, so she should be happy. But her father wasn't a very good liar. She'd only felt betrayed.

She would have still been waiting on her fifty-ninth birthday if she hadn't made her own plan. E.L. Taylor had been right. *Never believe those who say it can't be done. There is always a way to get it done. They haven't tried hard enough to find it. You will.*

"Cinderella is a terrible heroine for young girls." Eli crumpled up his cup and pitched it toward the trash can with just the right arc, just the right amount of force to land it in the barrel. "That story teaches girls to keep hoping all the garbage they're putting up with will magically disappear one day, so they continually put up with garbage. I don't want my sister to believe that the possibility of a wealthy prince in the future is worth putting up with any kind of abuse in the present."

Any kind of abuse...by her own family...

"Prince Charming could be poor, and he'd still be her choice. It's about finding someone who doesn't treat you like a servant. It's choosing your own friends, and making your own family, if you need to. It's having enough respect for yourself to be with people you can trust, instead of people who'll lie to you to keep you where they want you."

None of which she'd done for herself.

Eli's laugh was more like a scoff. "Self-sacrifice and servitude won't help you find any of that, either."

"Stop it." Mallory pushed herself off the bench and took a step away, desperate to put some space between herself and his terrible, horrible opinions. "You don't know what you're talking about. You don't understand anything."

"Mallory?" He stood, too, and had the audacity to look baffled. "We were talking about fairy tales. I was telling you that my little sister—"

"We were not talking about fairy tales." She stalked over to the trash can, scooped her cup off the ground and threw it into the barrel. "We were talking about heroes. *My* heroes."

"Childhood heroes. You must have outgrown Cinderella."

Eli had gentled his voice. He slowly put his hands into his pockets, as if she were a spooked horse, and he didn't want to make any sudden moves to upset her.

Too late.

Eli had been the mirror. Everything Mallory had thought reflected well on Cinderella looked tragic when she saw it on herself. Mallory had been a woman used, letting herself be used, until she'd stumbled from a fairy-tale story to a business manual that had forced her to stop waiting for that magical moment when she'd be sent to the ball—back to Masterson. If she hadn't been given that book as a birthday gift, whose house would she be sleeping in tonight, after she'd cooked and cleaned and administered the medicines, then cleaned up the food one more time when her great-aunt or grandfather was too sick to keep it down?

She thought she might be sick herself. What if she hadn't read that book? What if?

"I've got to go." She whirled around and clomped down the shallow wooden stairs as fast as she could, heading for the darkness, because she was about to bawl and she needed to do it in private. No one could see the worst version of herself. Her book said so, and her book had saved her.

There was no darkness in this part of the park. Everything was bonfires and Christmas lights. Mallory started to jog down the row of booths, weaving around the people in line at each one, desperate to reach the darkness beyond the stage.

"Mallory!"

She didn't want to talk to him. She was sorry she'd ever talked to him. She was—*damn, damn, damn.*

She was wearing his super-expensive gloves.

She stopped in her tracks and fumbled with the gloves, her vision blurring, her chest heaving as she fought to keep the sobs at bay—*not here, not now*—until strong hands, larger than her own, cupped hers together firmly but gently.

His voice was just as firm and gentle. "Please, don't leave yet."

Mallory lost her battle.

She started to cry.

Chapter Six

Never apologize for being right.
— How to Taylor Your Business Plan
by E.L. Taylor

God, he was an ass.

Eli had known it for some time, but this was terrible, even for him. He'd made this genuinely interesting, expressive, attractive woman cry.

"Don't cry," he said, a stupid command.

"I'm n-not." Tears ran down her face and she was doing something anxious with her hands.

He tried to hold them still. "I didn't realize your feelings were being hurt."

"This isn't about my feelings. This is about *you*, and your lack of feelings."

He had nothing to do with this drama over a fairy tale, but Mallory's face scrunched up as anger warred with sadness. If being angry with him stopped her tears, she was welcome to chew him out. Tears made him uncomfortable. Anger was easy to take.

Best to let Mallory get it over with. He tossed her some easy bait. "I have no idea what you're talking about."

She didn't yell at him to let off some steam. Instead, her tone turned icy. "You're so proud of not having a hero, of not ever having had a hero. You think that makes you superior to all the little girls who have hopes and dreams. I'm here to tell you, Eli, that it makes you worse." She threw her hands apart, knocking his away. "It makes you a man who has no one to aspire to be like, no dream to reach for. You're a man without any inspiration to keep growing."

He dropped his hands to his sides. *A man without any inspiration.* The world hadn't noticed any change in him, none at all. How had she?

Everyone knows women get emotional. She's throwing words around, angry at everything in general. It's a meaningless rant.

But the platitudes and excuses which had enabled him to ignore anyone else's inconvenient feelings had stopped working the same moment a small plane's propeller had stopped working. Mallory knew precisely what she was saying and to whom she was saying it. She'd listened to him tonight, better than he'd listened to himself.

She pulled his glove off her left hand, one clean

jerk. "So, who should I feel sorry for? Little girls who hope that being good will lead to a good life? Or you, a man who thinks he's too good to have a hero?"

He stood there, shocked. Mallory had summed him up accurately and succinctly: compared to hopeful little girls, he sucked.

He should say something. "I didn't—I didn't realize your feelings were—" *You already said that. Her feelings weren't doing anything. You are the problem.*

She shook his glove at him. "Here. Take it, take it. I have to go." She gave the other glove a vicious pull, then held the pair out in one quivering fist. "Take them, please. I need to go before I c-cry." But her tears were already falling. She was in pain.

He grabbed her wrist and tugged her close, wrapping her in his arms as if he could shield her, but her pain wasn't coming from something he could break or beat or buy. She tucked her chin and pressed her wet cheek against his neck, hiding her face. Sobs wracked her body.

He was appalled. It didn't seem right. It didn't seem fair. This lovely woman who'd demanded his attention, who'd laughed at his sullen silence, who'd spoken to the stars and to a fire and to a stranger, now was genuinely heartbroken. He wasn't certain why.

"P-people are staring. I want to g-go."

"Then, we'll go." It didn't matter *why* she was crying. It only mattered that she was.

He glanced around for a quick escape, then shepherded her in between two booths, keeping an arm around her shoulders and turning them both side-

ways to squeeze past a few propane tanks and cardboard boxes. The area behind the booths was darker,
just a grassy parking area for those who worked in
the booths. Quieter, too, because the speakers that
had begun playing prerecorded holiday music were
pointed away from them. Only a few other people
were back here, smokers taking a break, mostly. The
tips of their cigarettes glowed orange in the night.

Eli led Mallory in between two parked pickup
trucks. There, in semi-privacy, he leaned against the
side of one of the trucks and wrapped Mallory in his
arms again.

"I'm fine," she said, and then she set her cheek on
his shoulder, looking away from him, and gulped in
shaky breaths that did not sound fine.

He didn't know what to say, so he said nothing.
He had no idea how a cup of hot chocolate had led
to this situation. He didn't want to see her cry, but
as he held Mallory in her sturdy wool coat, he felt...
he felt... He didn't mind being the one she cried on.

Step one is to name your emotions. His therapist wanted him to work on that. Eli had consulted
a therapist a few weeks after the crash, of course.
He was no fool. People who faced near-death events
generally needed professional advice to process the
experience—and Eli's ability to sleep had been shot.

He'd hired a highly sought-after and very discreet
counselor. *Can you put a name to your emotion, Mr.
Taylor?* Terror. And in that final second, regret.

Mallory shifted a little, murmuring something
apologetic. Eli cupped her head in his hand lightly

to keep her as she was, so she wouldn't feel obliged to raise her head and step back if she didn't want to.

She didn't want to; she rested more heavily on his shoulder. He smoothed back a few strands of her hair, which were tickling his nose—a nuisance. Then he put his arm back around her and settled into her as she settled into him, and none of it felt like a nuisance.

Trouble?

It didn't feel like that, either.

When you can identify an emotion, Mr. Taylor, then you can accept it for what it is, no more, no less. As Mallory's breathing grew more and more calm, Eli looked at the stars over the silhouettes of the trees, and he felt calmer, too.

Calm was an emotion. There; he'd identified it. Like any other emotion, even terror, calm wouldn't last. He closed his eyes to soak it in while he could, the feel of another human being in his arms, the feel of having a person to hug.

His eyes flew open again. A hug. He'd almost forgotten it had a name.

There was nothing similar to it in his life. When he greeted his parents, his father shook his hand. His mother kissed his cheek. His brother and sister, twins born more than a decade after him, had turned eight during his freshman year at Masterson University. They'd rarely been part of his life once he'd left home for college.

The touches Eli gave and received were handshakes, firm ones that served the purpose of gauging a person's mindset or sealing a deal. When he made the time, there was contact during evening dinner dates—an arm offered in escort, or a hand on the small of a woman's back—followed by a night of sex.

He was relieved to remember that he'd had sex fairly regularly, before September. Not as often as people thought, but frequently enough. He wasn't some strange creature that existed in a world devoid of human contact.

But sex was not *this*. Sex had a goal. Every touch had a purpose: to entice, to increase arousal, to ramp up the craving for the climax, which then finished the need to touch. A shower. A drink. A civilized goodbye until next time.

He closed his eyes again. After a moment, he tilted his cheek toward Mallory's hair, seeking that tickle, that touch that didn't have any purpose.

At the hay bales, when Mallory had first grabbed his arm for balance, he'd practically shaken her touch from his sleeve the moment she'd let go. But after she'd lectured him, and after he'd seen her face in the firelight, it had felt different when she'd sat behind him and plopped her arms on top of his head. The sensation had been foreign, unexpected, but not unpleasant, in its way.

He'd grumbled about it, but he hadn't moved away. Maybe he'd wanted a touch that was neither business nor sex, without knowing he wanted it. Was that an emotion with a name? Was there a term for that kind of desire?

I like being with Mallory.

That analysis was specific enough for now. He wouldn't move away. He wouldn't shake off her touch.

He'd hold Mallory for as long as she'd let him hold her.

This was the most mortifying date Mallory had ever been on, real or fake.

Nobody wanted to have a big epiphany about the psychology behind their failures. Nobody wanted that to happen while they were at a holiday festival with a handsome man. Nobody wanted that handsome man to be the one who revealed how her old hero had led her astray.

Mallory was so angry at herself. Her hero hadn't even been real. Cinderella was only a character in a fairy tale that had been told centuries before the Brothers Grimm had written it down, yet Mallory had absorbed this nonexistent person's values: suffer patiently, voice no complaints. She'd let them influence her real life, of which twenty-nine years were now gone.

Mallory had been even angrier at the man who'd pointed out the obvious flaws in the fairy tale, but stating the obvious was all Eli had done. When she'd freaked out, he'd come after her. She'd castigated him for not having heroes, but he was holding her right now, anyway, and it felt incredibly good. He was as big and strong as he was broody and gorgeous. The way he glared at the world made her feel all the more protected in his arms.

It was an illusion. The strongest arms couldn't undo her past. Tonight, she could taste the shame and despair she'd felt two years ago, when she'd finished the last page of *How to Taylor Your Business Plan*, turned out the light and seen the truth.

Another shudder went through her. Eli tightened his hug. He didn't say everything was okay. He didn't tell her to pull herself together. He was simply here, holding her, and he didn't seem to be in any hurry for her to dry her tears and move on. She'd insulted him, yet he was being a nice guy...which meant she was the jerk, here.

Never apologize for being right, E.L. Taylor said.

Mallory hadn't been right.

When I know I'm the one in the wrong, I don't believe in making someone wait on my apology. That was what her grandpa would say.

Thoughts of her grandpa were making her homesick now, too. Knowing she'd have to leave the temporary security of Eli's strong arms and return to standing on her own two feet wasn't much of a motivation to dry her tears.

Eventually, they dried up, anyway. "I'm sorry," she mumbled, keeping her cheek on Eli's shoulder.

"Don't be," he said.

"Yes, I should be sorry. I said some harsh things."

"You didn't say anything that wasn't true."

He sounded so matter-of-fact about it, in a resigned way. *I know I'm uninspired.* Poor man. No wonder he was so grim.

"I failed to see that I was upsetting you. I should have recognized that you were defending Cinderella so passionately because she's your personal hero."

"She *isn't*." Mallory hiccupped, miserable on every level. "But she was. I think I've watched every movie version of Cinderella there is. She always keeps her dignity, but she never tries to leave, not until she meets Prince Charming. Her story did shape my thinking, without a doubt. You're the one who didn't say anything that wasn't true. You can't imagine how much I wish it hadn't been true. I wasted so many years emulating that exact kind of servitude to my family. I didn't realize it until it was too late."

"Too late for what?"

She picked up her head and moved back just far enough to look at his face, shocked that he couldn't see the obvious. "For what? Do you really have to ask that?"

He kept an arm around her as he brushed her hair from her wet cheeks. Her shame and regrets and misery built with each strand of hair he smoothed back, until, with an unbearable sincerity, he repeated, "Too late for what?"

The dam burst. Her words came tumbling out over hiccups and tears. "Look at me. Just look at me. I'm twenty-nine. I'm still in college. I live in a dorm. You can joke all you want and mock me for thinking that twenty-nine is ancient, but that's because you aren't in my shoes. You can't understand how it feels to be this far behind. You already have a house, and you have a career, and you could be married if you wanted to be, but you don't want to be, because men don't have to be married to get sex."

His eyebrows rose. "What?"

"It's true." She was talking too fast, but it was too hard to slow down. "It's true, my grandpa says so. He told me that when he was young, if you wanted to have sex, you had to find a wife. Marriage meant sex. It was a big proof of your manhood to have a wife. He says that's why men today don't get married right out of school anymore, because they can have all the sex they want."

"Ah... Okay?"

She swallowed bitter tears. "It never occurs to any-one to point out that women aren't getting married now, either, and it's not because they're home alone, wasting away as spinsters. They have careers, and they don't have to marry to get all the sex *they* want. Women like to have sex, too, you know."

He cleared his throat. "That's excellent news."

A second passed.

Mallory did a quick mental replay of her whole dam-burst. Somehow, Eli had kept a perfectly straight face. *Excellent news.* She gasped a laugh. Sort of.

"Is that a chuckle?" Eli dipped his chin to catch her eye. "You're trying not to laugh, aren't you?"

She gave his shoulder a weak push. "You're mildly funny, sometimes."

"Good." His smile was brief. "But I'm also insuf-ferable, sometimes. I want you to know that if I'd had any idea how important Cinderella was to you, I wouldn't have said anything."

She still had his gloves in one fist. She spread the fingers of her other hand wide, then turned her hand over, looking for signs of all the labors it had performed. There weren't any. She had nothing to show for years of caregiving. Nothing.

"I spent a lot of time trying to please a family that thought I was a convenience for them. Why did I allow that? I kept agreeing to their demands. I was *obedient*."

"Mallory." He brushed her hair behind her shoulder, then gave it a little tug, as if she were his sister. "Why do I find 'obedient' so hard to picture?"

She took the question seriously. Why hadn't Eli recognized that the woman arguing with him on the park bench was the girl who'd let herself get stuck with the work nobody else in her family wanted to do?

Because she wasn't that girl any longer. She'd made a plan for a different life, and it was working. Eli was seeing her at her worst tonight, but her worst wasn't as pathetic as it would have been two years ago. She looked into Eli's silver-blue eyes and saw that the Cinderella reflection didn't fit over her image anymore.

"I wish I'd met you on my twentieth birthday." She longed to reach up and push his hair back, the way he did himself. She wanted to trail her fingers along that heavily stubbled jaw. "If we'd debated fairy tales back then, I might have wised up sooner. In case you were wondering, I have wised up. You might find that hard to believe after this evening, but I wouldn't be here in Texas tonight, otherwise. I'd be freezing in Ohio."

"You said a friend gave you some advice two years ago, and you made some hard choices."

"Yes, he...he did." It was flattering that Eli remembered that. She needed to remember that she'd called a book *her friend*.

It was. Her business plan had saved her from her fairy tale.

"Tell me more."

She'd said that earlier, too. Eli's expression was hard to decipher. When he'd stood over her like this at the hay bales, he'd been looking at her like they needed to risk that public indecency charge. He was focused entirely on her once more, but this time, she wasn't certain... "Why?"

"We agreed to pretend to date your way. Talking."

They weren't in public. They didn't have to talk. He must realize that. "Are you trying to be nice to me because I was crying?"

"Not at all. I'm practicing my complete sentences."

He was more than mildly funny, really. She gave his shoulder another push.

As if she'd actually imparted any momentum, he fell back against the pickup truck and stayed there, settling in to spend more time with her.

"Hard choices?" he prompted.

"That's not a complete sentence." She was being difficult, and not entirely by accident. If she wasn't careful, she'd start thinking this was the beginning of a special something. She, the twenty-nine-year-old coed in rain boots and a pink peacoat, starting something new with him, the silver-eyed man in the pricey bomber jacket who had enough unconscious swagger for ten action heroes.

Not likely. Not even in the movies.

"Allow me a second attempt. Mallory, you made an earlier comment concerning a friend's advice and the resultant hard choices you made for yourself and the direction of your life. Share one or two examples with me, if you would."

"You're such a comedian. Who'd have thought it?"

He waited.

She supposed she could answer his question. If it made her sad, well, he'd already seen the worst.

"I had a long talk with that friend, then with myself, trying to get to the essential, underlying question. It was simple, really. 'Am I going to finish my degree?' Yes or no. I'd been waiting for my family's permission to finish college."

She kept her chin up, but she didn't look into the mirror of his eyes. She knew how weak that looked.

"I did need their money, but only because I'd let them convince me that all of the work I was doing was merely part of being a family member, not actually a job. Nobody else in my family was doing the nursing and caretaking, though. Just me. Was I going to finish my degree? The answer was yes, so I had to draw a line in the sand. I told them I wasn't willing to continue without a salary.

"My friend explained things in an unemotional way. I followed his directions to—" That sounded odd. She tried to cover for herself. "To have alternate in-home care options ready to present to them. I even made an appointment with them for us to sit down and discuss it, like I was pitching an opportunity to invest in a start-up."

"A start-up." The corners of Eli's eyes crinkled just a little, that tenth of a smile.

"I was the start-up. They could invest the money in me and get reliable live-in care at a bargain rate in return, or they could hire someone five times more expensive and I'd find someone else to invest in me. One way or another, the new Mallory Ames start-up was going to bring in some money, then turn it into a diploma."

"Well done."

His smile, his approval, his *interest* in her little tale were each their own champagne bubble. The effervescence was pleasant, but champagne wasn't powerful enough to make her forget the reality of where she was and how she'd gotten here.

"Don't think too highly of me. I meant I'd get a job at the Golden Arches or something. But if McDonald's had invested minimum wage in Mallory Ames, that would have been more money than my family had invested, and McDonald's would have gotten one heck of a burger flipper in return."

"Exactly. Well done."

"It was a bluff." Mallory ran her thumb over the cable-knit hat protruding from her pocket, over all the ups and downs and ins and outs. "If I'd moved out and gotten a job somewhere else, I would have had to spend almost every penny I earned on renting someone else's spare bedroom. To make sure it wouldn't come down to that, I only asked for a salary that would amount to this year's tuition. It wasn't even a quarter of what hiring a stranger would cost.

It was still so hard, though. I had just moved into my grandpa's house to care for him, so he was at the meeting, and his sister, my dad, my brother and my brother's wife. Five against one. But my—my *friend* had gone through every possibility with me beforehand. I was ready when the shouting started."

"Your family shouts?"

"Yours doesn't?"

She'd meant it flippantly, but curiosity made her pause for an answer.

"No."

She made a rolling motion with her hand. *Keep going, that's not a complete sentence.*

His lips quirked. "I haven't tried to hold a business meeting with them. My younger sister can be dramatic, if memory serves."

"My brother always shouts. People hate the noise and leave the room, so he wins that way. It's not a fair way to play the game, but I knew he'd do it. When he threw my paperwork back at me, I wasn't surprised. I'd presented actual contracts from a couple of caregiving services, and he picked out the fact that the professional caregivers were allowed to eat one meal a day away from their patient, but they had to pay for that meal. He acted like that invalidated every other point." Mallory imitated her brother's most patronizing tone. "'Haven't you noticed? You never have to pay for your lunch.'"

Eli made a rolling motion with his hand. *And? Keep going.*

"I told him this meeting wasn't about a sandwich. It was about a salary."

Eli actually made a sound of amusement—and approval. *Pop* went another champagne bubble.

"So, long story short, my dad took over. Instead of shouting, he got all weepy, saying he'd always wanted his little baby girl to be a happy homemaker, not the ungrateful woman before him. I kept pretending I was cool and confident. Once they realized the shouting and tears didn't work, they dropped that and started talking. From that point on, it was simple math. My salary request was so much less expensive than hiring someone to take care of Grandpa, it was an easy decision for them once they realized I meant business."

Eli looked serious in the starlight.

"No pun intended," she added.

He still looked serious. "Why do you describe yourself as pretending?"

"'Fake it 'til you make it,' that's my mantra."

"But why have you chosen it? I haven't seen any evidence that it applies to you."

"You're saying this after witnessing my crying episode, up close and personal?"

He crossed his arms over his chest. "You weren't pretending to cry."

"I know that." She crossed her arms over her chest, too, and leaned her back against the side of the pickup truck behind her. The trucks were parked so that a door could be opened for a driver to get in, but no farther apart than that. They spoke across the width of a truck door like they were speaking across the width of an executive desk. Mallory wanted that type of success, that financial security. Yet here she was, leaning against someone else's pickup truck, breaking rule after rule of her business plan, discarding everything that had worked for the past two years.

This was for one night only. They hadn't exchanged phone numbers or addresses, or even offered their last names. She might have mentioned hers in passing just now, but it wasn't like he was going to memorize every detail about her. He wanted a one-night, fake date, too.

She wasn't abandoning a good plan; she was pausing it. She looked at Eli in the soft, gray night and stopped pretending that she was any future version of herself.

"It's exhausting to keep up this big façade of being an energetic, goal-oriented person. You should see me at work. I've got a part-time campus job where I sit in a cubicle with an outdated desktop computer, and I type up things I'm told to type up. That's all there is to it, but I dress like I'm going to call a team into the conference room for a meeting. I'm faking it because I wish I had a job where I needed to wear business attire instead of rain boots and hand-me-downs." She tugged on the collar of her coat and sheepishly squinted at him through one eye. "I'm vain enough that I only kept the good hand-me-downs. It makes it easier to pretend I'm successful."

Eli remained serious, as if even that information wasn't trivial. "If you have a job that you perform in business attire, then you aren't pretending you have a job where you wear business attire. If your family shouted and cried, and you remained both unemotional and on topic, then you didn't pretend that you were cool and confident. You were."

"On the outside. My heart was pounding in my chest because I was so scared I'd fail. My heart was breaking a little, too. My grandpa was the person who could have ended up in a stranger's care if I'd failed. He was the last relative I took care of, and I enjoyed living with him the most. The irony was that he was the only person in the family who thought I was doing the right thing by threatening to find a job that paid something."

"Is this the grandpa who told you about men and marriage?"

"Yes. He taught me so much about life. I really miss him."

"I'm sorry for your loss." Eli said.

"Oh, he's not dead. He's ninety-three and kicking. He moved into an assisted-living apartment complex in August, just before I came down here to start the fall semester. He did that for me, so I wouldn't feel guilty about leaving him."

She had to pause for another breath. She couldn't cry on Eli again.

"He gave up his *house* for me. I still can't believe it. Before we moved out, he overheard me making calls to find a ride share to get from Ohio to Texas. He gave me his car. He signed the title over to me, so it wasn't a loaner car I'd feel obliged to return. He said he didn't need it anymore, because the assisted-living center provides shuttles to doctors and grocery stores and everything.

"I pretended it all made me as joyful as my grandpa wanted it to make me, but it tore me up inside. I didn't cry, though. I can usually hold my tears. There's just something about tonight that's been getting to me." She exhaled heavily. "I'm sorry you got stuck with all this crying."

Eli shrugged away her apology. "You don't make a very good Cinderella."

That sounded insulting. Cinderella was iconic, the perfect example of how a woman should be endlessly patient, never unkind. Cinderella was beautiful, too, the center of attention as she gracefully entered the palace in her sparkly blue—yikes. Maybe the glamour was a bigger factor than Mallory wanted to admit.

Eli looked stern, like a principal about to lecture a student who was wasting their potential, or a police chief about to dress down the rookie. "Cinderella only went to her ball because of someone else's magic. You're here, in the middle of your ball, because you earned it yourself with your own hard work."

"What?"

He didn't give her the *unnecessary question* look. Instead, he pushed himself off the truck and placed his hands on her crossed arms, cupping her elbows, pulling her up to stand in front of him.

"It wasn't Cinderella's type of hard work, doing whatever chores others dictated she would do. You are the one who determined what needed to be done, not your family. You worked hard on the right things to hit your goals."

That praise sounded excessive. "I wouldn't have managed it on my own, if I hadn't gotten good advice from my friend."

"People get excellent advice all the time, but that doesn't make them successful. You were smart enough to recognize which advice could work for you, and you were dedicated enough to implement it."

He spoke with authority, but there was something in his expression that said she wasn't his underling. She was important. She mattered. It didn't remind her of anyone else in any movie at all. This was just him. Talking to just her.

"Don't cry over Cinderella again. You aren't anything like her. It's very clear that she doesn't measure up to you."

Mallory looked at her leading man under the starlight, and she felt one last tear slip from the corner of her eye to roll elegantly down her cheek like a bit of movie magic.

Eli ran his finger up her cheek, stopping it in its tracks and whisking it away.

"I'm sorry I agreed to this fake date," she whispered.

"Why is that?"

"Because I would kiss you right now, if we were real."

Chapter Seven

Never be afraid to speak the truth.
—How to Taylor Your Business Plan
by E.L. Taylor

"Nobody wants a fake kiss," said Mallory.

Eli looked at the woman he wanted to kiss more than he could remember wanting to kiss a woman in a long, long time. Far longer than since September.

Mallory bit her lip.

"I'll take a fake kiss," he said.

"It wouldn't feel like a real one." There was a breathless note in her voice that affected him as much as that lip-bite.

Nevertheless, Eli let go of her arms. She'd had

an emotional evening, too much of it his fault. He shouldn't push.

But E.L. Taylor had habits that were hard to break. He could be ruthless when he knew what he wanted. He could also charm when he needed to charm, and he could balance those two things, because E.L. Taylor was a very good negotiator.

So, he let go, but he didn't step back. "In the pavilion, you said I couldn't know that heroes ought to be avoided, unless I'd met a hero in the past. The same logic applies here. You can't know if a fake kiss will or won't feel right unless you try it."

She lowered her gaze to his mouth, so with the taste of victory on the tip of his tongue, he moved a little closer, ready for that kiss. She had only to sway toward him.

Abruptly, she lifted her gaze—and her chin, too. "Who said I've never tried it before, Eli?"

You really think you're God's gift to women. Same tone of voice. No one else spoke to him like that, ever.

His smile wasn't intentional. "Fearless."

"I've got standards," she said.

"So do I. You exceed them all."

"Eli." She shook her head ever so slowly, a dimple appearing as she fought not to smile. "Eli."

It's Taylor.

If Mallory kissed him, she would be kissing an imposter named Eli. He wasn't playing fair. He was withholding information that would surely change the game.

But he *was* Eli. He had been more than half his life,

until he'd come here, to this town. Until, at age eighteen, he'd entered Masterson University and seized the opportunity to be someone else, a man of his own design: E.L. Taylor, the multi-millionaire entrepreneur, the hotshot with the model *du jour* on his arm, the man who had it all.

This September, he'd seen that for the lie it was. He couldn't defy gravity, and when he'd fallen from the sky, he'd known that his life, like everyone else's, could be lost on a dime. If Mallory kissed the real Taylor, she'd be kissing a man who'd nearly died without leaving behind anything that anyone would mourn. His stocks and homes and cars would not have ceased to exist. They would have been divided among his family by a law firm that would've charged an outrageous bill rate. Only Taylor himself would have ceased to exist, and nobody would have missed having him in their lives—not his terse conversation, not his cold companionship, not even his business acumen.

Mallory would be better off kissing the fake boyfriend. The real E.L. Taylor wasn't worth a dime.

"I only give real kisses." Mallory placed her hand on the side of his face, tentatively. He could feel the gentle hold, but not more, not through the bristles that he hadn't shaved in too many days. Then her thumb stroked a little higher, over his cheekbone, and he felt her cool skin touching his. She pushed a few of her fingers through his hair, smoothing back a piece that must have fallen forward, and his eyes closed in reaction, as if she'd stroked him somewhere much lower, much harder, someplace where the touch would have a purpose.

"Since you were kind enough to hold me while I cried real tears, here is a real kiss." She rose on her toes as she tilted his head down, and she placed warm lips just above his left eyebrow, on the spot she'd just bared with her fingertips. "Thank you for being so patient and kind."

She stepped back.

Eli Taylor stayed as he was, head bowed, humbled by a kiss that had no other purpose.

Mallory bumped into the pickup truck behind herself.

She'd done it. She'd touched him, she'd kissed him, and now she'd backed herself into a corner where the only gracious thing left to do was leave with whatever dignity she still had after crying her heart out with a stranger. She gave her cheeks one final wipe with the hand that had just touched Eli's face—his beard, his hair, all real, all warm.

Bodies… She'd spent so many years caring for bodies in distress, she'd forgotten that a touch could be warm and sexy, a touch between two people who were attracted to one another, equally vulnerable— but that wasn't the case here. Mallory hadn't seen any vulnerability in him at all. He was just this alpha male who said the perfect thing now and then.

This birthday party is a fantasy, remember? Time to go back to the dorm, Mallory.

She took her ski cap out of her pocket. The mitten

came out, too, and fell to the ground. She bent to pick it up, although, really, what was the point?

Eli bent to get it, too, so they ended up with an awkward moment, an attempt not to butt heads. His arms were longer, and he snagged the mitten before she did.

She'd been holding his gloves in her fist this whole time. "Here. I'll trade you."

She took her single mitten and slapped it on her jeans a time or two. The reason she'd stuffed it in her pocket when she'd first stood next to Eli was so she wouldn't look like a beggar with only one. She pretended she still had two, but just didn't want to wear them. "This is just too sandy to wear. I'll wash it later."

"You wore only one mitten when you first walked up to me."

So much for that little attempt at fakery.

"That peripheral vision of yours is really something, because you sure as heck didn't even glance at me while I was brushing the sand off my boot. I know, because I was looking at you the whole time, ready to give you a nice, fake smile. Yet somehow you noticed I was wearing only one mitten?"

He was back to the *unnecessary question* mode, apparently. The expression on his face wasn't as supercilious as before, though. It was awfully close to concern.

"Yes, I only have one." She tried to make it sound funny. "You know what they call a single mitten?"

"No."

She smacked it one more time, a mess of blue wool and sand. "A rag."

She'd thought it would sound clever in the context of their Cinderella conversation, but it fell flat. It was too true. One mitten was useless.

"Where's the other one?"

"At a fraternity party, apparently." She stuffed the mitten back in her pocket. "Better it than me."

"Frat boys?" He looked upward, picturing something in his mind. "Three of them, to the left of us. Kappa Lambda on one jacket."

"Is peripheral vision your superpower? I would swear you didn't look away from that bonfire for a second. I thought you were having a staring contest with it. You were winning, by the way."

His frown was so sudden, she thought she'd angered him.

"Is that a bad thing?" she asked.

He shook his head, a single, sharp no. "I assumed you were trying to make one of them jealous. They were frat boys. You looked like a coed. It made sense. But when I picked you up—"

"When you threw me on a hay bale."

"When I saw that you weren't that young, I assumed they couldn't be who you were avoiding. I stopped paying attention to them."

"You didn't see them flip me the bird?"

"Obviously not. I wouldn't have let that stand." He scrubbed his beard in an angry sort of way. Mallory imagined the rasp of those whiskers on his palm was stimulating—or punishing. "It's not an excuse, but I was distracted by…" He fell silent.

"By me? The *femme fatale* in the sandy rubber boots?" She laughed, mostly so he'd stop being so serious about it. He shouldn't feel badly for not challenging three guys who hadn't done anything in his sight.

"By having a large bird making herself at home on my head. If I'd seen them flipping—"

"This is excellent news. Maybe not as good as the other excellent news I clued you into tonight, but if you were that distracted, then you don't know how I responded. Please assume that I was far too mature to flip them off in return."

"Did you?"

"Oh, yes. I was quite brave, hiding behind you. If they'd gotten angrier, though, you could have found yourself in the middle of something you didn't know I was instigating over the top of your head. It wasn't fair of me to risk that happening to you."

He waved off her concern. "It's all part of the fake boyfriend duties. Anytime, Mallory."

And then, he winked.

That wink hit every note that made her body sing. Fun, sexy, confident, *intimate*, a wink meant for no one except her.

She looked away, down the row of pickups, for a breath or two. "You know, you can be really charming when you want to be."

"That's also excellent news. I feel pretty damned rusty."

"Nothing an oilcan can't fix. Practicing could help, too."

Pull me close again. Touch my hair again.

He didn't. She was rusty at the dating game herself, an understatement if there ever was one, but he sure seemed like a man who was into her. Then again, he kept his hands clasped behind his back, a soldier standing at ease, content to look at her and talk, no need to touch.

She had a need to touch, so she reached up to skim her fingertips across the forehead she'd kissed. "You don't have laugh lines, but you don't have permanent frown lines, either. You know how they wonder if a zebra is black with white stripes or white with black stripes? I'm wondering if Eli is an angry man who can be sweet sometimes, or if he's a very nice man who has something in particular to glower about tonight."

"I'm thirty-two," he said. "It's a little soon to have acquired either."

"But which are you on your way to getting?"

"I've smiled more tonight than I have in a year."

"Must be the hot chocolate."

"It's you."

The silence should have been electric, a prelude to more. *Ask me for my number. Kiss me in the starlight.*

Eli remained content to simply look at her. He'd stated a fact. Nothing more.

It was up to her, then. "If you'd like to practice smiling and being conversational, maybe you could come back another night. Or a lot of nights. I live here—I mean, near here, obviously—so I come here a lot of nights. I'll be coming here. I did, the other Decembers that I lived in Masterson. I like the Yule log." Mallory cringed inside. She sounded breathless and awkward, Baby announcing she'd carried a watermelon.

Eli practiced his rusty smile on her, the remote, polite one that gave her that déjà vu feeling. "This is my first and last night in the fake boyfriend business."

Mallory translated that too easily: *I won't be seeing you again.*

"But it's been a memorable night," he said. "Thank you for sharing your twenty-ninth birthday with me."

Goodbye.

Of course. She should have known, she *had* known, that she couldn't stay with a handsome man under a night sky forever. It was time to get back to the real world, back to campus, back to her dorm and its fluorescent ceiling light.

To get there, she'd have to walk down the row of booths where she'd stopped and cried in a stranger's arms. Some people would remember the girl who'd publicly bawled in a hard-to-miss Paris-Hilton-pink coat. They'd be curious as she walked by in the other direction, trying to guess how that had turned out.

She must still look like a mess. She nodded toward the light that came through the space between the booths. "I'm going to sneak over there and take one of their napkins. I need to wipe my face off and get my act together a little bit. You never know if you'll run into a professor or a coworker. I'd like to be able to fake like I haven't spent the evening on an emotional roller coaster."

Eli pulled a crisp white napkin from his back pocket. "Courtesy of the nuns. It came with the hot chocolate."

"Thanks." Mallory wiped her nose and face and tried not to compare the coarse napkin to the soothing way Eli had smoothed her hair off her cheek. The napkin went into her pocket with the mitten and the wish and the mini pine cone. No sense in making both of her pockets bulge out unattractively.

She pulled on her ski cap and did a little hasty hair-tucking, leaving it long down her back. "Okay, how do I look?"

"You look perfect."

She waved away his pat answer. "I mean, is it obvious I've been crying? Are my eyes bloodshot? It's probably too dark for you to tell here, but it will be light over there."

"You look perfect." There was just a touch of that *unnecessary question* tone in his voice. He'd declared her perfect. End of discussion.

She put her hands on her hips. "Seriously? My nose isn't even red?"

"It's cold outside."

"So, yes, it's red."

"You look perfect, Mallory."

"Then you're not a very tough critic."

"I'm a very harsh critic, and I choose my words deliberately. If something is perfect, then no part of it needs to change. You're perfect."

She sighed. "It's just as well this is only for one night. I couldn't keep up this pretense much longer."

"What are you still pretending to be?"

"Perfect on top of fearless, apparently. If you spent more than a few hours with me, you'd realize I was nowhere close to either one. The advice to act like I'm already the person I want to be sounds good, but it has a lot of pitfalls. That might be one thing to discuss with my friend next semester. He'll be here, at MU."

"We've already discussed it," Eli said, and in her fantasy, he sounded slightly jealous that she'd be continuing their conversation with someone else. "You aren't faking anything important."

"Just the business attire, huh? I must look pretentious in my cubicle, dressed more formally than everyone else."

"Only if 'formal' means a ball gown."

She was very sorry the evening had to end. "You're pretty perfect at lifting my spirits, Eli. Thank you for being my fake boyfriend on my birthday."

That seemed so inadequate for an evening that had been full of self-discovery, spent with a man who knew just how to comfort her, whether with a hug or a stern lecture.

Never be afraid to speak the truth.

She looked into his eyes one last time, wanting to see herself the way he saw her. "I hope we run into each other again."

Those eyes narrowed. "You're leaving?"

"I thought… We said this was for one night only."

After an eternal second, he didn't contradict her,

but his answer made her heart take a hopeful hop. "It doesn't have to be a short night."

She should leave. Her brain might continue to remember this was only a fantasy, but her heart just wasn't listening.

No, thank you. I must go. It was firm, decisive, final, and it would protect her vulnerable heart.

Instead, she waffled, gesturing vaguely toward the back of the stage and the booths. "We've done everything there is to do, really."

"The night is still young. What else do people do in Masterson to celebrate a birthday?"

"It's a college town. They hit twenty-one and drink themselves into oblivion."

"I was here for my twenty-first. I know that much. But you're an ancient twenty-nine. This is my first time back since I graduated. Where do the old folks go?"

"Very funny." She tried to be tart, but her heart was feeling bubbly—*The night is young!*—and Eli was jarringly adorable when he tried to be funny, a brooding James Dean breaking character, laughing in an outtake on a blooper reel.

"We could go to the Tipsy Musketeer. They're still the most strict about checking IDs, and they don't sell dirt-cheap booze, so there won't be a lot of college students there. Their live musicians are really good, too."

"I remember the place." But Eli was looking regretful or hesitant or something. "It will be crowded on a Saturday night."

So that was it. She should have put two and two together sooner. He'd chosen to be all alone out by the hay bales. He'd spent their first fifteen minutes on the pavilion bench looking at every passerby as if they were his personal enemy—and he'd hidden his face with his cup more than once. As bold and confident as Eli seemed to be, he wasn't comfortable in crowds.

"Or, if you don't want to walk all the way to Athos Avenue, we could stay here," she offered, giving him distance as an easy excuse rather than whatever his issue was with crowds. "I'm up for another cup of hot chocolate—oh. Never mind. I'm not trying to get you to spend more of your real money on your fake girlfriend."

"The nuns aren't charging enough to break the bank. Besides, we both could use another chance to hold a hot cup to warm our hands."

"You could just put on your gloves."

He began pulling one on. Unlike her, his larger hand needed to ease its way into the tight leather. "You could put on your mitten."

"It's too sandy. I'm not going to look dorky in one mitten and have sand itching me in between my fingers, too."

He fastened his right glove with the snap at his wrist, looking so damned James Bond cool that Mallory barely registered that his gloves must have been custom-made to fit him so perfectly.

"In that case, here." He picked up her left hand and put his left glove on her, like he was dressing a child.

"What are you doing? Are you going to make us both look dorky?"

He held out his bare left hand. She placed her bare right hand in his, and he laced his fingers between hers. They stood together in between the trucks, holding hands. "There. Now we'll both have two warm hands."

"My hand must feel like an icicle in yours."

"Not for long."

That unconscious arrogance, that certainty that he could handle anything physical, like warming up her hand quickly with his own, made Mallory's heart hop and flutter every which way.

Eli started walking toward the booths, holding her hand. She fell into step beside him and savored the sensation of being in sync.

He led her past the boxes and around the propane tanks. They walked into the light, and not one person at the festival looked at Mallory with concern or pity. Only envy followed her on their way to the St. Margaret's booth.

Eli paid for their drinks with a folded bill, which he handed to the nun with a murmured, "Keep the change." As they walked away, Mallory carried her cup in her gloved hand. So did Eli—such a coincidence. He took her bare hand in his once more, and her heart hopped and bubbles popped—not a coincidence at all.

Behind them, the nuns burst into excited twitters, sounding just like her heart.

"Either they're very excited to see us holding hands," Mallory said, "or you gave them a really big tip."

"I wanted us to be set for refills the rest of the night. We can trade gloves and hold a hot cup with our other hands next." Eli gave her hand a squeeze, a move as casually intimate as that wink.

Hop. Pop.

"Let's get out of this crowd," Eli said. "We're going to get bumped and spill our drinks any second now. We're flirting with danger."

I know I am.

Eli was being so charming, it was going to be hard for a real guy to live up to it on a real date. She had a feeling a fake kiss with Eli would set a new standard that any real kiss wouldn't be able to match. It was a good thing she didn't do fake kisses.

On the other hand, she'd broken half of E.L. Taylor's rules tonight.

Before she returned to reality, why not break one of her own?

Chapter Eight

Never allow yourself to be rushed into a decision.
—How to Taylor Your Business Plan
by E.L. Taylor

They were moving into the adult portion of the evening.

Alcoholic beverages were being drunk. Adult dancers had taken the stage. Eli glanced around the mostly child-free, late-night crowd, shaking his head. The adult portion of anything in Masterson was still shockingly wholesome.

The dancers on the stage were performing German folk dances, a lingering bit of culture from the German settlers who had established towns throughout Central Texas in the 1800s. The stage had been set with a tall maypole, made slightly less anachronous in the month of December by sporting red-and-white ribbons. It was slowly turning into a woven candy cane as men in lederhosen circled in one direction and women in dirndl dresses circled in the opposite direction. The men and women never touched. Wholesome.

Because a large number of Spanish and Mexican people had settled Texas, too, the hungry members of the audience were using their German beers to wash down burritos. And because Texas had been and still was cattle country, those burritos were stuffed with a cowboy standard, barbecued beef brisket. All the facets of Texas blended in a wholesome harmony.

There wasn't much seating available, so the fat branch of a live oak, sprawling low along the ground, was being used by Eli and a dozen other people as a place to sit. He sat closest to the massive trunk, using it as a shield from curious eyes. Eli had the surprising, astonishing Mallory Ames sharing his seat, sitting between his thighs. He'd bought her one-dollar hot chocolate with a one-hundred-dollar bill. He'd hugged her when she'd cried. He'd held her hand as they'd looked for the best spot to sit and talk, because talking was what she did on dates. Nothing that came close to public indecency.

Because they didn't have the tree to themselves, whenever Mallory had something to say, she'd turn her head and murmur it to him. He'd tilt his head to hear her better, and the closeness of her lips to his cheek made him acutely conscious of the possibility that this time, this comment might be the one where the words on her lips became a kiss on his cheek.

Shockingly wholesome.

The bonfire was at his back, so he benefitted from its light, but he didn't have to visually fight the flames. Distance made all the difference, in fire and everything else. Taylor's money was in a bank far away, but Eli had a few hundred-dollar bills in his pocket. Taylor's residences were in Dallas and New York and Monterrey, but Eli was renting a single-family home here in Masterson for the coming semester, a house which had a tree with a rope swing in the front and a porch that overlooked a lake in the back. His superyacht was berthed somewhere along the coast of Greece, but a rowboat lay at the ready by the rented home's dock.

Distance mattered most of all with Mallory, because there was none. *Mallory*—this woman, this incredible person who laughed and cried and talked to him as she made herself at home on his lap—Mallory was the reason he didn't want the night to end.

From the first moment she'd walked up to him, she'd touched him almost constantly. She let him touch her in return, not a sexual *carte blanche*, but he could sit beside her with his arm across the back of the bench. He could hold her hand. He could loop his arms around her waist as she sat on his lap on the branch of a century-old tree. It was so wholesome, so innocent, yet so addictive, satisfying a craving he hadn't known he had.

Can you identify that emotion, Mr. Taylor?

Mallory shifted in her sideways position. Her legs were over his left thigh and her backside was in the vee between his legs, pressing against his inner right thigh. He could feel her muscle flex as she moved, feel her softness against his inner thigh as she relaxed once more. Her denim jeans rubbed and rested against his denim, two thick layers of material that kept their bodies from actually touching. Being denied the feel of her skin, yet being able to feel the intimate motion of her body against his, created an unexpected level of eroticism, here in a small town's park.

She turned to murmur another little something to him. "I think the accordion player has a thing for one of the dancers. He checks her out every time she circles past him, and she's giving her skirt an extra little swirl to show off."

Her upper lip grazed his cheek, a millimeter of her touching a millimeter of him for the space of a single syllable as she spoke. Would this be it? Would this comment end with a kiss?

The distance between them held as she whispered her secret observation, no kiss, not yet—but a fraction of a second before she turned back around, she took a quick little breath. Had that been intentional? Had she snuck in a taste of his body heat, tempted herself with the warmth of his skin?

He'd never in his life wanted to kiss a woman this badly. He'd never imagined it was possible to want to kiss someone this badly.

She wanted to kiss him, too. She'd almost kissed

him a half dozen times this evening, at the hot chocolate stand, between the parked pickups and, yes,
over by the hay bales. He knew her expressions better now, enough to know he hadn't been wrong then.
She wanted to kiss him, but she wouldn't let herself do
it, because she'd told him she didn't give fake kisses.

It wasn't possible for Eli to receive any other kind.
Eli was a fake.

No matter how far Taylor distanced himself from
his real life, he was E.L. Taylor. He always would be,
until the day he didn't narrowly escape death, whether
that happened in seventy years or tomorrow. He was
withholding information from Mallory. He was playing the game unfairly.

Mallory slipped her left arm around his waist,
making herself comfortable. Tomorrow, she would
still be Mallory, wearing business attire to her campus job and studying in her dorm. He would wake up
alone in a six-bedroom lake house and be E.L. Taylor.
Loneliness.

Taylor had spent October and November naming
the feelings he'd known in the years before the terror
of the plane crash: anger, impatience, tension, disgust,
triumph. But he'd overlooked *loneliness*. Even his
expensive therapist had missed it, but it was easy to
identify, now that Mallory had made it go away this
evening. He'd been lonely as E.L. Taylor.

Emotions didn't last forever, not terror, not calm,
not loneliness. But loneliness had been around the
longest, so it was hard to imagine it as temporary. It
wasn't: all the warmth they were building between

them would freeze when he admitted the truth—when he admitted he'd lied. He would be lonely again after this evening.

"Do you see it?" Mallory said under her breath. "Watch."

Taylor—no, he was Eli, for tonight—Eli watched what Mallory wanted him to watch, glad to delay the inevitable. Onstage, the accordion player was looking right through the dancers in front of him for someone else. A female dancer caught his eye, and she gave her apron an extra swoosh, flipping it up a little higher and showing a little more stocking-clad leg as she sashayed past the oompah band, peeking over her shoulder to be sure that one particular musician had appreciated it.

"I see it," Eli said.

Mallory made that rolling gesture. "Practicing, remember?"

He gave an exaggerated sigh. "Why yes, Ms. Fearless, I do see it. It's fascinating, like one of those bizarre mating dances between two birds. Two very large, very German birds."

She pressed into him harder for just a moment, the tree-branch equivalent of her earlier shoulder shoves. "Very funny."

The idea that anyone found him funny was amusing to him, so he had a bit of a smile on his lips when she turned her head toward him and said, "Seriously, you—"

She blinked, a flash of feminine lashes covering a moment of surprise—at what? His smile? Of course he smiled when she was close. With another little catch of her breath, she turned back to the stage to finish her sentence. "You have your moments."

No kiss. Not yet. So close, but they were on a fake date. If he made this a real date, she'd kiss him. He was certain of it.

There was no such thing as a real date with a man who lied about his identity. He was certain of that, too.

Eli silently cursed. If he wanted to make this a real date, if he wanted her to kiss the real man, he was going to have to take her aside after this show, walk with her out to the dark so nobody would recognize him before he had the chance to tell her himself, and then confess that he'd been lying all evening.

Surprise. That would be her first emotion, but then what?

E.L. Taylor was a half billionaire and a half-dozen other things she wasn't expecting. He wasn't a loner; he was popular wherever he went. He wasn't an anonymous guy in a college town; he was a leader in the world of venture capitalism.

Someone farther down the branch got off, making everyone sway for a moment as the tree adjusted to the lighter weight. Between his thighs, he felt Mallory use the muscles in her backside and legs to hold onto him, not the tree. She trusted him not to fall and take her down with him.

She was so relaxed around him, a woman with nothing to hide. She knew which was her public persona and which was her private, and she'd shown him both tonight. He respected her self-awareness.

He wasn't there yet. He had to force himself to dig deeper than surface-level. He wasn't popular; he was famous. The people who looked up to him as a leader were the owners of the start-ups Eli had chosen to invest in. He was resented by those he hadn't helped, feared by those who knew he could buy them, sell them or ruin them at will. He didn't make friends in his line of work.

But he was rich. In his experience, being rich made up for a lot of flaws in every aspect of life. He rarely spent any time with his family, but his parents could live in Monte Carlo because of him, and his siblings, who were twenty-one now, had cars and college degrees and trust funds. He'd heard no complaints about his inability to make Thanksgiving dinner this year. Or last year. Or the year before.

Went it came to girlfriends, being rich was their favorite thing about him. Not being a completely selfish bastard in bed was their second favorite. He couldn't recall a girlfriend having a third favorite thing about him.

You're mildly funny.

Without money, without sex, Mallory liked him. He didn't want to lose that, but the truth would come out. E.L. Taylor couldn't hide on campus for a full semester. She'd see him sooner or later, if only as a face on a poster for the lecture series.

He hugged Mallory a little tighter. She ought to

hear the truth from him, which meant he had to tell her tonight.

The German dancers began turning their circles in the opposite direction, undoing all their weaving. The maypole's ribbons unraveled at a steady, rhythmic pace. Eli's time was running out.

It would be okay. She was going to be angry that Eli had been a trick, even a test, but then she'd be delighted that Taylor was rich. It was always okay, when one had money.

Eli studied Mallory's profile, imagining the way her face would take on that avaricious gleam he was so accustomed to seeing on other faces, the one that let him get away with so much.

He couldn't picture it. When he told her the truth tonight, no greedy glint would come to her eye—but she would know he was looking for it. He'd made it clear that her heroine, Cinderella, wanted wealth to solve all her problems.

He cringed now at the way he'd accused her—accused every little girl, which meant every woman, since they'd all been little girls—of wanting to latch onto Prince Charming for the castles and gowns his money could buy. In Mallory's version of the story, Prince Charming didn't have to be rich. *It's having enough respect for yourself to be with people you can trust,* she'd said, before he'd made her cry, *instead of people who'll lie to you to keep you where they want you.*

He'd lied from the start to keep her with him, to use her as a light in another dark night. Eli wasn't her

Prince Charming. *Choose whichever set of earrings you like* wasn't happiness in her book, but it was all he had to offer. Money, lies, and crippled emotions.

Over, under, around and around the dancers went, unweaving the ribbons until they finished with a twirl that detached them completely. The maypole stood bare. The people applauded.

Eli accepted his fate. This date was for one night only. In a few months, he'd leave Masterson and return to his usual life. He'd fly to Manhattan, he'd return to Dallas, he'd take a business trip to Tokyo, but he'd remember this one night and that one pure kiss. He'd wonder where Mallory was and how she was doing.

And who she was with.

"Tell me about this friend of yours who's coming next semester. Is he still in Ohio now?"

He felt the change in her body, an increase in muscle tension.

"My friend." She traced the seam of her jeans with her finger. With his glove. "My friend would be very disappointed in me if he saw me this evening."

"I imagine if you were my friend, I wouldn't be thrilled to have you spending an evening with another man, either. Not even on a fake date."

"It's nothing like that. He's been my coach."

Sure, it isn't. He'd bet her coach saw it differently. Eli took a moment to brush her hair behind her shoulder as if it had been caught between them. Then he put his arm back around her with a silent F-U to the guy in Ohio. *Eat your heart out, friend. Tonight, for these hours, she's mine.*

"He's very adamant that you should never put all your faults and doubts on display."

Eli shrugged, unimpressed. "That's nothing more than the code of the male locker room. Everyone pretends they'll win the game that day, even in the middle of a losing season."

She turned abruptly in his arms. "Ha. I caught you. That's just faking it until you make it. You've done it, too."

He raised an eyebrow at her, but it was hard to be supercilious in the face of her playful enthusiasm. "I said that was the code of the male locker room. I didn't say I lived by it."

"He does. I do, too, but I pretty much broke that rule five minutes after I met you. I don't know what it was about sitting on that hay bale behind you—"

"Leaning on top of my head."

He hadn't stopped her, because it hadn't felt bad, and not entirely unfamiliar—in a flash, he realized why. The sensation had been similar to carrying his little sister in a piggyback ride. He'd forgotten all about that, until this second. When he was a teenager and they were little children, his brother and sister had climbed all over him like he was their jungle gym.

"—staring at the bonfire. I guess staring at the fire is more likely to make you think deep thoughts than staring at these guys doing this slap-yourself dance.

This is the silliest-looking dance, you have to admit. I couldn't cry about anything right now if I wanted to."

He was aware she was laughing, but the images in his head were too vivid to ignore. His brother, his sister, piggyback rides... Old memories he'd buried so deep, he'd forgotten them. A black lake, a fiery explosion... New memories he wanted to bury deep, but couldn't.

"I shouldn't joke about that, should I?" Mallory sounded subdued.

Eli had to pull himself back to the conversation. Mallory had turned toward him more fully. There was a little wrinkle between her eyebrows as she waited for him to answer her.

"Joke about crying?" he asked, trying to pick up the thread of the conversation.

"I don't want you to think I'm ungrateful. You had to deal with a pretty big crying episode, and you were very kind. I think I cried so hard because I've haven't cried for two years, not since my friend explained all the ramifications of losing your composure like that."

Eli's sister used to lose it every time he had to return to college. He'd pull out of the drive as a little eight-year-old girl wept for him, and he'd feel like a monster for making her wail. He'd stopped coming home as often after his freshman year, only visiting on the big weekends like Thanksgiving, just so he wouldn't make her cry more times than necessary. To this day, he preferred anger to tears. Tonight, he'd tried to get Mallory to rant and rave at him, rather than cry.

He never cried. He hadn't even cried with relief when he'd gotten out of the plane wreck alive. He'd held Mallory to his chest tonight, though, as she'd cried hard enough for the two of them. Maybe he'd felt calm when she'd regained her calm because he'd finally stuck it out long enough to see that crying wasn't as frightening as he'd thought for so long. How could he have been so damned afraid of tears?

Man up. Big boys don't cry. Never let them see that they've gotten to you, son.

Of course, that was it.

It angered him that Mallory's friend was making her afraid to cry, too.

"For two years, you haven't let yourself cry?" he asked.

"I used to lose it over every little thing. Christmas movies. Greeting card commercials. The frustration of trying to get medical records sent to the right hospital."

"One of those things is not like the others."

"I know. But that was before I, um, I met my friend. I decided not to let myself cry about anything, ever. If I won't cry at lost-pet posters, then I won't cry when I'm under pressure to present an important paper at work, someday. I just stopped crying, cold turkey."

"That sounds wrong. What kind of friend prohibits another friend from crying at all for two years?"

"That was my idea. His was not to cry in front of anybody."

If Eli had the chance to go back and hug his eight-year-old sister before he got in his car and returned to college, he'd stand in the driveway and hold her until her tears dried up and she could wave instead of wail. He would have felt better during his drive back to Masterson for having done so. Instead, to avoid feeling bad, he'd avoided coming home to someone who'd wanted a piggyback ride.

That had been the wrong decision, and only now did he see how steep the cost had been. He looked into Mallory's eyes as the loss hit him.

Bye-bye, Eli.

Then he breathed again and cupped the side of her face in his palm. "I don't think this friend's advice is good for you."

"Why not?"

"He sounds like an idiot."

Chapter Nine

Never make the same mistake twice.
                    —How to Taylor Your Business Plan
                                            by E.L. Taylor

"He's *not* an idiot."

Mallory pulled away from Eli's hand with an angry jerk. This was her birthday fantasy. She was not going to let him ruin it by insulting yet another hero. He'd been right about Cinderella, but E.L. Taylor was different.

Eli persisted. "Your friend doesn't know what he's talking about."

"How can you say that? I told you the whole story. He taught me everything, so that I could navigate my family dynamics and get something productive done."

Eli lowered the empty hand that had been cupping her face. "Is it possible he's being manipulative with your emotions by telling you not to react, not to cry?"

"No. It's not."

He's E.L. Taylor, okay? Not an idiot. Also, he's too busy making millions to bother manipulating me.

Eli was dying to say something else, she could tell. He even opened his mouth, thought better of it and closed it.

The crowd broke into applause. The dancers took their bows. The couple beside them on the branch left, probably unwilling to let Mallory and Eli's quietly tense exchange dampen their festive evening.

Eli sounded sincere. "I'm concerned, but I don't want to randomly criticize anyone's hero. Cinderella taught me not to, earlier. It occurs to me that this guy might be your real-life Prince Charming. In that case, your fake boyfriend is jealous, and you should take his words with a grain of salt."

"Oh. That's a very sweet thing to say." Mallory realized she'd touched her fingertips to her heart, like she was a Disney princess. Goodness gracious.

"Somebody's been hitting me over the head with an oilcan all night. I'm glad to know it's working."

That was so charming. She ought to answer a sweet comment like that with a sweet kiss. The gap left by that missing kiss felt awkward to her.

Eli tapped her knee. "So, is he your real boyfriend? You so sagely pointed out that if you'd had a real boyfriend here, you wouldn't have needed a fake one.

That doesn't mean you don't have a real boyfriend somewhere else. Like in Ohio."

"I sincerely doubt he'd ever be interested in me that way."

He's E.L. Taylor. Also, he's too busy making millions to bother dating an in-home caregiver from Ohio.

She was really embarrassed now for having been too embarrassed at the beginning of the night to admit that she thought of a business book as her best friend.

"He's lucky to have someone who jumps to his defense so quickly," Eli said.

She was stuck with her little white lie now. "I defend him because he does mean a lot to me, but not the way you're thinking. His advice pulled me through a really dark time in my life. I might have stayed stuck forever, reliving my past in my head over and over. He showed me that I had to forget about all the years I'd wasted up to that point."

"That doesn't sound right, either. Don't cry? Forget about your life prior to meeting him?"

"Not *forget*. That was my word, not his." She reached up to wriggle her ski cap into place a little, as if that would get her brain working. She was making Eli more concerned. A concerned man was not going to think about her as a desirable woman. If she was going to break her rule and enjoy a hot kiss with this fake boyfriend, she wanted to make it a good one. A kiss of lust, not pity.

She slid off his lap and the tree branch. She stood and faced him, their eyes on a level, so he could see that she was telling the truth. Mostly. He wasn't going to think sexy thoughts about her if she revealed that she loved a book.

She began with the basics. "Never look back."

Eli looked at her sharply.

"That's what he actually said. Not 'forget about the past.'"

Eli came as close to rolling his eyes as a fierce man could. "That is the most overused, trite advice out there."

She glared at him. "I'm trying not to jump to his defense, but you don't have to make it so difficult with your eye-rolling and your insults."

Eli didn't so much as blink for a beat, but then that tenth of a smile touched the corner of his mouth. "Touché."

He crossed his arms over his chest, but it wasn't a negative gesture. He was giving her all of his attention, anchoring himself in place to listen until she was done, and that was a very, very sexy thing for a man to do.

"I thought his advice was wrong, too. Not just 'never look back,' but all of it. He couldn't possibly know what it was like to be me. But I had nothing to lose at that point, so I tried to do things the way he recommended."

She turned her hands palm-up and shrugged. "It worked. I used to daydream about how wonderful my senior year would have been at twenty-one, but the more I wished I could have already graduated, the more likely it was that I would never graduate.

Once I stopped looking back at the goals I hadn't met, I had nowhere else to direct all my energy, except toward the goals I wanted to meet in the future. It worked. Here I am."

Her explanation must have been better this time. Eli's scowl hadn't returned, although his smile had faded. Poor man, so grim.

"That was an excellent explanation of a frequently meaningless phrase," he said. "You should write a book."

"Ha. No." She laced her fingers together, gloved and bare. "I'm pretty sure it's already been written."

"When we sat on the hay bales, you said you aren't as happy as you thought you'd be, now that you'd gotten what you wanted."

The man didn't forget a thing she said. Sexy.

"That's what I planned to think about tonight, all by myself at the Yule log. Then Kappa Lambda and some wet sand and a stolen mitten and this growly statue that turned out to be an interesting man kind of distracted me, but I think I found my answer tonight, anyway."

She stepped closer, standing in between his knees, and placed her hands on his crossed forearms. Bodies—his was so steady, so solid. She'd been touching him all night, wanting to remind herself how to touch a body that didn't need her to fix it.

"I think the reason I'm not happy is because I'm constantly looking forward. The moment I started this semester, I started looking forward to the next semester. When I think about next semester, I'm planning how I'll manage to speak to the right people and get the right things approved, so I can move to the next goal after graduation. Looking forward is more productive than looking back, so it might be the best way to have a successful career, but it's not ever going to bring me happiness."

"What will?" His voice was a low, delicious rumble. They were standing so close that he didn't need to speak loudly at all. It was a heady feeling, being welcome in his personal space.

"Cinderella got this part right, I think. The key is finding your own people. Someone who is kind to you. Someone who enjoys being with you, maybe someone who says you're perfect even when you know perfectly well that you're not. A champion when you're down. An ally. A friend."

She ran her fingertips over the cheek she'd whispered against during the show, then let her thumb rest on his lower lip. "If this was a real date, I would have kissed you about ten times already."

The lip she touched changed shape, slipping into a smile under her thumb. "I thought you spent your real dates talking."

"I do. I spend real ones and fake ones talking. But I only kiss when they're real. It's a shame this is a fake date, because I've never kissed a man with a beard before."

"If this was a real date, I would have shaved for you."

He smiled wider when her thumb skipped across

his lip, a devilish, arrogant smile. He knew he'd flustered her.

She pretended he hadn't. "I don't know if I'd want you to shave. It's hard to imagine what you'd look like without this." She squinted one eye and pretended she was imagining him without the beard, but she was just admiring him. He did broody and untamed so well.

"Mallory." His mouth was serious now. He was going to say something she didn't want to hear.

She pressed her thumb against his lower lip again. "But if you shave for real dates, then the only way to kiss you with a beard is on a fake date. I happen to be on a fake date."

"You're toying with me, Mallory."

"If this is a game, can I choose my prize? Say, a fake kiss with a man who has a real beard?"

"If you like." He stood, and she took a step back. He was tall, strong, an alpha male fantasy in real life. He could pick her up and take her somewhere, anywhere he wanted to, but he only stood over her as she leaned her back against the tree's massive trunk. The stage lights were bright on the other side of the tree, but she could see enough of him, here in the shadows.

He placed his hand on the bark, right beside her head, and braced his arm, reminding her of the opportunity she'd missed by the hay bales. This spot wasn't nearly as private, but if he kissed her the way she wanted him to kiss her, she'd stop thinking about anyone else in the universe, anyway.

"Or," he said, commanding her attention away from his mouth, back to his eyes.

"Or what?"

"Or, you could spend a weekend in my bed. I'd pick you up on a Friday with a clean shave, because a gentleman shaves for a woman. It's much more pleasant for her when she doesn't want me to be a gentleman, and we risk that public indecency charge somewhere along the way, because she's decided she's too impatient to make it to my place. Then…"

Mallory stopped breathing.

Eli leaned in, murmuring words over her lips, her cheek, her ear. "Friday night…happens. Saturday, all of it, day and night. By Sunday evening, you have this beard once more, to do with as you please, anything we haven't done yet, or everything we already have."

Her heart pounded. "Are you toying with me?"

He paused.

"No," he said gravely. "I don't think I am."

He wanted her, genuinely. A weekend in his bed. Such a big part of her wanted it, too, but she couldn't do this for fun, extending a fake date into a weekend fling. She liked him too much. She had a heart. So did he.

"Eli, Eli." She closed her eyes against the passion smoldering in his. "Can you make this evening turn into something real?"

She felt his pause.

"No, I don't think I can."

Just as she felt her heart start to break, he said, "Not yet."

Chapter Ten

*Never fall into the trap of hearing only what
you want to hear.*
—How to Taylor Your Business Plan
by E.L. Taylor

Mallory opened her eyes.

The man who had just whispered the sexiest words
any man had ever whispered to her pushed himself
away from the tree that was keeping her upright after
she'd melted.

Eli shoved some of his hair back. She hadn't even
gotten to mess it up—not yet, anyway.

"When?" she asked.

He shook his head like he didn't know. That was
okay, because she didn't know what she was asking,

exactly. When would he ask her out on a real date? When would he kiss her, unshaven? Shaven?

When would they spend a weekend in bed?

Her whole body had gone up in flames as he'd whispered those words over her skin, because damn if the part of her that would say *I'm not that kind of girl* was utterly losing the battle with *How far away is your place?*

Her place was a dorm. She had tests to study for. Classes to attend. School, that thing she'd planned for and worked for and left everything behind for— that was real. This was a one-evening fantasy, not a one-night stand. Not a weekend with a gorgeous man who'd let her do anything she wanted to with his strong, healthy body.

Eli unzipped his leather jacket and held out his hand. "Want to take a walk?"

"Please." She pushed off the tree, grabbed his hand and started walking, taking big strides, burning off some of this heat.

Was he as hot and bothered as she was? She needed to watch where she was walking in the dimly lit field, but she took her eyes off the ground to peek at him. Their eyes met, and they both laughed, more than a little sheepishly.

"Well," she sighed, "that was a dumb game to play on a fake date that forbids kisses."

"Yes, it was."

She waited a few strides. "You won, by the way. I hate to admit it, but that was exceptional. No wonder you think you're God's gift to women."

Eli threw back his head and laughed, really laughed, and it was contagious and wonderful, and this was the best date Mallory had ever been on, real or fake.

"Where are we going?"

"I'm open to suggestions," Eli said.

"We've pretty much covered the festival. I'm hot-chocolated out. Maybe there will be another musical act."

"All right."

But they kept walking away from the stage, hand in hand, leaving the crowd and the light behind until it got too dark to walk easily. Their steps slowed to a stop.

As if they hadn't been silent for the last few minutes, Eli picked up the conversation. "What were you thinking of doing with me by the hay bales?"

"I was thinking of doing the same thing I was trying to do with you by the tree, Fake Boyfriend with a Beard, but you're playing hard to get."

Mallory was just able to see his face in the starlight. She tilted her head and pretended to be coquettish, which, according to Eli's logic, meant she was actually being coquettish. She batted her eyelashes, which made her feel coquettish whether he could see it or not.

He sounded amused. "You weren't trying to kiss me by the hay bales."

"I thought about it."

"You were pissed off because I was going to kiss

you. The opposite of this moment, where you're pretending to be pissed off because I didn't kiss you."

"Pretending? I'm honestly curious about the beard, and my curiosity has been denied."

"Allow me to refresh your memory. You stuffed my gloves into my jacket, told me you had planned to show me something that didn't require any money, then told me I was a jerk, so forget it."

"Oh, *that*."

"Yes, that. If I'm back in your good graces, let's do that. What is 'that'?"

Since they were facing one another, they were holding both sets of hands now, and Mallory gave them a little swing. "I'll answer your question if you answer mine."

"Trouble," he said on a sigh.

"Allow me to refresh your memory from five minutes ago, when you said, 'not yet.' What are you going to make real, and when?"

"That's two questions—ow."

She'd squeezed his hands hard for doing that big-brother smart-aleck thing again. "But I'm cute," she added through gritted teeth, "so you'll answer two questions."

"Cute is the wrong word—don't squeeze. Pretty. Vivacious. Expressive."

"You mean talkative?"

"Indomitable."

"Ooh, good one. Is sexy in there?"

"Passionate. About many things."

"Yes, but how about sexy?"

Mallory was laughing too much to sound sexy. The darkness made her feel uninhibited. She could say anything, and if she made a fool of herself, it didn't matter because Eli would only be in her life for one night. She'd have no witness to either her weaknesses or her silliness once they parted ways.

Her laughter caught. She didn't want to part ways.

Eli brought their clasped hands up between their chests. Like a large and lazy lion, he dipped his head and ran his jaw along her knuckles.

The sensuality of him, the reality of him, called to her body and filled her mind. It was her birthday, and she was too old to be Cinderella with a sweet prince. She wanted the seduction of the dark, Jane claimed by a legendary man in the wild, Christine spellbound by a phantom.

She tipped her head toward Eli with some vague intent to nuzzle him while he savored the rub of her knuckles on his jaw, but he lifted his head and let go of her hands. She heard his calm inhalation, a steady breath, a deep voice. "Yes, sexy. So sexy, it's killing me."

She spread her fingers wide, her hands freed by his. This was not the time. This was not the place. But this was the man.

"That's excellent news," she murmured. She was rewarded with his laughter and relieved that he broke the spell for her.

She was thinking too dramatically. This one evening was enough. It was a wonderful night. They were having fun, and her life would go back to normal tomorrow. All her plans and goals would still be there, unchanged. *Happy Birthday, Mallory. Stop worrying and enjoy your party.*

She tugged at the hem of her coat, squaring it up. "Seriously, this time. What are you going to make real, and when?"

"Seriously, Mallory Ames—" of course, this man had caught it, the one time she'd used her last name "—I'm in no hurry for this fake date to end, because there will never be another night like this. But when it ends, I want it to end with a good-night kiss. And since you don't do fake kisses, it will have to be real. Me, kissing you, no games."

"I see. When will this happen?"

"When I can't stand not kissing you any longer."

It was intoxicating to be with him. "Then, when the fake date ends with a real kiss, will that be the start of a real date?"

"I don't think it can."

"Why not?"

He didn't answer.

She wouldn't let him go back to being a silent statue, not with her. She placed her hand on his hard arm. "You do see that the phrase 'I don't think it can' means it might happen?"

"It might." Those two words were said in the authoritative voice of *Never*. Subject over, move on.

"Oilcan." Mallory squeezed his arm.

Eli smiled, breaking his statue stance, but it was a sad smile, not even one-tenth sexy. "It might, but even then, it won't be the same as this. Nothing will ever be the same as this, and in the words of a pretty, vivacious, expressive, indomitable, passionate, fearless and perfect woman, this is exceptional."

"You forgot sexy."

"I'm trying not to dwell on it. Thank God you're in a thick wool coat. Take my glove, too. Cover up that naked hand."

It might. She didn't want to hear anything else, not her own voice reminding her that she'd worked for two years to get here, and *here* didn't include an emotionally intoxicating love affair. *Never abandon a good plan.*

Eli's voice returned to the amused, charmed, the perfect man of her fantasy. "Now, tell me what you're going to do to me. Or with me."

"We're going to go make a Christmas wish at the bonfire."

"That sounds very wholesome."

"I'm going to try to make you desperate to kiss me the entire time."

"That won't be very difficult."

Nothing will ever be the same as this.

But the next thing might be even better.

Mallory would find out when Prince Charming finally kissed her good-night.

The fire grew larger.

Eli kept walking closer, Mallory's hand in his own once more.

The sick feeling in the pit of his stomach made him angry. The anger was why he'd come to the park tonight. He knew why the fire sickened him, of course. He'd escaped burning wreckage as water had filled the cockpit. The death he'd faced would have been gruesome, burning up, drowning, both.

His therapist had suggested giving exposure therapy a try if this avoidance of fires continued more than a few months. He'd have Eli begin by looking at fires that were smaller, contained, limiting the exposure to a few minutes. Then a few more, until the sight of flames would no longer cause a spike of anxiety.

Anxiety. He'd let the therapist name that one.

It didn't matter what it was called, Eli was not going to spend months timidly facing little candle flames. The announcements for this Yule log lighting had been on every gas station pump when he'd filled his motorcycle after he'd driven to Masterson. He'd left his staff to deliver his Aston Martin and a more anonymous Ford pickup, but the motorcycle had been his excuse not to fly. This festival had been his excuse to face a bigger fire than he could have built himself. He'd come tonight to face it and be done with it, in one grand episode of exposure therapy.

But a woman in a pink coat and blue hat had stood next to him and started talking. She'd grabbed his arm, argued with him, and even lain on a hay bale to talk to some stars. She was so damned distracting while he was dwelling on demons. Then she'd slid down his body, and he had come alive.

So, he'd lied to keep her by his side tonight, just so she'd make him feel better. Just like her father had done. Just like her aunt and her brother and all the others who were not the key to her happiness. She thought Eli was different.

He wasn't even Eli.

"What are you going to wish for?" She sounded upbeat as they got closer to the fire.

"I'm not going to make a wish."

"You can't go back to just brooding at the fire."

Brooding was a good euphemism for coming to grips with a near-death experience. He liked it. It wasn't exposure therapy. It was brooding.

"I'll watch you make your wish," he said.

I'm going to use you as a way to associate something pleasant with fire.

He was a real prince, all right.

"The table that's selling the wishing papers is over there," she said.

"Selling wishing papers?" It sounded absurd, and it gave him somewhere else to vent his turmoil. "Someone came up with a great marketing scheme to defraud the good citizens of Masterson out of a few pennies."

"Ah, that's the fake boyfriend I first came to know and love and knock upside the head with an oilcan."

Eli chuckled. He actually chuckled as he got closer and closer to a *fire*. That was the kind of miracle Mallory was. He wanted to scoop her into a bear hug and spin her around.

He wanted to kiss her.

Not yet.

He had to tell her the truth first, but he wasn't ready to stop being Eli.

"The wishing papers are free, just to blow your skeptical mind. They do ask for a charity donation, but that's only if you can afford it."

If she only knew... But she'd know soon enough, and it would change everything for her, for him, for them.

"They make super cute blank notes, and they tie a little greenery or something organic to it, to make it easier to throw. The air's always swirling around the fire. Without the weight, everyone would fold up their papers and try to sail paper airplanes at the fire, and you'd have wishes going every which way." Her free hand went every which way, demonstrating out-of-control airplanes. She looked cute, although he'd told her that was the wrong word to describe her, but she was so cute that it took him a second to realize she was talking about fiery airplane crashes.

He needed to keep Mallory in his life. He wanted her to be the woman he made the time to see.

If you need those earrings for next week's event, get them. An arm offered in escort, a hand on the small of her back, a night of sex. *I'll be in Tokyo tomorrow, then back through LA for two days. Let the staff know which dates you'll be in Manhattan. I'll see you then.*

She would never fit into his life. He had to let Mallory go.

Not yet.

She was so into the moment. "I had a great professor my sophomore year. She went through the origins of all kinds of holiday traditions. Throwing the greenery onto the Yule log had nothing to do with weighting wishing papers. Greenery represented life, but you have to wonder, why would you want to burn up life?"

Burn up life. He ignored the roaring flames and concentrated on the little dip in the center of Mallory's upper lip.

"For centuries, you see, *life* was the polite way to refer to desire. Arousal. Sex. Animal appetites. Life."

He nodded. "I get the picture."

"I was trying to get you to picture kissing me."

"I never stop."

"Me, neither, but you're still holding out?"

"It's not time to say goodbye. I can last a long time."

They continued to walk closer to the fire.

"Sorry," Mallory said with a giggle. "A man who lasts a long time was kind of... Anyway. Where were we?"

"The Yule log." For the hundredth time tonight, he could feel a smile teasing the corners of a mouth he'd thought had forgotten how to smile.

"The burning of the Yule log was a winter purification ritual. To atone for all your carnal sins, you could speak them into the greenery, toss them on the log, burn them up and start the new year as chaste and pure as the winter snow."

"I doubt Masterson is ready to have all its residents whispering their dirty secrets into pine boughs."

They'd reached the table. There were only a few scraps of paper and those ubiquitous golf pencils left.

The donation jar was nearly full. It was about to get a one-hundred-dollar bill, anyway. Eli took a moment to fold it so Mallory wouldn't see the number on the bill.

"Don't I know you from somewhere?"

Eli froze at the too-familiar question.

"I'm sure I've seen you before," the female table attendant cooed. "Masterson is such a small town."

He kept his head down, folding the money slowly, *not yet, not like this, please don't let Mallory find out like this.*

"I'm not from Masterson." He didn't make eye contact with the woman as he placed the bill in the donation jar. He knocked a few pencils off the table and bent to get them, buying time, *not yet.*

Mallory's arms came around his neck from behind before he'd stood halfway back up. What was she doing?

"I'm ready for my piggyback ride," she announced.

Ah. He played along. It had been over a decade, but it was like riding a bicycle to stoop low, reach a hand back behind each of her knees and stand.

Mallory lurched over his shoulder awkwardly, a move that let her arm block his face while she chatted up the attendant. "He came to town just for my birthday. He's the best."

Did Mallory know he might be recognized? Did she already know?

The attendant sounded cooler. "Well, good luck."

"Let's go," Mallory muttered.

"Aren't you supposed to take a piece of paper?" Eli muttered back.

"I got one before I met you tonight. It's been in my pocket this whole time."

"Then what was the tip for?" Not that he'd miss it, but he only had so many hundred-dollar bills on him.

"I didn't tell you to put money in the jar. If you don't want to make a wish, just grab some greenery. I'm sure you have a carnal sin or two in your past you can whisper into it."

"Nothing to repent."

"Sounds boring. You can wish for a more exciting year." She reached down and grabbed a pine bough. "Giddy-up."

He carried her closer to the fire, relieved, exasperated, loving the weight of her on his back, hating the blinding yellow blaze in the night. It was hard to ruminate over it—or anything—with Mallory's arms around his neck.

"You're choking me."

"Sorry." She let go and slid down his back to a stand.

He turned around to face her the second her toes touched the ground. "Why did you do that? Hide my face?"

Please, God, let her have known all along.

He would kiss her right this second if she said she hadn't wanted the public to recognize him, if she'd known all along he was E.L. Taylor—if *that* man was the one she meant each time she said *You're mildly funny.*

"I was trying to substitute for your coffee cup."

"You...what?"

"Whew. This fire is really putting out some heat." She twirled the pine bough, peeking up at him as she spoke. "You used your cup to hide your face tonight, more than once. You didn't want to walk down the row of booths. You kept leaning back on the branch to keep your face in the tree trunk's shadow. When you knocked those pencils off the table, I knew you weren't comfortable with someone seeing your face. It's not a big deal to me. I wanted to help."

She didn't know who he was.

"That was—" It was so hard to keep the disappointment out of his voice. "That was very thoughtful of you."

It had been very generous of her to use her own body to shield him through an imagined phobia.

It was the wrong type of anxiety: he was using her to feel alive in the presence of a bright fire and a black night. He was using her to avoid being E.L. Taylor, the man who'd so ruthlessly killed off all the parts of his life that hadn't fit his vision of being the man who had it all.

He didn't.

Eli had more. Eli had piggyback rides. One-dollar cocoa. Tree branches and silly conversations. Darkness and seductive conversations. The ability to soothe a friend when she felt so sad, she cried. Eli had received a single, real kiss. But it was all too new, too fragile to hold on to if he lost her. He would fall right back into being E.L. Taylor.

"I don't know why you hide your face," Mallory said, brushing his cheek with the pine bough to catch his attention. "It's a very handsome face, and even the thickest beard and shaggiest hair can't change that. Your eyes will always be Paul Newman blue. I hope you add laugh lines. Not frown lines."

She did not know just how fake of a fake boyfriend he was. He was going to have to tell her and kill a perfect night. But, before they parted ways, he was going to kiss Mallory—*he* was, not this imaginary Eli.

Me, kissing you, no games.

Unless she slapped him in his handsome face, called him the liar he was and walked away.

He did have a wish, after all.

I wish this evening could have a better ending than I deserve.

Chapter Eleven

Never abandon a good plan.
> —How to Taylor Your Business Plan
> *by E.L. Taylor*

There was a crowd around the white picket fence.

The adult crowd took turns pelting the Yule log with their wishes—or trying to. The heat of the fire created its own little wind system, which caught the ribbons and leaves on the papers and diverted them from their target. People lingered after throwing their wishes to watch the crazy acrobatics their neighbors' wishes performed.

Eli would have to snake his way through the crowd to get Mallory up to the fence for her throw. He felt the danger of it. *Don't I know you from somewhere?*

"I don't want to join their reindeer games," Mallory said. "Let's go around the sandpit to the other side. It's too hot this close to the fire, anyway." She unbuttoned her pink coat and started walking, certain he wouldn't disagree, probably certain he would be relieved.

Eli gritted his teeth at her thinly veiled attempt to shield him from a weakness he didn't have. But, since he did need to avoid the crowd if he wanted to have her all to himself, he could say nothing.

He escorted her along the long line of volleyball courts with a hand at the small of her back. Her coat was unbuttoned, but the double-breasted peacoat style didn't fall open. Still, he got a glimpse of a thin, white sweater underneath, a delicious peep, as erotic as catching a glimpse of lingerie.

"You know…" She was uncharacteristically hesitant. "My friend who's coming to MU next semester…? He's got a lot of good tips for how to make plans to handle obstacles when they arise."

That bastard. Eli prayed he never saw the two of them together, her and her little Ohio friend strolling across the campus.

"Like what?" he asked. "Don't cry? Forget they're there?"

She snapped her mouth shut at his caustic questions.

Damn it. He hated that guy.

"Does he even have any accreditation in psychology or psychiatry?" Eli asked. *Never take advice without considering the source.*

"No. Do you?"

He frowned at her petulant tone. "I'm not the one who is advising people on how to deal with their families and handle their emotions. If he doesn't have credentials, then he's a quack with all that 'Don't cry' stuff."

"Yes, you are advising me how to feel. You just advised me to distrust his advice, although his advice is working for me. I think it could help you, too."

"The face thing isn't what you think it is. I'm okay there." He had issues everywhere else.

"He wrote a book," Mallory said, an earnest disciple defending a god. "I hate that I called you a man without inspiration. I hate that you agreed it was true. Maybe you'd be inspired by the same book that inspired me."

Eli stopped and looked at her closely, wanting to see every nuance in her expression. He had a memory for detail, and he knew how she'd looked just before she'd pitched that crumpled cup at the barrel and cried over Cinderella. She looked almost as frustrated again, now.

"This guy is your hero, isn't he?" Eli was jealous. Flamingly, blazingly jealous.

"His book changed my life. He's going to be a featured author this semester. You don't have to be a student to go to a book signing. You could come with me and meet him, too."

"Meet him, too? You've never met him?" All that searing jealousy was smothered so quickly that Eli laughed in relief. "Who is he? Dr. Phil?"

She rolled her eyes.

He reached out to tug down her ski cap. "Never meet your heroes. It's one of the oldest adages around for a reason. He can't live up to your expectations. He's going to disappoint you. It always happens that way."

Ask any entrepreneur who couldn't convince me to invest in his start-up.

She fixed her hat as if he hadn't straightened it right. "I'm not going to meet him as my hero. I'm going to meet him as his equal."

"You're Dr. Phil's equal?"

She turned on her heel and marched off, a complete ninety-degree turn from where they'd been headed.

"Whoa. No, no, no—I didn't mean it like that." He caught her and turned her in his arms to look into her eyes, because if he'd made her cry again, he was going to hate himself.

She looked furious, thank God.

"I don't appreciate you laughing at me."

"I wasn't, I swear I wasn't." He caught her to him in a quick hug, then held her just a little way from himself, cupping her face in his two hands. He ran his thumbs over her perfectly beautiful, perfectly dry cheeks. His thumbs had to feel cold to her, because her cheeks were warm, like her heart. Her personality.

Warm. It wasn't an emotion. It was this woman.

"I'm laughing at the idea that he could be *your* equal. Nobody can compare to this person I'm looking at right now. You're like a bright piece of a star in this world. I was standing alone in the dark tonight, and this star just dropped out of nowhere and landed right beside me, and I'm so damned lucky that I got to be with you." He kissed the cold cheek under his thumb. He kissed her nose, he kissed the corner of her eye, which should only earn laugh lines in her life.

"Eli." She said his name like a litany. "Eli, Eli."

It's Taylor. He froze as he was, cupping her face in his hands. *It's Taylor, the man who's been lying to you. The man who divides his time between Manhattan and Tokyo, not a college town. The man who wears suits and ties, who has a sharp haircut, a shaved face. I have no friends. I've lost touch with my family. I've been crippling myself emotionally to fulfill my business goals, and I didn't realize it until I plunged from the sky into a lake.*

"Eli." She had stars in her eyes as she touched his face, too. "It might work out? It might? There is no way you can say these beautiful things to me and think that I wouldn't change my plans to be sure they included you."

The stars in her eyes were the reflection of the bonfire at his back. It could warm him, or it could burn him.

It's Taylor.

He rested his forehead on hers. "I don't know how to make this night turn into something real."

"You know how. You said it yourself. You just kiss me, and I'm yours. Me, kissing you, no games."

She was right. The game was over. To hell with Eli and screw Taylor, he was just himself, a man who wanted this woman. Now.

"Come with me." He grabbed her by the hand and headed into the darkness.

"To where?"

Somewhere private. He was going to have to tell her who he was, and then he was going to kiss her with everything real he had, until she couldn't think about his lies or his money or anything but him.

Afterward, he was never going to let her go. He had money, damn it. He could get anything he wanted, even a girl who thought Prince Charming would still be her choice if he were poor.

There was nowhere private to go in this park. Every tree had a couple under it, every bench was being used by the adults of Masterson, who weren't as wholesome as he'd thought. The hay bales were too far away, but it was a sure thing that another couple had already found dark privacy behind them, anyway.

"Right here." He stopped in the open field and turned to her in the dark, stepping close, ready to give her his real identity in the quickest and most passionate confession he could manage, but she didn't wait for the first word.

Mallory kissed him. She pulled him close, holding him tightly, stepping on his foot in her rain boot.

He didn't care. Her coat was open, so he could slip his arms around her waist for the first time. After a night of thick denim and thicker wool between them, this was so much more access, so much more to touch, that it felt like a great intimacy to feel the curve of her waist under the softness of a white sweater.

They deepened the kiss, mouths opening, tongues mating, tasting, wanting more.

"All right, folks. That's enough. Park closes in half an hour."

They broke the kiss and turned toward the voice, still clinging to one another tightly. Eli cursed in disbelief. A uniformed officer was walking toward them with his arms wide open, herding all of the kissing couples out of their cozy hideaways.

"Take it on home, everybody. We're closing this part of the park. Head toward the main gate, folks. Last call at the beer tents. Don't drink if you're driving."

"Oh, my God." Mallory squeezed Eli so hard her voice came out in a squeak. "We're going to get arrested for public indecency."

With a burst of laughter, Eli picked her up and spun her around under the stars.

"Don't make me dizzy. I've never tried to outrun a cop before."

"Let's go. I know a place we can use as our hideout." He set her down and took her hand. He'd take her to his rented house. He'd tell her everything there, and then he'd make love to her for hours in a four-poster bed, until the sun rose over the lake. Someday, when they made love by the Aegean Sea, they'd agree the lake had looked more beautiful.

Mallory tugged him in the direction of the bonfire. "I don't care where we go, as long as I get to make my wish first."

"As you wish."

"You're getting funnier."

They stopped at the edge of the sandpit to the side of the fire, away from the crowd, and she pulled her paper wish out of her pocket, holding up a folded square with a pine cone tied to it. "You'll notice I don't have any greenery on mine." She lowered the paper and said in a stage whisper, "Very boring year." Then she held up the pine cone again. "I wrote this when I first got here, hoping for a more exciting semester, because my friend would be on campus and everything."

"Yes, the inimitable Dr. Phil."

"Very funny." She bumped him with her shoulder, a move he hoped she repeated ten thousand more times in his life. "But I can tell it's going to be a more exciting year than I dreamed. I've already narrowly escaped the cops."

He wanted her in every way, all at once. He wanted her body under his hands—*hurry up*. He wanted to stay here and flirt over wishes—*take your time*. He wanted her, full stop.

"Does the pine cone represent any other type of overindulgence in your near future?" he asked with a wink.

"A pine cone means I passed my science classes, and I understand the concept of aerodynamics. Those green boughs are like fans. Everyone's missing when they throw tonight because they're trying to throw fans. This will make a better missile."

The air near the sandpit was swirling as the fire's heat hit the cold air. One of those swirls took the paper right out of Mallory's hand. She tried to grab it. Missed. The pine cone pulled it down to land with a thunk in the sandpit.

"Serves me right for bragging," she said.

"I've got it." Eli crouched down and reached for it, only one corner close enough to touch with his fingertips. He snagged it and shook the sand off, making it unfold. As he turned toward Mallory, her handwriting was clear in the firelight, simple words written in dark pencil lead.

I hope E.L. Taylor will like me.

He stared at it.

His first thought was *Of course, I do.*

But he hadn't told her his real name yet.

His second thought was *She knew all along, thank God.*

But she hadn't. She would have told him when she'd helped him hide his face.

He finally saw the truth. Her hero was him. Her book was his book.

It couldn't be. He didn't mention families. He didn't tell anyone not to cry. What the hell would that have to do with business planning?

Never show your doubts to the world.

He'd written that, yes, but he hadn't meant that she shouldn't talk about her worries with her own grandfather, for God's sake. She was going to be so embarrassed when he taught that chapter. He'd seen the two years of tears she'd bottled up by mistake. He'd touched them with the fingertips that held this paper.

She snatched the paper away. "You didn't read it,

did you? If you tell anyone your birthday wish, it won't come true. It's not that I'm superstitious, but I want everything to go just right next semester. Two years is a big investment." Mallory was blushing now, her color high in the bonfire's light.

If she only knew… But she'd know soon enough, and it would change everything for her, for him, for them, even more harshly than he'd known it would.

She folded the strip of paper and wrapped the pine cone's ribbon tightly around it. "I'm still going to throw it. If the birthday wish mojo is gone, I've still got the Christmas thing going for me."

She raised her arm, took aim, and threw it hard at the Yule log.

Bull's-eye.

It turned to ash almost instantly, becoming part of the smoke that carried it out to the universe.

"Well, that's that." Mallory sighed beside him, her face turned up to the smoke and stars. "I guess we'll just have to see what happens next."

Chapter Twelve

The End.

—How to Taylor Your Business Plan
by E.L. Taylor

Eli lingered under a pecan tree near the main gate.

Mallory was happy to linger with him. This particular pecan had been strung with multicolored Christmas lights. They looked beautiful in the night, and they didn't cast much light on the two people below. That was probably why Eli had stopped here, to keep his face in the shadows, waiting for the bulk of the crowd to clear the main gate before he took her… somewhere. With him.

She remembered his seductive words, his husky

voice when he'd spoken over her skin under the massive oak tree. *And then, Friday night…happens.*

She'd melted into a puddle then.

She could melt so easily now, if only Eli didn't look so grim.

"The crowd will clear out soon," she said.

He remained silent.

"Are you worried about something?" *Because I am.*

Eli was studying her as if she were some exotic bird who had landed near him.

No, I'm your very own piece of a star.

He broke his silence with words that sounded portentous. "I meant what I said, that you had no equal. This man who wrote a book you believe in—"

"I won't get a complex over Dr. Phil, I promise." She tried to lighten the tone.

"You're determined to meet him, although conventional wisdom tells you not to."

She didn't know if he was asking her or telling her this. "The rest of 'never meet your heroes' is 'wait until they are your equals.' I think we're equal enough. He has a college degree from Masterson. I almost have a college degree from Masterson. He also has a Harvard MBA, but still, we're equal-ish. When he was twenty-nine, he owned dozens of companies and sat on the board of dozens more. Now I'm twenty-nine, and I have the idea for a company."

"I wasn't aware of that."

She clapped her hands together, ready to break this strange mood. "Look. I know you read that wish, so we both know who I'm talking about. It might seem like a long shot, but I think I can convince E.L. Taylor to invest in me. I told you I'm faking it, but only some of it. There's no way I'd want him to know that my family was able to manipulate me into that huge gap between my junior and senior years. He'd be concerned that I could be that gullible again about something that would affect a new company, but I absolutely know I won't be. Everything else, all the research, all the numbers I've run, everything will be solid. I have a good chance."

Eli's intense scrutiny was unnerving.

She tried for humor. "Nobody needs to know I'm wearing my grandmother's clothes or my sister-in-law's shoes."

When that didn't get even one-hundredth of a smile, she slipped her arm around his waist, just to prove to herself that he was no longer that remote man who'd first shaken her touch from his sleeve.

"It was a dumb wish, wasn't it? I should have said I hope he'll give me a specific amount of venture capital. I was feeling emotional, I guess. But if you think about it, nobody invests in someone they can't stand to be around."

"Your goals aren't dumb." Eli stepped away and turned to face her squarely. "Why did you trust me with all of this tonight? A perfect stranger?"

"Eli, what are you talking about, exactly? I feel like I'm missing something here."

"You told me your doubts. You let me see your tears."

"The tears happened despite myself. Then I told myself that it wouldn't hurt anything if you saw me at my worst, because you were going to disappear after tonight. I'm so glad you're not going to disappear now, because you've brought out the best, too. I didn't know I could have as much fun as I've had tonight."

"But it was fun for one night," Eli said. "A fake date from the start."

"Yes, but now that we've ended our fake date with a real kiss…" She trailed off at his expression.

"That was the goodbye kiss, as we knew it would be."

She stepped close and put her hands on his chest. "It was real. You, kissing me, no games." She tried for a smile. "Until the cops came."

He softened the tiniest bit. "We said 'it might' turn into something real, and I'm very sorry it didn't."

She slipped her arms around his waist, locking him in tight. "We've been happy together, all night. Talk to me. Tell me what happened."

"Fearless Mallory." He reached behind his back, grasped her wrists and freed himself, but he didn't let go of her. He bent his head and rubbed his cheek along her hand, just once. A farewell.

A whisper was all she could manage. "You're breaking my heart. Don't disappear. Won't we see each other again?"

"If we do, you won't see me the way you do now, not the way you have tonight. You may not like me at all. I want you to know, I'll never forget the perfect date that Eli had with Mallory. There will never be another night like this. Thank you."

After a brief, hard squeeze of her hands, he let go and walked away.

"Eli!"

He kept walking.

What can I do? What should I do?

"Wait. I have your gloves." She held out her hands, palms up, begging him to come back and get them. "Eli!"

He glanced back over his shoulder. "Keep them."

Then he merged into the crowd and left her under the pecan tree, all alone.

Taylor straddled his bike wearily. Every limb of his body weighed a ton. It didn't matter. The next time he saw Mallory, she would hate him.

He wouldn't be Eli. He'd be Taylor. *E.L. Taylor.* Mr. Taylor.

He wasn't anyone's hero.

The farther he drove from the park, the darker his thoughts got. No Mallory, no light—there was nothing to distract him any longer from cold reality. He was the empty, callous son of a bitch who stared at fires and couldn't sleep. And when Mallory Ames came to find him in January, she was going to be devastated to learn that her hero was nothing more than that. *Never meet your heroes* might have been the only intelligent advice he'd ever given.

He came to an intersection and stopped. To the right was Greek row, the street where most of MU's fraternity and sorority houses were located. A little flicker of something came back to life inside him. It wasn't joyful, but it made him feel alive. He turned right.

It was obvious which house was Kappa Lambda. They'd erected ten-foot-tall Greek letters on their lawn to identify themselves. Judging by the crowd on the lawn and the number of people with red Solo cups in their hands, the odds were that at least one of those letters would be knocked flat on its face before the night was through.

Taylor killed the engine and took off his helmet. Then he just sat, one foot on each side, keeping the bike balanced, waiting until he saw them.

Mallory had asked him if his peripheral vision was a superpower. Others in his past had remarked on his ability to recall visual details. He just had to recall the scene, and it was like looking at a photograph. He could zoom in on different details, like the three fraternity brothers in burgundy hoodies, one in corduroy pants, one in khaki board shorts, one in jeans. White sneakers on all of them.

There they were.

He waited, knowing he was out of place, knowing the people closest to him on the lawn were starting to point and whisper. When the three boys spotted him, Taylor kicked the bike's stand into place and dismounted. The three lacked his ability—and Mallory's ability—to fake being cool and calm under stress. The moment they realized where they'd seen him tonight was comically obvious.

Taylor walked directly toward them. The party-goers in his way scattered like minnows as a shark swam through their school. Girls then stopped at a safe distance to devour him with their eyes. The boys pretended they didn't notice him, so they wouldn't have to challenge his right to walk where he wanted to walk.

Taylor stopped less than an arm's distance from the three he'd come for. "Allow me to introduce myself. I'm E.L. Taylor."

They were mute.

"This is how it's going to go down. First, you're going to hand me my girlfriend's mitten. Second, we're going to have an educational conversation about the appropriate way to ask a woman to spend her time with you. Lastly, and this one will be in effect for the rest of your time at this university, when you see me anywhere on campus, including your own fraternity house, you'll get out of my sight. Are we clear?"

They exchanged nervous glances with one another, quickly coming to the correct conclusion that they should go along with anything E.L. Taylor suggested. After all, he was known for his plans.

"Let's begin. Step One."

He watched as two of them scrabbled in their pockets while the third hissed, "Do you still have it?"

Taylor held out his hand, and the mate to Mallory's lonely mitten was placed in his palm. "Step Two. How many times should you invite a woman to spend the evening with you?"

They looked at one another again. The one in corduroy ventured a timid answer. "None?"

"Once, boys." Taylor gave them the same look he gave someone who was about to be fired for gross incompetence. "You invite her out once. If she says yes, you have the chance to show her your best side, such as it is. If she says no, then leave her the hell alone. Don't be a pain in the ass and ask her out ten more times. Don't be a criminal and stalk her. Once."

They mumbled some *yes, sirs.*

"Step Three," Taylor said.

They stared at him. He gave them a minute to let their beer-soaked brains recall the itinerary he'd laid out.

He unzipped his jacket and tucked Mallory's mitten into the inner pocket. Then he zipped it up and looked at the boys who were still gaping at him.

"I said *three.*"

They turned tail and ran.

Eli returned to his bike, put on his helmet and checked his gas gauge. He already knew he wouldn't sleep tonight. He might as well burn up another tank of fuel.

The cursor blinked on Mallory's computer screen. She changed it from a white arrow to a black one.

She watched it for a moment, a stationary thing, unexciting. Uninspiring.

It's not supposed to be inspiring. It's a cursor.

She changed it from a black arrow to a hand.

Eli, where are you? Are you okay? What happened?

She'd gone to the Yule log three nights in a row, Sunday, Monday and Tuesday, hoping he'd be there. He hadn't been. She shouldn't go tonight.

She changed the cursor back to a white arrow.

She probably would go, anyway.

"Is that him?" The woman in the cubicle to her right, Gladys, was a full-time employee, not a student. Her whisper was full of excitement, like she'd just spotted some juicy gossip. That was how Gladys always sounded, because she always sought out juicy gossip when she should be working.

Mallory stared at her screen glumly. It wasn't like she had room to criticize. She'd been staring at cursors for ten minutes.

"It can't be." The answering whisper came from another cubicle. "But whoever he is, I'm glad he walked in the door."

Mallory ignored her coworkers and got back to typing. This basic data entry was simple drone work that did nothing to divert her from reliving a goodbye under Christmas lights. And reliving it. And reliving it, daily, during the longest week of her life.

"Is he in a motorcycle gang or something? Say yes. That look is hot."

"He's hotter than a man has a right to be, already. He doesn't need to dress it up in leather, but I'm not going to complain, either."

"Oh, I hear you. Totally agree."

Mallory looked around. The excitement spreading from cubicle to cubicle was almost tangible. Everyone had stopped working, men and women, both. At the end of the row of cubicles, even Irene, the senior administrative assistant, had opened the glass door of her office and come out to see…something.

Mallory gave up and stood. Whoever had just walked in was causing enough of a stir that it might take her mind off *him*.

It was him.

Eli had found her. She must have said enough about her job for him to deduce where she worked. He'd *searched* for her.

With a little skip of happiness, she headed down the row of cubicles. He was walking toward the dean's office, his expression deadly serious. She wanted to head him off before he asked her boss if a woman named Mallory worked here.

His profile was just the same as when she'd first seen him. Stern, even grim. Silent, even while he was being greeted by the dean, shaking the hand he was offered.

Shaking hands with the dean?

Mallory stopped.

Irene stepped away from her glass door with her most gracious smile for—for *Eli*. She gestured toward the door of a currently empty private office, the one that was reserved for January and the arrival of the Executive-in-Residence.

The woman sitting in the cubicle where Mallory had stopped reached up and tugged on her sleeve. "Don't you dare go ask for an autograph. Irene will kill you."

The warning was unnecessary. Mallory couldn't

go anywhere. She was sunk shin-deep in quicksand, and going under.

Her Eli, her rugged and sexy and unsmiling Eli, who could be so charming if he only had a little oil-can for that rust, *that* Eli walked down the hall with Irene and the dean. As the dean kept up his effusive welcome, Eli turned his head and looked right at her. No flicker of surprise, no jolt of recognition crossed his face.

He hadn't needed to look her way at all, because he'd probably seen her just fine in his peripheral vision. But he'd turned his head; he wanted her to be certain that he knew she was there. Then he turned away.

Eli had no intention of acknowledging her, for he was a multi-millionaire, and she was a student working part-time to pay off her tuition.

They were not equals. He had already known that on Saturday night. She had not.

E.L. Taylor followed the dean into his new office and shut the door.

Chapter Thirteen

Learning Objective: Establish the parameters within which the business will operate.
            —Senior Year Project *by Mallory Ames*

"I quit."

Mallory hissed the words under her breath.

The pointing-hand cursor blurred with her tears.

You must continue to play when the game isn't fair, or you'll never win.

There was no game left to play. She'd wanted so badly to meet him—a man who'd written a book which stated that she should never meet him, not unless she waited until they were equals. She'd been so determined to break that rule. For two years, it had inspired her to take action.

Meet E.L. Taylor? *Meet him?* She'd kissed him, damn him.

It was so horrifically clear. She'd been open and honest with him, more than she'd been with anyone, even with her grandpa. She'd confessed to everything, from being a fool for her family to raiding her dead grandmother's closet. He was the one person who knew that every detail about her, even her appearance, was a lie.

She'd babbled to the stars about birthdays and wasted years, while he'd sat silently on the next hay bale over. She'd drunk hot chocolate next to him— oh, what a fool she'd been, saying she'd buy him a cup if she could. She'd been so careful not to make him spend too much. *Just the hot chocolate. I don't need a cookie to go with it.*

It had amused him, no doubt. He'd enjoyed spending an evening with a woman who was too dense to realize who he really was.

He was the hero whose philosophy she'd passionately defended throughout the evening, and he had egged her on, challenging her to explain his own rules. But after he'd read her wish, his mood had changed. He must have realized his little masquerade had gone too far. He'd left her under a pecan tree before she could fall in love with him and slobber all over him like a loyal Labrador.

I quit.

She wanted to scream it.

She couldn't. She had nowhere else to go, nowhere else to live, no way to get there if she did. She'd given everything up to be here at Masterson University, right here, right now. She couldn't quit. She'd starve.

Those were real-life stakes which the great E.L. Taylor had never faced. His *face*. She'd helped him to hide his face from a perfectly nice charity volunteer who'd started to recognize him.

Why hadn't Mallory recognized him?

She dove under her desk for her backpack, jerked the zipper open and dug for her book. His book.

She flipped the book over. The photo on the glossy book jacket was so familiar to her. Eli didn't look anything like it. Even now, she had to know what she was looking for to see any resemblance. His eyes in the black-and-white photo weren't that startling silver blue, of course. Just a dark gray. Too dark— the photographer must have touched them up so they wouldn't appear too light or white.

That smile—so polite, so empty. Nothing like Eli when he threw back his head and laughed.

She glared at the photo, her eyes blurring again, of course, because she was upset, damn it. She had seen this smile on Saturday night. Early on, when he'd stiffly suggested she return to her friends and family at the festival, this practiced, cold smile had given her a moment of déjà vu. Through the beard and shaggy hair, through the flames reflected in his eyes and the bitter set of the lines in his face, she'd recognized that empty smile.

Yoga breaths. She couldn't freak out in her cubicle.

She shoved the book into her backpack and placed her hands on the keyboard. She was on the clock;

she'd better work. She needed this job, because she needed the financial aid package it was part of. She needed the financial aid to cover her tuition and discount her dorm, because she needed to finish her degree, because she needed the clout it would give her when she met with investors. It was all a cascade of steps. E. L. Taylor had taught her that.

The very last step was supposed to have been his investment in her new business. She'd designed a better way to match caregivers and clients, a better way to meet the needs of both, but there was no conceivable way she could present it to him now. He'd be able to point to every part she'd already told him was weak. He'd laugh at her.

No, he wouldn't laugh at her. She wouldn't give him the chance. She would never speak to him again.

One minute later, without having pressed a single key, she dove under her desk again for her backpack and pulled out her book. The man in the photo was different in more ways than being clean-cut and clean-shaven. His expression was untroubled, unconcerned as he paused to look into the camera. It was the same expression she'd seen in his photos in business journals.

Nobody else in her family enjoyed *Shark Tank* and its discussions of valuation and equity, but Mallory had watched clips of her hero's guest appearance on her cell phone. He'd been polished, remote, somewhat amused.

The man she'd met last week was hardened. It had been a struggle for him to interact with her at all, at first. She'd left him to his brooding, but he'd come after her, offering to buy her hot chocolate, wanting a chance to speak in complete sentences to a fellow human being. His sense of humor and his charm had gotten rusty with disuse. Because...

Why? What had made the man in this photograph turn into the angry man she'd run to for protection?

I don't care. He lied to me.

She tossed the book onto a stack of completed paperwork in the corner of her cubicle.

That pile wasn't going to get any higher today. Mallory couldn't sit here until quitting time, waiting for the office door to open and Eli to walk out.

Eli. Had that been a joke, too? E.L. sounded close to *Eli.* That must have made it easier for him to keep up the pretense.

She was a dunce.

Mallory logged out of her work profile. Students were allowed to modify their work hours for academic necessities, when exams needed to be studied for and special projects were due. She had a special project: find a new hero.

She zipped up her backpack and headed for the door, leaving her book behind.

"Mallory. Mallory!"

Mallory jumped a mile at the tap on her shoulder. She'd started wearing headphones after last Wednesday, when *Mr. Taylor* had surprised everyone by appearing weeks ahead of schedule. The music prevented her from listening for office doors opening and closing down the hall as the bigwigs like Mr. Taylor came and went at their leisure. This had made her a little less tense throughout the workday. She blended right in with the other interns who'd been doing it all semester.

Still, she was embarrassed that her supervisor had to physically tap her on the shoulder to get her attention, even if her peers had to be tapped all the time. Her peers were generally nineteen.

Mallory tugged on the string to her earphones, letting them fall into her lap with a little plastic clatter. "I'm sorry, Irene. Could you repeat that?"

Irene handed her a set of forms. "I need you to complete this, print a fresh copy and deliver it to Mr. Taylor."

"Oh...no. I can't. I'm busy."

Irene looked at Mallory's monitor. "Busy doing what? Processing transcript requests? For goodness's sake, take care of this first. Mr. Taylor is waiting."

Mallory dutifully spread the forms out on her desk, but the moment Irene's office door clicked shut, Mallory opened a desk drawer and pulled out her mini cosmetics bag, the one she kept for touch-ups throughout the day to maintain her professional appearance.

She'd been having huge debates with herself every morning on what to wear. Nothing as mundane as deciding which blouse would go with which skirt. Instead, she'd had to decide if she should wear business attire at all. She changed her mind daily.

Eli—Mr. Taylor—knew she wasn't required to

wear it. He knew it was her silly way to pretend she had a job that required her to dress like an executive. Since he knew she was faking it, she should no longer try to fake it.

On the other hand, she was so angry with Mr. Taylor for all the wisecracks he'd made about not meeting her hero if they weren't equal, she was going to dress like an executive if he was going to dress like an executive.

The daily debate gave her an outlet for her angry emotions. She pulled things out of her microscopic dorm room closet, tossed them on her institutional twin bed, made a mess and blamed Eli. She was afraid if she stopped dwelling on the trivial and started remembering how he'd hugged her while she'd cried, her tears would start again and never stop.

This morning, dressing like an executive had won. She completed the forms in a ridiculously easy five minutes, hit Print, and touched up her powder and lipstick.

Ready to enter the lion's den? You can do this.

Mr. Taylor kept the blinds on his glass door closed. She hadn't seen him since he'd walked into the office last Wednesday and given her the shock of her life. She braced herself for the sight of him, then knocked.

"Come in."

She hadn't braced for the sound of his voice. Her heart fluttered like a wounded bird in her chest. *Come in* was spoken by the same voice that had said *There will never be another night like this one.*

She couldn't think about that. She had to deliver these forms.

There was nothing to it. She merely had to turn the doorknob, walk steadily across the carpeting in her sister-in-law's cast-off classic pumps, place the forms on the corner of the executive desk, refuse to think that it was about as wide as the space between two parked pickup trucks in a dark field, turn around and leave.

She did it.

"Miss Ames."

She had her hand on the doorknob, ready to pull it shut behind herself.

"Stop."

She did not.

The door shut.

Taylor threw his pen onto his desk, cursing under his breath.

Now he was going to have to come up with yet another stupid task to get her back in here. He couldn't walk out to the open reception area's cubicles and strike up a conversation. Everyone would be listening. Everyone would wonder how in the world they knew each other, which was precisely what they needed to talk about.

He glared at the door that hid her from his view.

He knew she hated the sight of him, but he did not hate the sight of her. It had been a week since he'd first walked into the offices of the university's school of business. In that week, Mallory had stayed hidden in a cubicle that was almost in the back corner of the open reception area. He hadn't managed to be within speaking distance until now, when he'd manipulated her to make it happen.

He stared at the door. For perhaps six seconds, she'd been here, live and in person. He could recall the image now, every detail, an image so different from the others he had of her.

She'd been so very pretty in the park while dressed in pink, but she was stunning in a professional environment. Her hair was smoothed into an updo. Her trim skirt and tailored blouse looked as good today as they had in the days of Jackie Kennedy and *Mad Men*. If he hadn't known they were her grandmother's clothes, he never would have guessed.

She wore black high heels. Red lipstick. It wasn't a high-maintenance look, but a professional, powerful look. Stud earrings—pearls. A ring on her right hand, a blue stone, a tiny chip of a thing, nothing like the rocks he could provide. It was probably her birthstone. She'd turned twenty-nine this December, and he had been there for it, her fake boyfriend for one night. He wished it could have been more.

You knew from the start it was only one night. So did she.

Yes, so had she—but she was furious with him, anyway.

In his mind's eye, he focused on her face, looking for the nuances, until he had to admit that she did not look furious. Fury was an emotion that required effort and energy. He'd paid his therapist enough to buy a sports car to spell that out for him. Mallory had been only going through the motions just now.

He couldn't unsee the straight line of lips that should be curved, the flat affect on a face that should be expressive, the dead eyes of someone who was performing a chore solely because they had no choice. That was the very definition of servitude.

That was Cinderella.

With a groan, Taylor put his elbows on his desk and dropped his head into his hands. He couldn't force her to perform tasks as if he were the wicked stepmother and she was the scullery maid.

For the entire coming semester, he was going to be aware she was perhaps forty feet away from him, but he might never catch another glimpse.

He picked up the forms that had wasted her time and dropped them into the trash can.

Chapter Fourteen

Learning Objective: Given an unexpected scenario, explain how the business will remain operational.

—Senior Year Project *by Mallory Ames*

The janitor would unlock the inner office.

Mallory would know it was time for her mission to commence when she heard the vacuum sweeper shut off. Wrapping up the cord would take the janitor a minute, then he would pick up the trash can, bring it out to the main office space and empty it into his large bin on wheels. Since he cleaned the Executive-in-Residence office last on his rounds, he'd roll the large bin past the cubicles and out the main door, then return to fumble through his keys, relock the inner offices and leave for the day.

While he rolled the bin out, Mallory would have two minutes to sneak in and out of Mr. Taylor's office, like Tom Cruise stepping over laser beams, *Ocean's Eleven* trimmed down to *Ocean's One*.

She needed to return a pair of gloves without seeing, speaking to or in any way interacting with their owner, the liar who had amused himself by watching his devotee break every rule in his book. Unfortunately, the man she wanted to avoid had begun working late hours. He was always still at his desk when she left for the day.

Not today. He'd left just before the janitor had arrived. The moment he'd walked out the door, Mallory had taken the gloves out of her backpack and hidden them in her lap. It was time for her to get rid of her last trace of Eli.

Closure.

The vacuum sweeper went quiet. Mallory gave the buttery leather one last caress. The bin rolled past her. She made short work of the distance between her cubicle and Taylor's office, walking with confident strides, even if their length was clipped by her pencil skirt. She set the gloves on his desk—but they looked too obviously out of place there. The janitor had just dusted. He might notice that they hadn't been there two minutes ago.

She picked them up and looked around, but every surface was clean and uncluttered. The gloves would be obvious anywhere.

The desk chair wasn't pushed in all the way. She ran around the desk to drop them on the seat, pushed the chair in, and turned to leave. No, the chair shouldn't be pushed in. She pulled it out to where it had been, rushing now, then turned to the door— which Irene was blocking.

"Hello," Mallory said, faking calm confidence like her life depended on it. "I was just leaving for the day, unless there's anything else you need from me."

"I need you to come up with a good explanation for whatever it is you're doing in Mr. Taylor's office."

It sucked, having a sharp boss.

Never be afraid to speak the truth.

Shut up, Mr. Taylor.

But Mallory followed the advice. "I was putting Mr. Taylor's gloves back where they belong."

"I saw you pick them up from his desk just now. I haven't had the staff sign the nondisclosure agreements yet because we weren't expecting Mr. Taylor until January, but not entering his office after he's locked it is common sense. You cannot go poking around an office after its occupant has left for the day, especially when that office is occupied by a celebrity."

"I'm just returning his gloves." Mallory picked them up. "Look. They're just gloves."

"How did you get his gloves, if you didn't just pick them up off his desk, which I'll remind you I saw you do? Why would you have his gloves in the first place?"

The park, the hand-holding, the bonfire, the wishes—Mallory hesitated a moment too long. Irene lost her patience.

"There is no circumstance that excuses this. I'm

sorry to see you go, but I have no choice. You'll need to get your personal belongings from your desk. Your belongings, not anyone else's."

Mallory's life crumbled before her eyes. "Please. I'm begging you to believe me. I had his gloves legitimately. Without this job, I will lose my dorm. I will literally be out on the streets."

A male voice interrupted, slightly amused, supremely confident. "I didn't see the memo that there would be a meeting in my office after five."

Irene was as flustered as Mallory, but Mallory hoped she hid it better.

"Mr. Taylor," Irene said, getting out of his doorway by coming into the office, allowing Mr. Taylor to enter as well.

"Irene." He acknowledged her with a nod as he walked to his desk and picked up his mail. "How are you doing, Miss Ames? I hope the gloves were warm enough."

Her heart was pounding as hard as it had when she'd faced her family and negotiated a salary. She faked the same calm confidence now. "Yes, they were."

He held out his hand.

She put the gloves in them. "Thank you, Mr. Taylor."

"Anytime. I did try that table-side guacamole, by the way. Great suggestion." Then he held up his finger as if to stop her from answering, when she had absolutely nothing to say, and he gave Irene one of

those *don't waste my time* looks. "Did you have anything for me?"

"No, Mr. Taylor."

"Thank you." He said it like *you're dismissed*.
"And Irene, I trust Ms. Ames is still gainfully em-
ployed? I didn't overhear everything, but there's no
reason to fire someone when it was my idea for her
to borrow my gloves. I was going into a restaurant as
she was coming out. It was a cold enough night that I
had come in my car. I noticed she had no gloves and
she was going to walk somewhere on campus." He
questioned Mallory. "Your dorm?"

"No, it was the library." She could pretend with
the best of them—which would be him.

He turned back to Irene, seeming to be supremely
bored with the detail he'd asked for to add some authenticity. "She told me to get the guacamole, and I
told her to wear my gloves and give them back once
she found hers. Any questions?"

"None."

"Good." He turned his back on Irene. "Can you
stay a minute, Ms. Ames?"

Irene left and pulled the door shut.

Eli's—Mr. Taylor's—blue gaze was piercing.
"Why are you avoiding me?"

The panic she'd just endured left a fine tremor
in Mallory's hands, in every muscle. She wanted to
collapse. She couldn't. She was speaking to her hero
like they were equal.

Equal-ish.

She leveled her own no-nonsense gaze on him.

"Let's see if I can remember. You lied to me about your identity, kissed me, then dumped me and walked away without a word of explanation. That sums it up."

"It wasn't the best time for an explanation. I knew I would see you again on campus, and I had every intention of having this conversation with you when we were neither outdoors, cold, nor emotional."

"How nice for you to know that you'd be speaking to me later, but *I* didn't know that when you walked away." She stabbed herself in the chest with her own finger, right over her heart, right where it had hurt so badly that night, and every night thereafter, when she'd wondered where he'd gone and fretted over how he was feeling.

"Mallory, I am so sorry."

She hadn't intended to let her pain show. She reached for her anger, instead. "You're so sorry for what? For stringing me along? For enjoying an evening pretending you weren't a multi-millionaire, so you could get your kicks as Joe Average, putting dollar bills in donation jars? You stood there in the parking lot and watched me *cry*, and then had the nerve to give me that pep talk about how I wasn't pretending all these wonderful traits, while you were the one who was pretending the whole time."

"For that, I am not sorry, because nothing about that conversation was pretend."

"You know I'm faking my way through life at the moment, but it's because I'm aspiring to a better standard of living. You don't do it to sink to a lower level. You aren't supposed to fake that you're enjoying a

cup of hot chocolate at a stupid small-town festival."
With a stupid small-town girl.

"I did enjoy the hot chocolate."

"You're obscenely rich. Astronomically rich."

Eli—Mr. Taylor, damn it—paused for a moment
before answering. "I'm at a loss here. What does
being rich have to do with my enjoyment of a cup of
hot chocolate?"

"Because you're used to better. You've probably
had the very finest handcrafted chocolate, melted just
so by a pastry chef at a Michelin-starred restaurant."

He looked irritated at that. She'd guessed right.

"You must have thought I was such a naive little
girl, championing the quality of the nuns' hot chocolate, as if I'd ever traveled to France or Switzerland
and knew how it compared to what the world has to
offer."

"Is hot chocolate the issue you want to discuss?"

"Why didn't you tell me who you were? It seems
cruel to string me along when you knew that I was
your—your *fan*. A fan of your book."

"How could I have possibly known that? Be fair.
It wasn't as if you were wearing an official fan club
T-shirt. That doesn't exist, by the way."

"You're not funny."

Something flashed across his expression, something like surprise or…or hurt. She couldn't possibly
hurt the great E.L. Taylor.

"When did you figure out that I was your biggest fan? Because you most certainly knew when you

ditched me." The moment she asked, she knew the answer. "My wish. You saw my wish."

He nodded. "And up until that moment, I didn't know your friend and hero was me."

"It wasn't you. It was an image of you I had invented in my head."

"The timing is important. When you remember that night, remember that everything before you threw that wish happened before I knew you were a fan."

"No wonder you wouldn't kiss me."

He came around the desk to stand in front of her. He didn't touch, didn't reach for her, but he stood quite close, with an intimate quiet to his voice. "I distinctly recall kissing you. It was the kiss of a lifetime."

She felt it all again, that hum of arousal, the way joy and hope had made everything feel like magic, but she was standing before a supremely confident E.L. Taylor in his natural environment, a businessman conducting an after-action review of a transaction. He was no rusty Tin Man. He didn't need an oilcan. He needed nothing from her at all.

"I meant that you wouldn't kiss me goodbye after that wish. That earlier kiss wasn't for you, Mr. Taylor. It was for Eli, a man who never existed. The joke's on me."

"Fearless." He said it more to himself than her.

She turned away and walked to the door.

"Mallory."

Her hand was on the doorknob, but this time she paused.

"Your wish did come true, you know. I do like you."

She walked out of his office and stopped at the first place she could, the kitchenette. Her hands were still shaking. She fussed with the coffeepot, although it was empty and clean for the night.

It was over. That had been it, the closure everyone touted. One big conversation to tie it all up with a bow. She'd tuck it away with the rest of her life that she couldn't allow herself to look back upon.

She needed to think ahead. She had bigger problems than a lying millionaire. This morning, dressed for work, she'd been stopped at the dorm building's exit by a simple fluorescent green paper taped to the door, the notice that her dorm would be closed during the winter break.

All the buildings on campus would be closed for sixteen days over the winter break, from the offices to the classrooms to the dining halls, a cost-saving routine on most college campuses across the country. No dorm supervisors, no janitorial staff, no electricity to heat a six-story building for over two weeks. When Mallory had made her budget two years ago, she'd forgotten all about the need to find alternate housing during the winter break. She'd flown home for Christmas, the cost of the ticket split by her separated parents, so she hadn't paid any attention to the dorm closure as a freshman, sophomore, or junior.

This year, it was an issue. She had no way to get back to Ohio, not after selling her car. Her grandpa needed every penny of his retirement funds to pay for the assisted-living facility. Her brother would make her grovel if she asked for plane ticket money, and then there was a fifty-fifty chance he'd say no, anyway. Mallory needed to find a local place to stay—a free place to stay, because free was the only thing in her price range.

She heard a private office's glass door opening. Who else was here after hours, besides Irene and Mr. Taylor? Her poise was razor thin. If Mr. Taylor came into the kitchenette, her ability to stay calm and confident would fail the test.

She escaped to the ladies' room, which was nicer than her dorm's. Really, the office had almost everything except a bathtub and a bed. Too bad she couldn't just move in here for the winter break, but the office buildings were closed during break, too. Besides, Irene would flip.

Mallory poked her head out of the ladies' room to be certain the coast was clear. She went back to her cubicle, put her pumps in the backpack that no longer held a man's gloves, pulled out her old ballerina flats, and left to walk across campus to her lonely room in the dorm. Instead of looking back on those moments of closure with the man she'd known as Eli, she began to plan how she'd locate free living arrangements.

What was one more obstacle? Her Taylor-built plan was made of little else.

Chapter Fifteen

*Learning Objective: Given two alternatives,
choose one and justify its benefit to the business.*
—Senior Year Project *by Mallory Ames*

"There's this woman…" Taylor tapered off.

He shouldn't have brought her up. Mallory had nothing to do with the plane crash. Nothing to do with nightmares. Nothing to do with the brother and sister he ignored or the fortune he paid attention to, nothing to do with the fame that came easily and the friendships that didn't, nothing to do with teaching a book he no longer believed in. It had nothing to do with goddamned anything else in his goddamned world.

But God, he wished it did.

His therapist, whom he was supposed to address as

Scott, like they were friends instead of doctor and patient, prompted him through the encrypted video connection on his phone. "There's a woman who does what?"

"She…she's…interesting." Taylor would not wince at his own wimpy reply. He shifted his position in his armchair, a ridiculously easy-to-spot bit of body language that made him wish this was an audio call, not video. He'd chosen to sit in the master bedroom's bay window for this session. There'd been no need to go into the office on campus today. There never had been a need, other than checking on Mallory.

"Is she new in your life, or is she one of the people in your past?" Scott asked.

"New."

Mallory would have made that rolling gesture and whispered *oilcan*.

The therapist accepted one word as a complete sentence. "I'm assuming this woman has the potential to be a romantic connection?"

Taylor gave a grunt of agreement. That was one way to put it. The other was that he was crazy about her. She was special, unique, unequaled in his world. He wasn't thinking about a polite dinner; he wanted her in his bed, to lose himself repeatedly and to discover her continuously, for that weekend he'd described as she'd leaned against an oak tree in the dark. For more than a weekend, more than a week. For as long as he lived.

He was insane. He and Scott had already established this, although Scott chose other words.

"Breaking out of the social isolation you built is

the goal, of course. But this is a risky time to imagine yourself in love. Your social isolation has been long-standing. The traumatic event only revealed it. Choosing a new companion is one of those life decisions that should be avoided during a period of grieving and recovery after any trauma. You've done excellent work in identifying your emotions. Now is the time to rebuild the earlier, essential relationships you allowed to lapse, rather than creating new connections."

Apparently, the psych world didn't approve of multitasking. Taylor did. His new connection to Mallory had helped him recognize how far he'd distanced himself from his siblings, why he'd done so, and what the consequences had been. Being with her for one night had been as productive as ten therapy sessions.

"Love can come later," Scott said. "You need to focus on the issues you've already uncovered since September."

Taylor didn't label anything *love*. That was his therapist's word, along with *the traumatic event*, which sounded complicated. Taylor had to remind himself they were talking about a plane crash, horrific but simplistic. A machine had stopped working while he'd been in it, nothing more, nothing less.

He challenged Scott's theory. "Love should wait? And yet, you encourage me to get my brother and sister to love me again." He immediately held up a hand to correct himself before the therapist could. "You're encouraging me to be better at loving them." *After ten years of neglect.* "If love and connections are what the traumatic event revealed I was lacking, what's the difference? Being better at loving is being better at loving."

"The difference is that you already love your brother and sister. You've loved them their whole lives, even if you were burying that emotion for much of that time. This new woman would require you to create a new emotion. I recommend that you acknowledge to yourself that she is interesting, but now is not the time. A symbolic gesture of farewell can close that side road, and you can keep driving in the right direction. A note, flowers, whatever seems appropriate, based on how much you've already invested in the relationship."

It had been a fake relationship from the beginning. Taylor wanted to ask if he should send fake flowers, but he knew it would sound snide.

Bitter. That was an emotion.

As Scott congratulated him for attempting to contact his siblings yesterday, Taylor looked out the window. The entire lake was empty, not one boat for the half mile he could see. The water was flat, ideal for crew, but it was too cold to row. The only craft available to row were a cheap plastic kayak and a clunky fiberglass rowboat, anyway. He should buy himself a racing shell.

"Your text messages to your siblings successfully opened a channel of communication. At our next session, I'd like to discuss your comfort level with trying to reach them live, either through a phone call or video chat. It's unfortunate they'll be in Monte Carlo with your parents for Christmas. If you want to attempt the plane flight, I'll support you."

No way in hell was Taylor getting on an airplane.

"That's a low priority." Taylor sounded so unconcerned. Mallory would say he was just faking it until he made it. She'd be right.

Maybe one day he'd genuinely be unconcerned about flying. If not, he'd fly, anyway. Sooner or later, he would have to travel somewhere beyond the reach of his motorcycle.

"Our next session will be in January," Scott said. "If you feel isolated over Christmas, volunteering at a soup kitchen or other charitable activity can be rewarding in a different way than making a financial donation."

Taylor's security team would love that. With great wealth came the greater risk of being taken hostage by those who wanted that wealth. His private security detail gave Taylor a wide berth at his direction, but he knew they were on the perimeter of his home. If he should obey a sudden impulse to pop into a soup kitchen on Christmas Day, they'd scramble and keep up, but it would be unfair of him to do that to them— and to the soup kitchen. Why should they let him take over someone's job after walking in on a whim?

Scott was in earnest. "Giving the gift of yourself is a gift to yourself."

Such flowery nonsense. Worse than Taylor's own published platitudes.

Scott recapped the issues. Taylor focused on the lake rather than on a brother who didn't text back, a sister who did, and an interesting woman who no longer saw anything in him to admire. He wanted to be on the lake. He wanted to taste the cold water in the air. He craved the feel of a perfectly balanced oar in his hands, but a cheap plastic one would do. In the kayak, he would be the machine that created the speed—not a motorcycle's engine, not a sports car, not a plane. He'd be a machine that would not break. He needed only his own two arms.

Only two arms—those were the limbs that the pilot still had use of. Taylor had reviewed the hospital bills for the month. The wheelchair costs were unchanged from the previous month. No new charges for crutches or a walker. No improvement, then, despite the cutting-edge methodology that the pilot was going through to regain the use of his legs.

Crew required the full body to row, arms and legs, but a kayak was all about the arms. Taylor would send the pilot a kayak, so he could be the machine that flew over the water. Taylor would text his sister back and try his brother again. He would give Mallory real flowers to close an interesting chapter they'd stopped writing on the first page.

He ended the call and tossed his phone onto the nightstand. It knocked a knitted blue mitten askew.

He wouldn't fall in love with his one-night-only fake girlfriend. He'd been through a traumatic event. Now was not the time.

He straightened the mitten.

Not yet.

He'd send those flowers, but he wouldn't say goodbye. *Not yet* meant it might happen, still.

It was time.

"You can do this," Mallory told herself. She swung her backpack over her left shoulder. Nothing new there. She always carried her backpack, just like every other student of every age. It wouldn't arouse any suspicion.

Then she picked up the bedroll she'd made, Girl Scout style. She'd laid her clean clothing out on her warmest blanket, then rolled it up and tied it in place with her belt. It might look odd on a security camera, but she knew the chances of anyone pulling security footage from the dean's office were slim. She'd carry it low by her thigh, just in case.

Lastly, she picked up the grocery bag of granola bars and all the other nonperishables she'd eat while she camped out in her cubicle, looking for a better place to stay. When she found it, she'd leave the administrative building through a fire-escape door. Those opened from the inside, even when locked on the outside. If she failed to find a place, then staying in a chilly building without electrical power was not going to kill her.

All students had to be out of all of the dorm buildings by seven. Mallory had timed her departure so that she'd arrive at the office building just before five. With luck, everyone else would have already skipped out early for the holidays. If not, she'd hide in a toilet stall when security made their final sweep before locking up the office building. It was far from ideal, but desperate times called for desperate measures. Having her plans blow up at the last second qualified.

Mallory had aced her last exam this morning, then she'd caught up with her new friend in her microeconomics class, Jacinda. She was a younger woman—wasn't everyone?—who'd assured her that her parents would love to have her use their spare bedroom for the holidays. Jacinda had a car, too, so Mallory had a free way to get there. It had been a perfect solution for the winter break housing situation.

"Hey, good news," Jacinda had said, just hours ago. "My parents will refund the cleaning fee in January."

The cleaning fee? That was how Mallory had found out that the spare bedroom was listed on a room-share app. She'd misunderstood what Jacinda meant by *Sure, my parents have a spare room, if you need one.*

Mallory was expected to pay $30 a day, plus the $50 cleaning fee.

She didn't have $530. If she did, she wouldn't give it to anyone's parents. She'd buy a plane ticket to Ohio and go see her grandpa. Everything that could go wrong in December had gone wrong, and she was tired of surmounting obstacles. She needed a friendly face. She needed to be with somebody who loved her.

Mallory breathed through the tears that threatened as she stepped into the dorm's elevator and pressed the button for the lobby. She would not cry, because she'd returned to her no-crying-at-all-over-anything policy. The doors opened with a chime. Mallory walked confidently to the front desk, signed her name on the dotted line and officially checked out of her room until January.

There was no turning back now.

She crossed the almost deserted campus and walked into the office building like it was just another day at work. The cluster of cubicles was a ghost town. She headed down her row with her groceries and her bedroll, telling herself the emptiness wasn't creepy at all.

It was her first time in the office in over a week, because students were not allowed to work during final exams. She'd been grateful to spend a week without listening for the nerve-racking sound of a private office's glass door opening. Final exams were less stressful than dodging E.L. Taylor.

There were dead flowers on her desk.

Mallory set her grocery bag on her chair, kicked her bedroll under her desk and dropped the heavy backpack on the floor without taking her eyes off the flowers. The arrangement must have been stunning when it was first delivered. Nothing ostentatious, but a variety of small, unusual blooms arranged in a petite crystal vase. The card was still tied to a ribbon around the vase. No plastic pitchfork, here. This was luxury that fit in a cubicle.

She only knew one person who could afford luxury. Dead petals showered her desk as she lifted the vase to untie the ribbon. The vase was shaped like a pine cone. That seemed—that seemed romantic. Sentimental, at least. He remembered that she'd carried a pine cone in her pocket that whole night.

She tore open the vellum envelope and read the single sentence: *Because I had the time to buy you flowers.*

Every detail of that night was etched on a piece of her heart that she didn't know how to erase. When he'd tossed her up to the top of the hay bales—to safety—she'd told him that wasn't how he should act on a date. He'd said, "There wasn't time to buy you flowers." It had been her first hint that he had a heart and sense of humor trapped underneath that hard exterior.

Oh, Eli, Eli. Why couldn't you have been real, instead of Taylor?

"Mallory."

She whirled around, hiding the card behind herself.

There, straight out of the pages of *Forbes*, stood the country's most successful venture capitalist, E.L. Taylor.

The beard was gone. His hair was styled very well, shorter, devastatingly perfect for his strong features and newly revealed jawline. He wore impeccably tailored slacks, a bespoke dress shirt—it had to have been tailored for him, to fit the width of his shoulders and taper to his waist so well. His watch was understated, for a Rolex.

The last trace of Eli was gone.

"What are you doing here?" he asked curtly.

She did not know this man. In voice, in demeanor, in appearance, he was *the* E.L. Taylor. This was the legend she'd toiled for two years to meet.

Be careful what you wish for; you might get it.

Mallory challenged the one and only E.L. Taylor. "You first. What are you doing here?"

"They're locking up the building tonight for the rest of the year. I came to get my gloves." His voice was flat. He owed no explanations to a peon in a cubicle.

"If you'll excuse me," she said, trying to sound unemotional and flat, just like her former hero, "I have things to do."

"Do you need a ride this evening? You have extra bags."

"No, thank you. I'll—I'm just going to leave them here until next semester."

It had been the smallest hesitation, but he narrowed his eyes for a moment. He took in her casual clothing—more comfortable for sleeping in—and the grocery bag. Then he crouched down, a flex of masculine thighs and backside in those civilized slacks, and looked under her desk.

"You decided to keep a bedroll in your cubicle until January, with a stash of granola bars. Why?"

"It's none of your business."

"Answer me."

"I already did." Mallory found that very satisfying to say. She'd have to adopt that *unnecessary question* thing from her hero. Former hero.

"The dorms close today, too, I assume. Most people who find themselves homeless would choose to sleep in their cars. Why don't you?"

She laughed at his audacity. What did he know about homelessness? "I would have to own a car. My grandfather's car was my one-way ticket to school from Ohio. Then it became a year's meal plan at the dining facility."

"The dining facility which will be closed until January."

She owed him no explanation. He could glare at her all he wanted to. She would not flinch.

But then, to her shock, he smiled that one-tenth of a smile. "Mallory Ames, you are not the paragon I thought you were. You are stubborn to an asinine degree, and you need to learn how to ask for help."

"I'm doing very well. I don't need help."

"Don't prove my point so quickly." His lips quirked—*quirked*, the jerk. "You have nowhere to stay, and I'm renting a six-bedroom house just outside town. I won't make you ask. I'll just answer you. Why yes, I do have a spare room. You're welcome to use it. I happen to have my car today instead of the motorcycle, so grab your stuff. Let's go."

She didn't move. "That would violate a fraternization policy."

"You're not my student. You haven't even signed up for one of those mentorship coffee-and-donut gigs. I suspect that when it's my turn to be the speaker for the Thursday guest lecture series, I will stand behind that podium, and you will not be in the theater."

The mentorship coffees were exclusively for graduate students and well-heeled alumni. Mallory had volunteered to serve the coffee as a way to be in the room where it happened, as the saying went. She'd un-volunteered after the dean had shaken Eli's hand.

"The semester hasn't started. I'm not on the faculty yet. Do I need to keep demolishing your stubborn opposition to the offer of a place to sleep for the winter break? A place, I might add, that won't be having its electricity shut off? Winter is cold, even in Texas. The house is big enough that you can continue to avoid me with very little trouble."

Mallory tried to come up with a brilliant counter to his offer, but that tenth of a smile made him look like Eli, distracting her from the debate.

"If you don't accept this offer, then, at some point in the next week, you will be caught by a security guard on his rounds. Being charged with trespassing is not nearly as good a story as being charged with public indecency."

"You're not funny."

"But I am right."

"I can't live with you. Let me be the one to point out that we've kissed. It's too personal."

He tipped his head to the side, looking more relaxed, not less, now that she'd addressed the elephant in the room. "Kissing generally is."

"This isn't going to be that weekend in your bed you described."

"There are six bedrooms, Mallory. I won't go into any but my own. Since we're being refreshingly blunt here, if you choose to go into mine, I won't kick you out."

"Don't hold your breath."

"I'm not." He picked up her bedroll, grocery bag and backpack. That tenth of a smile took on a shade of sadness. "I told you that you'd never see me the same way again."

Chapter Sixteen

Learning Objective: Identify the similarities and differences between an established business entity and your own prospective company.
—Senior Year Project *by Mallory Ames*

The house wasn't the grandiose palace Mallory had been expecting.

It was a sprawling split-level which spread along its piece of the lakeshore from one wooded boundary to another, taking up almost all of its cleared lot the way a teenager stretched out on a twin bed that was just a little too small for him. There were formal living rooms, two of them, as well as a more casual family room, a sunroom, a game room, two offices, a home gym and a massive back porch. Stairs led up to some rooms and down to others. Passages connected the wings that had been added as the house had grown over the years. Just as he'd promised, Mallory was able to avoid her host without any effort at all.

The only indication he was aware of her presence was a note she'd found on the kitchen counter: *Eat something besides granola bars. Help yourself to anything. The kitchen gets restocked on Wednesdays.* She'd made herself an omelet and left the handwritten note on the counter, aware that just a month ago, she would have been thrilled to have an E.L. Taylor autograph, let alone an entire note. Now, it was just a note from a guy who'd left half a pizza in the fridge.

He'd written on the cardboard box, too. *Yes, I have had pizza around the world, and yes, this one is very good. Reheat in the oven. Don't microwave. Ruins it.*

On her third night in the house, in the middle of a thunderstorm, the power went out.

Mallory took the book she'd been reading—a sweet Christmas novel, a respite after reading so many textbooks this semester—and her cell phone to use as a light, and tiptoed out of her bedroom. She began making her way to the downstairs family room, the one room in the house that had any holiday decorations, for a little ambiance while she finished her novel.

The family room was divided from the kitchen by a breakfast bar with eight barstools. The kitchen and family room combined to make one open space, but it still felt more cozy than the rest of the house, particularly because there was a fireplace in the family room.

The mantel had been decorated with ornaments and garlands that exuded all the holiday warmth of a department store display. Mallory was certain the decorations had been part of the kitchen restock. Some enterprising company probably included it with their regular December deliveries: a dozen eggs, a gallon of milk, a six-foot garland, four bows.

The fireplace had also been stocked with kindling and a charmingly photo-ready pile of logs. This storm was the perfect time to use it. The fire would provide light to read by, so she could save her cell phone battery. If the power stayed out for a long time, the fire would keep the room from getting too chilly. Besides, Mallory hadn't had the chance to build a real log fire in years. If she was going to live here for two weeks, she might as well enjoy the amenities.

She reached the half staircase that led from the hallway with all of the bedrooms down to the family room. Her flannel nightgown covered her from her neck to her toes, so she was warm. More importantly, the nightgown was super modest. If she encountered the other resident of this massive house, she wouldn't be embarrassed by anything other than the flannel's pink bunny print.

She stopped on the stairs. There was already a fire burning, but nobody was around.

It was irresponsible to light a fire and leave. It didn't seem like something the brilliant E.L. Taylor would do. She took the last step down and tiptoed toward the kitchen, thinking he might be there, but it was only a black space. All of the appliances with their glowing digital clocks and touchpads had died with a crack of lightning.

"What are you doing?"

Mallory spun around with the book clutched to her chest. She could see over the back of the couch, now that she was in the room. Taylor was stretched out on it, staring at the fire, not at her.

"You scared me to death," she said.

He didn't say anything, so after standing there awkwardly for a moment too long, Mallory turned to go back up the stairs.

"You should stay and read by the firelight." He hadn't taken his eyes off the fire, but he'd seen her book with that super peripheral vision, apparently.

"I don't want to intrude," she said.

"Please. Intrude."

There was something in that *please* that made her step closer to get a better view of him over the back of the couch. "Are you okay?"

He shut his eyes, blew out a breath, then turned his face toward her and opened his eyes. "Yes."

She looked at his face and thought, *No*.

She should go. She was trying not to dwell on either Eli, who'd never been real, or Mr. Taylor, whom she avoided like the plague, but she never stopped thinking about this man, for better or worse. Sharing this room with him wasn't going to make her think about him any more than she already did, so she might as well stay near the fire. Her bedroom was pitch-black and would soon grow cold.

She held up her book. "The couch is the closest to the light, and you're kind of hogging it."

He sat up.

Mallory sat down.

They remained side by side in silence for an eternity. Mallory went through the motions of reading her book although she was far too aware of *him*, the physical presence of the man next to her, his body strong and healthy, his whole demeanor unhappy.

"You're staring," he said, without looking away from the fire. His five-o'clock shadow was just enough to add a touch of Eli to his appearance.

"My book is boring. There's nothing else to look at."

Do you miss being Eli? Do you miss holding hands with a girl in a blue ski cap?

She needed to stop thinking like that. It was like asking an actor if he missed being a movie character. E.L. Taylor had given an Oscar-worthy performance, but he was not Eli.

"I don't know what to call you," she said. "Mr. Taylor in the office, of course. What should I call you here? E.L. Taylor is a mouthful. Do you go by E.L.?"

"Just Taylor."

"Okay."

"You can call me Eli."

She closed her book. "I don't think you're trying to be mean right this moment, I really don't, but it's not nice for you to remind me what a sucker I was. I'm not going to keep calling you by a fake name. It's not cute."

"It's not a fake name. I was Eli growing up. I still

am, to my immediate family. If I see them." He closed his eyes and turned his head from the fire toward her again, such an odd way to look from one thing to another, but the end result was the same, Paul-Newman-blue eyes gazing into hers.

"I don't know why I told you Eli when you asked me my name, but it wasn't intended to trick you into being a sucker. You weren't one, anyway. A sucker gets taken advantage of and loses something of value. Their money, their car. There has to be something they get suckered out of."

"I didn't know who you were. You took advantage of that by staying anonymous."

"To get what from you? What did I trick you out of?" *My heart.*

With the firelight on his face and the shadow on his jaw, he looked so much like Eli, it hurt. She wished she didn't still like him as Taylor.

She pulled up her feet to sit cross-legged, smoothing pink flannel bunnies over her knees. "You amused yourself at my expense."

"Mallory." He said her name with such disappointment, like he was a student he'd expected to give a better answer. "When I read that wish and saw my own name, did I strike you as being amused?"

"Can't you see what a fool you made of me? I told you all my plans and all the flaws in my plans, all the mistakes I made. I laid it all out for the man who wrote 'Never divulge more details than necessary.' Your book taught me to anticipate what might go wrong, so I would never be taken by surprise. How did my face look when I realized which office you were being shown into? I'm floundering now. I broke all the rules that had been working for me, and I don't know how my plan is going to turn out."

"That book wasn't intended to dictate your life."

"Yes, it was. It's an advice book. You can't conduct your business one way and your personal life another. Either you believe in moving forward, or you don't. You believe in setting goals, or you don't. You make hard choices, or you don't."

He sat forward, elbows on his knees, and scrubbed his face with both hands. "I wish I'd never written that book. It's caused me nothing but grief."

How could he hate a book that had been so important to her? A book that he wrote?

"It made you a lot of money. It made you famous enough to be on TV, and that made you even more money. You dated beautiful, famous women. A rock star. A supermodel."

"Like I said, nothing but grief." He kept his head in his hands, but another smile touched his lips. "I see you've been doing your research."

Busted.

For two years, she'd only researched him by reading articles and interviews in her local library's copies of *Forbes* and *Harvard Business Review*. She hadn't been interested in his personal life. That would not help her move forward with her plan, and she'd been so very strict with herself about putting all her effort toward her goals.

But after Eli had walked into the dean's office and

shocked her to her core, she'd made up for lost time. The first candid shirtless photo she saw had made her jaw drop. How unfair that the one day of her life she'd gotten to sit on his lap, they'd been in winter coats.

Tonight, he wore long plaid pajama bottoms and a close-fitting, short-sleeved T-shirt, exposing his arms to her sight for the first time. He looked great in photos, but being only a couch cushion away as those defined muscles bunched and flexed and stretched the sleeve of that T-shirt was something else—the difference between looking at a photo of a tropical ocean and actually standing on the shore with her toes in the hot sand. She didn't touch the water either way. But, in person, the possibility was right there, if only a wave would lap a little higher on the shore.

Most of the photos had been taken at black-tie events. The man looked good in a tux. So did the women who got to be by his side. He didn't need a caregiver from Ohio as a girlfriend.

Pretend you're equals.

She shrugged and waved one hand, a princess in pink bunny print. "Feel free to research me back."

"How?" He dropped his hands and sat back. "I can't just look at a thousand photos of you on the internet. I tried."

"You tried?"

"Of course. I came up empty. I have to do my research some other way." He turned sideways on the couch and laid his arm across the back of it, giving her all of his attention, while she split hers between his blue eyes and those incredible arms.

"I have to look at you whenever I can in real life instead of photos. It's not often enough." He tapped his temple. "But I've got pictures up here of Mallory crossing the campus in her blue jeans. I see Ms. Ames killing it in the office in her pencil skirt. I can tell a lot about the kind of day you're having by the way you walk."

She frowned. "When do you see me walk?"

"When you leave the office, you take the sidewalk that goes past the east side of the building. My side. On the days I pretend I have a reason to come into the office, I wait for you to walk by before I leave, except that one night. You were still there, but the janitor had started cleaning the offices, so I finally left, but I sat in my car a while, waiting for you to come out. You didn't. I went back in and found you and Irene in my office."

Mallory could still taste the fear that she'd been on the brink of losing everything. "I was being fired. You were very smooth with your excuses."

"You played along flawlessly. I thought it was better to give her a story she could accept. I know how the rumor mill would have worked if I'd told her it was none of her damned business how you'd gotten my gloves, which is what I wanted to say."

"I didn't thank you then. Let me thank you now. Without that job, I would have lost my financial aid package. I would have had to drop out."

"You will never have to drop out."

"What does that mean?"

They stared at one another through one lightning flash. Another.

Taylor dropped his gaze to his thigh and flicked imaginary lint from his plaid flannel pants. "There's money in your student account, if you need it. If you don't, let it sit. The school will give you the remaining funds when you graduate and they close out the books."

"I *don't* need it." She'd worked for two years to achieve success on her own terms, and now the man who'd inspired her to do so was telling her she could give up, take some free money and be just fine?

Aren't you proud of me for doing this, E.L. Taylor? I made a plan exactly the way you taught me to. Do you think I can't complete it?

"I can do this," she said. "I *am* doing this."

"It's just twenty grand." He spoke evenly, but he sounded angry.

"Twenty grand?" It was a breathtaking amount. She could move out of the subsidized dorm, rent an apartment, and still have enough to buy a used car and more. "I can't accept that much. I can't accept any amount."

He laughed, sort of. "You're consistent. You didn't want me to give you money for hot chocolate, either. Take the money. It won't hurt me. Good God. I hit the half-billion mark this year."

She sucked in a quick breath. Five hundred million dollars? It was an unfathomable amount of money.

"And still, people I care about won't take my money. I have to pay bills for them when they aren't looking." He drove his hand through his hair. "Why won't any of you take the money? It isn't tainted. I haven't made it by doing anything illegal or immoral. I won't miss the money."

"The point isn't that the money won't affect you," Mallory said. "It affects me."

The rain pelted the windows, a force of nature that dumped water whether the people below wanted or needed it. She'd be a fool not to use the money, but it didn't make her instantly happy. Twenty thousand was a sudden deluge in a land where she'd painstakingly constructed irrigation ditches in the sand.

"'Never let anything take you by surprise,'" she quoted. She laid her hands in her lap, palms up, empty. For now. "I failed to predict the possibility of an influx of cash at this stage of the plan. I'm a terrible student of E.L. Taylor, it turns out. He tested me, and I wasn't ready for it."

Taylor sounded resigned. "You'll modify your plan, and you'll use it to its best effect. That's the way you are. It's been refreshing to know a woman who'd prefer college tuition instead of another set of earrings."

"Twenty-thousand-dollar earrings?" She sounded sour. Jealousy was not her best self. "Be real."

He lifted the hand that had been resting beside her shoulder, tucked a strand of hair behind her ear, then gently touched the shell of the ear he'd bared. "Yes, for real. But those women have slept with me."

"Unlike me." Her voice was supposed to sound firm, not husky. Not jealous.

"You and I are something different. What's between us isn't courteous, consensual sex."

"What is between us?"

She wouldn't have dreamed she'd be asking this even a half hour ago, but this storm, that *Please, intrude*, his frustration that money wasn't a simple gift for her and for others—*people I care about*—combined to make an invulnerable man seem vulnerable. It crept into her heart just enough to make her feel a little vulnerable, too.

"I don't know what we have, Ms. Mallory Ames. I haven't put a name to it, have you?"

"No, Mr. E.L. Taylor, I have not."

His voice was quiet, reflective. "If we shared a bed, I think we'd be lovers, not people who date and have sex when their schedules allow. We'd want each other every night. We'd share our days, a meal, a conversation, anticipating those nights." He leaned closer and gently pressed his thumb on her lower lip, the way she'd done to him as they'd shared the tree branch. It was, she realized now, a touch that was more intimate to receive than to give.

"I can only learn so much from seeing you on a faraway sidewalk. If I want to know more about you, and I do, then I have to talk to you on stormy nights. I have to listen to what you say, and what you don't, and watch the expressions on your face as you do and don't tell me about yourself. I need to learn you differently than I've learned anyone else in my life, because there's more here, and it's very real. I want to be with you just like this tonight, to talk with you like a lover, even if you never become my lover."

His fingers trailed over her hair. Her heart tripped and her skin heated, a familiar sensation, so like her night with Eli when she'd fallen under his spell in the shadow of the massive tree, when he'd told her she could do with him as she pleased. *Anything we haven't done yet, or everything we already have.*

It had sounded so sensual despite being in the middle of a park, no place for a seduction, so they'd broken their mood with a laugh, agreeing that it was a bad time and place to play that game. She hadn't known there was another game being played simultaneously, that the man toying with her had been E.L. Taylor, pretending to be someone else.

He touched, very precisely, the imitation pearl stud in her earlobe, one he could and would so easily replace with a real pearl, for any lover.

He was toying with her again. She knew for a fact he could manipulate others, he could sound sincere when he was not, he could fake anything.

She stood and snatched up her book. "I've had enough of that game. You're very good at it. Stop practicing on me."

"No—Mallory, stay."

"Really, Eli?" *Damn it—that shadow of a beard.* "I mean, really, Taylor? Good night. I leave you to your fire and all of the abject misery that comes with writing a wildly successful book and hitting the half-billion mark and—and having sex with glamorous women you shower with twenty-thousand-dollar earrings. You poor man, it all sounds so grim."

As she headed for the stairs, her peripheral vision was just good enough to see Taylor fall back on the couch to resume his sprawling position in defeat.

She made her way back to her bed by the flashes of lightning, pushed open the door and dove for the mattress, landing facedown so she could muffle her cries in the bedding, and nobody would know how weak she was, except herself.

Chapter Seventeen

*Learning Objective: Describe the effect which
a volatile market would have on your business.*
—Senior Year Project *by Mallory Ames*

Taylor jackknifed upright, awakened by the hideous crack of thunder. He tried to get his bearings in the darkness. He was still on the sofa. The room was black except for the orange glow of a few dying embers. There was no storm outside the window, but he'd heard thunder.

Not thunder. There'd been an explosion. He was supposed to be doing something, a task that meant life or death. What the hell was it?

Water was part of it, he knew that, so he stumbled in the darkness from the couch to the kitchen island to the sink, knocking over a bar stool on the way. He couldn't stop to pick it up—he needed to do something with the water.

He cursed out loud, and the sound of his voice was real. He held on to the edge of the sink and turned on the tap. The water felt real. The dream—it had been the dream again, of course. It always started the same, with him in the air, unable to muster any vestige of awe at the dark landscape below as he watched the headlights of miniature cars traveling in straight lines, exactly as he'd felt on a real September night.

Then a propeller had stopped spinning, black water had come rushing into focus. *Terror.* He'd seen clearly—too late, too late—that he'd lost everything important to his soul years before he'd lost his life in a single second of deafening impact. *Regret.*

Only he hadn't died.

He'd come to just seconds later. Water had been pouring into the broken cockpit, bringing with it a rush of cold, clean-washed air, which he'd been so desperate to inhale below the toxic smoke of the burning fuel that had cost him $150. He'd clawed his way out of his seat belt and ducked under the water.

He cracked his head on the plane's controls, reached out blindly, felt a human body, a leg in jeans. The pilot was here. The pilot wasn't moving—was he dead, this supposed friend, this person from his past? Taylor couldn't let the body burn up.

He groped frantically in the dark, lungs bursting under the water, but there was no air above the water, either, so he kept going until his hand hit the pilot's seat belt buckle. He could feel the heat of the fire right through the water. *God—God, I'll boil alive.*

With an explosive effort that drew out every last bit of energy remaining in every last cell of his body, he launched himself over the controls toward the pilot's missing door. His head broke the water's surface, his lungs sucked in the unbreathable black smoke, and he rolled onto his back, dragging the pilot's body with him. Taylor's arm was his oar, his hand was the blade. Catch, stroke, recover, catch, stroke, recover— the rhythm must be kept while muscles strained. *Ignore the pain, cross the finish line, break that record, more, faster, take the pain, winning is everything.* The air became breathable, the fire more distant, with every stroke of the oar, every pull of his shoulder muscles.

Then the fire went out. Through the grit in his eyes, he strained to see the plane, but it had vanished. The water was black, the air clear. The plane must have sunk, and Taylor would sink, too, if he stopped for even one stroke, weighed down by the lifeless body he was dragging along. Catch, stroke, recover.

His ears were ringing from the sound of metal sheering on impact. He couldn't hear the sound of his own strokes, his own grunts of exertion. He didn't hear the woman in the canoe until she was on top of him, a little grandma who paddled like hell while Taylor hung onto a rope she'd wrapped around his arm, once they'd both realized he was too exhausted to lift the pilot's body into the boat, too exhausted to climb in himself without letting go of the pilot.

"Are you okay? I heard you crash into something and shout."

Taylor gripped the edge of the sink. He could hear. He could hear the woman speaking.

"Taylor, do you hear me? Are you sleepwalking? Hey, Eli. It's me."

The ringing in his ears cleared instantly, for it was only a phantom from the crash that had left him deafened for days. A phantom could not exist in reality, and reality had just walked up to his side, a barefooted woman wearing a nun's habit made of flannel with pink bunnies.

Pink bunnies. Mallory. *Oh, thank God.*

He let go of the sink and grabbed Mallory for dear life, hauling her against his chest and burying his face in her hair. The long strands tickled his nose as he breathed in too hard, too fast. They stuck to his wet cheeks—damn it, his cheeks were wet—and he welcomed that nuisance, he craved that touch that could do him no good, except to bring him back to his body and his place in the world, in this kitchen, holding Mallory.

He was alive.

Now, what was he going to do about it?

"You're doing a shot of tequila?"

The disbelief in Eli's voice sounded better to Mallory than the anguish had.

She kept an eye on him as she sliced a lime into quarters. She'd picked up the toppled bar stool and pushed him onto it a little while ago, after he'd told her the terrible story about the plane crash. She'd stoked the fireplace to get some light and heat in the room, hurrying because she didn't want to leave him at the cold breakfast bar, alone.

As soon as she was within arm's reach, he'd pulled her close to stand between his knees, and he'd kept his arms looped around her waist. He'd watched the fire as he'd told her about the pilot who couldn't walk. She'd felt his crushing guilt in every word, and she'd held his head in both of her hands as she'd pressed her cheek to his, smooth against rough. The warm tears had been hers, that time.

"You're really doing a shot of tequila?" he asked again.

Mallory pushed aside the lime slices and plunked a bottle of very high-end tequila on the breakfast bar. "I assume that is a rhetorical question."

She watched Eli's face, but the fire was behind him, so it was hard to see if she'd gotten even a tenth of a smile.

Relax. Smile. You need to loosen up.

If she wasn't able to help him smile, that was okay. He was allowed to feel any way he wanted to feel as far as she was concerned. He'd survived a wreck, a fire, a near-drowning.

She felt raw enough just hearing about it, just holding him through the memory of it. This man, who'd been so important to her in one way for two years, might never have become important to her in a different way this December. He could have ceased to exist. She would have spent her twenty-ninth birthday hiding in a festival crowd she didn't want to be in. She would have had no one to tell her Cinderella wasn't as self-reliant as she was. She wouldn't have known what it was like to kiss a man with her heart wide open under a starry sky.

He was right: it had been the kiss of a lifetime. She'd almost never had it. That alternate Mallory wouldn't have known what could have been.

She sat on the bar stool next to his and put her head on his shoulder. He didn't move away or shake off her touch.

"Why haven't I heard about this? Wasn't it in the news?"

"I kept it out. It's not good for business."

She picked her head up. "How do you keep something like that a secret? Aren't there official investigations?"

"There are. Money fixes things." He put one finger under her chin and gently closed her mouth. "Legally. Reports can be redacted for the public for all kinds of excuses that lawyers are paid well to come up with. It's a business investment to have them do it. The news would have hurt a dozen fledgling companies who are depending on my reputation in order to get off the ground."

She'd accused him of not knowing how to correctly *fake it 'til you make it*, but he knew how. He had to do it, or other people with dreams like hers would suffer.

She ducked her chin, embarrassed that she hadn't seen this before. "'Never show weakness.' You have to appear invulnerable all the time."

"E.L. Taylor does, yes. That's part of my job, but I've been just the same as you."

She raised her head at that. "I'm embarrassed I ever tried to say we were equal-ish."

"We're two peas in a pod. I told you my book wasn't intended to apply to your personal life, but I was applying it to mine, too. I was so focused on creating E.L. Taylor and then maintaining E.L. Taylor that I lost touch with my family. I can barely remember people I was friends with when I was younger. Eli Taylor forgot that being the invincible E.L. Taylor was a job, not a life."

He laced his fingers in between hers. "This girl in a blue ski cap sat on a hay bale next to me once, clapping her boots together to get the sand off them, and she said she was pretending all the time, too. But she's not my equal. She's wiser. Already cautious about spending an entire life pretending to be someone she isn't. She told me that being who you really are, flaws and all, might be a better way to live, but if you never try it, you'll have wasted your only chance to find out."

She nodded, too touched to speak. He remembered everything she said. He paid attention to her. He treated her like a lover whether or not she ever slept with him.

"The moment before I knew I was going to die, my thought was, 'I wasted it.' I'd gotten to live for thirty-two years, but I'd wasted them. I wasn't leaving behind anyone who would grieve for me. I know that sounds selfish, but that means I hadn't invested myself in other people. Their businesses, yes, but not people. No one would miss me at a family dinner, because I never visited my family anymore, anyway. No one would miss my sense of humor, because I never relaxed enough to be even mildly funny with anyone." He picked up their joined hands and rubbed her knuckles along his jaw as if it were the greatest luxury in the world to do so. "No one would miss holding my hand. I'd wasted my life."

"But now you won't."

"You'd think I'd be like Scrooge after the ghosts visited. He saw the error of his ways, threw open the windows on Christmas morning and everything was fixed, just like that. I'm afraid it doesn't work that way. But I found a decent therapist. I'm making progress."

"Progress? Even when I didn't know you were E.L. Taylor, you were very E.L. Taylor-ish. How are you going to stop being that?" She used their hands to push him in the shoulder. "You're not going to swagger into the office and leave all the women sighing in little melted puddles anymore?"

"You're kidding."

"Not kidding. You definitely have swagger. You should keep that part." He had the sexiest tenth of a smile she'd ever seen, and she was getting to see it right now. It made her heart hop and flutter. She didn't waste any energy trying to stop that unstoppable hop.

"I made progress because I made contact with my sister. We've texted this week."

That was sobering. "That's the first time you've talked to her since September?"

He let go of her hand and picked up a lime slice, evaluating it in the firelight. "The first time in more than a year. They're almost eleven years younger than I am."

"They? Two sisters?"

"A brother and a sister. Twins. When I went off to college, they were starting third grade. They turned twenty-one in October. Decided to do it in Vegas."

"That sounds like fun."

"I didn't go. It was after the crash, but..." He set down the lime. "See? It's not like a magic wand just fixes everything."

"Cinderella never knew how easy she had it."

"You're mildly funny," he said, and she smiled, since he couldn't. "I didn't want to fly. The therapist said that was normal. It won't be an issue unless I get to the point I think I'll never fly again, but for now... normal. But that wasn't the only reason I didn't see them. It's awkward to be around them. I don't know how to make up for so much neglect.

"They're twins, so they're extra close. I told myself they didn't need me, so it wasn't that bad if I didn't go home and spend time with them during college. Those visits got more rare as I began being the businessman instead of the person. It's hard to suddenly say, 'Changed my mind. Let's be family again.' I'm making progress, though. Thank you for that."

"What did I do?"

"You cried on me. You made me feel like I had

some potential to be... I don't know. To be there, if somebody needed me. After Eli had a perfect night with Mallory, he knew that even if the twins no longer needed him, he still needed them to know he was around, in case they ever did. So I texted them. She answered. He didn't."

Mallory put her head back on his shoulder. His definition of progress was so paltry. *This poor man, so grim.* "What else did your therapist tell you?"

"If I stare at enough fires, they won't make me feel sick anymore. And I should be very careful to not fall in love with you."

She closed her eyes, one moment of pure emotion, not good, not bad, just an intense pulse, the inseparable blend of hope and fear, love and grief.

Then she picked up her head and picked up the bottle of tequila. "That's enough for now. I don't know about you, but if I'm going to spend the rest of the night watching a fire until it burns itself out, if I'm going to do that while someone I care about talks to me like a lover, even though we're not supposed to become lovers, I definitely am going to need a shot of tequila first."

She poured one glass and picked up a lime slice. Eli—because he'd always been Eli, deeply buried but abruptly freed by a terrible crash—pushed the second shot glass toward her with a smile that was at least two-tenths of a full smile.

"Hit me up, bartender."

She poured while he made his way through the dark to the stove, coming back with a shaker of salt.

He kissed the back of her hand, then sprinkled salt where he'd kissed. He licked the side of his finger with a wink that brought back all of that buzzy, aroused feeling she'd gotten accustomed to on her twenty-ninth birthday, then he salted that spot, too.

Eli began the traditional toast. "Remember, life is always easier when you take it with a grain of salt."

They licked the salt.

"And a shot of tequila."

They threw back the shots.

Mallory finished the toast as fast as she could. "And-a-slice-of-lime." She shoved the lime in her mouth to ease the tequila's burn.

Then she and Eli sat on the floor in front of the couch and stared down the fire, together.

Taylor woke up on the floor.

He could tell it was daylight because the sun was trying to come in through his eyelids, but he wouldn't let it. He kept his eyes shut, and drifted back to sleep.

He drifted awake a minute or an hour later. With his eyes shut, his brain cataloged all the spots on his body that had been in contact with the hard floor for too long. In every house he owned, every interior designer scattered luxury pillows on a carpet in front of a fireplace for comfort. Taylor knew from hard experience that pillows were never that damned luxurious after an hour on a floor, let alone a whole night. He preferred a bed, always, with or without a bed partner.

Speaking of which…there was a woman, breathing softly, using his chest as a pillow.

He cracked open one eye and saw pink bunnies.

Mallory. Holy smoke. *Mallory.* It all came back to him. She'd spent the entire night with him. How had he gotten so damned lucky?

There'd been no sex, of that he was certain. His body would be flying from the endorphins, still. His heart would be—well, he didn't know how his heart would feel once it got its heart's desire, because that had never happened before. And it hadn't happened last night, because when it came to Mallory, he hadn't found the names for the emotions he felt toward her.

He opened both eyes and looked up at the Christmas decorations peeking over the edge of the mantel. There'd been a shot of tequila. Before that, the dream. He hated that dream. Hated it every time. But this time, it had ended with Mallory to hold on to. Talking. Tequila. A fire that hadn't transformed itself into anything except a couple of small logs in a modest fireplace. A woman falling asleep with her head in his lap while he wrapped a strand of her hair around the finger he'd used for the tequila salt. He'd unwrapped the strand, wrapped a different strand, over and over, until he'd fallen asleep, too. All in all, a damned good night.

Would have been better on a bed. This floor was hard.

Mallory was soft. In her flannel, she felt like the ultimate teddy bear, so wholesome, even with her thigh thrown over his. He reached down to move her leg and encountered her bare knee. He lifted his head an inch—a reflex—and saw Mallory's very bare, very sexy thigh draped over him. Her nun's habit of a nightgown was completely bunched up around her waist. If he picked his head up higher, he'd probably see what she wore below the waist, under her clothes—so hell, yes, he lifted his head.

Nothing. She wore nothing, unless one counted a scrap of black lace that didn't begin to cover the round curve of her backside, the very last thing he would have guessed lay under pink bunnies, a pink coat, a blue ski cap, a *thong*, good God, he'd never been so hard in his life.

"Yoo-hoo. Anybody home?"

What the hell? A female voice. Was it Wednesday? Had they come to restock the kitchen?

"Eli, are you here?"

Eli. The only woman who called him Eli was sound asleep in his arms. Except for his mother, who was in Monte Carlo. Or his sister, who lived hours from here, but sounded like she was in the hallway.

"This house goes on forever. Have we been down this hallway yet? This must be the last of the bedrooms."

His brother's voice. He hadn't even texted back.

Eli couldn't believe they were here, his brother and sister. He couldn't believe they were about to walk in on him—him and Mallory, sleeping together. At least he was dressed a T-shirt and pants, and Mallory's nightgown was modest—oh, *crap.*

It was instinct to try to cover her up as his siblings burst into the room, which was how he was caught with his hand spread over Mallory's bare backside as his sister jumped off the bottom stair and threw her arms open wide. "Ta-da! Merry Chrisss...oops!"

Chapter Eighteen

Learning Objective: Define the term "rapid-growth firm."
—Senior Year Project *by Mallory Ames*

"I was shielding you from their view."

"By putting your hand on my butt?"

"Yes. Your underwear is too small."

Mallory rolled her eyes. This was absolutely, positively, the worst possible way to wake up, ever. She was never going to recover from this, *ever*. She was going to be beet red from now until the day she died.

Eli had taken her aside to give her a quick update on just who these people were, but it had quickly become a hissing match between the two of them. His brother and sister were pretending to ignore them while sitting at the breakfast bar with their backs to the cold fireplace.

"I thought you'd only just exchanged your first text message in a *too small* eternity. How did you not know they'd stop by? Do they live in Masterson?"

"We live in Dallas," his sister said cheerfully, turning around in her seat to address her older brother. "We came in your jet. You said we could use it in your text, so we're using it."

Mallory was startled. His sister had heard their angry whispers from across the room.

Eli cursed softly.

"Heard that," his sister said. "Oh, look what's for breakfast. A bottle of tequila. Good thing I turned twenty-one. *In Vegas.* You should have been there."

Eli grimaced. "I forget how good her hearing is. It's freaky."

"So, you have freaky wide-angle vision or whatever, and she has freaky hearing." Mallory addressed his little brother, who was also six feet tall. "What freaky sense do you have?"

"None at all. I'm just normal." He said it with a smile, but it was subdued. Perhaps he felt like the odd man out in this trio of siblings.

"Good. Then I like you best." Mallory marched her bare-footed self over to the bar stool next to him and sat down. "I'm Mallory Ames, by the way, and I am never going to recover from this first impression. I'm very sorry for…it."

"I'm TJ," he said. "You were asleep. He's the one who should be very sorry for…it."

"I didn't let you onto the property unannounced," Eli said drily. "The security guard is the one who'll be very sorry for…it."

TJ scowled, which made him look more like Eli. "He's the guy you sent to Vegas to keep an eye on us. He knew who we were. Don't fire him."

"I'm Eli," his sister said. "My name is really Eleanor Elizabeth. You can call me Eliza. But Eli is pretty close, and when I was little, I wanted to be just like my brother." She made a face at TJ. "My cool brother, so I made everyone call me Eli, too."

"That's so cute." Mallory turned to check on Eli— her Eli. He looked baffled, as if he had never seen any of the three people who were sitting at the breakfast bar before. She had to make a *get over here* motion with her hand behind TJ's back.

Eliza was perfectly capable of carrying the conversation if everyone else was too embarrassed, subdued or baffled to do it. "I got named after two great queens. Eleanor Elizabeth. Lucky me."

TJ sighed. "You do this every time."

"TJ got named after Roman emperors. Tell us what TJ stands for, TJ."

"Tacitus Jovian."

"Wow," Mallory said. "I've never met a Tacitus Jovian before. What does E.L. stand for?"

"He wouldn't tell you?"

Everyone looked at Eli.

"She never asked. It's Erasmus Leonardo. I got the Renaissance geniuses."

Everyone looked at Mallory, who tried valiantly

to nod as if that was a perfectly ordinary baby name. "Well. Now that we've all been introduced, I'm going to slink away in humiliation and find something to wear that might be a little more dignified in case our paths cross again. It was nice to meet you. I'm sorry the power's still out. I hope you three have a good time together." She headed for the half staircase.

Mallory's hearing wasn't amazing, but Eliza wasn't trying to whisper, either. "She's not leaving, is she? Your date ends first thing in the morning after a fun night of tequila? I like her. You should try talking to her when you're not in bed."

"I do talk to her. She's staying here for the holidays."

Eliza sucked in a happy-sounding breath. "Oh, that's exciting. Go get dressed, too, so you can both show us around. Hurry up. No hanky-panky. We're only here until seven tonight. Then TJ and I are taking your jet to Monte Carlo. We're not as good as you are at getting out of Christmas with the parents."

Eli knew he was doomed the moment the twins spotted the two-person kayak.

"You have to race us. Rowboat versus kayak." Eliza turned to Mallory to keep her in the loop. "If there are Taylors and boats, there must be a race."

TJ picked up one of the oars and gave it a spin. "If we're not competing, we're not a family."

Eli wasn't imagining a touch of bitterness there. Or was he? He turned to Mallory.

She only smiled at him as if they were a happy

little couple, because they were faking it once again. They'd discussed it out of Eliza's earshot, which meant they'd had to go to another room and shut the door.

Mallory had objected: *You only have one day. I'll be in the way.*

He'd begged. *I need you to hit me upside the head with that oilcan if I screw this up. I don't want to screw this up.*

The oilcan reminder had softened her up a little. *We'll just behave like friends, right? I mean, we are just friends. Not lovers.*

Mallory, they're going to think it's weird if we're all stiff and formal with each other, old buddy, old pal, considering how the day began.

I can't do fake kisses with you.

How about real hand-holding?

Deal.

Since the power was still out, they'd all eaten Mallory's granola bars for breakfast. Nobody had washed theirs down with tequila. Then they'd all started their tour of the house, worked their way outside, skipped past the empty stable, and zeroed in on the dock.

"Do you need to do some warmups?" Eliza asked him. "Given your advanced age?"

"Athletes always warm up." Eli swung his arms, big swings to loosen up the shoulders, as Eliza stood still. "The smart athletes do, at any rate. If you capsize, it's not my fault that you have to fly to Monte Carlo tonight in wet clothes."

TJ handed his sister a life vest. "Mallory has to get in the rowboat."

Mallory didn't think so. "There are oars only for one person. I'd just be deadweight. A rowboat is slower than a kayak, already."

Eliza snapped her life vest shut. "Exactly."

They agreed to row and paddle out to a buoy, which gave everyone a warm-up. They'd race from the buoy back to the dock.

Eli made sure Mallory was situated, then he pushed off, put the oars in the oarlocks and set his feet. It was like riding the proverbial bicycle, although he hadn't been on the water in years. Easy as pie.

Until he took the first real stroke. Catch—put the oar in the water at just the right angle. Stroke—pull the oar through the water. Release—lift the oar out of the water, bring it back to the start position. *Catch, stroke, release.*

This was not his first time on the water in years. He'd been on the water, in the dark, in September. *Catch, stroke, release.* Dragging a pilot whom he'd thought was dead. If he'd released his hold on what he'd thought was a corpse, the pilot would have drowned. Eli would have murdered him without knowing it. *Catch, stroke—*

He let go of an oar. It started to slip out of the oarlock. He caught it. Too many years of training didn't abandon him, even now, while he was out on the water where explosions made him deaf, where he couldn't hear the voice of the woman in the canoe.

"I can row us back to the dock," said a different voice.

Mallory.

"You don't have to be out here if you don't want to be out here. I'm on your side, whatever you want to do."

It was the voice of the woman he loved. Eli could hear her, and thank God, he could hear her, because he loved her.

Can you name that emotion, Mr. Taylor?

He was so done with that. The emotion was love, as obvious to him now as the oars in his hands, but naming it, knowing it, wasn't enough. He wanted to act on that emotion. He needed to get over *the traumatic event* before he could do so, or else he might drag Mallory under, too. He was sick, literally sick, and very tired of waiting to recover.

His therapist had been good, setting him on the path, pointing him in the right direction, but that pace wasn't going to work any longer.

He was E.L. Taylor, damn it, and he gave advice to people, too. He advised those who were ready for change to determine their core question and use that to make their plans. For Mallory, it had been *Are you going to finish your degree?* Eli knew his core question now. *Are you ready to recover?*

The answer was yes.

He looked into Mallory's eyes, and he started rowing.

The rowboat was nothing like a racing shell, clunky instead of sleek, but the basic motion was the same. The resistance of the water against the blade, even the sense of creating speed were there. It felt good. Then it felt great. Then Eli won the race.

His sister pouted while he gave her a hand to pull her up onto the dock. "You are such a show-off."

"Show-off? *Show-off?* You forced me to row."

Eliza smirked at him. "Oh, I read this great book. It says 'Never say someone made you do it. You and only you control your actions.'"

Eli trapped her arms in a bear hug from behind and picked her up before she could react. "It does not say that. You lost the race. You're going in."

She put up a good fight, he'd give her that, and when he held her over the freezing water, she got in a really good kick on his left shin, which hurt like the devil and also made him proud. She was still as feisty as she'd been in third grade.

But a lot bigger. He set her down on the dock. "If it wasn't December, you'd be going in. Watch out when the weather gets warmer. When you least expect it, I'll be collecting this debt."

Her face lit up. "This summer? I can come and live with you here this summer? My master's degree is a year-round program, but I get almost the whole month of June off. I could bring my horse. That stable's just sitting empty. I'll bring two. We could ride."

Eli felt terrible—and honestly, a little claustrophobic at the thought of having his family moving in with him, bringing their animals, consuming his time. "No. That won't work. I'm just renting this house for a few months."

There was a terrible moment of silence.

Eliza shrugged. "It was just a thought."

But she looked like a six-year-old whose Barbie had just lost an arm. Eli knew that, because she'd once brought him her Barbie and its arm to fix. He'd laughed at the sight, and she'd immediately pretended she didn't care if it ever got fixed, because it was just a dumb doll. He'd fixed it, but she'd never brought him another broken toy. It was shocking, how much damage one could do in a thoughtless moment.

Eliza started to leave the dock. He'd told her no, that he wouldn't spend the summer with her. He hadn't meant it that way, just like he hadn't meant to laugh at a plastic doll with one arm.

He tried to explain. "I have Tokyo on my schedule almost every other week this summer. I don't have any reason to rent this house in June. It's nothing personal."

Eliza kept walking. It was too late, the damage had been done.

No, damn it. I have to fix this.

"The rental agreement is only through May," he said to her back. "I couldn't stay through June if I wanted to."

Eliza turned around. "You could own this house by June. If they didn't want to sell it, you could make them an offer they couldn't refuse. You have the money to do anything you want. The only reason you won't have this house in June is because you don't want it. You don't think it's worth what you'd get in return."

She walked away.

Damn it.

He turned to his brother. "I don't know what she means."

TJ only shrugged and walked off the dock, too.

Eli watched them go. They didn't need him. He felt the loss, but he also felt the fairness of it. How many times had he walked away, back to college, back to Wall Street, leaving them behind, making them feel unwanted? If he'd known how it felt...

It felt terrible.

A hand took his. "I don't know what that was about," Mallory said, "but I'm so sorry." She laced her fingers with his, and stayed by his side. His friend.

I love you.

He couldn't say it, not yet. He needed to figure out where he kept going wrong in his other relationships.

"It's about money. I screwed up something with money again." He had to laugh or else he'd cry out of sheer frustration. "I paid for their whole Vegas party, anything they could wish for, but they seem pissed off every time they mention Vegas. You're pissed off that I gave you money. Nobody ever seems to want it when I try to give it to them, but now Eliza is pissed off that I won't buy this particular house. She said I would think it wasn't worth what I'd get in return. What in the hell would I get out of owning this house besides a place for her to stay in... June... I'm an idiot."

He turned to Mallory, appalled at himself, relieved to have cracked the code, embarrassed not to have done it sooner. "It's her. What I'd be getting in return if I bought this house is *her*. I'd get her company for the summer. But I told her I wouldn't buy the house, so she thinks I value her less than a house. Than a house. That's crazy."

But that was it. From a very young age, Eliza must have thought every decision he made reflected her value to him. She wasn't worth the cost of a trip to Vegas to see her on her birthday. She wasn't worth the financial loss if he left a business consortium in Berlin to be at her high school graduation. Every time he hadn't shown up, she'd assumed something else had been worth more than she was. What else could she have thought?

"Would she be happy if you bought it?" Mallory sounded doubtful. "You won't be here in June."

"I don't know her very well anymore. She was so little when I moved away from home. She just wanted piggyback rides from me. She wanted...my time."

Mallory bit her lip.

"Do you think that's still it? That's—that's amazing. Does she still think I'm cool to hang out with?" The thought made him laugh. Mallory thought he was funny. Could Eliza think he was cool?

"She could come to Tokyo with me in June. It's a little crazy there. These executives, these icons of industry, do karaoke for hours. I don't, but God, it would be great to have her come with me. She'd love it. I think she would, anyway."

Mallory was absolutely beaming at him. He was blown away by her beauty in the December sunshine.

He squeezed her hand. "What are you so happy about?"

"I'm smiling because you're smiling."

He was smiling, wasn't he? "I need to go talk to my sister."

Mallory gave him one of those little shoulder shoves. "Go get your sister back," she said.

So he did.

This was the most bittersweet date Mallory had ever been on, real or fake.

The sun was setting, but the front porch faced west, capturing enough warmth for them to sit there, all four of them, waiting for the car that would take the twins back to the airport.

"Are you going to come in June as well?"

Eli was speaking to his brother, not to her.

Mallory could have melted at the effort Eli was making to reach his brother, it was so touching. But the question made her wonder where she would be in June. She looked at the trio of Taylors sprawled on the steps, and tried not to picture herself here.

A wistful pang was still a pang.

TJ only answered Eli with a shrug.

Eli looked at his watch. "You know, we're running out of time. There could be a half-dozen good reasons for you to be giving me the silent treatment, TJ, but I wish you'd give me one to work on. What's going on?"

TJ heaved a sigh. "I don't have a problem with you. You followed in Dad's footsteps. Did what was expected of you. I'll have to remind him he got at least one son to stay in the family business."

"When you tell him what? What are you planning to do?"

"I'm teaching. By June, I'll be teaching in India at a boarding school for girls. It's been in operation for years now. I saw a documentary on it when I was a freshman, and I'd never forgotten it, so I applied for the job. They provide top-notch educations to girls in the most poverty-stricken communities. It's astonishing how much impact there is on the whole community by educating just one girl. There's a socioeconomic ripple effect that—" TJ cut himself off.

"It sounds fascinating," Eli said, and Mallory could hear the sincerity in his voice. "If you need anything at all—"

"Nope. I'm sure they need money. I'm just not here to ask for that."

Mallory remembered their stormy fireside chat. *People I care about won't take my money. I have to pay bills for them when they aren't looking.* A school in India was going to be the beneficiary of some major grants very soon. Poor Eli—it wouldn't bring his brother any closer to him, but it was all Eli thought he could do. TJ didn't want to travel to Tokyo or even stay in this house in June. He had plans.

TJ flicked acorns off the steps. "You know Dad. It's going to be a merry Christmas when he finds out. He doesn't approve of teaching. There isn't a lot of money in it."

"I approve of teaching." Eli made the announcement, and the twins both looked at him in surprise.

Mallory gave Eli their signal, making that rolling motion with her hand. *Keep going.*

"Do you know what I'm doing here? Either one of you? It was in the Masterson alumni news."

Eliza threw an acorn at him from her seat on a lower step. "If you don't know that neither I nor TJ went to Masterson, I'm going to throw you in the lake."

Eli put his hand on her head. "Vassar." He nudged TJ with the side of his shoe. "Columbia. Of course you don't know what I'm doing, because I didn't tell you, and that's my fault. I'm working on it."

Mallory could have laughed at the matching expressions of shock on the twins' faces—but they weren't her siblings, and this wasn't her family. She needed to remember that.

"I'm teaching at the university. Only for a semester, but I'm going to have MBA students in a classroom. Between you and me, TJ, teaching is now part of the family business. If Dad's unbearable about it, you've got my jet at your disposal. Go have a merry Christmas somewhere else. Or here. You could come here."

Eli glanced Mallory's way. She knew he wanted to know if that had gone well. It sure seemed to her like TJ wanted someone to back him up on his career decisions. Eli had figured that out quickly, once TJ had started talking. She nodded at Eli and tapped her heart lightly.

Eli winked back.

Mallory felt more in her heart than bubbly champagne. She felt like she belonged.

Except she didn't. She liked Eli's brother and sister. She liked Eli so very much, and he liked her. But that was where it ended.

Before his waking nightmare, he'd spoken to her about talking like lovers, but not making love. She'd told him to stop seducing her, and she'd stormed out of the room. That had been the end of that. After his terrible nightmare, he'd held onto her for a long time, but he'd flat-out told her he was being careful not to fall in love, that it would be bad for him, psychologically, right now. She'd fallen asleep watching the fire with him, but there'd been no kisses. No more attempts at kisses. They'd held hands today, but only because he wanted to put on a good show for Eliza and TJ.

January would come, and they'd see each other in the office now and then. Maybe a lot. But she wouldn't be his girlfriend, and she wouldn't be part of his family. There was no point in sitting out here now, watching them like a child with her nose pressed against a toy store window, getting a glimpse of what she could not have.

Mallory excused herself as she should have done more firmly at breakfast. "I'll let the three of you have a few minutes to say goodbye."

"Wait a minute." Eliza, of course, had something else to talk about. "I think it's amazing that you didn't know my brother was a stud when it came to rowing and fencing. What did you first see in him? Where did you guys meet?"

Mallory implored Eli silently. *I told you I didn't want to be your fake girlfriend. Don't make me lie.*

Eli turned his palm up. *What's the problem?*

At their silent exchange, Eliza's face fell. "Dumb question, huh? I always forget that he's famous now. It was bad enough when he was rich. Rich and famous? Everyone he meets is already predisposed to like him. It's too easy for him."

Mallory was offended. "Not me. He didn't tell me who he was at all. I had to find out the hard way."

Eli settled back on the stairs. "I think we should tell them the truth, Mallory, my dearest, darlingest cupcake."

He did?

"Okay," she said, not knowing if it was okay or not. "You go first."

"I met Mallory at the annual lighting of the Yule log in the town park. She walked right up to me and started talking. Must have been something she liked about the way I looked."

Mallory shook her head at Eliza. "It was really dark, and he was doing this whole wild-man thing with his hair, and he had a beard. I didn't know who he was. He said his name was Eli. Not Taylor. He bought me hot chocolate, which cost one dollar, so you can't say I was dazzled by all the money he spent on me."

"Actually, it was one hundred dollars. I only had one-hundred-dollar bills on me."

"You—you paid one hundred dollars to drink a cup of hot chocolate with me?"

"I bought you two cups."

"Two hundred dollars?" Mallory was appalled. It didn't matter how much money Eli had. Two hundred dollars for hot chocolate in a paper cup was outrageous. "Don't do that. It's crazy."

"The nuns would beg to differ, I'm sure."

His sister looked between them like they were playing ping-pong. She settled on Mallory. "So, if it wasn't the money or the fame, what did dazzle you?"

"Yes," Eli said, clearly enjoying himself. "What did dazzle you?"

"We talked."

"You talked," he corrected her. "I listened."

"Really? It was hard to tell you were listening when you were doing that whole statue imitation, staring at the bon...fire. Oh."

The look they shared was one of a kind. Only the two of them knew what he'd been going through when she'd walked up to him. Only the two of them knew how they'd spent last night, staring that fire down together. It wasn't sex or even a kiss, but it was an intimate bond.

"We both talked, and some of the topics were serious, and he was very patient and kind when I got all choked up." She was getting choked up now.

Eli looked away, all nonchalance. "She wept like a waterfall on me. Very sexy first impression."

"He refused to shake my hand when I introduced myself."

"She got mad at me after she finished crying, because I wouldn't tell her that she looked bad."

Mallory crossed her arms. "He picked me up and set me on top of a hay bale without even asking."

Eli huffed out a sigh. "So, I'm not supposed to buy her things, and I'm not supposed to tell her she's pretty. She's really hard to date."

Eliza and TJ both stared at their big brother.

Eliza recovered first, turning to Mallory with a beaming smile. "Well, I love you!"

Chapter Nineteen

Learning Objective: Define the term "mature firm."

—Senior Year Project *by Mallory Ames*

"How long did your therapist say that reconciliation should take?"

Eli smiled at Mallory's pert question. "I don't want to be too smug about it. The fact that Eliza and TJ showed up on my doorstep probably accelerated the timeline by six months. The fact that they seemed pretty…open? Is that the word for it?"

"Openhearted. Your brother and sister are very openhearted people."

"Good word. The fact that they are so open-hearted with me, even TJ, probably skipped another six months. They get the credit. I'm grateful, though. Today was a really good day."

"You didn't wake up with strangers looking at your bare butt."

Ah, this woman made him laugh. Eli looked down at Mallory's pretty face as she lay with her head on his thigh, looking at the fireplace.

He stretched one leg out as he sat on the floor, virtually in the same position as the night before. Nothing seemed harrowing tonight. The power was on, and they'd found a string of twinkling lights in the garland on the mantel and plugged them in. They'd done a shot of tequila for the fun of it, instead of hoping it would ease strained nerves. The fire looked like a fire to him, although they'd been smart about it and were burning only one log at a time. If he should start to feel anxious, it would be easy to extinguish. So far, he felt great.

And, yeah, his brother and sister didn't hate him. What a difference a day could make.

"He wanted you to spend twelve months reconnecting with your siblings? What kind of snail's pace is that?"

Eli brushed a strand of hair off Mallory's forehead as she frowned. "Want to guess how long I was supposed to look at little fires before I moved on to medium fires?"

Her sleepy eyes opened wider at that. "You showed him. You went to the biggest bonfire of the year, you rebel."

"That didn't exactly work. It was kind of hellish, actually, until you showed up."

"Mmm. And then you did it again here, anyway, by yourself."

"Also hellish, until you showed up."

"So, which one of us is not the paragon we thought the other one was? Someone around here was labeled 'stubborn to an asinine degree.'"

"I told you, we're two peas in a pod."

He was smiling down at her when she looked up at him and said, "I really like you."

Game over. This was the woman. His one and only.

A piece of a star just landed next to me. I'm so damned lucky that I get to be with you. He wanted to say that out loud to her once more. And this time, he didn't want any of his own insecurities to mar their happiness under a starry sky.

She was almost asleep, her whole body going slack. His whole body was not slack.

"One thing left," she mumbled. "Your pilot."

Eli's drowsy desire was doused as effectively as if he'd jumped off the dock into the December lake water. The pilot was in a wheelchair because of him, trapped.

Eli was trapped with him; he could see that now. He'd been waiting for the wheelchair to disappear, hoping that he hadn't permanently injured this distant friend. That day might never come. The wheelchair might never go away. If he couldn't face that, if he allowed that piece of *the traumatic event* to fester, his heart would never be whole.

He needed it to be whole. It could be cracked and patched, because scars made things stronger, but it had to be whole. His to give. God willing, Mallory's to receive.

He sighed and lay back on a luxurious pillow that wouldn't feel luxurious by morning. But he had a sleeping Mallory in his lap, a fire burning safely in front of him and a long night ahead of him.

He needed to make a plan to see—not the pilot. Owen. Owen Michaels. He needed to drive down to Houston and meet with Owen in person. He owed it to the man to give him the chance to give him hell for the damage he'd done.

Eli was ready to recover, and baby steps weren't his style. Forget the drive. He might as well fly to Houston.

Eli swept into the hospital, his open trench coat flaring out behind him, a man on a mission in a suit and tie, his armor for battle.

He'd just defeated one obstacle. Completing the flight from Masterson to Houston hadn't been much of a challenge. The luxury jet was nothing like the tiny prop plane that had bounced on every air current. Either that, or Eli had just been too keyed up about facing the man he'd put in a wheelchair to spare any energy worrying about the airplane. It had been anticlimactic, in its way.

Mallory had poked about the cabin, once she'd realized he wasn't particularly fazed by the flight. She'd been amused by the luxurious bathroom with its shower. Delighted with the pastries that had been arranged for their breakfast. When she'd made a joke about joining the Mile High Club, he'd completely forgotten he had any problems in the world for a minute or two.

Some day...

But they were in the hospital now. Owen Michaels was expecting them. Eli wished he knew what to expect in return.

"Slow down." Mallory pulled back on his arm. "These pencil skirts limit my oh-so-confident strides. How do you swagger into a hospital and know which way to go?"

"My assistant sent a floor plan."

He slowed his strides for the woman by his side. He'd worn business attire, because he wouldn't lose his composure as E.L. Taylor. He knew how to meet the expectations others had of him when he wore a suit and tie. Mallory was wearing a skirt and heels to match his business attire, because...

Because she was his friend. He hoped the journey from friends to lovers would be brief, because he wanted her more than he'd ever wanted a woman in his life.

He paused outside the correct room. Mallory had her hand tucked in his elbow. She squeezed his arm. "He's probably apprehensive about this meeting, too."

For once, Mallory turned out to be wrong.

Owen was unabashedly glad Eli had come. Mallory stayed awhile, a star by his side, and then she stepped out. Eli shut the door after her and walked back to Owen. The time for real talk had come.

Looking down at the man in a wheelchair got to him. They'd been about the same height on the airstrip, two big men buckling into a tiny cockpit, oblivious to how they'd get back out.

"Owen. Let me say this. I appreciate your courtesy this morning, but I don't know how you can even talk to me. The guilt is mine. I know it."

"Whoa. Hold up. What are you guilty of?"

Eli gestured toward the wheelchair. "This. All of this."

"Sit down, man." Owen rolled his wheelchair over to a table.

Eli sat. Eye to eye, he saw that Owen was still the same formidable man who'd once pushed hard to make his crew team.

"You got me out of that cockpit alive. You swam me to safety. You may think it's terrible that I'm sitting here, but it is the God's honest truth that it's a miracle I'm sitting here at all. You saved my life. You were a hero that night."

Eli wasn't impressed with that assessment. "I'm a good swimmer. I'm in shape. That doesn't make me a hero."

"No, it doesn't. Look at Adrienne. That canoe-paddling angel is in her late seventies and barely five feet tall. She pulled us both to shore."

"Exactly. That's a hero. She had no quit in her. She could have called 911 and waited on the shore, and nobody would have thought poorly of her. She jumped in a damned canoe and tried to get to the plane before it sank, just in case anyone had survived."

She'd refused Eli's financial reward, too, saying she'd only been doing the right thing. He'd paid off her mortgage, anyway.

"One-hundred-percent agree," Owen said. "But that's you, too. You could have escaped from that cockpit and swum to shore, and nobody would have thought poorly of you. You didn't do that."

Eli took a slow breath, the same kind Mallory had taken so many times in difficult moments. *Two peas in a pod.* He needed to match her determination.

He gave voice to the worst truth. "You wouldn't have been in the air in the first place if it weren't for me. You only flew me because I'm E.L. Taylor."

Owen laughed at that. "Sorry, I'm not a big fan. On the crew team, I didn't even like you that much. You didn't know who the heck I was that day, did you?"

It was not the response Eli had expected, but he rolled with it. "Actually, you did look vaguely familiar. That's unusual. A thousand times, I don't know the person who swears they know me. I looked you up in the yearbook, after. I remember you now. You were a sophomore when I was a senior."

"Don't worry about it. I couldn't name the sophomores on the team when I was a senior, either. You didn't make me fly you anywhere that day. I only flew you because I needed someone to cover the fuel costs. I wanted to log some more hours."

Then it was Owen taking the big breath, bracing himself. "I was the pilot. I don't think you really get what that means. It was on my shoulders to make the flight as safe as possible. Sometimes, it's not possible, and then it's still the pilot's job to preserve life."

"Your skill set us down in one piece, mostly. Thank you."

"Your skill pulled me out of that wreckage. Thank you."

They looked at each other a moment longer.

Owen shook his head. "Well, look at us, a couple of heroes sitting here at a table without a damned beer in sight."

"I'll bring the whiskey next time."

"You do that. Seriously. This is far from over, and it's been brutal, but I'm going to walk again."

If sheer willpower could do it, Eli knew Owen would walk. If not, that wouldn't stop him from having a good life.

Eli might even be able to help out in more ways than paying hospital bills. "It's come to my attention that I have a bad habit of just dropping gifts on people whether they want them or not. While you're working on your recovery, would you want to give a few top of the line kayaks a test run?" Eli barely hesitated. "With me? I need someone to race against."

He didn't make friends in his line of work. That didn't mean he couldn't make friends at all.

"Hell, yes." Owen held out his hand.

Eli shook it, fully aware that a friendship was an incredible gift to receive in the face of a tragedy. "In that case, I look forward to giving you a new kayak for Christmas and then immediately kicking your ass in it."

Owen laughed. "You can try. Merry Christmas."

The private plane was posh.

Mallory could appreciate it, but she couldn't enjoy it. Not with Eli sitting next to her silently, concentrating deeply on something she wasn't part of. The private jet seats were full-size recliners, so being next to him wasn't as close as she wished it were.

He'd tossed his suit jacket aside and sat, looking out the window, his chin resting on his fist, Rodin's *The Thinker*—or just a man who'd done a lot this week to think about.

"How are you doing?" she asked in her most gentle, most positive tone, the one she'd used with the people whose bodies were so very sick and in need of comfort. She craned her neck a little bit, trying to see what had him so entranced.

Eli dropped his hand and looked her. Blue skies reflected in his blue eyes. "It's beautiful out there. This isn't as comfortable as a tree branch, but you could sit with me, and we'd be able to see everything together."

He really was okay. She'd thought so, but it was good to know he thought so, too. Because if everything else was good, there was one thing that could be better.

Once she was in his lap, she told herself to take a deep breath—and went for it. "Excuse me, Mr. Taylor?"

That took his eyes off the view. He looked at her with one eyebrow raised. "Yes, Miss Ames?"

Oh, he did deliciously bossy so well.

"I would like to review my policy on kisses."

That made him set his hands on her waist. "Please do."

She fiddled with his loosened necktie for a moment. "I want to redefine a real kiss, because as you know, that's the only kind I allow."

He settled back in the seat, a powerful man at leisure, but under her hands, she could feel the rise and fall of his chest. Under her thighs, she could feel the tension in his.

"From now on, the criteria is simple. I have to want to kiss the person badly, and he has to want to kiss me, too. I have been dying to kiss Eli for days. He bought me a hundred-dollar cup of hot chocolate and told me I met all his standards."

"I told you that you exceeded them."

In his voice, she heard everything she could have wanted to hear. Warmth, admiration, affection—desire. This was going to be wonderful. He wanted her as much as she wanted him.

She ran one finger over his shoulder, over the polished cotton of his dress shirt. "Eli kissed me only once, but it was the kiss of a lifetime. I'm not sure what happened, but he hasn't tried to kiss me again. I'm going to have clarify that all kisses from him qualify as real and are quite welcome. But in the meantime, while we're on the plane, I wondered if you, Mr. Taylor, would like to kiss me? Because I don't really care which name you go by. You are always you, and I would like to kiss you, oh, so badly."

"Ms. Ames. *Mallory.* From now on, and I do mean for the rest of my life, I'm Eli Taylor. Both names. And all of me would very much like to kiss *all* of you. But I'll start with your perfect mouth."

She could hardly kiss because she could hardly breathe, she wanted this so badly. Their lips met, softly. Pulled away again, slowly. She kissed his lower lip, which had smiled under her thumb, and she kissed the corner of his mouth, which was far too busy returning her kisses to smile at the moment.

He tapped the center of her upper lip with his finger, then kissed her there reverently. Then her cheeks, her eyelashes.

With a little breath, she turned so she would be chest to chest with him, one bent leg against his hard stomach, which was only possible to do if she let her pencil skirt ride up very high. Her breath was all shivery as she ran her fingertips down the smooth shirt that hid his hard chest from her view—for now.

He placed one hand on the side of her neck, his thumb on her jaw, and held her head steady as he stared her down, not angrily—oh, no—but seriously. His other hand drifted over her hip and her bunched-up skirt to slide over her backside, finding mostly bare skin and a little bit of lace.

The breath left his body. The fire burned in his eyes. He was putty in her hands, a glowering, gorgeous man at her mercy.

"Please tell me, Eli Taylor, that the pilots don't leave that cockpit."

"They don't."

"Please tell me that we aren't landing soon while you take me wherever it is we're spending the night."

It seemed to take him a great deal of concentration to look at his wristwatch. "We have at least two hours."

"In that case, this would be the ideal time and the most elegant place with the most beautiful view for us to stop talking like lovers and actually become lovers."

Chapter Twenty

Final Grade: A+
— Senior Year Project, *Mallory Ames*

She'd never seen Eli so anxious.

She'd expected him to be very, very relaxed after welcoming her to the Mile High Club, but instead he was at the mirror over the sink in the jet's spacious bathroom, fixing his hair and straightening his tie. Then he turned around and eyed her critically, head to toe.

"Um…" He looked at her updo. "Maybe you better re-twist that bun. Your lips are a little puffy. I don't suppose we can do anything about that."

"*Eli.* Why are you so worried about our appearance?"

He cleared his throat and looked a little sheepish. "It's Christmas Eve. This is supposed to be your Christmas present."

"I loved it. Can I have another?"

He tapped her on the nose. "You'll notice we've been in the air awhile—or maybe you were too busy to notice—but we've been heading north this entire time. You were looking for a place to stay for your winter break, and I thought you might want to spend your time off with your grandpa. In Ohio."

"Grandpa? We're going to land in Ohio?" She threw her arms around Eli and kissed his cheeks soundly, feeling more like a little girl and less like the *femme fatale* she'd just so successfully been.

Eli was kind of holding her off, like she was an exuberant, large puppy. "Yes. He's expecting us. I just had no idea I'd be meeting him after so thoroughly messing up his granddaughter's hair. And makeup. And clothes." He looked chagrined. "This is not a good look. I mean, this is a fantastic look, but it's not a good look for Grandpa. I'd like to meet him, if that's okay with you. I have to leave tomorrow, Christmas night. I always line up business in Asia over the holidays, but this will be the last year for that. Christmas should be family time, now that I have a family again. But you have a family, so I thought you'd like to be with them."

He sounded nervous. Mallory was stunned, but this was as close to babbling as she'd bet E.L. Taylor could get.

"I can send the jet to bring you back to me on January sixth. I know that's a long way away, and I only asked you to pack an overnight bag for this trip. I thought I was being clever that way, to get you to pack your personal makeup and stuff, but I know you need more clothes and coats for a couple of weeks in Ohio. I'm not trying to dump a big gift or a lot of money on you without checking with you first, but in this situation, it wouldn't be much of a gift if I sent you somewhere with only one change of clothes."

He *was* nervous. It was unbearably sweet.

"There are suitcases on board, ready for you. Nothing crazy, just two weeks' worth of clothes and shoes and whatever, just to get you by. I kept my word and didn't go into your bedroom, but I sent the housekeeper in to get some clothing sizes for my assistant. Anything that doesn't fit or that you don't like you can get rid of. Maybe your sister-in-law would like your hand-me-downs."

"Are you done?" Mallory asked.

"Yes."

She launched herself at him and kissed him over and over. "You're taking me to see my grandpa for Christmas. Thank you, thank you, thank you."

"If that's too expensive, I have another gift that didn't cost me any cash." Eli reached into a pocket of the coat he'd hung on the door and pulled out a blue mitten. "The boys of Kappa Lambda were very cooperative when I stopped by their party that night."

She pressed the mitten to her heart. "I can't believe it."

"I'm sorry."

"For what? This is a wonderful gift. It cost you

more than money. You spent your time and—and I'd bet your swagger and everything else you have that isn't money to get this back for me."

"I'm sorry because I shouldn't have kept it so long. It was all I had of you for a little while. It's been my lucky charm. It worked for this flight, didn't it?"

He cupped her face in his hands and kissed her passionately, because her lips couldn't look *less* kissed, anyway.

It was Epiphany, January sixth, and the last of the Yule log was being burned tonight to officially end the holiday season.

Tiny tots ran wild around the park, unable to contain themselves while waiting for the Three Wise Men to arrive with a real camel and bags of candy.

Mallory could hardly wait to see Eli. The last time she'd seen Eli had been Christmas Day. He'd given her one more gift: he'd set up indefinite payment for her grandfather's assisted-living apartment. Eli had asked her grandfather's permission to do so. Grandpa had insisted that he had funds to last through September, so it wasn't necessary. He'd worry about September when September came. Eli had explained that Mallory would be at ease if she knew her grandfather wouldn't have to move from a place where he'd made so many friends. It wasn't charity for Grandpa, but a gift to make Mallory happy. That had been a winning argument. E.L. Taylor was a very good negotiator.

After her grandfather had fallen asleep in his recliner during the football game on TV, Mallory had been truly sorry to whisper to Eli that she had nothing to give to him.

Eli had winked. "You could give me an interesting new start-up to invest in."

They snuck out to have a second round of pumpkin pie in the dining room, and she'd pitched her caregiver-client matchmaker concept. She'd asked him for twenty-thousand dollars in return for a twenty percent share of her company. Eli had countered with twenty grand for thirty percent. They'd shaken hands on twenty-five percent.

Eli had needed to leave for Japan. Mallory had ridden with him to the airport. Limousines were private enough for making love, she'd learned. If her lips had been a little puffy and her hair had been a little messy when the limo returned her to her grandfather's apartment, Grandpa had been kind enough not to say anything. He'd just patted her hand and said her new fellow seemed to be smart and respectful. He approved.

Her father hadn't quite believed she was dating somebody as rich as her brother kept claiming E.L. Taylor was, despite the fact that she and Eli had talked every day by phone. Her brother had been even less polite to her than usual, because jealousy didn't become anybody. Her sister-in-law, however, had swallowed her pride and graciously accepted the cast-offs from Mallory's new wardrobe.

Mallory was glad to be back in Texas, gladder still when the chauffeur took her from the tarmac to the town park. "Mr. Taylor said you would know where to meet him."

There could only be one place Eli was waiting. She headed for the bonfire at a brisk walk, taking confident strides. She skipped the crowd and headed for the darker side of the sandpit. When she caught sight of Eli, she ran.

He scooped her up and spun her around under the starry sky.

"I missed you," she said between kisses. "Take me home and make love to me. Hurry, or we might get caught for public indecency."

"I don't care where we go, as long as I can throw my wish first." Eli pulled a folded piece of paper out of his pocket. He held up the pine cone that was attached to it by a ribbon. "Aerodynamics."

Eli threw the wish up in the air, straight up toward the stars. It came fluttering down, spinning in a little helicopter motion as the pine cone pulled it down to earth. He caught it and held it out to Mallory.

"You're supposed to throw it onto the Yule log," she said.

"You need to read it first, or it won't come true. I read your note before you threw it one month ago, and it came true. E.L. Taylor likes you."

Mallory unfolded the wish.

I hope Mallory Ames will like me.

"Oh, Eli. I like you. So much more than that."

Eli kissed her, because he could. Because he needed to kiss her, to hug her and hold her hand, to live the rest of his life with her touch.

For just one more minute, though, he needed to let go. He stepped back and pulled another folded wish out of his pocket. "Once upon a time, I wrote a book that said you should never meet a hero, somebody who inspires you, unless you were their equal. You inspire me, Mallory. I want you in my life, which means we need to be equals. That means you would have to love me, because I love you. With all of my heart, Mallory, I love you."

"Oh, Eli, Eli. Yes, we're equals. I love you with all of my heart, too."

He'd never wanted to kiss a woman so badly. So he did.

She kissed him back as the air swirled around the bonfire, until he whispered over her perfect, beautiful lips. "I want to spend the entire weekend in bed with you, but I have one more wish in my pocket. Let's see if this one comes true."

He stepped back and threw it up to the stars, higher than the one before.

Mallory caught it on its way down. She unfolded it with trembling hands. In the firelight of the Yule log, she read, *I hope Mallory Ames will marry me.*

One perfect, happy tear rolled down her cheek, because a dream was coming true. She lowered the note and saw E.L. Taylor, her very own Eli, down on one knee with a ring in his hand.

"When I came to see this Yule log on the first day of the season, I was a man who had nothing. Money, yes, but nothing worth living for. Then a star fell from the sky and landed right next to me, and I've been so incredibly lucky to be with her. Mallory Ames, you are my light and my happiness. I hope you are my future. Will you do me the honor of becoming my wife?"

"Yes, yes, yes."

He slid the ring onto her finger and kissed her hand.

"Please stand up, Eli. I'm afraid I'm going to cry very hard in about two seconds, and I'm going to need a hug."

Eli stood and wrapped her in his arms. "That's what I'm here for. I'm going to love you forever, Mallory Ames."

She nodded her head and sniffed back happy tears. "That's excellent news."

* * * * *

MILLS & BOON

Coming next month

TEMPTED BY THE TYCOON'S PROPOSAL
Rachael Stewart

'Come with us, Sophia—come with us to Iceland.'

Her eyes shot open and she gazed down at him, hardly daring to believe the question and knowing at the same time that she couldn't. The thought, the idea of being surrounded by her fear, by the past, by the snow... She shook her head and shifted beneath him to remind him of her body, of what she wanted in that moment. What he so wanted too.

'You can't ask me that, Jack. Don't ask me that.'

He raised himself up over her, his elbows planted either side of her body to bear his weight. 'Why not?'

'Because I can't. We can't.'

He kissed her until she was breathless, panting. 'Why?'

'We don't even know they'll be available for Lily's birthday yet.'

'That doesn't matter. They will be available at some point and I want you to come.'

She shook her head, the emotions clawing at her throat and her chest, making it hard to breathe. 'We both know this has to end and that the longer we spend together with Lily, the more likely it is that she will become attached too.'

His eyes were so serious now as they blazed into

hers. The 'too' spoke volumes; it told him that fear protected her own heart, but did it protect his as well?

'That's not the whole truth, is it?' he pressed, probing for more, probing for her to admit that she feared being faced with her past. All it took was one harmless-looking snowflake, the ice forming over her windshield, and the shivers would start.

'It's enough.'

He shook his head, one hand stroking her cheek and catching a tear she hadn't known was there. 'You need to stop living in fear of your past, Sophia.'

He kissed her to soften his words and she clamped her eyes shut over the rising swell of emotion within. 'You've taught me that; you've made me realise that avoiding a base, avoiding London, is running from it. And by doing it, Lily has suffered.'

She kept her eyes closed as the tears refused to stop. He was right. She'd been a hypocrite to tell him the same and not realise it was exactly how she'd been behaving all along.

'Come with us. Not because I ask you, not because it would make Lily happy to have you there… Come because you want to. Come because you are ready to move on from it.'

Continue reading
TEMPTED BY THE TYCOON'S PROPOSAL
Rachael Stewart

Available next month
www.millsandboon.co.uk

MILLS & BOON

THE HEART OF ROMANCE

JOIN US ON SOCIAL MEDIA!

Stay up to date with our latest releases, author
news and gossip, special offers and discounts, and
all the behind-the-scenes action
from Mills & Boon...

 millsandboon

 millsandboonuk

 millsandboon

It might just be true love...